Unscheduled Valor

Andre Sierra

Andre Sierra Publishing

Print ISBN: 9798319225436

Dedication

To my wife, **Heather** and **My Sons**, whose unwavering support and love have been my guiding light.
This book is for you.

To **Joe Rogan, Jack Carr,** and **The Joe Rogan Podcast.**
Your conversations sparked the inspiration for this journey.

To **Caleb** and **Kevin,** for your helpful insights with the book's editing.

And

To **John** and **Paul,** for your helpful technical knowledge for the story.

Thank you.

Contents

Outside of Baghdad – Sunday 10:00 p.m. Iraq Time
Brigadier General Roger Sloan scanned the warehouse activity while his buyer inspected the military equipment he brought to sell. An armored Humvee, armor-piercing rounds of ammunition, RPGs, and advanced communications gear were spread out under the dim glow of fluorescent lights.

Hassan, the group leader Sloan dealt with in several previous transactions, ran his hand over the Humvee's armor-plated hood. "General, are you sure this won't be missed?" Hassan asked.

"I'm certain of that, Hassan," Sloan stated. "Like I've said before, with the military doing its equipment drawdown from Iraq, things just happen to get misplaced due to routing errors all of the time," Sloan said as he smiled. He had done this hundreds of times over the years and knew just how to navigate the complexities of military logistics. "It's just about knowing how to file the ... right ... paperwork."

Hassan looked at Sloan and said, "I will give you two hundred and fifty thousand dollars in cash for everything, as agreed." He motioned for one of his men to bring over a duffle bag.

Sloan took the bag and carefully counted the money, making sure that everything was there. *It appears to be satisfactory as usual, I can always count on Hassan to pay what he agreed he would pay. I wish all my buyers were like him.*

After he counted the money, Sloan directed his men, private contractors that he had hired and paid very well for their discreteness, to begin helping Hassan's men load up the crates of equipment into trucks Hassan had brought.

Leaving that task to supervising NCOs, Sloan returned to base. He sat in his office and unlocked a small safe next to his desk pulling out a printed list of all recently transferred supply personnel, complete with their login credentials. Sloan flipped through the pages to the most recent transfer. *Ah, Staff Sergeant William Finley, freshly rotated out to Bahrain a week ago; well, Sir, it seems you'll be doing some late-night inventory modifications for me. Let's see who else we can use. Here we go, LT Riley Parker; you went to ... Fort Stewart a few days ago. Excellent, you'll do as well.*

Sloan logged in to the inventory system using the still active logins. He began to weave a trail of what seemed like actual transfers of the equipment that he just sold off. *Alright ... it looks like we'll be sending this Humvee back to the States, I just need to swap the VIN with one of these destroyed Humvee VINs and we're good. OK ... what's next ... Ammo ... OK ... I just need to modify this ammunition count. Wow, we really fired off a lot of rounds at the range this week. I may need to talk to someone about that.* Sloan smiled, amusing himself.

Sloan had done this so many times in the past that he didn't even have to come up with new ways to manipulate the system. Consistency in the lie was key. He knew how to work the system to make it all seem legit.

As he was about to finalize the last update, he saw Major Natalie Wright's account activate in the system. *Why the hell is she logged in at this hour?*

Major Wright was one of his logistics supervisors. *She should be asleep.* He pulled up her audit logs to see what she was up to. *She's going through Sgt Finley and LT Parker's recent inventory transactions. Interesting ... I'll have to pay her a visit; she's probably in her office right now. Let's go see what she's up to.*

Three Buildings Over – Monday 12:00 a.m. Iraq Time

Sitting in a dimly lit office, Major Natalie Wright sat at her desk, staring at her laptop screen. Her hands trembled as they hovered over the keyboard, her eyes glued to the screen, staring at the rows of information. The Major had spent 20 years of her service in military logistics. As she scanned through the data, she knew something was very off.

My God, she thought to herself as she reviewed the list of recent inventory transactions. *Finley changed this in-service Humvee's VIN. It looks like he swapped it out with a destroyed one. And ... now it's marked for shipment back to the States? I don't know why someone would do that ... and ... Parker adjusted the ammunition numbers from the firing range ... at 11:36 p.m.? There was no way that many armor-piercing rounds were used in just a week. They use cheap ammunition in training.*

As The Major dug deeper, she noticed other login IDs still active in the system that should have already been terminated. *Why the hell are all these user IDs still active? And why do they have recent activity? I better figure out why and what is going on here.*

Wright decided to start looking into past transfers. She started to become concerned—not just about the equipment but also about the large amount of ammunition inventory that had been manipulated. *Why would someone change the ammunition counts like that? Especially the armor-piercing rounds. Those things are powerful enough to shred even military-grade body armor. That much ammunition just doesn't go missing, it could easily outfit a small army. I need as much evidence as possible. I need to figure this out and find out who is doing this.*

Wright began to type quickly, her fingers dancing across the keyboard, as she started backing up files to her thumb drive. Suspicious equipment transfers that did not match the transfer records. Adjustments to inventory counts that were logged from sites that were already decommissioned. Ammunition quantities that made no logical sense when looked at closely. With each record found, the pattern started to stand out more and more. What she saw wasn't just a simple clerical error during a drawdown; this was something more. Someone was deliberately manipulating the system.

Suddenly, the sound of her office door being opened startled her. *Who the hell?*

She instinctively moved her hand to her sidearm as she looked up. "Oh! General Sloan," she said, relieved. *What the hell is Sloan doing in the office at this hour?* "You're here late, Sir. Is there anything I can help you with?"

The General smiled while scanning the Major's face. *She's up to something, I can see it in her eyes.* "At ease Major." Sloan began to speak, "It would seem I'm not the only one burning the midnight oil, Major. I see you're doing an inventory check. Have you found anything interesting in those reports?"

Something in the way he said it caused a chill to run down her spine. "No Sir. I couldn't sleep so I figured I'd get some work done. I'm going over our daily equipment transfer reports. Just as you've directed me to do."

Sloan stepped a little closer, the light from the door casting his shadow over her. "Thorough as always, Major, all of these transfers due to the drawdown are causing unforeseen complications. Easy for things to ... get lost in transition." *People sticking their noses where they don't belong can get lost as well ...*

Looking directly into his eyes, Major Wright said, "Yes, Sir, but not this much equipment. Not this systematically. Especially the quantity of ammunition inventory that has been modified."

Sloan's face seemed to change almost instantly to a darker look. *She's looking into the ammunition inventory; this isn't good. I need to squash this right now.* "I would be remiss if I didn't tell you to be careful about digging too deep, Major. Sometimes, things are just better off left alone. For everyone's well-being. You know we're under intense deadlines to wrap this up, we'll be eviscerated by Washington if we miss our deadlines."

Wright looked at the General and replied, "I see, Sir." *What the hell does that mean? Did he just threaten me?* Suddenly, she felt uncomfortable and a little afraid.

"As your superior officer, I'm just giving you some good advice. I value your service and attention to detail." As Sloan made his way out of Wright's office, he stopped at the door, looked back, and said, "Oh, and Major. Make sure you delete those files. That's an order."

"Yes, Sir," Wright responded. Making sure to hide her surprise at the request.

After the General left, Wright sat in her office, her heart beating fast in her chest. *It has to be General Sloan. The way he was looking at me. The visit to my office at this hour. This just got dangerous. I need to think; I need to report in; that is what I need to do.*

Her hands were shaking as she reached for her encrypted phone. She had spent several weeks researching and gathering information, building backups, and creating redundancies. Could this be the evidence that her team was directed to find? *If I don't have enough evidence now, when will I?*

Washington, D.C. – Sunday 4:15 p.m. EST

Senator Katrina Long sat at her desk in her office, stacks of military oversight reports surrounding her. She looked out her window as the Capitol building dome shone in the late afternoon sun, reminding her of the oath she had taken and sworn to protect. Her eyes were weary from the long hours of reading reports, but something continued to bother her about them. *Why are we losing so much equipment? Where's it all going? This drawdown from Iraq should be cut and dry, yet ... these field reports show everything is above board. Something just doesn't add up ...*

The intercom on her desk buzzed. "Senator, you have an urgent phone call from Major Natalie Wright on line one."

Major Wright's exactly who I need to talk to. Senator Long reached for her phone and answered it. "Senator Long speaking."

"Senator, this is Major Wright." Speaking low so as not to be overheard by prying ears. "I did some investigating like you asked my unit to do, and I discovered something troubling. I'm calling you directly because I think we're running out of time. I was just confronted by General Sloan a little while ago."

General Sloan confronted her? That's odd, Long wondered to herself as she listened.

Major Wright began to describe the issues she found in detail. As she did, Senator Long typed on her laptop, taking down all the information in a flurry of keystrokes. Making sure to take note of all the relevant information.

"Senator," the Major paused for a moment before speaking again. "I'm going to have to remove myself from this situation. The General is on to me. I can't keep snooping around. He instructed me to delete files before he left my office a little while ago. We may need some help, maybe from the outside."

The Senator leaned forward before she spoke, thinking about all of the details she had just learned, pondering the implications. "I agree, Major. You're in a volatile situation here, but I think I may have a solution. Let me work on it. Thank you for all the information. I'll be in touch. And Major, be careful. If you have to get out of there, find somewhere safe to hold up until we can get you some help."

After ending the call, Senator Long sat there briefly, reviewing everything Major Wright shared with her. *General Sloan, what are you up to, and what are you hiding? I never liked him. He was always a smug son of a bitch and very resistant to my inquiries. Well, Sir, let's see how you like it when I make your life very uncomfortable. I think it's time we figure you out.*

"Susan," she said over her intercom.

"Yes, Ma'am," came a reply.

"Can you please schedule a call with Captain Angelique Phillips down at NAS Jax in Jacksonville, Florida, ASAP," Long replied. "And please clear my calendar for the day. Thank you."

"Will do, Senator," Susan replied.

And now, for a little bit of transparency, shall we? Senator Long, with a fire lit within her, picked up her phone and dialed another number from a card that she had hidden away in her desk for just this type of situation.

"World News Network, Mark Smith speaking."

"Mark. This is Senator Katrina Long. I may have a story that you might be interested in," she said.

"Senator Long, How nice to hear from you. I'm all ears; anything that piques your interest must be good." Mark replied.

The Senator began to speak, "As you know, I sit on the Senate oversight committee managing the drawdown in Iraq. I've come across some concerning information about our military's logistics. With your permission, I'd like to draft a letter to the Joint Chiefs for clearance to embed

WNN with a Marine unit in Iraq. The official purpose of you being there is to report on daily life on base, covering patrol missions and other standard everyday activities. It's to show the American people how we're carrying out the Iraqi withdrawal. But the real reason I want you there is to cover the equipment inspections that will be taking place."

"Interesting. What do you need me to do?" Mark said.

"Be ready for a call from Public Affairs as soon as this is signed off, and be ready to go as soon as possible."

Mark smiled before he replied, "Thank you for thinking of me, Senator; I won't let you down."

Senator Long hung up the phone. She was already planning the next steps in her mind. Completely unaware of how her actions would set in motion a chain of events that would captivate a nation.

Chapter 1

A Morning in the Martinez Household

The smell of sizzling bacon and freshly brewed coffee filled the Martinez house on a sunny Monday morning in Jacksonville, Florida. James Martinez was in his early forties, with salt-and-pepper hair and a beard to match. He had laugh lines around his eyes, indicating that life had been good to him. He stood in front of the stove, flipping pancakes while keeping an eye on the clock.

"Breakfast is up!" James called out to his kids, who were up stairs getting ready for school.

His wife Elena stood behind him preparing school lunches for their children. She steadily chopped up fresh fruit and snacks for the kids' lunches. Her dark hair was pulled back in a messy ponytail, and her oversized T-shirt seemed to flow around her as she moved around the kitchen.

"What do you think the odds are that Miguel makes it downstairs before his food gets cold?" Elena asked with a smile on her face.

James chuckled. "I'd say they're pretty low, but there's a first time for everything. Right?"

Their daughter Sophia came bounding down the stairs as if right on queue, her backpack slung over her shoulder. She was eleven years old, going on twenty, and the epitome of an organized and punctual person.

"Morning, Mom! Morning Dad!" she said as she slid onto a bar stool at the kitchen island. "Oh, man! That smells amazing, Dad!" she exclaimed.

James placed a plate of bacon and eggs with a side of pancakes in front of her. "Breakfast is served, Your Highness," James said with a wink. "You need to fuel up for the day, and there's no better time than breakfast."

Glancing at the clock, Elena let out a sigh. "I better go check on your son, I swear that kid is never on time for anything."

Right when she moved towards the stairs, a hazy-eyed Miguel came stumbling down the stairs and into the kitchen. His hair stuck out in wild tufts, and his T-shirt was on inside out. He was not as organized as his sister; in fact, he was the complete opposite.

"Look who decided to grace us with his presence if it isn't Prince Sleepy Pants." Sophia mocked while pointing her fork in his direction.

10-year-old Miguel responded to his sister with a grunt, climbed onto the bar stool, and laid his head on the cold countertop.

"Come on, bro," James said, putting a glass of orange juice next to Miguel's messy hair. "Here's a little pick me up to get you going. You need to get that brain of yours fired up for school."

Elena had returned from getting dressed for the work day, one she would be spending just down the hall in her office.

Running her hand over her son's hair as she passed by, she said, "I hope you plan on combing this mess before you leave for school, mijo. The neighbors are going to think you are homeless or something."

"I swear, this boy could sleep through a hurricane." James chuckled.

"Wait ... what? I'm awake, I'm awake ..." Miguel mumbled, finally raising his head off the countertop. "I was up late learning about building stuff for my school project."

Sophia snorted and rolled her eyes. "You mean up all night playing Minecraft with your friends, right?"

"Hey, it's the education edition!" Miguel argued, suddenly wide awake.

James quickly intervened before the two of them started arguing. "Alright, alright, let's simmer down. Less yapping out of you two and more eating. We got things to do today."

As they all ate breakfast, James pulled out his phone and began checking what he had scheduled for work today. "It looks like a regular Monday. We have a Teams Conference call at 10 with my logistics group over at NAS Jax, and then I have a few inventory reports to check out for the 1st Marine Logistics Group's incoming equipment transfers."

Elena, now packing up the last of the kids' lunches, asked, "Are you still liking the work-from-home life, babe?"

With a content smile, James paused for a moment and then replied, "I'm definitely glad that I don't have to sit in Jacksonville morning traffic anymore. But I need to go into the office tomorrow though, to meet with the team. We have a big project coming up. We're streamlining logistics for the equipment going from Jax to Camp Lejeune."

Sophia, always the curious one, said, "That sounds pretty complicated, Dad."

"Sometimes it can be mija, but that makes it that much more interesting. Every day is a new problem to solve," James said to her.

Elena smiled at James' excitement for his job. "And to think, you were worried about leaving your cushy corporate job to become a civilian employee for the military."

James, remembering his hesitations years ago. "The best decision I've ever made. Well, it's a close second," winking at Elena.

Changing the conversation, they started to focus on the day ahead. Sophia, the more active one in school, had a science club meeting after school. And Miguel had been nagging about trying out for the local junior soccer league.

"So … Mom, have you decided if I can join the junior soccer league? Tryouts are today!" Miguel asked.

Looking at Miguel's still messy hair and inside-out T-shirt, Elena said, "I don't know Miguel. Are you sure you can handle getting up early enough to make it to practice?"

"Heck yeah, I can!" Miguel insisted, now all of a sudden full of energy. "I'll even start getting up extra early to prove it!"

Sophia snickered. "This is going to be good. Are we placing bets on this?"

Miguel just squinted his eyes in her direction as if mentally trying to get her to stop talking.

After finishing breakfast, James paused to gaze out the back window of their home on Jacksonville's Westside. Beyond a line of oak trees, a lake shimmered in the morning light, bringing a quiet sense of peace to him for the life he and his family had built here.

"What a great morning!" he said. "What do you guys think about taking the RV out this weekend? How about we head out to Hanna Park to camp and hang out at the beach for a couple of days?"

"That sounds great to me!" Sophia said with excitement.

"Can we bring the fishing poles so we can do some fishing?" Miguel asked.

"Heck yeah, we can man!" James said, looking at Miguel.

They continued their morning routine. James and Elena worked together to pack the kids up and get them out the door for school. As the kids went out the door to catch the bus, they said their morning goodbyes. When the door finally closed shut behind Sophia and Miguel. James and Elena stood there, sharing a quiet moment of silence.

"Another day of living the life," James said as he pulled Elena in for a quick kiss.

She looked up at him and smiled. "Living the life, with a side of chaos. I wouldn't have it any other way."

Before heading to their offices, they took a few minutes to go over each other's schedules. Elena, who was an independent realtor, had a client showing in the afternoon. They coordinated who would pick up which kid and worked out what was for dinner that evening.

As they headed to their offices, James looked back one more time at Elena, thinking to himself. *How'd I get so lucky?*

James walked into his office, settled into his perfectly worn-in office chair, and sat there for a moment, feeling a sense of satisfaction with his life. His job with the Defense Logistics Agency was a challenging but definitely rewarding career.

He oversaw marine equipment movements from NAS Jacksonville to all points within the nation. It was both challenging and rewarding, and it gave him a sense of purpose. The stability of everything allowed him to have this great life with his family.

He reached out to his laptop and turned it on, his monitors coming alive with the logo of the US Marine Corps. He began to mentally prepare for his conference call with the group he worked with.

They were a mix of servicemen and women along with a few civilians, all working together like a well-oiled machine. James prided himself on being able to navigate the two worlds with ease. He grew up in a military family and had been around military bases his entire life. This gave him a unique perspective on the military and how to interact with military personnel.

James glanced at a framed photo on the wall next to his desk as he waited for his email to open and update. The picture had been taken not too long ago on a day trip to the beach with the family. He smiled, recalling that day as if it were yesterday. They had spent most of the day body surfing on the waves and building sandcastles. It had been a great day, for sure.

The all-too-familiar notification sound of incoming mail brought James back to the present. James glanced back at his screens, expecting to see the regular Monday emails and calendar invites. Instead, an email subject line at the top of his inbox caught his eye.

"High Priority: Overseas Assignment Opportunity."

Chapter 2

The Assignment

The sound of an alarm going off filled the air. Lisa Chen reached over and fumbled for her phone to turn it off. *Is it 5:30 a.m. already?* She yawned and then put her phone back on her nightstand and looked around her barely lit, almost closet-like-sized apartment in New York City.

Lisa lay there for a moment and thought to herself, *another day of local stories about city council meetings and potholes.* "This should be fun," she said sarcastically. Stretching, she sighed and then rolled out of bed. *Reporting on these lame stories is not where I thought I'd be in journalism at this point in my career. Oh well, a job is a job. I just have to keep going.*

She went through the motions of her morning routine. Taking a quick shower, rapidly applying makeup, and putting up a messy ponytail that somehow looked almost intentional, she caught her reflection in the mirror and thought. *I'm 28 and one of the youngest reporters at World News Network's local station. There has to be more for me to do than these local news stories ...*

* * *

At the same time, Lisa was getting ready for work. Lisa's boss, Mark Smith, was already in his office at WNN's main building on the other side of the city, scanning through several emails and reports from the night shift crew, when suddenly, a notification went off on his phone, pulling him away from what he was reading. Mark glanced at his phone and noticed an encrypted message from an unknown number on his Signal messaging app account. He picked up his phone quickly, seeing the message timer counting down, he tapped on the message, his eyes narrowing as he read the text:

"The Joint Chiefs have approved my request for WNN's embedment. Expect a call from Public Affairs shortly. – SL" 5, 4, 3, 2, 1. And then the message was gone, having been automatically deleted by the app.

Mark felt the excitement building up inside him as he considered the possibilities of this story. This could be the big break he'd been looking for.

Mark quickly saved the number under something less obvious just in case anyone had a peek at his phone. Knowing better than to keep conversations like this open in the app, he thought about all of the implications and possibilities. He recalled several conversations he had about the issues going on with the current drawdown in Iraq and the unexpected call from Senator Long all but confirmed it.

If there really was an issue and his network broke the story, this could be the news story of a lifetime. Mark leaned back in his executive chair and thought about his next moves. He was very aware every step needed to be carefully calculated and planned.

* * *

Back at Lisa's apartment, she sat in front of the mirror at her dressing table, staring at her reflection. "Today's the day. Today's story is the one that changes my life." She repeated this self-affirmation to herself every morning, more out of habit than conviction at this point.

As she prepared to leave, Lisa grabbed her go-bag, which was always packed just in case something crazy broke. She picked up her tumbler, already full of freshly brewed coffee, and headed out the door. She locked the door behind her and headed for the subway.

The subway car was crowded as usual, with people heading to and from work. After leaving the subway and walking a few more blocks, she finally made it to the news station. Waving to the security guards at the front desk, she made her way to the elevators and headed to the newsroom floor.

Leaving the elevator, Lisa quickly walked to her desk, pulled out her laptop, and settled in. She scanned through her emails for any breaking news stories or changes to her assignments for that day. *Another boring day ...*

She glanced around and caught sight of the TV screens on the newsroom wall, most of them showing local traffic and weather, but one of the TVs displayed a competitor's news channel. It was broadcasting footage of a conflict that was going on in the Middle East and she found herself drawn into the story on the screen. A combat journalist was talking about something in the background, but she could barely hear what was being said.

"Chen!" a familiar voice broke her concentration. "You're with me today. The city is filling potholes on 5th Avenue. It's going to be awesome." He said sarcastically.

Lisa managed to suppress a noticeable eye roll as she grabbed her notebook and followed her cameraman, Steve, to the company van. *Great! These boring reports are what I work so hard for, reporting on road maintenance and trying to make it sound riveting and "sexy" for the morning viewers.*

The morning passed by in a blur of annoyed commuters yelling at her, the horrible burning smell of lava-like asphalt, and some crazy city worker who seemed to think Lisa was personally responsible for all the traffic delays in Manhattan.

By the time she got back to the news station, she was dirty and sweaty and questioning many of her life choices.

Halfway through editing her pothole story, she felt frustrated. *There has to be more than this,* she thought. *Trying to make road maintenance sound interesting is a huge waste of my time.* Just then, her phone vibrated with a text message from the executive producer: "My office. ASAP."

Lisa's mind raced through several thoughts: *Am I in trouble? Did someone complain about my reporting? I guess I'm OK if I get fired from this miserable job covering potholes ...*

Ever since joining WNN, she had constantly requested to be given more challenging assignments and volunteered for every opportunity that came close to hard-hitting journalism. Despite it all, she had been relegated to reporting on the local news. But she never gave up; she used every story, no matter how boring it was, as a chance to hone her skills.

Lisa took a second to calm herself. She ran her fingers through her hair, smoothing it as she headed to Smith's office. When she arrived, Mark was on the phone. He held up one finger, signaling her to have a seat.

"Yes, Ma'am, I completely understand. We would be proud to show the American people the work of our troops during this crucial time," he said. "Absolutely, we will handle this with the utmost care that it requires. Thank you for giving us the opportunity," Mark said to the person on the other end of the phone call.

A big smile crossed Mark's face as he hung up the phone. "Lisa, that was the Public Affairs from CENTCOM and they have just granted us a clearance to embed with a US Marine Corps unit in Iraq. Not just any embedment, I'm talking about live broadcasts and real-time coverage of the Middle East operations. We are going to show the American people what is really happening on the ground over there."

Lisa's mind began to race from the implication of the information she just heard. "Why us?" she asked.

Mark looked at her and shrugged. "They told me it is part of a transparency initiative to cover the current drawdown. But between you and me, there is more to it than Public Affairs is letting on. We've got a whistleblower who informed me that there could be an opportunity to uncover something huge."

"What are your thoughts on sand?" Mark asked with a smile.

"Sand? I ... What are you getting at? I guess it's fine. Why?" She asked, surprised by the question.

A slow smile spread across Mark's face as he leaned back in his chair. "How would you like to give up all those great pothole stories for some Middle East action? We've got a great opportunity here, and I think you are the right journalist for this job."

Lisa's heart nearly leapt out of her chest. "Go on, I'm listening," she said, trying to hold back her excitement.

Mark leaned forward. "I want to be upfront with you, Lisa. This isn't going to be all fun and games. Where you'll be going will be dangerous and unpredictable, and it'll push you to your limits, both mentally and physically. But it's also the kind of assignment that can catapult someone's career to the next level. We need someone who's sharp, adaptable, and isn't afraid of anything. I believe that's you. What do you think? Are you ready to make history?"

Lisa didn't even give it a second thought. She just replied. "When do I leave?"

Grinning from ear to ear, Mark said, "That's what I wanted to hear," he slapped the desk excitedly. Then his expression turned serious for a moment. "Lisa, what I'm about to tell you right now does not leave this room. Do you understand?"

Lisa nodded her understanding.

Mark leaned in and spoke just low enough for Lisa to hear. "Three days ago, I received a call from my source in D.C. They're the ones who set this story up."

Mark pulled a key from inside his suit jacket, unlocked one of his desk drawers and pulled out a file, sliding it across to Lisa. "These documents were delivered to me anonymously. They show that we've got a high-up source in military logistics who's claiming that there's systematic theft of military equipment going on in Iraq. We're talking about millions of dollars in vehicles, weapons, and other high-tech gear vanishing from inventories without a trace. The source believes this goes all the way up the chain of command."

Lisa began scanning the documents.

Mark continued. "So, officially, you'll cover daily life on the bases and patrol missions, you know, the standard embed reporting. But my source also tells me that there's going to be a civilian logistics specialist assigned to investigate these so-called discrepancies. Your real assignment will be to follow their investigation in secret and see where it leads. But you can't be conspicuous."

"Does CENTCOM know that we know about the discrepancies?" Lisa asked.

"No, CENTCOM is unaware that we know about the equipment inspections. They think they are just sending us over there to get some good PR. Lisa, you could be the one who breaks one of the biggest stories of the decade by uncovering this corruption that's happening right under the government's nose."

Mark paused for a second before continuing. "And here's the best part. We're going to broadcast key parts of the mission live around the world. There will be no delays, filters, or commercial breaks. Just raw, real-time reporting of whatever you find."

Lisa's eyes grew wider. "Live? Are you serious?"

Mark nodded. "Yes, ma'am. Welcome to the future of live on-location military reporting, kid. We'll be pushing the boundaries with this one, giving the American people and people around the world a real-time glimpse into what is happening on the ground in Iraq. We'll be the first ones to accomplish something like this. It'll be groundbreaking." Mark paused while Lisa processed it all. "I'm going to need you ready to leave in a couple of weeks. You think you can handle that timeline?"

"Of course, I'll start making preparations. Thank you for this opportunity Mark, I won't let you down." Lisa said as she stood up.

"I know you won't! Exciting times Lisa!" Mark said.

As Lisa left Mark's office, her mind raced a thousand miles per hour. She made her way to the break room to review everything she had just heard. Her hands were shaking as she poured herself a cup of coffee, walked over to a nearby chair, sank into it, and pulled out her phone.

The lock screen on her phone showed a recent picture of her parents. Her dad was in his Army uniform, and her mother was glowing proudly next to him. Lisa's father, Colonel David Chen, served three tours in Afghanistan before retiring a few years ago. Listening to all of his stories is what inspired her to want to become a military correspondent.

Looking down at her phone, Lisa dialed her mother's number. She picked up almost immediately.

"Lisa? Honey, is everything okay? You don't usually call us at this time of the day," her mother asked.

"Everything is okay, Mom, I promise. Is Dad there with you? Can you put us on speaker so he can hear me?" Lisa asked.

There was a moment of silence, and then she heard her father's voice coming on the line. "We're both here, sweetheart. What's going on? Are you alright?"

"Yes, I'm okay, Mom. Dad. I … I have something to tell you both. I just came from my boss Mark's office, and he offered me a new assignment. It's a big one. It looks like I'll be heading to Iraq."

The silence on the other end seemed to last forever. Finally, Lisa's father spoke first. "They want you to go to Iraq and report from over there?" he asked.

"That's right, Dad," Lisa replied. "We'll be assigned to one of the Marine Corps units that are being deployed to Iraq real soon. We'll be doing live broadcasts of our stories while on location there. CENTCOM wants us to cover some of their operations in real-time."

Lisa could hear her mother take in a sharp breath. "Live broadcasts?" There was a pause before her mother continued. " Sweetheart, aren't they still fighting over there? I was just watching the news earlier today. I just ... I'm worried about you going over there and being in the middle of all of that. Isn't it going to be dangerous?"

"It will be, Mom. But I can handle it. This is the opportunity of a lifetime for me. I've been waiting for this kind of break for a long time. Reporting on these types of stories is one of the main reasons I became a journalist." Lisa told her mother.

Her father's voice came through. "Listen, Kiddo ... conflict zones aren't anything like you have seen on the news segments or on TV shows. It's unpredictable and chaotic. Even when you think there isn't anything going on, the stress from what could be going on can be a lot. It can wear you out mentally and physically."

"I understand, Dad," Lisa said. "But this is something that I believe I have to do. I want to show people around the world the harsh realities of what is happening in the Middle East.

Just like you and I always talked about, making sure people know the real stories.

"Well, it sounds like your mind is already made up. Just promise us you'll keep your head down and stay safe." Her dad said before continuing. "I also want you to know that we are very proud of you, Kiddo, and all of the accomplishments you've achieved so far."

"I will, I promise, and thank you, Dad. It really means a lot to me to hear you say that. Okay, well, I need to get back to work. I still have to go over a few more details and finish up the assignments I have now. But I'll talk to you both soon, and I'll let you know if anything changes. I love you both so much," Lisa said to her parents, trying to hold back her emotions.

"We love you too, sweetheart." replied her mother.

After ending the call, Lisa sat for a moment, letting the reality of it all sink in. Then, with a new pep, she headed back to her desk. There was a lot to get done and not a lot of time to do it.

Over the next few days, Lisa's life got even busier with all of the preparations she had to complete. She was put through crash courses on combat zone safety, learned about all the equipment she would be using, and attended several briefings on the current situations in Iraq.

Lisa was given access to a small TV studio, where she practiced stand-ups while wearing body armor and a helmet. The extra weight initially threw her off balance, but she eventually got the hang of it. She also had to learn to project her voice differently. Her new cameraman, Tom Ballard, had embedded many times in his career. He gave her pointers on how to move around and speak while staying safe.

"Now remember, Lisa," Tom told her during one of their many practice sessions. "The story is just a story; It's not as important as your life. If I tell you to get down, I need you to hit the deck immediately. No hesitation at all, got it?"

In Lisa's last briefing, Mark went over the final details of her assignment. "Remember, your main focus will be on the day-to-day operations of the base and the men and women serving there," Mark explained. "We want to show people here at home what life is like for our troops on the ground in the Middle East."

Mark pulled out an updated version of the file he had shown Lisa previously. He began laying out new photos and documents he had recently received from his source. "I'm being told there might be some irregularities in the inventories. Our source says the person doing the inspections should be headed there at the same time as you. Once you figure out who they are, it should be easy for you to keep an eye out for them while you are on the base. If you can dig anything up, it could be big. But remember, inconspicuous. Understand?"

Lisa nodded as she leaned in and began studying the documents. "Do you know what kind of irregularities they're talking about?"

Mark just shrugged. "It could be anything from a simple mismanagement to something more sinister. We don't know yet, that's our job to figure it out and report on it."

As he shuffled around the documents, Mark picked one up and handed it to Lisa. "Don't freak out, but I'm being told there's also been an increase in insurgent activity in the area. We want you to look into it and see how it affects the operations for the drawdown, exit, and troop morale."

Lisa nodded, making a mental note as she scanned the document. "And what about the live broadcast aspect? How often do you want us to do them?"

"We're looking at doing at least one live segment a day, possibly more if there's significant action going on. When we're close to the equipment inspections, we want as much of that live as possible. It's a risk, broadcasting from inside a base in real-time, but we've got the go-ahead from CENTCOM, so ... they seem to think this PR thing is a good move," Mark said.

Later that evening, while Lisa was sitting at her desk going over the list she had made for everything she needed to get done before her trip, her roommate Jess appeared in the doorway.

"So, you're really going to do this, huh?" Jess asked.

Lisa nodded without looking back. She carefully went back over her list to make sure she hadn't forgotten anything. "Yeah, I really am," she replied.

Jess was quiet for a second and then said, "Just ... Be careful over there and come back in one piece, okay? Who else is going to appreciate my bad jokes?"

Lisa chuckled and then turned to face Jess. "I'll do my best. And hey, maybe I'll pick up some Arabic jokes while I'm there. Expand your repertoire of bad jokes."

They both laughed and talked for a little while longer. As they said goodnight to each other, Lisa really began to feel the reality of this assignment sinking in. She would be leaving behind the comfort and safety of her New York life for the dangers that could possibly await her in Iraq.

Chapter 3

The Opportunity

The sound of James Martinez's alarm pierced the darkness of his bedroom as James mumbled something inaudible before rolling over for his phone on the nightstand to shut the alarm off. It was 5:45 a.m.. He lay there for a moment longer, gathering all the willpower needed to get out of bed and face the day.

Beside him, his dog Max had managed to weasel his way onto the bed. The dog was spread out as usual, taking up most of the space. Elena's spot was empty. She was always up and out of the house before 5 a.m. to make it to her morning workout classes at OrangeTheory Fitness. One time, she had tried to talk James into going with her in the mornings, and he just responded with, "Are you trying to kill me?" James knew what kind of workouts they did there and he was not interested in that, at all.

Looking at the clock, it was now close to 6 a.m. He knew Elena would be returning soon and would probably chastise him for still being in bed. With that in mind, he swung his legs off of the bed and slowly made his way to the bathroom.

James was halfway through brushing his teeth when he heard the sound of the garage door opening and then closing softly a few seconds later. The sound of their home alarm chirp echoed throughout the house as the door to the garage opened and then closed. He could hear Elena's footsteps as she made her way up the stairs.

Suddenly, she appeared in the bathroom doorway, her face flushed and glowing from her intense workout. "Good morning, my love," she said, giving him a quick kiss on the cheek. "Kids still asleep?"

James nodded while rinsing off his toothbrush. "They should be. I hate not being here when they get up."

Elena squeezed his arm. "I know you do, babe. But they understand. It's only once a week. They sure will miss you cooking them breakfast, though. They always make sure to let me know that, when you are not here," she said, smiling.

James smiled back at her and then headed down to the kitchen. James moved with purpose in the kitchen, brewing fresh coffee and putting together his lunch while Elena came down the stairs and gathered her dog-walking gear. They danced around each other with practiced ease, going over bits of information about the day ahead.

"Miguel has soccer practice after school," Elena reminded him. "I should be able to pick him up on my way back from my last showing."

James nodded as he packed the rest of his lunch into his lunch bag. "Got it. Sophia has her study group after school, and she said she would take the bus home, so she should be good."

Elena clasped the leash around their golden retriever Max's collar. "I better get this guy out before I take a shower.

If I don't see you before you leave. I hope you have a wonderful day. Love you!"

"Love you too, be careful," James replied, watching as she headed out the front door, Max leading the way.

Twenty minutes later, James was in his truck, backing out of the driveway. He was just beginning to drive off when he spotted Elena and Max returning from their walk. They exchanged waves as he drove past.

The morning traffic wasn't too bad. James made it to work with plenty of time to spare. He pulled up to the security gates at Naval Air Station Jacksonville, presented his ID, and was waved through.

James pulled into his building's parking lot and made his way inside building 400. He took the elevator to the third floor. The office was nice and quiet at this hour. Most of his co-workers wouldn't arrive for another half hour. He liked having the place to himself. It was peaceful, and it gave him a chance to get organized before the day's chaos began.

After unpacking his laptop and getting everything set up, James logged into the network and immediately checked his email. As he scanned through it, he noticed there wasn't anything urgent. It was just a mix of the usual number of constant memos and meeting requests.

For the next hour or so, James went down the rabbit hole of inventory reports and spreadsheets. The Defense Logistics Agency's work might seem boring to most people, but James found satisfaction from the constant dance of the complexities of moving military equipment around the globe and here at home. Every line item in his spreadsheets represented actual equipment that servicemen and women around the world depended on. It all mattered to James.

At 8:45 a.m., a new email pinged his email inbox. It was from his department's supervisor, Commander Jack Barnes: "James, Please see me in my office ASAP."

James raised an eyebrow slightly, surprised by the email. It wasn't like Jack to be so formal or urgent. James saved all his work and made his way to Jack's office.

As he got closer to Jack's office, he could see through the window that Jack wasn't alone. He slowed momentarily when he noticed that Captain Angelique Phillips, the base commander, and Colonel David Reeves, head of operations for their site, were also in the office. *What are they doing here?* James thought to himself.

James knocked on the open door frame. "James, come in. Could you please close the door behind you?" Jack said to him.

James did as he was asked, trying to keep his composure and his face neutral. *Man, something must be going on if the Captain and Colonel are also here.*

"Good morning, Sir, Captain Phillips, Colonel Reeves," James said, nodding to each of them while shaking each of their hands.

"James, thanks for coming so quickly. Grab a seat," Jack gestured to the chair in front of his desk. He waited for James to get settled before continuing. "James, did you happen to see the email about the overseas assignment opportunity that was just posted?"

James nodded. "Yes, Sir. I briefly skimmed it, but I haven't had a chance to really take a look at the entire email yet."

Jack looked at the others, exchanging glances before continuing. "Well, a situation has presented itself that might interest you. We've come across some ... issues ... with equipment inventory discrepancies at a few of our bases in Iraq."

Colonel Reeves spoke next, "To be clear, Martinez, we're under the impression that it's a clerical error. But given the nature and value of the equipment involved here, we need someone with your expertise to go over there and take a look in person. We need someone who'll be thorough and who knows all of the systems inside and out, someone who can spot errors that others might miss."

James nodded, taking it all in. *Is this really happening?* He thought to himself. "And you want me to go over there and do this?" James asked.

"I recall, in some of our past conversations, you expressed your interest in possible overseas work. James, your hard work and attention to detail here has demonstrated to everyone's satisfaction that you'd be the best candidate for this assignment." Jack replied.

James thought about it. *An overseas assignment in Iraq? This is crazy! But it's the opportunity I've always thought about, a chance to do more than sitting in this office all day. But it could be really dangerous ... What about Elena and the kids? What would they say? How would they react to this? I'd definitely need to talk to them about this first.*

James carefully thought of what to say before he spoke. "I ... I'm honored that you'd consider me, Sir, can you tell me more about what I'd be doing over there?" he asked.

Jack smiled and then began to go over the details of the assignment. "All of the inventory discrepancies that we've noticed seem to involve a series of equipment transfers between a few of the bases in Iraq. Looking at it on paper, it all looks up to snuff, but when you begin to cross-reference them with the on-the-ground inventories, things are just not adding up. And then we see large write-offs after counts."

Colonel Reeves interjected, "We're not talking about a small amount of money in lost equipment. We're talking about millions of dollars. Humvees, ammunition, tactical gear, and technical equipment. Some items are showing up in inventories where they shouldn't be, and others are just missing altogether."

James tilted his head, thinking, his analytical mind activated, spinning up the possibilities. "Could it be a glitch in the software or possibly in the tracking system? Or maybe some sort of lag in the system causing the information not to update the databases?" asked James.

"Honestly, that's what we initially thought," Captain Phillips said. "But we had the help desk go through the system and they ruled out most of the obvious issues that usually come up. That's where you come in. We need eyes on the ground. Someone independent who can physically verify the inventories, go through all the paperwork, and interview the personnel."

Leaning forward, his eyes locked on James. Jack began to speak. "You have a talent for spotting patterns, James. Remember all the discrepancies you found in the Blackhawk parts transfer last year? That's the kind of insight we need."

James nodded, remembering it in detail. It'd been a minor error that was easily overlooked. Still, it led him to a massive discovery of a logistical issue that, if left unchecked, could've grounded over half of the Blackhawk fleet for weeks.

As he listened to more of the assignment details, James felt that familiar excitement he once had for this type of assignment starting to build up once again. This was the kind of challenge that he'd always wanted to pursue.

He thought back to that first year on the job at the DLA when he'd volunteer for every project, especially the ones involving overseas operations. The intricate dance of global military logistics and the challenge of ensuring that the right equipment got to the right place at the right time had always fascinated him.

One specific memory stood out to him all the time. He'd been working late one night, going over inventory reports for a base in Germany, when his old supervisor stopped by his desk and said, "Great job, Martinez. You know, if you keep this up, you might find yourself over there one day. Overseas opportunities are a really great life experience. Being able to see the world and get paid for it—nothing better than that!"

James looked up. "You really think so? I'd love to have that opportunity. I'm always checking for open positions."

His old supervisor chuckled, "Just remember that some places aren't all excitement. It can be long hours, really tough conditions, and a lot of responsibility. But for the right person, it's definitely the chance of a lifetime."

Hearing those words stuck with James, fueling his ambition for years. But as time passed and he'd settled into his family routine with Elena and the kids, that inner fire had dimmed. But now, he was presented with that dream again.

Pulling James out of the haze of his excitement, he heard Jack speaking.

"This assignment would initially be for about six months, with the possibility of extending longer if needed," Jack explained. "You'd be stationed and housed at Camp Liberty in Baghdad, but you'd also need to travel to other bases as well. There are a lot of risks involved, of course, so I'm not going to sugarcoat it. We'll make sure that you have military protection any time you travel, and you'll also be required to undergo training before you go."

James just nodded while he listened, going over it all in his head. *Six months or longer? This would be a long time to be away from Elena and the kids. And being in Iraq ... definitely not a great place to visit, especially for Americans.*

He thought about all the news reports he saw recently, the stories of IEDs, insurgent attacks, and the recent drone attacks that were going on due to the region being so unstable.

A wave of fear started to build up in James' stomach, but alongside that fear, excitement was building up and pushing that fear back down. *This is not just about going on some vacation or about advancing my career. If there really are all of these equipment irregularities, it could put American lives in harm's way. Servicemen and women in the field depended on having the equipment they needed when they needed it. If I could make sure that happened, then it's my duty to help.*

"James, are you still with me?" Jack's voice broke through the fog of his thoughts. "We know this is a lot to take in. You don't have to make a decision right now. Go home and talk it over with Elena. We can give you until the end of the week to give us your answer. Is that satisfactory to you?

James steadied himself. "Yes, Sir, that should be fine. I really appreciate the opportunity, and I'm definitely interested. But, like you said, I need to talk it over with my wife first. This would be a huge change for my family, and I need to make sure they'd all be on board with all of this."

Nodding in approval, Captain Phillips spoke. "That is a wise decision, Martinez. This isn't something to take lightly. But I do hope you'll seriously consider it. We need your talents and skills over there."

As the meeting wrapped up, James stood to leave. He felt like he was in a daze. The typical Tuesday in the office he'd expected had just turned into a pivotal moment in his life and career. As he made his way back to his desk, his mind was already running through the possibilities. James imagined himself in Iraq, sifting through all of the inventory lists, putting together a complex puzzle of the missing equipment.

But then his thoughts went to his family. He thought of Elena's face, of Miguel and Sophia. *How are they going to handle this? Could I really be thinking about leaving them for six months or longer? And would I really be prepared for any dangers I might face over there?*

James sat in his chair. His stare pierced through the screen that was in front of him. He had a lot to think about and not a whole lot of time to do it.

Later that day, in the break room, sitting with a cup of coffee, James let his thoughts drift. He recalled all the conversations he had with his old Marine buddy Chez, who'd served several tours in the Middle East.

"It's not just the physical danger, James," Chez had said, his voice serious. "It's the mental toll as well, the constant need to be on guard at all times. You'll see things that you never wanted to see. You'll have to deal with situations that could mean life or death for you and the people around you

... it changes you, man." Chez had paused for a moment before continuing, "And the toll that you'll put on your family by not being around, it's not just about risking your life, it's also about risking the life you've built for yourself here."

James understood those words now more than ever. The possible risks were not just physical but also mental and emotional, stretching way past the time he'd be there.

He began to go over all the questions he had in his mind. *Could I handle missing the kid's birthdays? And what about Elena? How would this affect her? Could I put her through all of this? Would she be able to manage the kids alone if something happened to me over there?*

James shook his head, clearing out all the doubts and worries. He knew he had to go over the risks more thoroughly. James decided to speak with Captain Phillips one more time. He knew that she had firsthand experience in Iraq and could provide him with a little more insight on what to expect when he got there.

James walked up to the Captain's office and lightly knocked on her open door. Captain Phillips looked up from her work, "Yes Martinez, what is it?"

"Captain, if you've got a few minutes, would it be okay to ask you a few questions?" James asked.

"Of course, Martinez, come on in and take a seat. What's on your mind?" she asked.

"I was hoping you could help me understand a little bit about what the conditions would be like over there. What are the risks, not just from the hostile insurgents there, but what would daily life be like over there, and what impact might it have on my family?" James asked her.

Captain Phillips sat back in her chair; lines were etched around her eyes as she thought carefully about her reply. "It's a tough place, James. You'll be stationed at relatively secure bases. But you'll also have to be prepared for the unexpected to happen. There are still IEDs hidden on some of the roads around there, and indirect fire and other events are sometimes a daily occurrence around Iraq."

The Captain paused momentarily, letting James take in what she had just said before continuing. "The mental toll can also be real on someone who hasn't experienced this before. You might have to see or hear things and possibly have to make decisions under pressure that you could never have imagined you had to do before." She paused, letting it all sink in. "I'm not aware of your family situation, that's something you have to figure out together but I can tell you that it'll be hard on them. Calls home help with that, but the time difference means you're up when they are asleep, and vice versa. It's definitely a strain on your relationships."

Listening intently, James began to imagine scenes of all the scenarios she described.

"But," Captain Phillips continued. "This is also a very tight-knit community. The military takes care of its own. You'll have the support you need when you return. From the base for you and your family. We have lots of programs like counseling and networks for spouses. Those aren't just for people in the military but are also to support our civilians who travel overseas. It's not easy, but it's possible to manage it with the right support."

James took it all in gratefully and then thanked her for her time. His mind was now a little more at ease. Returning to his desk, he couldn't help but wonder how his wife would react to this little adventure.

The rest of the day went by in a blur for him. He went through all of the motions of his usual workload, reviewing reports, answering emails, and hopping on a few conference calls. But through it all, his thoughts were somewhere else. They constantly kept going back to the meeting and the decision that he had to make. *Man, this is hard,* James thought to himself.

When James finally looked down at his watch, he was startled. It was already 3:45 p.m. *Holy crap, where'd the day go?* Then he remembered Miguel's soccer practice. *Yes! This could be the perfect time to talk to Elena about this. Seeing Elena and Miguel would help put this all in perspective for me. Yeah, that's what I'm going to do!*

Chapter 4

The Decision

The drive to the soccer fields went by pretty quick. Before James knew it, he was pulling into his community's sports complex. *And there's her car, parked in its usual spot.* He smiled to himself. *I can't wait to see the look on her face when she sees me here. It's going to be awesome, at least until we discuss the day's events.*

The late afternoon sun was warm on his face as he walked up to the soccer field where Miguel was practicing. He spotted Elena almost immediately sitting on the bleachers just behind where Miguel's team was, her attention was focused on Miguel who was warming up with his teammates on the field. James carefully climbed up the steps. *Man, I hate climbing up these bleachers. I always feel like I'm going to tumble to my death.* James eventually got to where Elena was and sat down beside her.

"You mind if I sit here, ma'am?" he asked with a grin on his face.

Elena turned, her face lit up with surprise and excitement. "Babe! What are you doing here?! I didn't expect you to make it, but I'm so glad you did." They shared a quick kiss. "How was your day at the office?" Elena asked.

"It was good. It was busy as usual, but it was good," James replied. *Alright, wait for the right moment to tell her; be cool, James. Ask her how her day was.* "How has your day been?" he asked.

"It was hectic. I was running all over the place today. But it turned out good, I think these buyers for that house over off of Frost Street might sign today." Elena replied

"That's awesome." James said.

They then turned their attention to the soccer field, where the coach attempted to organize the kids into their practice drills. James and Elena sat in silence for a few minutes, watching Miguel run through passing drills.

James sat there working up the courage. *Alright, we've sat here long enough. Say what you need to say, James.* He finally said, "So, something very interesting occurred at work today."

Elena turned towards him, raising an eyebrow. "Oh really-ly? Do tell."

James nodded, trying to hold back the nervousness in his voice. "Yes, ma'am. Your husband has been requested, at the highest levels, to accept a temporary posting overseas. The heads of my DLA department want me to fly out to Iraq and assist the DLA team there with some inventory issues they're having on a few of their bases."

"Oh my!" Elena said, opening her eyes wide in surprise, "Iraq, huh? Wow, that's ... that's pretty big news, babe. How long would you be gone for? What would you be doing while you were there?" she asked.

"Well, the gist of it is, with the military's drawdown from Iraq coming up, the military has been trying to take an inventory count of what equipment they have deployed there. While they were in the process of doing this, they ran into some inventory discrepancies. So, the DLA wants someone from the outside to come in and take a look. Investigate what's happening and identify the issues." James explained

"I see, and … how long would you be gone for?" Elena asked, her face showing signs of concern now.

"Well, initially, the assignment is for six months, depending on how long it takes me to figure out what the issues are. But it could take longer. How long? I'm not 100% sure, but you know me, babe. I get things done, so I'd be shooting for no longer than six months," James said confidently.

"Six months … that's a long time." Elena said, looking back out to the field.

James could see that she was thinking about it as she sat there quietly, her eyes looking out at Miguel, but she was clearly trying to process what James had just said.

Elena thought back to when they first met. It was on a blind date arranged by some friends they had in common at the church she attended. James was so animated back then, talking about his dreams and how he wanted to make a difference in the world doing something he loved. She had fallen in love with that passion, that sense of purpose he had. Now, she saw it in his eyes again, but it came with a considerable cost she hadn't fully considered back then.

Finally, after a minute or two, she turned back to him with a small smile on her face. "This sounds like a huge opportunity for you, right?" she asked.

James nodded. "Yes, it is, babe. But it's also a huge decision for our family. I'd never even consider it without all of your support."

Elena reached out and squeezed James' hand. "I remember not too long ago after you started working for the DLA, how passionate you were about the idea of working overseas someday. I can see that fire has been lit again in your eyes."

She paused before continuing. "I'm very proud of you, babe, for wanting to make a difference and being willing to take on this difficult challenge. But ..." Her voice lowered a bit. "I'd be lying If I said that the thought of you going to Iraq didn't scare me just a little bit. It's a big step for not just you and me but also for the kids."

James looked out at the field, staring into the distance, squeezing her hand back. He looked back at her and said, "I know. To be honest, I'm a little scared, myself."

Elena smiled. "We're in this together, Sir. Whatever you decide to do, just promise me that you'll really think it over—not just the opportunity but the risk as well."

"I will, I promise," James assured her.

Elena smiled and kissed him on the cheek. "How about this? Let's talk about it over dinner tonight. We can loop in the kids and make this a family decision. How's that sound?"

James felt a rush of love and gratitude for this amazing woman beside him. "That sounds great to me. Thanks for being such a great person. I love you very much."

Later that evening, as they all sat around the dinner table. James decided to bring up the subject again, but now with his kids. Sophia and Miguel sat there listening as their father explained the opportunity that was offered to him.

Finally, when he was done talking, Sophia had the first question. "So, you'd be gone for six months? or possibly longer?" she asked, her fork paused halfway to her mouth.

"That's right, mija. It's a long time, I know. But time will fly by faster than you know it." James replied.

Miguel spoke next, with a little bit of concern in his voice. "But isn't Iraq really dangerous? I saw online ..."

James held his hand up, gently cutting him off. "It can be dangerous, mijo," James admitted. He didn't want to withhold the truth from his kids. "But I'd be on highly secured military bases most of the time I'm there. It'd be rare for me to have to leave the base, and even if I did, I'd have a lot of protection."

"Your dad would be helping to ensure our servicemen and women have all the equipment they need to stay safe. It's a very important job," Elena added.

Both of the kids seemed to sit there and mull it over for a bit. Sophia, always the analytical one, started asking questions about how they'd stay in touch. "Would we be able to talk to you over Facetime?" Sophia asked.

"I'm pretty sure we'd be able to do that, mija. I'll have access to the base's Wi-Fi, so I should be able to talk to you over FaceTime just fine. I can always email and call you on the phone as well." James replied.

Miguel was much quieter. Eventually, he spoke up. "You'll be very careful, right, Dad?"

Seeing Miguel's concern, he motioned for him to come over and gave him a hug. "I'll be super careful, mijo. I promise."

"We're proud of you, Dad," Sophia said, coming around and giving him a big hug.

Miguel gave a thumbs up in agreement. "Yeah. You'll be a real-life hero!"

James chuckled, "I don't know about that, but I'll definitely be doing my part to help them fix whatever problems they need me to fix, buddy."

After putting the kids to bed, James and Elena relaxed on the couch, going over the rest of the details of his trip.

"We'll need to see if your passport needs to be renewed," Elena said, starting to take mental notes. "And we'll need to check to see if there are any vaccination requirements for going to Iraq. Remember that time your father talked about all the vaccinations he had to get when he went to Vietnam. Do you think you'll need any special gear?"

James just smiled at this remarkable woman. How fast she switched into planning mode always amazed him. "When I go into the office tomorrow to let them know my decision, I'll get a list of requirements from them. Thank you, babe, for everything. Your and the kids' support means the world to me."

Leaning in and kissing him softly on the cheek. Elena said, "Just promise me you'll be careful over there. And call us as much as you can."

"I promise I will," James said, pulling her close.

Laying there in bed that night, James thought about the assignment. *This is going to be pretty hard. I'm going to have to make sure I do some digging into the databases before I head out. That way I'm prepared for whatever issues I find. I'll need to check out the internet and see what kind of problems are going on over there in Iraq right now. I think the last thing I read was something about drone attacks on some of the bases. I'll need to look into which ones. Can I handle being away from them for six months? Man, I hope so. Once there, I'll have to do it.*

He thought about how this might change their easy and happy family life. *Elena will have to take on more responsibilities at home and possibly rely more on her parents. Should I suggest that she hire someone to help around the house? What about the kids? Would they be forced to grow up a little bit faster? Will they learn more about independence in ways they might not have had to if I wasn't leaving?*

Whatever was going to happen, he knew he had a short amount of time to help his family prepare for his absence.

Chapter 5

The Game of Shadows

Brigadier General Roger Sloan walked through the quiet halls of his headquarters at Camp Liberty. The unease from his encounter with Major Wright earlier in the week, and the fact that she was accessing the logistics databases at the same time he was, still had him on edge as he made his way to his office.

The air was hot today as it always was. *Why is it always so damn hot in this God-for-saken place? It always smells like dust and diesel.* It was a constant reminder of where he was. Outside, he could hear the sound of the call to prayer from a nearby mosque that carried through the air.

When he finally got to his office, he went straight to his desk and began typing away on his laptop, pulling up Major Wright's access logs. As the logs came up, Sloan clenched his jaw as he reviewed exactly what she was looking into. *She's been looking at all of my transfer records, looking into the inventory discrepancies, and all of the shipping manifests. It would appear that she's putting together some kind of report, possibly to be used against me.* Continuing to read it became abundantly clear. *She's documenting everything. Why? For whom? Who's involved? Good questions but no answers.*

Sloan leaned back in his chair, placed his hands behind his head, and thought back to his earlier days when he was in military intelligence back in the 90's. *Those were the good old days when I was back in Eastern Europe. That's where I learned the art of manipulation and control, some of the primary necessities of maintaining a secret. Those lessons were priceless, but they came at a cost … All the damn faces of the people I had to sacrifice always haunting me, all of the lines I had to cross. This operation now is just like those; it's all about my survival and maintaining the power that I earned all by myself over all these damn decades. But … now, this fucking Major Wright is trying to screw it all up for me.*

A sudden ring from his secure phone brought him back. "Sloan," he answered.

"Sir," Colonel Richards' voice came over the phone with a hint of urgency. Breaking away from his thoughts. "Sir, we've got a problem that requires your immediate attention."

"Make your way to my office now, Colonel," Sloan ordered.

Sloan went back to reviewing Wright's access logs while waiting for Colonel Richards to make his way to his office. Sloan had to give her some credit. She'd been very careful. Each of her queries was on point, and they were all properly logged. Nothing that would raise any red flags in the system with a regular user. But put them all together, and …

A knock at the door pulled him out of his review. "Come."

Colonel Richards made his way in, quietly closing the door behind him. He walked up to Sloan's desk and saluted.

"At ease, Colonel," Sloan said.

"Sir, I just got word that the DLA is planning to send someone to investigate our equipment transfers and do an inventory spot check. The orders came over from CENT-COM this morning," Colonel Richards informed Sloan.

Sloan looked up from his screen, his face hardening. "On whose authority?"

"It was signed off by the Joint Chiefs, Sir, just this morning," Richards said, dropping his voice slightly. "It looks like Senator Katrina Long has been pushing for more oversight during the drawdown. She's been very vocal about full transparency since the last committee hearing. They're sending out a civilian specializing in data analytics and forensic audits. He's based out of NAS Jacksonville. The memo said his name is James Martinez, Sir."

General Sloan's fingers danced across this laptop keyboard with ease. *Who the fuck is James Martinez? Sloan thought to himself as he pulled up Martinez's file along with his performance record. It was impressive: top ratings across the board and multiple commendations for solving complex logistical issues. This guy is good.*

"Civilian, huh?" Sloan said with amusement as he scanned through James' file. "This is ... typical D.C. bureaucracy." He recalled the last time he had to deal with some nosy civilian auditor. *What was that jackass's name again? Phill ... Bill ... Something stupid ... that guy was just a glorified accountant from New York who had no clue how logistics worked. I believe he ended up at some out-of-the-way place; I forget where I had him reassigned to. Was it Utah? Something like that, for basically finding a few clerical errors. The guy was an idiot, but this Martinez seems different. Interesting ... this was the kid that fixed our blackhawk parts supply issue last year; god damn did that save our bacon. Well, Mr. Martinez, bring it on, my friend. But still, an inner warning urged caution. There are still a few possible unknowns involved. I need to work on them all ASAP.*

"There's more, Sir," Colonel Richards went on. "Public Affairs called a little while ago to let us know that, unrelated, they're sending out a small crew of journalists from the World News Network."

Sloan looked up and asked. "Have you confirmed this?"

"Yes, Sir. I just verified with them this morning. Public Affairs is placing the journalist with a Marine Corps unit that's currently being rotated out here. WNN has been approved for standard coverage along with approval to do live broadcasts from the field. Public Affairs wants them to report on daily operations, patrol missions, and human interest stories. They think it'll be a great PR opportunity. They're set to arrive in a couple of weeks along with Mr. Martinez." Richards reported.

"My personal opinion, Sir, I believe there's more to it then they're letting on. The timing of it all doesn't seem to add up. I believe the senator is behind this as well." The Colonel said with concern.

Sloan sat back, tapping his fingers on the arm of his chair.

Looking at Richards, Sloan asked. "Colonel, you wouldn't happen to have seen Major Wright recently?"

Richards tried to recall if he did or not before responding: "No, Sir, I can't say that I have. I didn't see her at the morning briefing. I went by her quarters concerned afterward, but they were empty. Her laptop was gone, and most of her personal items were cleared out. Is it right to assume that she was transferred, Sir?"

Sloan, withholding the truth from Richards, slowly nodded. "Yes, she was needed for another assignment. She had to ship out quickly. I signed off on her transfer yesterday, and she was scheduled to head out this morning. I was just wondering if she'd made it out OK. My apologies for not giving you a heads–up, Colonel."

Sloan sat there thinking to himself. *All of this extra fucking scrutiny had to be because of her. Wright is no halfwit. She had to have known the risks before she started digging around. I imagined she would have found a good place to hide by now ... Fucking coward ... She could be anywhere, in the city, or maybe on her way out of the country where she thinks she's untouchable ... But no one is untouchable ... I'll find her ... She may think she's smarter than me, but that's her mistake and it'll be her downfall. Hmm, she would have planned an exit strategy right after I caught her digging. Especially if she and the senator are working together against me ... I need to figure out who her allies are around the base and how far her network of spies stretches.*

"Alright, let's make sure that we make our guests feel welcome when they arrive," Sloan said to the Colonel. "Thank you for the report, Colonel. You are dismissed."

Colonel Richards gave Sloan a quick salute and left his office, closing the door behind him.

Sloan, now alone, leaned back in his chair, rubbing his hands together. He was going back over everything, one issue at a time. *This James Martinez is one thing, but hav-*

ing to deal with this damn journalist and live feed being broadcast from my bases ... this is going to be an immense pain in my ass. Fucking senator sticking her nose where it shouldn't be. This complicates things significantly. I'm going to need to make some adjustments to my operations.

He pulled out his encrypted burner phone and opened a secure messaging app. He quickly started typing out a message:

"We need to move the timeline forward on inventory crate 347. Clear the rest out before 0600."

Then he created a new message to another contact:

"We need to rotate some of the teams out, move team Alpha away from Balad, and move the Delta team out of Liberty. We have eyes incoming, and I want everyone out of sight while they're here. Get this done ASAP."

After each message was sent and received, the messages were auto-deleted.

He created one more message:

"Hassan – We need to meet tonight. Location Tango. Priority delivery. I need to move up the regularly scheduled delivery due to some complications that have arisen and are being handled."

Hassan immediately confirmed the message with a thumbs-up, and then it deleted itself.

Sloan had created a highly organized network that ran like a well-oiled machine. Each team knew its role without seeing the entire picture of the operation.

Sloans' hired private contractors would disappear like wraiths in the night, their paperwork showing routine transfers to other bases as they were shuffled around. Their weapons and equipment would vanish and be untraceable through dozens of offshore shell companies and phony requisition paperwork.

Pulling up a map on his screen, Sloan studied a list of bases Martinez would likely visit. Each one had to be carefully prepared for Martinez's arrival. Sloan would need to ensure that inventory records were cleaned, certain personnel rotated out, new ones rotated in, and contactors hidden away.

But his main concern was the places between the bases. The out-of-site zones were where his trucks moved at night, where most of his shipping containers changed hands, and where money was exchanged through channels that might be visible to official audits.

Sloan stood, stretching his legs as he walked over to the window. Going over the backup plans he'd have to make, the calculated risks and opportunities around him.

Let them come. He thought to himself. *Sometimes, the best place to hide something is in plain sight.*

Turning back to his laptop, Sloan began to draft a message to his logistics team:

"Good morning, Team. We have some visitors inbound from the States. They'll be conducting some inventory audits within our operations. Let's make sure that they have our full cooperation. Every file, every record, every base they want to visit. Keep me posted on all of their activities on and off the bases."

A sinister smile formed on Sloan's face as he hit send.

Then Sloan double-clicked on another file, opening it. It contained his entire network of private military contractors who worked with a no-question-asked policy, local tribe leaders paid handsomely to look the other way during his operations, corrupt border officials at every border crossing, and even a few military personnel who had no idea what they were actually getting into.

Each had no idea about the other, and they were all managed separately, so no one person, other than himself knew the scope of the entire operation. He had spent years creating this web and was not about to let some civilian unravel it.

Reaching once again for his secure phone, he dialed a number from memory. The phone rang, and the person on the other end picked up immediately. "We may have a situation here. Our friend Senator Long is sticking her nose where it shouldn't be. She is sending the media out here. It's nothing urgent yet, but I need you to stay alert. I'll be in touch if anything changes."

After hanging up the phone, Sloan looked back at his laptop. He studied James Martinez's profile picture. The man had an intelligent face and keen eyes. *I have a feeling this isn't going to be a simple matter of bureaucratic oversight getting in the way. I'm going to have to be smart about all of this.*

"Well, Mr. Martinez. I welcome you to Iraq with open arms." Sloan said softly. "Let's see how good you really think you are at figuring out puzzles."

Sloan decided to draft one more email, he began drafting orders that would overwhelm the civilian investigator with so much information while revealing absolutely nothing substantial. *The games have just started. Mr. Martinez and I plan to win.*

As the sun rose higher in the sky over Baghdad, Sloan displayed a slight smile on his face. His operation was built so carefully, piece by piece, brick by brick, and contact by contact. He hadn't gotten this far to be undone by some logistic specialist who thinks he's good at his job or by some ambitious journalist, and definitely not by some D.C. senator up on her high horse demanding oversight over everything.

If James Martinez turned out to be as capable as his record suggested, Sloan thought, *There are always other methods and solutions to my problems.* For now, General Sloan would play the ever-so-gracious host, watching from afar and waiting to see each move his opponents would make.

The game of shadows was about to begin.

Chapter 6

A Family's Last Adventure

Cruising through the morning fog on I10 East, James Mart-niez was in the driver's seat of the family pickup truck that was pulling their RV. Elena sat next to James, her hands wrapped around a warm cup of coffee, her long hair pulled back in a ponytail. In the back seats of the truck, Sophia and Miguel were huddled under a warm blanket. They were still trying to shake off the sleep from having to get up so early.

James caught Elena looking over at him, and they shared a smile, silently acknowledging this rare moment. Most of the time, their kids would complain about being up this early, but not on these trips. Their excitement always out-weighed the complaints.

"You know," Elena said, "I was just thinking about the first time we went camping when we first got the RV and we tried to boondock with it. Do you remember that? When we got lost trying to figure out where the campsite was that we found on that boondocking app?"

James gave a slight laugh, the memory popping up in his mind. "How could I forget that day!? We ended up setting up camp and later discovered it was some old man's backyard."

"Yes! And he came out waving his cane at us, yelling at us to get off his lawn." Elena added, laughing. "I thought for sure that guy was going to keel over because he was so mad."

James and Elena laughed so hard that it caught the kids' attention. "What are you two laughing about?" Sophia asked.

As Elena retold the story to the kids, embellishing it just a little bit with a few dramatic gestures that had Miguel laughing uncontrollably, James felt a warmth spreading throughout his body. *These are the moments I'll miss the most while I'm gone. I'm going to miss them so much. Alright, enough of that. This weekend is about making memories, not about being sad. Pull it together, James.*

As they approached the entrance to Hannah Park, the sun began to warm the air causing the morning fog to finally lift. James steered his truck and RV toward the entry gates, pulling up to the ticket window for their campsite paperwork. After passing through, they drove to their assigned spot and backed in.

"Alright, it's time to get set up, team Martinez," he said before continuing. "Let's work on getting unhitched and the campsite set up. Miguel, you and I'll get the RV plugged in and the truck unloaded. Sophia and Mom can handle getting the slide out and the AC going. Let's move like we have a purpose, people!"

With everyone's tasks assigned to them, the family moved just like they'd done many times on previous trips. While James and Miguel were working on getting the truck unloaded, James could hear Sophia and Elena inside the RV going over the meal plans for the day.

"Dad," Miguel said suddenly, pausing while he was standing in the back of the truck handing something to James. "Do you think we'll still be able to take trips like this when you get back from your trip?"

James stood there for a moment, caught off guard by the question. He'd been so caught up preparing to leave that he hadn't even thought about what would happen when he returned. "Of course we will, bro," he said, reaching up and running his hand over his son's head. "In fact, I'm counting on you to keep your mom and sister in tip-top camping shape while I'm gone. Do you think you can do that for me?"

Miguel looked up with pride in his eyes. "Absolutely, you can count on me!"

"I know I can, mijo! Now, let's get the rest of this gear unloaded so we can go fishing and catch some dinner. I bet you there are some big bluegill under that dock at the campground lake just like last time," James said.

As the day continued, they all fell into the familiar rhythm of their camping life. James and Miguel went to the lake to fish, while Elena and Sophia went on a hike on one of the park's many trails.

Later, they all met back at the campsite for lunch. Elena had packed sandwiches and fruit for all of them. While they sat there eating their lunch, they began one of the many camping traditions that they inherited from Elena's family. They started singing a Spanish lullaby called "Cielito Lindo," which they had adopted for their trips. Sitting in their chairs around the campsite, they all began to sing together.

Down from the Sierra Morena mountains,
Pretty little darling, they come,
A pair of black eyes,
Pretty little darling, they're contraband!
(Chorus)
Oh, oh, oh, oh,
Sing and do not cry
Because singing cheers up,
Pretty little darling, our hearts.

That mole that you have,
Pretty little darling, near the mouth,
Don't give it to anyone,
Pretty little darling, it's for me to play with.
(Chorus)

The bird that leaves,
Pretty little darling, its first nest,
Comes back and finds it occupied
Pretty little darling, that's what it deserves.
(Chorus)

An arrow in the air,
Pretty little darling, launched by Cupid
As he was playing,
Pretty little darling, I was the wounded one.
(Chorus)

From your house to mine,
Pretty little darling, there is no more than one step,
Before your mother comes,
Pretty little darling, give me a hug.

The song's melody brought a sense of culture that felt grounding for all of them. With all of the changes that were coming it gave them a sense of comfort. They Laughed throughout the song and the verses, which created a moment of pure joy for them all.

"You know my mother used to sing this all the time when I was just a little girl when we went camping," Elena said when they were finished singing.

"We know, Mom, " Sophia said as she giggled. "You tell us that every time we sing the song."

"Do I?" Elenas asked while poking at Sophia

"YES! You know you do!" Sophia said while laughing.

They all had a good laugh about it, and after lunch, they all decided to go to the beach for a swim in the cool water, which was a welcome relief from the Florida heat.

This is the life, James thought to himself as he listened to Sophia's excited squeal as he tossed her through the air into deeper water. He smiled as he watched Miguel's determined look as he raced his sister. James watched as Elena relaxed in the water and floated on her back, her eyes closed against the sun.

James watched his family having a great time and began thinking about what he might miss while he was gone. *I'm going to miss moments like these. Sophia is going to grow up just a little bit more while I'm not here, and I'm probably going to miss most of Miguel's soccer games ... I'll make it up to them.* He promised himself.

As the evening came, they all gathered around the campfire. James was manning the grill, cooking up the fish he and Miguel had caught earlier at the docks. The smell of freshly seasoned fish being cooked over an open flame drifted through the air.

"Oh man, that smells so good, Dad," Sophia said with a big smile while licking her lips, ready to eat.

"Oh yeah, I can't wait to eat. Dad, which one is the one I caught?" Miguel asked.

"I believe it is this one right here, mijo." James pointed at the large bluegill at the end of the grill.

"That's a big one, Miguel. Good job on catching that one, mijo!" Elena said proudly

Miguel, now with a big smile on his face, said, "It was a fighter, Mom! It took me a long time to reel it in."

James looked at Elena, nodding, "It sure did, but he got it in, and now we have dinner!"

When the food was ready, they filled their plates with the day's catch and all the sides they wanted.

"So, Dad," Sophia said as she sat down to eat, "are you starting to get nervous about leaving for Iraq?"

James paused, taking in the question. His voice almost betrayed him more than he had intended. "I think I'm ready, mija. I've been working out a lot of the details while at the office. Planning and getting all the things I need to get done before I go. It'll be a big change for me, and I'll have a lot more responsibility than I do here when I get over there. But I'm also excited about this opportunity to help."

"What are you going to be doing over there again, Dad?" Miguel asked, his mouth full of fish.

Smiling at his son, James replied. "Well, mijo, I'll be there to help investigate some inventory issues that the team over there is having with some of their equipment. They want me to make sure that our servicemen and women have all of the equipment they need to do their jobs."

James began to think of a good way to put it, "It's like ... imagine if we came out here on this camping trip and realized that we had forgotten all of our camping supplies. My job is to make sure that doesn't happen to our troops over there."

"But why'd they pick you to go?" Sophia asked, pressing the issue. "Couldn't they just have found someone else, someone without a family?"

Seeing James struggle with the onslaught of their kids' questions, Elena came to his rescue. She chimed in before James could answer. "Your father has a special talent for solving really complex problems and seeing patterns where others might miss them. Do you remember last year when he was able to figure out why the school's bus routes were always running late?"

Sophia and Miguel nodded.

"It's something like that," Elena explained, "But on a much larger scale. Your dad will use those same skills to help ensure the servicemen and women have all the necessary equipment they need to do their jobs." She paused, her eyes meeting James'. "But we'll definitely miss him, right? So we'll need to be strong for each other."

"Okay," Sophia said, sounding a little sad. "I'm just going to miss you a lot, Dad."

"I'm going to miss all of you so much as well, mija," James said to her, feeling the guilt building up inside of him.

As they continued their conversation, they talked about everything from the details of James' upcoming deployment to Miguel's latest soccer game, James sat there feeling a deep sense of gratitude for what he had.

Later that evening, as the fire began to die down and the kids went inside the RV to watch TV, James and Elena hung out a little while longer, looking up at the star-filled sky.

"You know," Elena said quietly, "When you told me about this assignment, I was really scared. But now, seeing you with the kids and hearing you tell them about your work and the work you'll be doing ... I'm very proud of you, James." She said, her voice catching.

James gently squeezed her hand. "I couldn't do any of this without your support," he managed to say. "You and the kids ... you're my rock. No matter where I go, that'll never change." He looked up at the stars, wondering if he would see the same ones in Iraq. "I wish that I could make moments like this last forever."

As they sat in silence, the sounds of the wilderness around them, James felt a sense of peace finally settle over him. The fear of what might come was still there, lingering deep down. The weekend didn't go exactly as they planned. There had been no grand speeches, no perfect moments of fatherly wisdom. Instead, it was messy and wonderful all at the same time. It was full of small, precious moments that made up his family life.

Before they went to bed, James called out to the kids to join him and Elena by the fire. James pulled out his phone, wanting to capture one last moment of the four of them, their faces illuminated by the firelight. "For when I need to remember this moment," he said.

The next day, they'd pack up and head home. They'd attend their routine service at Rise Church of Jacksonville, where the music and pastor's Adam and Rebecca Peterson's up-lifting words would bring James a small sense of hope. But he also knew that the sermon would also speak of trials of faith that were tested by distance and danger as they usually did. It was a subtle reminder of what lay ahead for him.

Then would come the final preparations, the hard-to-say goodbyes. But right now, under the Florida sky, James was exactly where he needed to be. With his family, the people he loved the most in this world, making memories that would stay with him and sustain him through whatever trials lay ahead.

Chapter 7

Departures

James Martinez stood outside the security checkpoint with his family at the NAS Jax airfield in Jacksonville, Florida. Elena and the kids were there with him, saying their good-byes before he went through security. Elena was busy on her phone going over the checklist that she had created to make sure that James didn't forget anything.

"Passport?" Elena asked James.

"Got it right here," James replied, patting his chest pocket on his shirt.

"Meds? You got the sunscreen I packed you? Did you pack enough underwear as well?" Elena almost sounded like she was interrogating him.

James just laughed as he pulled her in for a hug. *What would I do without her?* He thought. "Yes, ma'am, I got it all. I double-checked my bag after you triple-checked it before we came. I can't believe how fast these last couple of weeks went by."

Sophia, who had been standing right next to James with tears starting to well up in her eyes, said, "Don't forget to FaceTime us as much as you can, okay, Dad?"

James looked down at Sophia and saw how emotional she was getting. *Oh man, I hope she doesn't cry. This is harder than I thought it would be.* James knelt down, wrapped her in a big hug, and softly said, "I will, mija, I promise, as much as I can every day. I love you so much. Thank you for being so brave." James gave her a kiss on the cheek.

James turned to Miguel, who was standing next to Elena. "Come here and give your old man a hug, mijo."

Miguel wrapped his arms around James, resting his head on his shoulder. "I'm going to really miss you, Dad. Please be careful. And like Sophia said, you have to make sure you call us every day if you can."

"I will, mijo, I promise." James gently pulled Miguel away so he could look him in the eyes. "You're in charge now. You're the man of the house while I'm gone. It's up to you to take care of your mother and sister, okay? Can you do that for me, buddy?"

Miguel nodded as a big smile crossed his face, wiping away tears. "Yes, Sir! I can do that."

"Good, I'm counting on you." Looking at both kids now, "You two be good for your mom while I'm gone, okay? I love you both very much." James said, with a bit of emotion now in his voice.

"We will." both of the kids said at the same time.

James stood up and looked at Elena, who now had tears running down her face. He walked over to her and gave her a hug. "I love you so much. I'll be back before you know it," he said, kissing her on her cheek.

"You better! I love you. Have a safe flight, and be careful. Text me when you land so I know you made it there safely", Elena said.

"I will. Okay, I need to get to my flight now. I love you all. I'll call, text, and FaceTime all of you every chance I get," James said as he picked up his bags and headed to his flight.

Turning around one last time before going through the security gates, James gave one last wave goodbye to his family. James sighed, *Man, I'm going to miss them so much.* He took a deep breath calming himself before heading to the gate. *Am I doing the right thing?... It's too late now to have reservations.*

While James sat at the gate waiting to board, he started going over things in his head. *Alright, what do we know? A lot of the data I was given isn't adding up when I reconciled it against past purchases. So, that would mean something is happening in the system that's causing these issues. Could it be a supply clerk who doesn't know how to do their job?*

This is going to be a huge challenge for me, but they wouldn't have picked me to do this if they didn't think I could figure it out. James pulled out some of the briefing documents from his bag to review. *This is a lot of data. I need to find a good starting point. I need to get into the mindset that these aren't just numbers. They are all pieces of a puzzle that I need to put together to figure out what's going on.*

When it was time to board the plane, James walked out of the gate onto the airfield. The Florida humidity clung to him as he walked up the stairs to board the plane. James looked back one last time to take in the view of home. *This is the last time I'll see home for the next 6 months. You never know how much you're going to miss home until you're actually leaving it.*

James entered the plane and found his seat. He pulled out his phone to make sure it was in airplane mode. As the phone came on, the photo he'd taken with his family on their camping trip a couple of weeks ago was on his lock screen. James just stared at it and smiled. *I'll be back before you guys know it, I promise.* James looked out the window as the plane was taxiing down the runway for take-off. As it started to lift off the runway, he watched as the Jacksonville, Florida, landscape receded beneath him. *I hope they have AC in Iraq ...*

A couple of hours later, James arrived at Dover Air Force Base. After the plane landed, it taxied to a safe area where everyone could disembark. As James left the plane, the heat from the tarmac washed over him, and the sun almost blinded him. So he put on his sunglasses, which were hanging around his neck to shield his eyes from the sun. When James reached the bottom of the stairs, he scanned the arrival area to see if he could locate his contact.

Standing near some double doors was a young Airman holding a sign with the name "Martinez" written on it. James made his way towards him and introduced himself. James reached out his hand and said, "Good morning, Airman. I'm James Martinez. I'm guessing by your sign that you're here for me."

The airmen shook James' hand and replied, "It's a pleasure to meet you, Sir. My name is Airman Fields. Welcome to Dover Air Force Base. I'll be in charge of escorting you to the guest lodging area. You will spend the evening here at Dover and then catch your departing flight to Iraq via

Kuwait tomorrow morning." Airman Fields took James' bag and said, "Please follow me, Sir. The car is this way."

While driving to the lodging area that was located on the other side of the base, James looked out the car window and was amazed at how massive the base was. *Holy cow, this place is huge.* The entire base was alive with activity. The sound of jet engines and shouts from aircraft personnel filled the air. The roar of the jet engines was deafening as they flew overhead, taking off, heading somewhere unknown.

"Is this your first time at Dover, Mr. Martinez?" Airman Fields asked James.

"Please, call me James," James replied politely as he nodded. "Yes, this is my first time here, actually. This place is way bigger than NAS Jax, I can tell you that. It's very impressive."

Smiling proudly, Fields said, "Yes, Sir. Dover is home to the 436th Airlift Wing. We handle a significant portion of the East Coast strategic airlift operations. But the thing we are probably best known for is that we are the main location for our fallen service members returning home. The base also supports most of the global mobility and refueling missions through the Air Mobility Command for the East Coast."

"Really? That's good to know. You learn something new every day!" James said, taking it all in.

Airman Fields pointed out a few key locations around the base to James while driving and passing various buildings. *A lot of these buildings remind me of the ones at NAS Jax.* James thought to himself.

After pulling into the lodging area where James would be staying, Airman Fields helped James get his bags out of the car. "It was a pleasure meeting you, Mr. Martinez ... I mean James. I hope you have a safe trip to Iraq. And again, Welcome to Dover Air Field," Airman Fields said while shaking James' hand.

"You too, Airman. Thanks for the ride!" James replied.

James walked up to the front desk and went inside to check in. A young lady was waiting for him. "Mr. Martinez?" she said.

"Yes, ma'am, that is me," James replied.

"Welcome, Sir. We have been waiting for you. I have your room information and keys all ready for you." The young lady said.

She then showed him how to get to his room on a little map and then handed James his keys.

"Thank you for all the help," James said to her before making his way to his room. As he entered the room, he thought, *This place smells like it was just cleaned. At least they have the AC running for me. It's a little small, but it'll do for one night. I guess I better get used to these types of sleeping arrangements.*

Later that afternoon, after James had settled in, there was a knock at his door. *I wonder who that could be?* He closed the file on the briefing material he was going over, got up, and answered the door.

A stern-looking Sergeant stood in his doorway and began to speak as soon as he saw James. "Mr. Martinez? I'm Sergeant Rodriguez." He extended his hand to shake James' before continuing. "I'll be your liaison during your deployment to Iraq. Once we are in country, you'll be handed off to your DLA contact, who will be your guide for the remainder of your stay there."

James shook his hand and said, "Nice to meet you, Sergeant Rodriguez. Please come inside."

The Sergeant entered the room, and as he removed his cover, he glanced around at James' things. *This guy brought a Backpack and suitcase, typical civilian. I wish they would give these guys better gear before they get here for deployment.* "I need to brief you on some security protocols. OPSEC is going to be very important over there."

James nodded and thought. *This Sergeant is pretty serious. I think I like him already.* "I understand, Sergeant," James replied.

"Good. Also, remember that any requests you may have will need to be cleared through the proper channels. Have you been debriefed on those already?"

"I have Sergeant," James replied.

"Good. The situation in Iraq is very complex right now, and we need to make sure you understand the risks," Rodriguez stated.

As Sergeant Rodriguez continued his OPSEC briefing, James carefully followed every word the Sergeant was saying. *This guy is very thorough. He kind of reminds me of myself.* James knew his assignment would require him to navigate certain military protocols, but this was next level.

Later that evening, after Sergeant Rodriguez left. James sat at a small table in his room, doing some work before he went to bed. James was on his laptop, logged into one of the databases that maintained the inventories for one of the bases in Iraq. As he scanned through some of the inventory files, the information he was looking at seemed troubling to him. *How could these inventory numbers be so off? One minute, they are correct, and the next minute, they are way off from the physical count that was performed. And why weren't any red flags raised earlier? A lot of this is just not adding up.*

James took out his phone, opened his note app, and started typing a few vital questions he would want to ask people, pondering each one as he typed them in. *This is going to be a hard one, maybe harder than the Blackhawk parts issue I figured out, but I should be able to get to the bottom of it. That is why they picked me, right? I know how to figure this stuff out.*

After James was finished, he swiped out of the app and looked at his phone. There on his home screen was a picture of his family. He sat there for a moment, looking at it. His eyes drifted to the top of the screen. *Oh man, is it midnight already? I guess it's too late to give them a call. The kids would already be asleep. Where did the day go? I'll just send Elena a text message and let her know I got here just fine:*

"I made it to the base safely, babe. Sorry for not texting you earlier to let you know. There was a lot going on when I got here. I'll try to give you a call in the morning if I can. Tell the kids I love and miss them. I love you too, by the way. Talk to you soon." James hit send.

The following day came quickly. Having stayed up way too late, James was moving around a little slower than he wanted to. He packed up all his things, hopped in the shower to rinse off real quick, and got ready for his departure. James' phone dinged while he was packing up his laptop. *That must be Elena. Yep, it is.*

Elena: "Good morning, Sunshine! I was so glad to see your text this morning! I was a little worried when you didn't message me to let me know you landed. But I figured you were probably super busy getting settled in, so I'll let it slide this time! The kids are already off to school. They said to tell you they love you. I hope you have a safe flight. I love you so much and am super proud of you! Stay safe, my love."

James smiled as he reread the text before replying. *Man, I love this woman.* "I'm about to head out the door right now to grab a quick bite to eat. I love you too, babe! More than you'll ever know. I'll text you before we lift off. Love you!" James hit send. James grabbed his stuff and headed out the door.

After he ate his breakfast, James ran into Airman Fields again. "Good morning, James! It's good to see you again, Sir. I was sent here to take you to the staging area where you will depart to Iraq from. My car is right out here."

"Morning! Airman. Lead the way." James replied.

At the deployment area, James joined other people who were also leaving for Iraq that day. *Wow, there are a lot of people heading out with us. Hopefully, there will be enough seats on the plane.* Everyone, including James, had to go through a small processing center. They all moved through each of the stations, doing medical checks. Security personnel verified each person's paperwork, and then there was a final security briefing.

A familiar voice boomed through the hanger. Sergeant Rodriquez called out to everyone there. "Alright, folks, listen up! We'll be issuing your gear next. You'll receive 4 pieces of critical equipment: 2 pairs of fatigues, a flak jacket, a helmet, and a rucksack. After you dress out, you must wear these on base at all times. Pack all of your other clothes in your rucksack, and you'll be able to leave any other civilian belongings you won't be needing in Iraq here at the Dover

Base. Once you are done kitting out, report back here and we'll move out to the flight line, where our C–5M Super Galaxy awaits to take us to Kuwait at 1100 hours sharp. Don't be late!"

James waited in line to gather the gear he'd be issued. *Well, I guess there is no turning back now, is there? This is crazy. Am I really about to catch a flight to Iraq?* Despite being nervous, he was ready for the challenge. He was on the edge of a journey that would change his life forever.

Chapter 8

The Long Haul

James made his way onto the airfield. The massive body of their C–5M Super Galaxy stood like a juggernaut on the tarmac. *Dear GOD! This plane looks like it's too big to fly. I've always seen them from a distance, but now, seeing one up close, it almost doesn't look real. With the cargo bay open, it kind of reminds me of the story of Jonah being swallowed by a whale. I bet the kids would have loved to see this thing up close.*

James strapped on his rucksack and fell in line with the other military and civilian personnel who were boarding the plane. Ahead of him, he spotted two other passengers who seemed to be struggling with their equipment cases. *Should I give them a hand? Sure, why not? I'll be a nice guy.*

"Do you need help with that?" James offered, stepping forward to help steady a case that was about to fall out of the young woman's grip.

"Yes, thank you so much," she smiled gratefully. "I thought I was in pretty good shape, but apparently not good enough to lug fifty pounds of gear." She stuck out her hand and introduced herself. "Hi, I'm Lisa Chen, and this is my friend Tom Ballard."

James politely shook her and Tom's hand. "Nice to meet you both, I'm James Martinez."

"Well, James, I really appreciate your help. It looks like we're all on the same flight. Shall we." Lisa said.

As they made their way up the ramp of the aircraft, Sergeant Rodriguez appeared from inside of the cargo bay with a clipboard in his hand. "Martinez, Chen, Ballard," he called out, checking them off his list. "Find your seats lined on the left side of the aircraft. Make sure to stow and secure your gear. It's going to be a long flight."

The inside of the C-5M had a far different look than any commercial airliner James had flown on before. There were canvas seats lining the walls of the aircraft, and large cargo pallets took up most of the floor space in the middle of the plane. James secured his gear and then decided to help Lisa and Tom secure their equipment as well before finding his seat.

As the engines fired up and came to life, Sergeant Rodriguez stood at the front of the cargo bay. "Alright people, listen up! The flight time to Kuwait is approximately 14 hours, and we're going to try to beat that. We'll make a refueling stop while we are en route in Ramstein Germany. We'll also be unloading some of this cargo in Germany. You will not be getting off the plane. Make sure your seatbelts remain fastened before takeoff and before landing. Does anyone have any questions?"

One Marine raised his hand. Rodriguez seemed to recognize the man because all of a sudden the Sergeant now had an irritated look on his face. "What's your question, Harper?" Rodriguez asked.

"Will there be an inflight movie, Sir?" Corporal Harper asked, who seemed to be holding back a laugh.

Now appearing even more annoyed, Rodriguez barked, "No, Harper, there will not be an inflight movie ... Does anyone else have any questions?"

Everyone in the cargo bay seemed amused by the interaction, which lightened the mood on the aircraft.

"If there are no more questions, I'll let the pilots know we're ready for takeoff," Sergeant Rodriguez said, turning as he eyed Corporal Harper one last time before heading to the flight deck to talk to the pilots.

The plane began to shake as it taxied to its designated runway for takeoff. A few minutes later, the engines spun up with a thunderous roar, as the aircraft barreled down the runway. The next thing they knew, they were airborne. The plane seemed to creak as the massive aircraft fought against gravity, climbing higher and hurtling into the sky.

As they leveled off and were able to unbuckle their seatbelts, Lisa decided to go over and talk to James. *This guy looks interesting, I wonder why he's headed to Iraq.* As she approached, she asked, "Mind if I join you?" and pointed to the empty seat next to James.

"James looked up from some reports he was going over and said, "Sure, have a seat." He motioned towards the empty seat with one hand and put his reports back in his bag with the other.

"So, James," Lisa began casually, "what brings you to Iraq?"

Just as James was about to answer, he noticed a logo on Lisa's jacket that displayed WNN. *She must be a journalist for WNN. I need to watch what I say. They said in the briefing not to talk to any press about official business while over there. They must have been referring to her. But small talk won't hurt.*

Smiling politely, James replied, "I'm with the Defense Logistics Agency, or DLA for short. I'm just heading over there for ... logistics things. Nothing super important. Overall, we just ensure our servicemen and women have what they need to do their jobs. Nothing too exciting." *I think that sounded good. Hopefully, she won't try to press me for more details.*

Lisa realized who James could be. *This must be the guy Mark was referring to. The person who's heading to Iraq to investigate discrepancies. I need to play it cool. I won't ask too many questions. Remember, be inconspicuous, Lisa!* Lisa smiled, seeming interested in this new information. "Routine, huh? Seems like a long way to go for a routine audit. I would think that one of the requirements upon joining the military would be knowing how to count," she said jokingly.

"Audit?" replied James. "I didn't say anything about an audit." James thought, *maybe I had said too much? I need to somehow change the subject.*

"Oh, sorry, I guess I just assumed that," Lisa replied, realizing she had overstepped. *Damn it Lisa, you're blowing it.*

"It's ok," James shrugged. "What about you? I noticed the logo on your equipment. I'm guessing that you work for WNN? What kind of stories are you hoping to cover while you're in Iraq?"

Lisa instantly realized her mistake. She chastised herself in her head, *Stupid logos. I knew we should have taken those off before we got this on the plane.* The element of surprise was gone, so she would have to hold off on her questioning for now. Lisa didn't want to seem pushy, so she decided to just tell him about the other parts of her assignment that didn't involve her following him around to see what he was up to.

James' strategy seemed to work. *Good, now she's changing the subject. It never fails. Ask someone to talk about themselves, and they'll take the bait.*

While James and Lisa were chatting, Sergeant Rodriguez approached them and said, "I see you two are getting to know each other now," the Sergeant said in a neutral type of tone. "Just remember, all interactions must be cleared through the proper channels, Chen," Rodriguez said to them both, more so to Chen. *I'm going to need to keep an eye on her. I can't have her just talking to anyone when I'm not around.*

"Oh, we are just chit-chatting. No interviews going on here, Sergeant, I promise," Lisa assured him. *I'm going to need to try to talk to James when Rodriguez is not around. I think the Sergeant is trying to get in the way of me asking some hard questions.*

Rodriguez eyed them both for a moment longer. *I'm definitely going to have to keep those two apart. There's no telling what Martinez might accidentally say to her.*

"By the way, Chen, I'll need to talk with you and your cameraman, Tom, about some embedded protocols I was instructed to discuss with you. Mr. Martinez, your DLA contact will brief you once you land in Iraq," Sergeant Rodriguez said to them before walking off.

The next few hours seemed to go by in a blur of small talk. Several people were in groups being briefed on their assignments, and several others attempted to find a comfortable position in the uncomfortable seats.

Lisa tried to probe James a little bit more about his assignment, but he carefully deflected the conversation to different topics, like his kids back home, what Lisa had previously reported on before getting this assignment, and a few other mundane subjects.

As the flight continued, James yawned, starting to feel a little tired. *Man, the hum of these engines is putting me to sleep.* And just like that James nodded off. Sometime much later, James was jolted awake from the aircraft hitting some turbulence. *Dear LORD! What was that? This damn turbulence is going to give me a heart attack.* Most of the others, including Lisa and Tom, were still asleep.

Sergeant Rodriguez made his way around the cargo bay, checking on everyone. Eventually he got to where James was sitting and asked, "How are you holding up, Mr. Martinez? Are you doing OK?"

James looked up at him while stretching out the kinks in his body. "I'm doing alright, Sergeant. Thank you for asking. How much longer do you think we have until we get to Germany?"

"I just came from the flight deck, and the pilots told me we're about three hours out, and then another 5 or 6 hours to Kuwait," Rodriguez replied. After a slight hesitation, the Sergeant decided to sit down in the empty seat across from James. "Is this your first time overseas?"

"Yes, Sir." James nodded. "First time outside the United States. How about you, Sergeant?" James asked.

Rodriguez's face softened a little bit. "This will be my second tour to Iraq; I also did two tours in Afghanistan." He shifted a little bit in his seat, trying to get more comfortable. "It's getting harder and harder to leave my family each time, though."

"Do you have kids?" James asked, grateful for the welcomed conversation to pass the time.

"Actually, I do, two girls," Rodriguez replied with a big smile on his face. "There's Maria, who's twelve, and Isebella's nine. Both of them are smart as a whip. My wife Kelly is a teacher, so she's on top of their education, so they come by it honestly." He paused before continuing, "How about you, Martinez? You have family waiting for you back home?"

James nodded his head while reaching into his pocket and pulling out his phone. He unlocked it and pulled up a photo showing it to the Sergeant. "This is my wife Elena, my son Miguel, who's ten, and my daughter Sophia, who's eleven going on twenty. This picture is from last weekend, we went on a camping trip." He handed the phone to Rodriguez.

"That's a beautiful family you got there, Martinez," Rodriguez said, looking at the photo. "This is the hardest part of the job, right? Leaving your family behind. But they are also why we do what we do." He handed James' phone back to him. "Your son plays soccer? Is that his team jersey?"

"Yes, Sir, he's really great at playing, too," James replied. *He caught that detail in the photo pretty quick. This guy is pretty sharp.* "Do your girls play any sports?" James asked.

"They both play basketball," Rodriguez chuckled. "I can definitely say they are both way better at it than their old man is. My wife used to play in college, so that's another thing she encourages them to excel in."

Sharing a quiet laugh, the Sergeant's expression grew slightly more serious. "Listen, Martinez. I know you said this is your first time over here, being this far away from your family and being in a possible combat zone. Just remember what we went over in your briefings. Always stay alert, and don't hesitate to ask questions if you need to. Remember your training, and you'll be alright."

Rodriguez stood up, about to head back to his duties, and said, "Try to get a little more rest. Once we are in-country, it may be a while before you get a decent night's sleep." He paused, then added, smiling, "And Martinez? Call me Rodriguez. We're not in briefings anymore, so we can drop the formality. Most people call me that anyways."

James, looking up at the Sergeant, nodded his head. "Thank you, Rodriguez. I appreciate the conversation."

Sergeant Rodriguez left to continue his rounds, as James settled back in his seat. *I really like Rodriguez; he seems to be a really good person. I'll have to tell Elena about him.* As James sat there, he thought about everything and eventually drifted back to sleep.

CHAPTER 9

THE LAYOVER

The arrival announcement came over the intercom, waking those who were still asleep. The C-5M Super Galaxy began to bank slightly as it descended into Camp Arifjan in Kuwait. James checked his gear to ensure everything was ready to go upon arrival. He looked over and saw that Lisa and Tom were doing the same. James shouted over the noise of the aircraft to Lisa, noticing the tense expression on her face, "Nervous?"

"Maybe, just a little bit! I can't believe this is really happening, you know?" Lisa said to James, laughing a little bit

I know exactly what you mean, James thought to himself.

The wheels touched down on the runway with a squeal of rubber and smoke jolting the aircraft and everyone inside. They were now on Kuwaiti soil. James looked out the window and thought. *Welcome to Kuwait, James. Next stop is Iraq. Alright, I just need to keep it together and focus on the task that has been assigned to me.*

The C-5M slowly taxied to the location where they would disembark and came to a stop. A few minutes later, as the engines slowly started to wind down, the rear door to the cargo bay slowly began to open. The heat from the runway invaded the interior, hitting them like a ton of bricks as they made their way out. The heat was intense, even though it was only early morning.

Sergeant Rodriquez held up his clipboard at the bottom of the ramp and spoke loud enough for everyone to hear him over the busy airport.

"Welcome to Camp Arifjan, people," the Sergeant announced. "We'll have a 24-hour layover here before flying out to Baghdad. Those of you that'll be flying out tomorrow will be shown to your temporary quarters, where you can get cleaned up and get some rest. I'll need everyone ready to move out at 0500 tomorrow."

James shouldered his rucksack and laptop bag and followed the escort through the unbearable heat of the tarmac as they walked toward the temporary housing area.

When James finally arrived at his assigned room, he went in and placed his laptop bag on the bed and placed his rucksack on the floor. He took this opportunity to shower and wash off the smell of the aircraft and sweat he had accumulated on the trip there. After his shower, James lay on the bed. *I'm just going to take a little bit of a nap. That was a rough flight.*

James woke up a few hours later. *Man, I feel so much better after that nap, but I have a feeling the jetlag is going to catch up with me at some point.* Looking at the time on his phone, James realized he hadn't eaten in a while and was feeling a little hungry. *I wonder what they have to eat around here.*

James got dressed and made his way to the dining facility. The large room was alive with activity, filled with servicemen and women and other personnel from all over the world. There was a strong smell of spices and food that he didn't recognize that filled the air. As he made his way to the food line, he noticed Lisa and Tom. He hesitated for a moment. *Should I go over and talk to them? Yeah, I think I will. I just can't let Lisa lure me into business talk.*

James approached Lisa and Tom and asked, "Mind if I join you guys?"

Stifling a yawn, Lisa nodded her head and replied, "Absolutely, we could use the company of someone else from the States, and besides, I think Tom is getting tired of talking to me already," giving Tom a wink and a smile.

Tom chuckled. "Don't let her fool you. She knows I enjoy our riveting conversations."

After going through the food line, where the kitchen staff dished out their selections, they made their way between the occupied tables until they found an empty one near the back of the dining facility. The metal chairs scraped against the floor as they settled in with their trays and began to eat. *This food either tastes REALLY good, or I was way hungrier than I thought I was.*

A few minutes later, Sergeant Rodriguez walked up and joined them. "Good evening, everyone," the Sergeant began. "Please don't forget that our flight heads out at 0500 local time. It'll be a shorter hop this time and should only take us about two hours to get to Baghdad International. Once we're there, we'll break into our assigned groups, and you'll all be transported to your respective locations."

"Sergeant Rodriguez, do you have any idea how long we'll have to wait at Baghdad International before we head out?" James asked.

Sergeant Rodriguez shook his head no. "That'll all depend on what the security situation is like there, along with transport availability. We could be there for a few hours or possibly a day. Just be prepared for anything. If there aren't any other questions, I need to head to the barracks to check on my men and get some sleep. Have a good evening, everyone."

After Sergeant Rodriguez left, the conversation changed to lighter topics, like how hot it was there. "I'm serious," Tom said, gesturing to his already sweat-soaked shirt. I'm going to return home looking like a raisin—a severely dehydrated, tanned raisin."

James nearly choked on his food after hearing Tom's complaints. "If the food is as good as it is here at the other bases, I might return home a few pounds heavier from all the good eating," James said.

They all seemed to get a good laugh out of that. James always had a knack for lightening the mood. "Well, I think I'm going to head back to my room and give the wife and kids a call. They should all be out of bed by now," James said while pushing in his chair and picking up his tray.

"A call home, that sounds like a good idea. I think I'll call my wife." Tom said.

Lisa stood up. "I should call my parents. My mom is probably bouncing off the walls, wondering where I am and when I'll call."

"I guess I'll see you both tomorrow, remember 0500! Don't be late!" James said.

With that, they said their goodnights and headed to their rooms. James made it back to his room and sat down on his bed, reflecting on his trip there. *Alright, just one more day of travel, and I'll be able to get to work. The sooner I work, the sooner I solve this problem and head back home.* After a few minutes, he pulled out his phone and opened a video chat. Luckily, the barracks had a pretty decent wireless signal.

He tapped on Elena's photo and hit the video call button. *Let's see if they are at home or out and about somewhere.* The phone rang a few times, and then Elena's beautiful face, which he was glad to see, popped up on his phone screen.

"What's going on, babe! How was the flight? Are you in Iraq already?" she asked.

"Not yet, honey. We're currently at Camp Arifjan in Kuwait for the night. We'll be heading out to Baghdad to-morrow morning. I was told it should be a fairly short flight from here," James replied.

"Well, I guess that's good. It gives you some time to rest up. How are you feeling after that long flight?" Elena asked.

James shrugged, "I guess I'm OK. I took a nap for a couple of hours when I got here, which seemed to help. I just got back from eating dinner. I might go over a few reports and then call it a night."

Just then, James heard a bunch of racket in the background. It was the sound of two kids racing down the stairs.

"Is that Dad on the phone?!" Sophia asked with excitement. "Dad! How was your flight? Are you in Iraq already?" she asked.

James smiled at seeing her face on the phone screen. "Not yet, mija, I'll be there tomorrow. We're just on a layover right now in Kuwait."

Then, the next thing James saw was the phone shuffling around, and Miguel's face came into view. "Dad, listen," Miguel said as he walked around with the phone. Sophia was in the background telling him to give the phone back. "I will in a minute, I need to talk to Dad for a second. Listen, Dad, I need you to log in to my Roblox account. Are you listening? Just nod your head if you are, OK, good. Log into my account, and I need you to buy me 2500 Robux. You know that I'm good for it. Mom has no idea how to do it, and she says that I have to wait till you get back home, so you need to do it. I can't wait that long, Dad. There is a special Blox Fruit on sale, and I need it! It's super rare, Dad."

There was another shuffling and some arguing as Sophia managed to wrestle the phone away from Miguel. The last thing he heard in the background was Miguel saying, "Don't forget to do it, Dad! It's important!" He also heard Elena in the background say something like, "You better not be bothering your father about those silly roboxes or whatever they are."

Sophia's face was now on the screen. "Sorry about that, Dad. Since you left, all we hear now is Miguel complaining about not having his Robux. He's such a silly boy. Anyways, we miss you so much, Dad. I love you. Please be careful over there. Here's Mom. Bye!"

Elena was now back on the screen, and James just smiled throughout the interaction. *Haha, I love that boy. He's crazy, but I love him.* This entire interaction made him miss home even more.

"I swear that boy has been driving us crazy since you left," Elena said with a smile.

"Tell him I'll take care of it before I go to bed," James said with a laugh. "How are you holding up, babe? Did your parents come by to visit and check on you and the kids?" He asked.

"They did. Mom brought over some Aroz con pollo for dinner, and of course, the kids tore it up as soon as it hit their plates. I think I had half a plate before they ate it all. Mom and Dad said they'd be back later this evening to eat with us again. But we're doing OK so far," Elena said.

"That's good to hear. I'd kill for some home cooked chicken and rice right about now. But I'm glad your parents are there to help out." James replied, feeling a little guilty as he said it.

"Well, get some rest, babe. You look a little tired. You need your rest for the flight tomorrow and whatever else they have planned for you. Don't stay up all night looking at reports! I know you, James Martinez! I know you better than you know yourself. Set an alarm for a decent time to stop working and go to bed. Do you hear me, mister?" Elena said firmly but lovingly.

James smiled big. *This woman really does know me better than I know myself,* "I will, babe, I promise. No staying up late."

"I'm going to hold you to that. OK, kids, say goodnight to your father and tell him you love him," Elena said.

"Goodnight, Dad! We love you!" he heard Sophia say.

As if on queue, Miguel's face was on the screen again as he tried to wrestle the phone away from his mom. "Dad, Dad! Don't forget about the Robux before you go to bed! Remember! It's important! Oh, and I love you and miss you. ROBUX Dad!"

Elena managed to get the phone away from Miguel finally. "I swear I might hurt this boy while you're gone. Please don't forget about his ... whatever it is he needs. I'm not sure how much more we can take of him. OK honey, get some rest. Call us the next time you get a chance. I love you."

Still cracking up from the entire interaction, James said, "I love you guys too. I'll call tomorrow when I get a chance and tell Miguel I'll take care of it when I hang up the phone. Talk to you later, my love."

After ending the call, James sat there for a moment, taking it all in. *Man, I miss those people. I better get those Robux for Miguel, or I might not have a son when I return ...* With a smile on his face, he pulled up the Roblox app on his phone that Miguel insisted he never take off and purchased the requested Robux.

James stayed up for a couple more hours making some last-minute notes and questions for his briefing tomorrow with the DLA group he would be meeting with. *Alright, and the last question is done.* As he finished typing in the final note, the alarm he set went off on his phone. *Right on time, that woman always has the best advice.*

James slid into bed. O*h my, thank the Lord, this bed is halfway decent to lay in.* He stared at the ceiling. *Seeing everyone so happy at home, I kind of wish I was there and not here. Although, I'd have Miguel pestering me constantly about getting the latest Blox Fruit ... Nah, I'll take that any day over this heat here. Just remember, we're here to do a job because you're the one who's right for it.* After a few minutes, James drifted off to sleep.

The next morning, after a quick breakfast, they were all once again gathered at the airfield. The sun was just rising as they boarded the C-17 transport plane. This plane was a bit smaller than the C-5M Super Galaxy they flew in on, but it still had plenty of room to spare. The predawn air was already beginning to warm up, giving them a preview of the heat to come.

The flight to Baghdad was uneventful. Looking out the plane's window, James could see the landscape below, a massive sea of desert stretching for miles. *Wow, I'm guessing that's the Tigris River snaking its way through the land down there. I should have brought my boat.* As they started their descent, James could see a large, stretching city coming into view. His heart began to beat a little quicker. Alright, it's *almost time to get this show on the road. Bring on the TPS reports…* James thought, attempting to amuse himself trying to relax.

Baghdad International Airport was busy with activity. Military and civilian aircraft were flying in and out non-stop.

After landing, Sergeant Rodriguez gathered everyone near the back of the transport's cargo bay. "Ladies and gentlemen, welcome to Iraq," he began. "Martinez, your DLA liaison is currently inbound. He should be here shortly to meet you. Chen and Ballard, you're with me. You'll ride with my team to Balad Air Base in about three hours."

James walked over to Lisa and Tom and shook both of their hands. He felt a little reluctant to part ways with them. They had sort of become a temporary lifeline in this unfamiliar place. "Well, I guess this is where we say, until next time. Good luck with your reporting."

Smiling, Lisa said, "It was good meeting you, James, and good luck with your … audit … I mean logistics things."

Did she just say audit again? James could swear he saw a slight twinkle in her eye. *Hmm, I'm going to need to watch out for this lady. She may know more than she's letting on, or the heat might be getting to me and I'm starting to become paranoid ...*

James just chuckled at the comment, waving it off. "Tom, stay safe. Take good care of yourselves."

"I will. Be careful out there yourself. Remember, hydration and sunscreen, or you know what will happen if you don't," Tom said with a smile.

"I have a feeling we might be seeing each other again at some point. Though, it might be under different circumstances," Lisa said. *Because I know exactly why you're here, James Martinez, you can't fool me ...*

There she goes again! Alright, she has to know something. Note to self. Avoid her while we're here. James just shook his head and laughed as he walked away.

As James walked towards the waiting area, he thought, *Well, here we are. This is definitely no longer a regular civilian job. This is something entirely different.* The heat from the desert was just a prelude to the challenges that were waiting for him.

Right now, the important task at hand was to meet with his DLA contact, and then he could start to piece together the complex puzzle of what was really happening out here in this hell-soaked desert. The adventure was about to begin.

CHAPTER 10

A Calculated Welcome

As James Martinez reached the terminal, Dave Simmons, his DLA liaison, was waiting for him. He was checking his phone with a frown on his face. *Great, now I have to deal with this shit, too …* Simmons looked up and noticed James walking his way. *About time this fucking guy got here.* He quickly stuffed his phone in his pocket and extended his hand. "James Martinez, I'm Dave Simmons. I'll be your liaison while you're here in Iraq," he asked.

James reached out and shook Dave's hand back. "Yes, Sir, that is me. Nice to meet you, Dave."

"Welcome to Baghdad, Mr. Martinez. How was your flight over? Not too bad, I hope," Dave asked.

"It was very long, but we made it, " James replied with a tired smile. *Thank God It was uneventful.*

"That's good to hear. Those long flights can sometimes be painful if you know what I mean," Simmons said, glancing down at his phone as it buzzed. "I'm sorry. I just have some last-minute security details coming through." *I don't know why he keeps messaging me. I know what I need to do, damn.* My Humvee is right over here." What do you say we head to the base and get you all settled in? It'll take us about 20 minutes to get there, depending on the traffic," Simmons told James while walking to the vehicle.

"We'll have you stationed at Camp Liberty. When you're not out in the field visiting the other bases, that's where you'll stay and work. It's our main base in the area. It's home to a large portion of our logistics operations," Simmons said to James.

When Simmons and James arrived at the Humvee, they climbed in, and soon they were off, leaving the fairly busy airport and heading to Camp Liberty. James looked out the window, checking out the scenery as they drove.

Dave's phone rang again, and he apologized to James before answering it. "This is Simmons."

"I want you to take him the long way around. Just say it's part of some new security protocols. We need to inconvenience him as much as we can. Make things a little difficult for him while he's here," came the voice on the other end of the call.

More of an inconvenience for me as well. "Yes, Sir. I completely understand. We'll take care of it, Sir." Ending the call, Dave turned to James. "We have a slight change of plans. We need to head to a different route to the base. Something about new security protocols. They're always changing things up at the last minute here. You know, making sure we're not always doing the same things, forming habits that can be used against us." *More like making my life as hard as possible.*

Dave easily navigated the Humvee through the busy traffic, its bulky armor seeming to rumble as they drove. James looked out the window. *Look at all this old architecture. They seem to be building new buildings too. The number of destroyed buildings is still remarkable; they look just like the pictures I saw on TV back home. I wonder how long it is going to take to rebuild this place.*

"It's all quite a site, isn't it?" Simmons pointed out, noting that James seemed amazed by it all. "It definitely has come a long way from what it once was, but there is still a lot to do." *And a lot of money to be made. Hopefully, this asshole doesn't mess that up for us.*

James nodded as he watched a group of kids playing soccer in a dusty lot next to a half-completed apartment complex. "It's ... not really what I expected at all," he admitted. *Honestly, I thought it would be a lot worse than it is.*

When they arrived at the first security checkpoint, they ran into some issues that caused a delay. The guard studied James' credentials with a frown. The guard picked up the radio.

"Control, this is Gate Three. I need to verify a CAC for one, James Martinez. It shows Special Access, but I'm not seeing it in the system." He listened for a moment. "Copy. Standing by."

James shifted his weight, exchanging a look with Simmons. *Well, this is just great. Now I get to sit here and roast in this Humvee. I wonder what the hold up could be?*

"Yeah, Control. I've got a Sierra Alpha clearance that's not matching what I'm seeing in the system." Another pause. "Roger that. I'll hold."

Five minutes stretched into ten. The guard made two more calls, his voice becoming increasingly professional—the kind of professional that meant someone higher up was now involved.

"Yes, Sir. I understand. No, Sir, just following the new protocols that went out this morning." He lowered the radio. "One more moment, fellas."

Finally, after a third call and some typing into his terminal. The guard returned James' CAC.

"Apologies for the hold-up," Simmons said, checking his watch. "This usually goes way smoother than this. Like I said before, new protocols in place." *This is mainly because you are coming over here and sticking your nose in everyone's business.*

"No worries," James replied. *It seems a little odd that they would change up all this stuff right when I got here ... Alright, James, let's not start going down a conspiracy rabbit hole just yet. It's all good.*

40 minutes later, basically twice the amount of time it takes to get there, they arrived at Camp Liberty.

"There it is," Simmons pointed. "Home sweet home for the next 6 months for you."

At the entrance, another guard studied James' credentials. He keyed his radio: "TOC, Gate One. We need to verify access for DLA inspector Martinez." There was a pause. Roger ... showing Special Access authorization." There was another pause. Copy, running it now."

The guard made one more check in his system before handing back James' CAC card. "Sorry for the delay, Sir. New security protocols. Welcome to Liberty." The guard said.

"No problem, that seems to be the theme for today so far," James said. *Two weird security checks in less than an hour of being in Iraq … nah, just a coincidence, James, nothing to see here …*

The barriers lowered with a mechanical sound as they drove onto the base. When they finally got inside, Simmons led James to his quarters. They were a small but private room—more than likely a luxury on a busy military base. Inside, there was a narrow bed on one wall, and on the opposite wall, there was a small desk for James to work at, along with a small closet.

"The base dining facility is two buildings west of this one on the left," Simmons explained to James. "The showers and latrines are at the end of this row. They are all public, so I hope you brought some sandals to wear. If not, you can get some at the PX, which is next to the dining facility. DLA offices are in the admin building. I'll take you there later this afternoon." He paused, checking another message on his phone. "Actually, they have moved up the briefing to 1600 hours." *Great, more games. This is going to be a lot of fun …*

"OK, get settled in, grab some food if you are hungry, and I'll meet you back here at 1530. Sounds good?"

"Sounds good to me, Dave. Thank you for everything," James said with gratitude.

After Simmons left, James began to unpack his things. *Alright, let's get all of this unpacked. I'm probably not going to want to do all of this later. My body is starting to feel a little tired … Maybe I'll take a shower, and that'll help energize me a little bit. But first, I need to hit the PX; I definitely didn't think about packing sandals to wear in the desert. Who am I, Moses? God only knows what is on the floors in the showers here.*

After hitting the PX, James headed to the showers. The cool water was refreshing, washing away the stress and sweat of the day's travel. After the shower, he dried off, put on a fresh set of clothes, and headed back to his room.

While sitting on the bed, James glanced at his watch. It was 1 p.m. in Baghdad. He grabbed his phone and pulled up his world clock to see what time it was back home. It was 6 a.m. in Jacksonville, Florida. *Elena should be awake by now. Let me give her a call and let her know I finally made it to the base in Iraq.*

Tapping on the FaceTime icon on his phone, he called Elena. After a few rings, her beautiful face appeared on the screen. She was breathing hard, trying to catch her breath.

"James!" Her face lit into a big smile. "I guess you finally made it?"

"Yes, ma'am, I got in earlier today," James replied. "I just got to the base a little while ago. How was your workout?"

Elena just laughed, pushing a strand of sweaty hair out of her face. "It was brutal! As always. How are you holding up after all that traveling? Are you remembering to take the vitamins I packed you?"

Oh man, here she goes about the vitamins. "I'm pretty tired but good. I have them all in my bag, I'll be taking them momentarily," James assured her. "Is it too early to talk to the kids?"

"Now, James, you know it is 6 a.m. These kids aren't getting up before they have to," Elena said, snickering at the notion. "So, how was the flight over? Were there a lot of people on the plane with you?"

"It was pretty long, but it wasn't that bad," James replied. "I met some new people and had a few friendly conversations. I had an interesting conversation with the Sergeant that was leading our group during the trip."

"Oh? What about?" Elena asked.

"Well, we got to talking about our families ..." James' voice softened. "You know, hearing him talk about being away from his kids. He's got two daughters around Miguel and Sophia's age. It really hit home for me. This is his fourth tour out here. And still, when he talks about his family, you can tell he really misses them a lot ..." James trailed off for a moment before speaking again. "It helped, you know? Knowing I'm not the only one feeling this way."

"Oh, wow. This Sergeant Rodriguez sounds like an interesting person to know, babe. I'm glad you found someone to talk to," Elena said.

"Oh, he definitely is. He seems to really know his stuff, but at the same time he is really down to earth as well. As we were talking about our families, it helped make all of this feel a little less ... overwhelming, to say the least. You can tell he's the type of person who tries to look out for people other than himself. A very selfless type of person," James told her.

"That's good," Elena said softly. "It makes me feel better knowing you've got people looking out for you while you are there. It helps me worry less about you being over there."

Looking down at his wrist, checking the time. James was reluctant to have to get off the call. "Well, I have a briefing I need to get ready for real soon. I hate to cut this short."

"No worries," Elena replied. "I'll let you go; I know you will probably be busy in and out of meetings all day, seeing how you just got there. Call again when you can, OK?"

"I will, I love you," James said. "When the kids wake up, give them a hug and kiss from me and tell them I love them and miss them."

"I will. I love you, too. Have a great day! Be safe! And don't forget to take your vitamins!" Elena replied, kissing the phone screen before the call ended.

James sighed as he turned the phone off. *Man, I didn't realize how hard it would be to be away from home. It has only been two days, and I already want to go back home. I'll be fine. I just need to focus on the task at hand and get to work.* Grabbing his bag with his laptop and other essentials and headed out the door and made his way to the dining facility.

When he got to the DFAC, it was packed. *This place is hopping; there are so many people here.* James got in the line and grabbed some food. Looking around for a place to sit, he spotted Simmons. H*mm, there is Simmons, I should go over there and eat with him.*

Walking over to Dave Simmons, James asked, "Mind if I join you, Sir?"

"Sure thing, Martinez, have a seat," Dave replied. *Great, just want I need. This guy trying to get all chummy with me.*

"So, Dave," James began to speak while digging into what looked like a delicious, homemade stew. "Where do you call home, back in the US?"

"I'm from Ohio," Simmons replied. "And, you? You're from Florida, right?" *Great, now I have to get to know this guy as well?*

"Yes, Sir, I was born and raised in Florida," James said. I can tell you the heat here is definitely way different from where I'm from. Over here, I feel like I'm in an oven and being cooked versus being steamed like broccoli back in Florida." *Did I say that right? The guy probably thinks I'm lame for saying that.*

"Oh yeah, it will certainly take some getting used to, but eventually, it isn't so bad," Simmons said, smiling. *This should be fun to watch. It took me a few years to get used to the heat here. There's nothing like watching the new people get burnt up in the sun.*

They sat there for a while, talking as they ate. James learned that Simmons had started as a supply sergeant before transitioning to becoming a civilian working for the DLA.

"You pick up a lot just being around here," Simmons said, gesturing with his fork. "After a while, you get to know who handles what, which procedures actually matter versus what's just on paper. It makes the job easier."

"I gotcha. Well, hopefully I can pick up some pointers from you." Said James.

Simmons checked his watch. "Well, Sir. It looks like it's time for our briefing with the section heads. Are you ready to get to work?"

James, wiping his mouth, nodded. "Absolutely, let's get this show on the road." *Finally, it's time to get to the bottom of all these problems they have.*

They picked up their trays, placed them on the tray return, and headed to the briefing room. The room was nice and cool, and the lights were dim. *Thank God the room has AC. That sun is killing me, man.* James thought as he entered the room.

James looked around the room, recognizing the attendees from the profiles in the briefs he was given. *OK, that's the base commander, Colonel Harrison. Sitting beside him is the head of the DLA, Laura Henderson. Man, that's a lot of files and folders on the table. I guess these people mean business when they say they want to get to the bottom of this.*

"Mr. Martinez," Colonel Harrison said warmly, extending his hand. "Welcome to Baghdad. I'm sorry your trip to the base was rougher than expected. I heard the extra security measures caused a few delays."

"Yes, Sir. It wasn't too bad. I understand completely. You can never be too cautious with security," James replied after shaking the Colonel's hand and then taking a seat at the table. *Although it did add an extra 20 minutes to my ride here, twenty minutes of sweating in a hot Humvee. If I didn't know any better. I would say it was intentional, and someone was trying to mess with me. This heat is already getting to me. I'm rambling on about conspiracies now. Keep it together, James.*

Laura Henderson, the head of the DLA section, spoke next. "It's a pleasure to finally meet you, Mr. Martinez. We have heard a lot about you," she said with a smile. My colleagues over at NAS Jax speak very highly of you. We began prepping for your arrival when we heard you were coming. I believe we have everything you might need already prepared for you."

Settling in, Ms. Henderson pulled up a series of slides she had created in powerpoint. They popped up on a large screen on the wall at the other end of the room. "So let's get into it, if that is OK with you?" she said.

"Sounds good to me. Please proceed," James replied. *Let the games begin ...*

"As you know, we are starting to uncover a lot of discrepancies in our equipment and supplies inventories as we began to do physical counts over the last couple of months," Ms. Henderson explained.

She flipped through a few more charts and showed a few spreadsheets on the screen. The amount of data seemed overwhelming. James watched as she kept flipping. *Holy cow, this is a lot of data ... But I should be able to work with this. There is always some sort of pattern to be found. There is nothing more fun than untangling a web of nonsense.*

"At first, we thought with all the clerks being rotated in and out, they were just clerical errors or maybe it was due to some misplaced invoices. But as everything began to look off and not add up, we realized we needed a fresh set of eyes out here to take a look. Maybe you can figure out what's going on. Major Wright was the first one to notice the issues but she's been transferred out so we won't be able to have any help from her."

"Ah, that's too bad," James said, referencing Major Wright's transfer. "Is there a reason you have been doing so many clerk transfers?" asked James.

"With the drawdown process beginning the implementation phase, there are lots of other places we're distributing resources throughout the system to handle operations," Henderson replied.

"That makes sense," James acknowledged. *Is it a bit odd that a clerk identifies an issue then gets immediately trans-*

ferred? I'm going to dig into this Major Wright when I get back to my laptop.

James pulled out his phone and opened his note app, which contained all the questions he had written down over the last couple of days.

James scanned through all of the questions. *Alright, which one was it? No, no, ah, here it is.* "How often have these types of discrepancies happened in the past?" James asked.

Colonel Harrison leaned forward and answered. "It's usually very rare, Mr. Martinez. However, as we began to ship all the equipment back to the States due to the upcoming drawdown, we started to notice the inconsistencies. We must start to account for every piece of equipment. We don't want to make the same mistake we did in Afghanistan during that withdrawal. We can't afford any ... misunderstandings. That's why you were sent here. To make sure we get this all cleaned up the right way."

James nodded. *So, no pressure. Got it. I think this should be fairly easy for me to figure out. I can already start to see some patterns emerging from a few of the slides. This is going to be a lot to go through, but I can get it done. This is right in my wheelhouse. I love this type of stuff.*

"What exactly do you want me to do here?" James asked.

Ms. Henderson, smiling, spoke up this time. "We want you to do a deep dive into everything, Mr. Martinez. Audit our processes, our paperwork, and our physical inventories. Turn over every stone. If there are gaps in our system or flaws we have not found, we need you to find them. You'll be given unfettered access to everything."

James looked once again at his notes. *Hmm ... not sure if I should ask this one or not ... to hell with it, why not.* "And if it turns out to be more than just system clerical errors?" James asked carefully.

The entire room fell silent for a moment. Colonel Harrison spoke next. "Then we need to know that as well, Mr. Martinez. But let's not go down that road just yet. For now, let's focus on operating under the assumption that this is just a logistical and clerical error, not a nefarious one."

"Sure, that's reasonable Colonel. It just wouldn't be the first time, ..." James responded. James made a few more notes on his phone. *The whole room went silent when I asked about it not just being a clerical error. Could it be more? Everyone seemed to clam up at the question. Could it be a conspiracy? I might need a tin foil hat for this one.*

"Can anyone give me the exact point in time you guys started noticing discrepancies?" James asked.

"We only discovered them starting a few months ago. That is when we started tracking them in more detail," Ms. Henderson replied, flipping to another slide. "It looks like it started out small, but then it looks like they have increased in how often they happen, and their values also increased."

As they continued going over all the data for the next two hours, it was an endless onslaught of reports, statistics, and other procedural details.

James typed in a few more notes on his phone as she spoke. *More slides, lovely. If I didn't know any better, I would think they were trying to overwhelm me with all of this stuff. Wrong guy for that trick ...*

As the meeting wrapped up, James thought to himself, *Oh man, that was a lot of slides. I thought I was going to be transported to another dimension at some point when they were all going by so fast. But this is the job, and I'm ready to show these people what I can do.* Making his way back to his room, James began to organize all the files he had been given.

Sitting at his desk looking at everything, he began to recall the briefing in detail. *Hmm, was it weird that everyone was so quick to give me all the information I needed? They also seem to be able to answer a lot of my questions and have explanations for them pretty quick. I have been working for the government for a good while now, and most of the time, it is like pulling teeth to get the answers I need. Everyone usually has to check with ten people before I get my answer. Humph, maybe they are just in a hurry and made sure they had everything I would need to get this resolved quickly.*

James continued sitting and thinking about everything. *Something is just not adding up for some reason. Maybe I just need to focus on the data for right now ... This is a ton of data, but I should be able to get through it pretty quickly. I wonder how deep these "discrepancies" go ...*

CHAPTER 11

ASSISTED DISCOVERIES

In his dim office, illuminated by the glow of his laptop screen, Brigadier General Sloan was sitting at his desk when he heard a knock at his door.

"Enter," Sloan said

In walked Dave Simmons, closing the door behind him.

"Mr. Martinez is all settled in at Camp Liberty," Simmons reported. "His initial briefing went as we planned. We gave him every piece of information we could dig up and more. I don't see how he will be able to sift through it all and figure out what is going on."

"Major Wright briefly came up, and the topic of clerk transfers," Simmons continued.

"How did the team respond?" Sloan replied, piqued. *Major Wright is exactly the wrong person I need Martinez knowing about. This isn't good. If he finds out Wright was never transferred ...*

"The team did well Sir, they pointed out that with the implementation of the drawdown, we need logistics operators repositioned to handle supply redistribution," Simmons reported.

Sloan acknowledged this information without looking up from what he was looking at on his screen. "Sounds good. What is the status of our other guests?"

"The journalist Lisa Chen and her cameraman Tom Ballard are en route to Balad as you instructed," Dave said.

Now, looking up from his screen, his eyes looked cold in the dim light. "Very good. I want you to make sure the journalist and Martinez are kept separated when at Balad. We don't need that reporter asking Martinez any probing questions." Sloan paused, looking at Simmons, studying the man. "You have been doing logistics for quite a while now. Is there anything we should be concerned about, as far as this Martinez goes?" Sloan asked, searching for any stone unturned.

"He seems to know his stuff. He's very detailed, very analytical, and methodical, but he'll only find what we want him to find. We'll keep him going in circles. I'll make sure he focuses on the discrepancies we want him to see," Simmons replied.

"Make sure that you do just that." Sloan's voice started to harden now. "We can't afford any unexpected problems or, God forbid, discoveries of our operations." *That would not be good for any of us.*

Simmons understood the implications all too well. "I suggest we head over to Balad as our first inspection site for Martinez. Their motor pool has enough legitimate issues to keep him fairly occupied for a while."

Sloan gave a thin smile. "Sounds good. Let's give our friend, Mr. Martinez, something of our choosing to investigate."

* * *

The sound of his alarm clock woke James up from a fitful sleep. James took a minute to focus, feeling a bit disoriented by the unfamiliar surroundings as we woke. *Wait, what? OK, I'm in my room at Camp Liberty. That was a weird feeling. Alright, I need to get up and get started on digging through those reports. We have things to do. Get up, James. No sleeping in on the first day on the job.*

James got out of bed and stretched. He grabbed his shower kit and headed to the communal facilities to rinse off the night's sleep real quick. Then he remembered something right as he was about to walk out the door. *Wait. Yep, I need my sandals for the showers. The last thing I need is some funk on my feet with all the walking around I'm going to be doing here.*

After his shower, James returned to his room and prepared for the day ahead. *Alright, what do I need to bring with me? Laptop, check, tablet, right here, and satellite phone. Let me check and make sure it is connected to my tablet and syncing up correctly. Alight, good on that. I think we got everything. You have got to love having the internet at all times for real-time updates.*

James put everything in his backpack, shouldered the bag, and headed out the door. He made his way to the dining facility to grab some breakfast before hitting the road. The DFAC was already busy when James arrived. *Holy crap, this place is busy. Ah, there's Simmons right over there in the back. It looks like he already got us some coffee and breakfast. I'm starting to like this guy already.*

Simmons had just finished sending an encrypted text to Sloan when he looked up and saw James walking over. *Well, look who finally decided to join me. This guy looks way too happy for my liking. This should be an interesting day, to say the least.*

"Morning, James," Simmons greeted him as James walked over. "I grabbed you a cup of joe along with some bacon, eggs, and toast. I hope you don't mind. The lines for breakfast can get pretty crazy this early in the morning."

"Oh man, I really appreciate that. I'm definitely hungry," James said, thankfully. *This food looks good and smells good. Nothing better than some bacon and eggs. It ain't Cracker Barrel, but it will do. Mmm, Cracker Barrel. I would love some of their pancakes right about now.*

"How did you sleep?" Simmons asked. *Hopefully as bad as I did. This guy has me all stressed out over this damn investigation.*

James just shrugged as he took a sip of what seemed like some strong-brewed coffee. "As well as expected, I guess," James answered. After taking a quick bite of some eggs, James asked, "So, what is on the agenda for today?"

Simmons leaned in as he spoke, his voice low despite all the noise in the DFAC. *Alright, I need to play my part perfectly. If I can gain this guy's trust, he will tell me everything he finds.* "We will head north of here, over to Balad Air Base. It should take us about an hour to get there. We can take a look at their motor pool. They seem to have a good amount of issues going on over there that we haven't been able to figure out. We can focus on the vehicle and communication equipment inventories they have stored there. If you are able to identify any patterns, it'll hopefully be the blueprint for everything else you'll find; lord knows it's stumped us so far."

James nodded as he shoved the rest of his breakfast into his mouth. *Man, I was really hungry. So Balad has some issues with their motor pool. I guess we already have our first problem to solve. They probably have a bunch of missing parts. Probably due to the mechanics improperly logging what they are using. Should be a piece of cake. Mmm, cake, I wonder if they have any here? Focus James!* Wiping his mouth before he spoke. James asked, "And do we have any plans after we wrap up at Balad?

"Actually, yes, we will be hopping on a transport plane that is heading over to Qayyarah Airfield West," Simmons replied, carefully weaving his story of deceit. "It is further north, near the town of Mosul. I just got a report over email late last night about some interesting things going on over there. You should have the same email in your inbox." *All thanks to General Sloan ...*

After finishing their breakfast, they headed out. As they drove to Balad, James couldn't help but look out the window of the Humvee and watch the Iraqi landscape go by. The urban scenery of Baghdad eventually gave way to a view of agricultural lands, with small villages spread out all over the place, with the occasional security checkpoint they would have to go through.

Breaking the silence during the drive, James asked, "So, Simmons, How long have you been stationed here in Iraq?"

Glancing over at James from behind the wheel, Simmons replied, "I believe it is going on nineteen months now. I came out here thinking I would just be here for a six-month rotation, but ..." shrugging with a smile, "The work keeps coming, and so I have just stayed on." *Nice job, Simmons, throwing in the six-month rotation part. That should freak him out a little bit.*

"Holy cow, that is a long time to be away from home," James said. *Holy cow! Did he say he was only supposed to be here for six months? And he has been here for nineteen? No way that is going to be me.*

"Yeah, but it's just me and my dog back home in Ohio," Simmons replied, "I gave my dog to my sister to take care of while I'm here. I don't have a wife or kids, so there's not much to force me to go back for. *Unlike you Mr. Martinez ...* But I get what you are saying. This place ..." He gestured at everything around them, "It grows on you, though. And you can't beat the hazard pay!" *And how good Sloan pays me.*

James chuckled and nodded. "What made you really want to stay?" James asked. *Am I getting hazard pay? I need to send an email to HR about that. I don't remember them talking about that.*

"Well, honestly? I feel like the work here really matters. Helping maintain the supply here has been crucial, as well as every inventory check and every supply delivery. It all adds up to something that I think is important." Simmons said while adjusting his sunglasses, attempting to hide his eyes. *Important, like making a boatload of money.* Simmons chuckled at that. "On top of that, the people here are actually pretty great. Both our servicemen and women, along with the locals. Once you get to know people here, understand their stories, what they have been through and are currently going through ... It gives you a totally different perspective of things."

Simmons glanced at his phone discreetly as he spoke, checking on Sloan's latest instructions.

Sloan's message read, "Make sure you update me on what Martinez is looking into and never leave him by himself."

Yeah, yeah, I got it, Sloan. Sloan must think I'm an idiot or something. Simmons thought as he finished reading the message.

"It sounds like you have really made some good connections here," James said. *Why does he keep looking at his phone so much?*

Simmons was amused at the statement but for other reasons. *If this guy only knew how many of my connections were part of General Sloan's network.* "You will, too, eventually. The military, all the contractors, locals, we are all part of the same agenda out here. *Sloan's agenda, and you were sent here to mess it up for all of us.* Speaking of which, you will definitely like the team over at Balad. Colonel Harrington runs a really tight ship over there, but she is also good people. She has been stationed there going on two years now."

They passed through another checkpoint and exchanged a few casual waves with the guards.

"You got any other advice for the new guy?" James asked.

"Actually, I do." Simmons nodded. "Make sure to take the time to learn the stories behind the numbers. Every piece of equipment, all the supply requests, there is usually more to it than what you see on some spreadsheets. I wish I had figured out that sooner when I first got here. *But don't look too far behind the story in those numbers. You might not like what you find there.*

As they continued north, James decided to open his laptop and review some of his findings from last night. *Let's take a look at those maintenance logs I flagged last night. Something was bothering me about them and the transfer logs that went with them. Hmm. Looking at these VIN numbers, they seem to not be matching for some reason. There is a Humvee with the VIN number #A789332 that was logged as transferred to Mosul on September 19th, 2023, but the same VIN number seems to be in the maintenance log at Balad some three days later. They are not just similar. They are identical.* Now having something to look for, James began digging deeper into the reports, finding four more instances of the exact same thing. *This is statistically impossible.*

James thought to himself. *These don't look like some kind of clerical error. VIN numbers are unique to each vehicle. There was no way the exact same vehicle could be in two different places at the same time. Unless ...*

James glanced over at Simmons for a second, who was focused on driving. James opened his Outlook and created an encrypted email as discreetly as he could. He kept the message brief and to the point.

"To: DLA Oversight Committee Group Email – Subject: Irregularity Report on Vehicles – URGENT.

ALCON, (all concerned)

While investigating the data given to me, I discovered multiple instances of duplicate VIN numbers in vehicle transfer logs. I have attached the reviewed documents showing the same units were logged at several different locations simultaneously. I recommend we send these findings over to my NAS Jax team for further review of all transfer records involving all vehicles in and out of Iraq.

Respectfully,

James Martinez"

James clicked on send before he could second-guess what he was implicating. He watched the email leave his outbox folder. *Message sent, no turning back now.* One thing James was unaware of was, who the exact recipients of that email group were. One individual in particular would see his email and trigger a response far beyond his control.

* * *

Brigadier General Sloan was sitting in his office when his email notification went off, alerting him of a new email. Reading the subject line marked Urgent, his face stiffened as he opened the email and began to read its contents. The email was from James Martinez and addressed to the DLA Oversight Committee. Sloan was not a member of the committee, but he had insisted that his name be added to the group email so that he might be kept in the loop about the progress.

Sloan scanned the email again. *This guy, James Martinez, is better at finding things than I anticipated. He seems to have uncovered my VIN number swaps fairly quickly. I thought I did a good job at it. The idiots around here never noticed. Apparently, I underestimated this guy's experience. No matter. These can't be traced back to me anyway.*

Sloan sat there for a moment, drumming his fingers on his desk as he worked through his options. *On second thought, this could turn out to be an inconvenience to me, it could pose a direct threat to my operations. I need to get this resolved, and it needs to be done quickly.*

Picking up his secure phone, he dialed Dave Simmons. "Simmons, we have a problem. I have decided to handle this myself. I'm heading to Balad. Keep that Martinez fellow occupied until I arrive. We need to take control of the narrative before things get out of hand."

Simmons, now with concern on his face as he drove, glanced over at James, who was looking out the window. "I understand, Sir. We will be at the motor pool in Balad shortly. We look forward to your arrival."

Sloan ended the call with Simmons, his mind kicking into overdrive, devising plans. *This email clearly shows me that Martinez is much sharper and more observant than I thought he would be. I need to make sure that while Martinez is at Balad he is properly managed and his attention diverted. I can't just leave this up to Simmons anymore. I need to handle this myself.*

As Simmons and James got closer to Balad Air Base, James admired its sheer size. *Holy cow, this place is big.* James thought to himself. They passed through security and found a place to park. Simmons guided James through security and then towards the logistics center. The constant thunderous sound of aircraft coming and leaving and the busyness of all the personnel gave the base this electrifying energy that you could almost physically feel.

"It is quite different from being at Camp Liberty, isn't it?" Simmons asked, noticing the surprise on James' face. "Balad is our busiest base here in Iraq. You will see why those inventory numbers matter so much here. So much equipment moves in and out of this place almost 24/7. Speaking of which, we should get started now. Colonel Harrington expects your preliminary findings by the time we head to Qayyarah."

"The motor pool is over this way. We can start over there," Simmons explained as they walked through the huge complex. *Right this way, Mr. Martinez, right over here where Sloan wants you.* "I believe there have been some discrepancies in the Humvee inventory that we may need to check out," Simmons said to James.

Over the next few hours, James dove head–first into what looked like a backlog of serial numbers, maintenance logs, and unorganized inventory sheets. *Man, all these reports are so disorganized, and there are so many of them. No wonder they have inventory issues here. I just need to establish a rhythm. I'll start by checking the vehicle's VIN numbers against that master purchase list I found, then I'll verify the current location of that vehicle. Then, notate any discrepancies.*

Simmons worked next to James, occasionally adding in any needed context about certain vehicles or on–base procedures, carefully trying to direct James' attention to only the minor issues they wanted him to find. Simmons thought to himself. *I don't think this guy is buying anything I'm saying. He seems to be locked in on these VIN numbers, which is not good at all.*

While reviewing the maintenance logs, something caught James' eye. *Hmm, there seems to be another pattern hidden here. It looks like there are some subtle inconsistencies in the service dates, and here are some weird transfer requests. Why would they request this? And what is going on with these duplicate entries in the logs that don't match?*

This doesn't make any sense at all. I guess you can overlook some of this if you weren't looking for it, but still ... Over the years, he had developed an instinct for these types of things, and seeing all of these inconsistencies were beginning to raise red flags.

Watching in the distance, unknown to James or Simmons, Major Natalie Wright was observing them. *That guy with Simmons must be the investigator that the Senator sent out to look into everything.* Major Wright had arrived at Balad a few days earlier. She figured if anyone needed to find something, it would be here. Most of the staff here didn't answer to General Sloan. She knew Colonel Harrington personally and knew the Colonel was a stand-up person. She would never get caught up in anything like this.

Wright continued to observe Martinez, eventually saying to herself in a low voice. "You're looking in the wrong place, Martinez. It is more than just missing Humvees." Watching him look through the motor pool records, she thought. *I need to somehow point him in the right direction, but how?*

Major Wright took out a scrap piece of notepaper and began to write down some information. She folded the note up nice and small. *Now, I just need to slip this into Martinez's pocket without Simmons noticing.*

Wright made her way down to the motor pool while at the same time keeping an eye on Simmons as she walked. She approached James, who seemed to be completely engrossed in what he was doing to even notice her. As she passed by him, she slightly bumped into him, making it seem like an accident. She was also careful to not draw any attention from Simmons in the process.

"Oh, excuse me. Sorry about that," Wright said. In that brief moment of contact, she was able to slip the folded piece of paper into James' pants pocket before continuing on her way without a word.

James looked up, but by the time he did, Wright was already making her way out of the motor pool. James just said, "No problem, Ma'am" *I'm pretty sure that lady just slipped something in my pocket. It was subtle, but I felt it. I won't look at it right now. I don't think that person intended for me to read it in front of Simmons.* James went back to what he was doing.

Simmons, who had in fact noticed this interaction go down, narrowed his eyes as he recognized who bumped into James. *Holy shit, that is, Major Wright. What the hell is she doing here at Balad, she went AWOL.* Wright may have been wearing a ball cap, trying to hide her face when she walked by James, but he knew exactly who she was.

Simmons debated for just a split second, torn between going back to watching James or going after Major Wright. *Should I go after her? If I don't and she gets away, Sloan will be pissed. Yeah, I'll follow and see where she goes. Besides, Martinez seems to be preoccupied with those crumbs we gave him to find, he'll be busy for a little while.* Simmons quickly went after her.

As he passed by James, Simmons said, "I need to hit the head real quick, I drank too much coffee, and it seems to have passed right through me. Just hang out here until I get back." *Don't you go anywhere, Martinez, or I'll kick your ass.*

James looked up, just nodded his head and said, "OK, no problem. I'll be here."

James stood there watching Simmons leave in a hurry. *That bathroom excuse was just lame. I don't think people realize how observant I am. I think it is because I have watched too many spy movies on Netflix—probably more than I should have. He sure does seem pretty interested in that woman who bumped into me. I'm pretty sure Simmons didn't notice whatever it was she gave me. I guess this pretty much confirms my thoughts about Simmons from when I first met the guy. He looked a little shifty when we first met. But I was trying not to judge a book by its cover, eh? That is what I get for trying to be a nice guy.*

Now alone, James looked around, making sure Simmons was out of sight. *Welp, let's see what I have in my pocket ...* James pulled out a piece of paper. *hmm, it is a note. Let's see what it says.*

"You are looking in the wrong place. Go to warehouse 9, on the east side of the base. Look for the crates labeled AP1 through AP35. Only trust Colonel Harrington with your findings. Simmons compromised. –M N.W."

After reading the note, James quickly crumpled the note and stuck it back in his pocket as he stood there for a moment. *Well, that is a little cryptic, but I guess I should probably go check out Warehouse 9. Should I wait for Simmons to get back? Nah, he would probably try to ruin all the fun. I better get a move on. He could be back at any moment, and he probably would be against me going to check it out.*

James looked around and noticed one of the motor pool guys standing around. He walked over to him and said, "Excuse me, do you think you could help me find warehouse 9? I'm with the DLA and working on the base inventory. I need to check something out in that warehouse."

"Sure thing, Sir. Follow me. I can drive us over there," the soldier replied, leading James to a truck. They hopped in and headed east towards Warehouse 9.

Arriving at Warehouse 9, James hopped out of the truck and thanked the soldier for the ride. He then made his way into Warehouse 9, where he was greeted by another soldier with a clipboard in his hand.

"Can I help you, Sir?" the soldier asked.

James looked at the soldier's rank and name tag and replied. "I hope you can, Sergeant Lyons. My name is James Martinez and I need to check out some crates in your warehouse. I'm doing an inventory spot check, and there are some crates that were flagged in Warehouse 9 for review." James lifted his badge around his neck for Sergeant Lyons to see.

"One moment, Mr. Martinez." Lyons pulled out his radio and proceeded to call the base commander for verification. "Colonel Harrington, come in. This is Sergeant Lyons. Over."

"Colonel Harrington here, go ahead. Over," The Colonel replied.

"Ma'am, I have James Martinez from the DLA here with me at Warehouse 9 requesting access to do an inventory spot check. Can you please verify he is cleared to enter the warehouse to perform this task? Over" the Sergeant said.

"Permission is granted, Sergeant. He has full access to anything on this base per orders from CENCOM. Over." replied the Colonel.

"Roger that ma'am, over and out," Lyons replied.

"OK Mr. Martinez, what are the crate numbers you need to review? I'll take you to them," the Sergeant said.

James smiled. *Hmm. The security measures here are pretty tight, so why would there be an issue in this warehouse if that were the case? I'll have to figure that out later.* "I need to see crates AP1 through AP35. They are supposed to be located in the right back corner of the warehouse."

The Sergeant seemed to cock his head slightly. *How does his guy know where the crates are located? He must have access to the warehouse database or something.* "Sure thing, follow me, Sir, and watch your step," Lyons directed as he began to lead the way

James looked around as they walked and thought. *This is a pretty big warehouse. I wonder how many crates are in it.* Eventually, James and the Sergeant arrived at the location where AP1 through AP35 were located.

Sergeant Lyons pointed at all the crates. "It looks like they are all here, Sir," Lyons said.

James walked up to the crates. *They all look fine to me.* Then he asked, "Do you know what is supposed to be in them?"

Sergeant Lyons looked at his clipboard, flipped through the pages, and stopped. "Armor-piercing rounds, Sir."

James' eyebrows raised. "I'm going to need to verify their contents, Sergeant. Can you get someone to open them up for me?" *This is not good.*

Lyons hesitated for a moment about the request but then pulled out his radio and spoke. "Marshall, Duncan, Walker, I need you to grab some crowbars and bring them over to section 4. We need to pop open some crates."

A minute or two later, three soldiers appeared with crowbars in hand. The Sergeant pointed at the crates, "I need you to open up crates AP1 through AP35."

"Sir?" Walker asked.

"Inventory spot check, Walker, that is all you need to know," Lyons said.

Private Walker shrugged and proceeded to open the crate labeled AP1. As the lid came off and Private Walker peered inside, he said, "Um... Sergeant, seems to be cinder blocks."

James, hearing this, walked up to the crate and looked inside. *Holy shit, this is not good at all.*

As the lids of the other crates were opened, the other soldiers said the same thing. By the time they were done opening them all, 35 crates of military-grade armor-piercing rounds were missing.

Sergeant Lyons pulled out his radio almost immediately. "Colonel Harrington, come in. This is Sergeant Lyons at warehouse 9. Over."

"Go ahead, Lyons. Colonel Harrington here, over," the Colonel replied.

Lyons hesitated for a moment, thinking fast. "Go to priority channel Zulu. Over." The Sergeant proceeded to adjust his radio channel to the correct private channel. A second later, there was a chirp as someone else entered the channel. Lyons, hearing this, said, "Authenticate, over."

"Foxtrot, Lima, Alpha, Alpha, Zula. Over," Colonel Harrington replied.

"Ma'am, we have a serious problem at warehouse 9 that requires your immediate attention. Suggest a low-key arrival. Over," Lyons said.

In her office, Colonel Harrington typed quickly on her laptop to pull up the inventory of Warehouse 9. Lyons requested her to move to a private channel, and the news that

James Martinez was on her base at Warehouse 9 had to be troubling.

As the inventory detail loaded, Harrington scanned through it. *Everything in that warehouse better be there or we are going to have a major problem.*

There was a brief moment of silence, and then the Colonel replied. "I'm on my way, Sergeant. You are to seal up the warehouse until 1 arrive. Nobody in or out. Over."

"Yes. Ma'am, locking it down right now. Over," Lyons replied.

Colonel Harrington sat there for a moment, thinking about what to do next. Then she picked up the phone and dialed a number. "Yes, Ma'am Colonel Harrington, how can I help you?" Master Sergeant Reyes asked.

"Reyes, I need four of your men to pick me up and take me to warehouse 9, now. This is a top priority," ordered the Colonel.

"Yes, ma'am, they are on their way now," Reyes said.

Hanging up the phone, the Colonel stood up and glanced at her laptop one more time. Then closed it. *I have a feeling this is going to be a fucking dumpster fire.*

"Martinez, the Colonel is on her way," Lyons reported back in warehouse 9.

"Great, thanks for that," replied James. "By the way, can you pull up for me really quick when the next scheduled count is going to be performed in this area of the warehouse?" James asked.

"Sure, let me pull the schedule," Lysons responded. "It looks like it is scheduled for tonight. The request was put in by the DLA group over in Liberty."

"Perfect, thanks for that," James acknowledged. *Guess we would have seen one of those infamous write-offs related to "discrepancies" tonight. How fortuitous. M N.W., who are you?*

CHAPTER 12

DIVERSION AND DECEIT

A vehicle was heard pulling up to Warehouse 9. The warehouse had been cleared of personnel. The only people left inside were James Martinez, Sergeant Lyons, Private Walker, Private Duncan, and Private Marshall. There was a knock on the warehouse door, as Colonel Harrington announced her presence.

In walked Colonel Harrington, flanked by four hulking MPs. James looked at them and swallowed hard. *Holy crap, those guys are huge. I hope they are not here for me.*

Colonel Harrington walked up to James and put out her hand. "Mr. Martinez, my name is Colonel Harrington. We have not met yet, but it would seem we are meeting now under some very precarious circumstances. I understand your spot check has turned up some troubling news."

James shook her hand and replied, "It is nice to meet you as well, Colonel, and yes, I would say we have very troubling news indeed. If you follow the Sergeant here, we can show you what we found." *I hope to God she is not involved in whatever this is and that those MPs are not here to take me away somewhere and murder me. Nooo, wait. What am I talking about? Get it together, James!*

Seeing almost all the blood drain from the Sergeant's face, the Colonel held up her hand to him. "It is OK, Lyons. I reviewed the staff records for the warehouse. I know you have not been in charge very long. Just lead the way and show me what you have."

Sergeant Lyons breathed a sigh of relief and led everyone back to the crates, leaving the MPs behind to guard the door.

As they approached the location of the crates, the Colonel noticed that all the crates were missing their lids. There were so many, too many. Walking up to the first crate and looking inside at what should have been filled with armor-piercing ammunition, the Colonel's heart began to race. Keeping her composure, she asked. "How many rounds are missing, Lyons?"

Sergeant Lyons, who was about to pass out by now, started flipping through his paperwork to come up with a number. But it was James who spoke up first, having already done the math.

"Colonel, if I may. You are looking at about ten thousand rounds per crate, give or take a few thousand, times thirty-five crates ... You are looking at around seven hundred thousand rounds of ... if I'm reading the crate designation correctly... 7.62 armor piercing rounds," James said. *That is a hell of a lot of missing ammunition. I think things just got serious.*

Private Walker who was standing nearby let out a low whistle at that news.

Colonel Harrington, now feeling weak in the knees, stood there for a moment. *How the hell could this happen under my watch? What the hell do I do? Think Harrington. I need to contain this fast.*

"Sergeant Lyson, seal these crates back up right now." The Colonel ordered. Looking at the other soldiers, she said. "Not a word of this to anyone, do you understand me? If I hear one word of this getting out, I'm holding you four responsible for it, and I'll have your asses thrown in the brig. Do you understand me?"

They all responded in almost perfect unison: "Yes, Ma'am!"

"Mr. Martinez, you are with me. Let's go," the Colonel said to James.

James, stunned at what he had just heard and witnessed, did not protest. He just followed the Colonel. *Oh man, this is not good at all. The look on her face tells me that she is trying to work this all out in her head. Is this where she takes me over to the MPs and has them take me back behind some shed and shoot me? Pull it together, man! You are not in some movie where they do that type of stuff.*

Finally, they stopped where they were alone. Harrington turned to James and said, "Mr. Martinez, thank you for bringing this to my attention. Please don't think I'm trying to stop your investigation. On the contrary, I want you to continue your investigations. But we need to keep this under wraps for now." She saw James begin to protest on that last part and held up her hand, stopping him for a moment. "I understand your concerns, but what you fail to realize now is we don't know how far this goes up. This means that you would need to be very high in rank in order to hide something like this from someone as high up as me. Do you get what I'm saying?"

James thought about it for a moment. *She is right. If this wasn't her, then it has to be someone much, much higher up than her.* Then James answered, "I completely understand, Colonel Harrington. I was actually going to agree with you." He pulled out the note that had been slipped into his pocket and showed it to Harrington.

She read the note and then noticed the initials at the end. "Do you know what these initials stand for?" she asked.

"I do not. I was hoping you could tell me who she was," James replied.

When hearing that it was a woman who slipped him the note, the Colonel was able to deduce precisely who she was. "Major Natalie Wright, I believe. I was told she was transferred out a couple of weeks ago. It would seem she was not. And this part about Simmons, do you believe her?" *Simmons? He is with the DLA and has access to the inventory system. But Simmons?*

James thought about it for a minute before answering. "Simmons has been my liaison since my arrival. He has given me all the data I need for my investigation, but looking back at it, it feels like he may have given me too much data. Like he was trying to bog me down with too much information ..." James paused for a moment before continuing. "Now, seeing this on the note, the empty crates, I would say yes. I believe he is likely in on what has been going on. I can't tell you who he works for or if he does work for someone, right now. I'm still working through it all, but I'm sure I can figure it out with time."

"What do you recommend we do with Mr. Simmons? Should I have him detained?" Harrington asked, seeking James' insight into the matter.

"I would say, leave him in play. He doesn't know that I have found these empty crates. I don't think he saw Major Wright slip me the note. If he had, he would have stayed with me and tried to see what was in it. So, as far as he knows, nothing is wrong right now," James said.

"OK, Mr. Martinez, we will do it your way for now, mainly because I'm trying not to bring too much attention to what is happening here. I suggest you email the DLA Oversight Committee, informing them of your findings and letting them know our plan. If they give you a hard time about this, you tell them you are just following my orders. Make sure you CC me on the email so they know I'm in the loop, and that should cover you," the Colonel said.

"Will do, Colonel. We will get to the bottom of this ASAP." In the meantime, I need to get back to the motor pool before Simmons sees I'm gone and starts looking for me. *If he hasn't already ...*

* * *

Meanwhile, having lost sight of Major Wright, Simmons returned to the motor pool only to find James not there. His pulse quickened, spiked by the panic. *Where the fuck did this guy go?*

He began asking around to see if anyone saw where James went. Finally, he found a Private who said he saw James leave with one of the other Privates. "Yeah, I think I saw him leave with Private Gay. He said something about needing to go over to one of the warehouses on the east side of the base," the private said.

Simmons' mind raced as he tried to recall what was over on that side of the base. *Shit, that's where Warehouse 9 is. That is the warehouse that had the ammo we removed and sold. If Martinez goes looking around in there, we are in deep shit.* Simmons felt as if the walls were starting to close in around him; the conflicting loyalties to his job, General Sloan, and the truth he knew was there in that warehouse.

Simmons brought himself back to the present. *I need to find Martinez and see if he found anything.* He quickly made his way towards warehouse 9, but by the time he arrived, he saw James exciting the warehouse with Colonel Harrington and 4 MPs. *Holy shit, is that Martinez with Colonel Harrington? Look at the size of those fucking MPs. Shit, shit, shit, are they going to come looking for me? No … There is no way they know about me. Or do they? I need to send a message to the General. We are so fucked right now.*

Simmons pulled out his phone, his hand shaking as his fingers flew over the screen, sending an encrypted message to General Sloan:

"URGENT: Martinez has discovered Warehouse 9 and the missing ammunition. He has already reported it to the base commander. The warehouse has been sealed off and put under guard. But there has been no commotion yet. I think they are keeping this under wraps for now."

The reply was almost instant from General Sloan:

"I'm almost to Balad. If the Colonel is keeping this under wraps, then this could play into our favor. Get Martinez back to the motor pool ASAP. Keep him under control. And Simmons, when I get there, I'm going to need a good explanation of how and why he was able to get to warehouse 9 when you were supposed to be watching him."

That last part made Simmons's blood run cold. *I'll come up with a good explanation later. For now, I needed to get Martinez back to the motor pool somehow.*

* * *

James finished his conversation with Colonel Harrington while walking her back to her vehicle. James looked at his watch. *SHIT, I 've been gone way too long. Simmons may already be back by now. I'll just tell him I had to use the restroom or something.* His steps were quick as he hurried through the paths leading to his destination.

Across the base, Lisa Chen watched from a distance, her attention caught by the sight of James walking away from the base commander, Colonel Harrington, and what looked like two very large military police. She scanned around and noticed two more standing in front of a warehouse. *I wonder what is going on over there? Why was James Martinez talking to the base commander after leaving that warehouse? Why are there two guards in front of it now? Did he find something while doing his "routine" inspections? I'll have to figure it out one way or another.*

Standing by a container, Simmons watched as Martinez walked away from the Colonel and appeared to be headed toward the motor pool. *Shit, I need to get to the motor pool before Martinez does.* Simmons took off in a light sprint back to the motor pool.

Lucky for him, Simmons was able to beat James back to the motor pool. He stood there for a moment, trying to catch his breath. *Now, I need to do some damage control. I need to figure out how Wright was able to tip Martinez off about the warehouse. That is the only way Martinez would have figured it out. It had to have been her.* Just then, Simmons' phone buzzed in his pocket. He pulled it out and read the message from Sloan:

"Working on a plan to contain this. We need to get Martinez away from Balad. Let's stick to the schedule. I have redirected the transport flight to Qayyarah; you will drive there instead, so make sure Martinez is in the convoy. Driving there should buy me time to get a new plan in motion."

Simmons looked up and saw James returning to the motor pool. Simmons looked at the phone one more time and then sent a reply:

"Copy that."

He put his phone back in his pocket and then walked over to James and asked, "Hey man, where have you been? I have been looking all over for you," trying to keep his composure. *Let's see how good this guy is at lying.*

Having thought about the excuse he would use on the way back, James didn't hesitate to answer. "I ran to the restroom and got lost, trying to find my way back. A lot of the buildings all look the same, or the heat is getting to me. Sorry about that. Everything OK?" He asked Simmons. *Hopefully he buys that. I probably could have come up with a better excuse, but sometimes, the simplest lie is the best one. There is no time limit on taking a dump.* James thought as he watched Simmons.

Simmons eyed James for a moment. *This guy has a good poker face.* "No problem. It's happened to me a few times as well. I'm glad you found your way back. I was about to come looking for you. Anyways, it looks like our transport plane to Qayyarah got diverted for another mission, so we will be catching a ride on a convoy that is headed that way." *That way, General Sloan has a chance to unfuck the shit storm you are starting.*

"Convoy? Is that safe? With all the insurgent attacks and all?" James asked, sounding a little concerned about the change. *Convoy? Aren't there IEDs all over the place on the roads out there? Man, I'm going to get blown up in Iraq. Why did I take this assignment again?*

"Yeah, it's safe. The route we'll be taking is regularly vetted given it's a main supply line between Balad and Qayyarah, and recon tells us there are no insurgents in that area," Simmons said calmly. "I take the route regularly to get out to the base, we'll be fine."

"I guess I better grab my stuff so we can head over to wherever we are leaving from," James said to Simmons, now eyeing him suspiciously. *This freaking guy is up to something. He is looking shiftier than usual.*

Simmons nodded and started walking out of the motor pool with James in tow. As they were walking, Simmons's phone buzzed again. He reached into his pocket and read the message on the lock screen. It was from Sloan:

"I'm here. Where the hell are you and Martinez? Meet me at the convoy."

Simmons swallowed hard. *Sloan sounds pissed. Hopefully, he can keep it together and not try to murder Martinez, or me, right in front of everyone.* Simmons put the phone back in his pocket and continued walking toward the convoy. When James and Simmons arrived, Simmons could see General Sloan walking towards them. The General walked up to James and introduced himself.

"Mr. Martinez," Sloan said, reaching out to shake James' hand with a smug smile. I hear you've been quite the detective." Sloan kept his voice low to keep the conversation private. "Thank you for having such a keen eye and uncovering this issue for us. We are looking into your recent findings as we speak." *Am I going to have to kill this fucking guy to make this go away? We will see how this all plays out when he is away from Balad.*

James shook Sloan's hand and found it a little too firm for his liking. Looking up into the man's eyes, they seemed a little too intense, to say the least. "Just doing my job, General." *Holy shit, this guy is intense; why is he squeezing my hand so hard?*

"Keep up the good work, Mr. Martinez. I can't wait to see what you find out at Qayyarah," Sloan continued, his tone seeming without emotion. "We need to make sure we uncover any issues we have ASAP. Every piece of the puzzle helps us ensure we are ready for anything. Have a safe trip, Gentleman." *And get as far away from here as possible. I need to figure this shit out ASAP.*

James nodded. *Was it me, or was that guy messing with me? I can't put my finger on it, but I feel like that guy seemed a little off. How did he get here so fast? And the way he thanked me sounded a little weird. Does he know about warehouse 9? Colonel Harrington said she was going to keep this under wraps. Could this guy be involved somehow? The Colonel said someone higher than her would have to be involved in order to hide that missing ammunition.* James thought as he looked at General Sloan.

After speaking with Simmons, Sloan finally stepped away. James turned away so as not to be seen and pulled out his phone. *I need to email the DLA Oversight Committee now while I still have a chance.* He pulled up his secure email and drafted a new message:

"To: DLA Oversight Committee Group Email CC: MAJ Wonda Harrington –Subject: Critical Findings – Ammunition Discrepancy

ALCON, (all concerned)

During my inspection of Warehouse 9 at Balad Air Base, I discovered a very troubling irregularity in the ammunition section. Upon physical inspection, multiple crates (AP1 – AP35) were found to be filled with cinder blocks, contrary to the inventory logs on file and bills of lading documents from receiving. I recommend immediate investigation and security review.

I have also received an inside tip about possible parties involved. I was told that Dave Simmons, my DLA contact here in Iraq, may be involved. At the direction of Colonel Harrington, who is CC'ed in this email, his detainment has been postponed. She has instructed me to carefully monitor his actions while she carries out an investigation and search for possible co-conspirators. I have agreed to go along with this at my own risk.

I have attached all my investigative documents and a picture of a note that Major Kathleen Wright secretly slipped to me, implicating Dave Simmons. This note is what directly led to the discovery of the missing ammunition at warehouse 9.

Respectfully,

James Martinez."

James hit send, and the email was gone in a flash. *What the hell have I gotten myself into?*

James had no idea that Sloan had stopped at the side of one of the buildings and was watching what he was doing. The General focused on James and watched him typing on his phone almost frantically. As soon as James was done, he put his phone back in his pocket and turned back to where the convoy was being staged.

General Sloan heard an email notification go off in his pocket. He pulled out his secure phone, tapped to open the email, and began to read it. *Damn it to hell! Martinez didn't just find discrepancies in the paperwork; he has physical proof. And now he has implicated Simmons in this fucking email. If Simmons is arrested, he will flip on me, no question about that. I can't have that happen. If the DLA were to start digging deeper, they would find everything I have done: the weapons, the vehicles, and other equipment I have sold off over the years. My entire network is fucked. Everything that I have spent years building it's all going to shit because of James Martinez ... I need to figure this out.*

Sloan began devising a plan. *I'll show you how smart you are, Mr. Martinez. It is time to take care of this problem once and for all.* He pulled out his other encrypted phone and dialed a number he had memorized. The person on the other end picked up almost instantly.

"That thing we talked about earlier, we are a go," Sloan said, keeping his voice low. They will be on the main road to Qayyarah today. Make it look random; leave none alive."

"Payment?" the voice requested on the other end, in a thick arabic accent.

The General looked at the phone, pulled up another secure app, and hit send. "Double the usual. I just sent half. Half now and the other half when the job is done."

"It will be taken care of. As usual, doing business with you is a pleasure, General Sloan."

The call ended.

* * *

In a small village just outside Mosul, Hassan looked at his phone and verified the General's payment. He then turned to his lieutenants.

"General Sloan has requested our assistance with a delicate matter. He would like for us to take care of a convoy that will be in route between Balad and Qayyarah, in the name of self-preservation." Hassan said with a smile on his face. "We are to set up an ambush for them along the road."

"Brother, this sounds like an opportunity for us," Ahmed, Hassan's right-hand man, said as he studied a map on the wall. "We have been training for months now with the Americans' equipment, which is now in our hands thanks to the greed of one of their own. Why waste this opportunity?"

Hassan eyed Ahmed, trying to figure out what he was suggesting. "What would you have us do?"

"All of the American bases are vulnerable. Their equipment readiness is compromised. Sloan has seen to that. If we strike now, not just this convey, but all of their bases. Balad, Liberty, and Qayyarah, all at the same time. Let this American fool think he is just arranging a silly little ambush. But Today! We strike at them when they least expect it. We take back what was taken from us!" Ahmed said, raising his voice.

Hassan stood there for a moment, pondering Ahmed's words. Then he slowly started to smile, "Make the calls, assemble EVERYONE, tell them. Today, we show our aggressors what it looks like when they arm their enemies!"

Seemingly on queue, Ahmed stood and began to shout:

For the cause, we rise!
For the fight, we stand!
With fire and steel,
We strike on command!
Allahu Akbar! Allahu Akbar!
Praise be to Allah!

Chapter 13

Ambush

Back at Balad, the sun was setting, as the convoy was preparing to depart. James, along with Simmons, hopped into one of the Humvee's. You could cut the tension with a knife. James' mind was racing. *Man, today has been nuts. First, I discover those empty crates; then this General Sloan guy suddenly shows up at the base. I get a note passed to me spy style by his lady Major Wight, of which I have no idea who she is or how she is involved in all of this, and on top of that, she warns me about Simmons's somehow involvement.* James looked out the window and watched Lisa and Tom get into another Humvee, wondering if they had figured out any of this was happening.

Sergeant Rodriguez appeared at the front of the convoy and proceeded to walk down the line of vehicles. Then he spoke, "Listen up, people! I want the civilian vehicles in the middle of the group at all times. Keep the formation tight, with no exceptions. The first sight of trouble, follow orders immediately. Are we clear?!"

In unison, James heard a chorus of "Yes, Sir!"

Rodriguez spotted General Sloan walking back up to the convoy. His mood seemed aggravated by something.

Rodriguez walked up to Sloan and asked, "General, why such a late departure? We usually don't head out this close to nightfall. We could arrive at Qayyara in the middle of the night."

"It will be fine, Sergeant. We have the route secured for you. I need these civilians in Qayyarah by tonight, no exception," Sloan said, his response firm.

"Sir, with all due respect, this is not standard operating procedure. It could put us all at risk," Rodriguez pointed out to the General.

Sloan's eyes seemed to almost bore into Rodriguez. "Are you questioning my orders, Sergeant?"

"No, Sir! General." Rodriguez said, now realizing he had maybe pushed too hard.

"Then you have your orders, soldier. I expect you to follow them to a T," Sloan said as he turned and walked away from Rodriguez.

James witnessed the entire exchange. *What the hell was that all about? Rodriguez seems to think we shouldn't leave this late. I wonder why.*

Lisa Chen, in her vehicle, also caught the exchange. Her journalistic instincts kicked in, telling her something was not right. She made some quick notes on her phone, connecting some of the dots from the events she witnessed earlier today.

The sun was beginning to drop towards the horizon as the convoy started to leave Balad. James looked out the window, watching the landscape change from a busy base to a quiet desert terrain, but his thoughts were far from peaceful. *I need to speak to Colonel Harrington without Simmons finding out. The incident with Sloan before leaving is beginning to make more sense to me now, and I can't help but have this strange feeling that I'm being led into some kind of trap. God damn it, why am I here, I miss home. I need to call Elena ... No, she is too perceptive, she might see my face and suspect something is wrong. Maybe I'll just send her a text, that should be easy enough. Short and to the point.*

James pulled out his satellite phone and pecked out a text:

"Hey babe, sorry I haven't had a chance to call. In-route via military convoy to Qayyarah. Will call as soon as I can. We are taking the reporting crew with us. Check WNN, they might be broadcasting our trip. The vehicles are really loud so I might not hear your reply if you send one. Love you, tell the kids I love them."

Back home, Elena was excited to hear her messages alert with a ding. After reading James' message, she felt a pit in her stomach. She wasn't sure why, but something in James' tone didn't feel right. She decided to text back. "OK! we love you too. Travel Safe. Will pull up WNN."

James saw her reply, tucked his phone into his flak vest, and said a quiet prayer.

* * *

"Hey," Lisa tapped Tom on the arm. "Did you see how Rodriguez was questioning that General?" she whispered. "And what is up with us leaving so late? Something is not right. We need to figure out what's going on."

"Yeah I saw all of that go down. We just need to be careful and try not to draw too much attention our way," Tom said.

"When we start filming, do not stop. There might be more going on here than we know," Lisa said.

After about two hours on the road, the convoy moved along at a decent pace. The Iraqi landscape seemed to just roll by as they traveled towards Qayyarah. Inside the second Humvee, James Martinez moved around uncomfortably. *Man, these seats suck in this Humvee. I wonder what Simmons and Sloan have up their sleeves out in Qayyarah. I'm sure it can't be good.*

"How are you holding up Martinez?" Simmons asked, glancing over from the driver's seat. *I need to figure out what Martinez knows. I'm sure Sloan has worked it out, but he hasn't messaged me with anything.*

James just faked a smile. "I have been on far more comfortable road trips than this one." *I don't understand how this guy can just pretend everything is good. We're finding some serious discrepancies, and he doesn't know it yet, but he's been implicated.*

In the Humvee ahead of James, Lisa Chen had gotten permission for Sergeant Rodriguez to go live and record the ride to Qayyarah. "I'm being told that we are currently about two hours out from Qayyarah Airfield," she narrated to the camera, her voice remaining steady despite how rough the ride was. The convoy is moving smoothly through the Iraqi desert. It demonstrates the military's ability to travel in such difficult environments."

Suddenly, the radio came to life, "All vehicles, be advised we are coming up on a zone where there have been recent reports of insurgent activity. Stay alert."

Having heard the alert on the radio, the tension inside the convoy vehicles seemed to intensify instantly. Looking back, James began to observe some of the soldiers in the Humvee directly behind them. *All the Marines back there are looking out of all the windows. What are they looking for? It looks like they have their weapons ready to start shooting. Oh man, this is not good. I have a bad feeling about this.*

* * *

Mitchell Hawkins, News Anchor at WNN in New York was getting a final touchup on his makeup before going live. He was adjusting his tie when the floor director called out "thirty seconds to air" over his earpiece.

Hawkins gave a thumbs up. His expression became serious as he went over his notes one last time.

A countdown started in his ear. "We are live in 5, 4, 3, 2, 1." The red light on the camera went red, and he looked directly at the lens.

"Good evening, everyone. This is Mitchel Hawkins reporting. Tonight, WNN News will bring you an unprecedented look at ongoing operations in Iraq. For the first time ever, we will be broadcasting a live feed from a military convoy using our new satellite feed. One of our correspondents, Lisa Chen, is on location. She has been embedded with a Marine unit in Iraq that is escorting some civilian employees as they make their way to Qayyarah Airfield in the western region of Iraq."

A screen behind Hawkins came to life, displaying a map of Iraq with a red dot indicating the convoy's current location.

"We will be going live with Lisa in a few minutes, but first, let's go over the current situation in Iraq ..."

* * *

Elena Martinez was settling in on the couch in Jacksonville, Florida. She had been impatiently waiting to see if there was going to be a broadcast ever since James' text, and mentioning WNN was embedded on the convoy. She turned on the TV and found the station immediately. *Oh my, this is so exciting. Maybe we will get to see James on TV!*

She watched as Michell Hawkins wrapped up his introduction and said, "Now, let's go to our live feed with Lisa Chen, who is currently in Iraq, traveling with a military convoy. Lisa, can you hear me?" Mitchell asked.

The feed switched to Lisa on the TV, and her face filled the screen. The camera seemed to bounce around, and you could hear the sound of the engines in the background. This gave the entire scene a sense of authenticity to what was happening on the TV.

"Yes, Mitchell, I can hear you," Lisa replied, her voice coming over nice and clear despite all of the noise in the background. "I'm being told that we are currently about two hours out from Qayyarah Airfield. The convoy is moving smoothly through the Iraqi desert, which demonstrates the military's ability to travel in such difficult environments."

On the screen, the camera seemed to pan around. Revealing the line of vehicles that were behind them. "We are traveling with a mix of servicemen and women, and a couple of civilian employees. One of them I met on the way to Iraq. His name is James Martinez, and he is a logistics specialist working for the Defense Logistics Agency"

Elena, after hearing her husband's name, leaned forward. Her heart skipped a few beats. *Oh my God! Did she say James' name! This is just crazy!* As the camera panned to the vehicle behind it, she could just make out James sitting in the passenger seat. A big smile formed on her face as she looked at him. *Oh my God! That is him!*

Then, suddenly, the entire image on the screen shook violently. A loud explosion rocked the convoy, making the TV's speakers rattle from the unexpected loud sound.

Elena could see the lead Humvee disappear in a cloud of smoke and debris as the camera caught it all. The camera seemed to shake violently again as another explosion was heard, and someone yelled that the rear vehicle had been hit. *What just happened!* Elena shouted.

"Oh, my God!" Lisa's voice was coming through the TV speakers, sounding panicked. "We are under attack! The convoy seems to have struck an IED!"

In the bottom right corner of the screen, Hawkin's face went pale, but he remained composed. "Lisa, can you still hear me? Can you tell us what is happening right now? Are you able to get to safety?"

The camera continued to shake, as smoke obscured a lot of the view. You could hear gunfire in the background. "We are taking heavy fire! We are taking cover!" Lisa shouted over the noise. Her face was streaked with dust. She had blood on her forehead from a cut. "The convoy is trapped. I can see soldiers returning fire, but the situation is very intense."

Her words were cut off immediately, muted by the sound of another explosion in the background. The camera fell, landing at an angle that only showed feet scrambling for cover. You could still hear Lisa's voice in the distance. "This is ... this is unlike anything I have witnessed before in real life. The entire convoy is being attacked. We need help!"

Back in Jacksonville, Florida, Elena Martinez sat there frozen, her hands over her mouth. "James," she whispered, looking around the chaotic scene for any sign of her husband.

* * *

Back at the convoy, it had become embroiled in complete pandemonium. There were explosions everywhere. The convoy had come to a grinding halt. The civilian Humvee's were trapped between the obliterated wreckages of the lead and rear Humvees. Heavy gunfire from a rocky outcropping peppered the sides of every vehicle.

"Martinez! Out of the vehicle! GO, GO, GO," Simmons screamed over the loud gunfire that was almost deafening. James was already out of his seatbelt and opening the door. He flung himself out, dropping out of the vehicle, his helmet flying off as he hit the ground. Simmons came flying out right behind him, almost landing on top of James. Glass and bullets flew all around them. Luckily, there was a roadside drainage ditch next to the road that gave them a fair amount of cover.

James looked up and saw a wounded Marine lying in the road near the front of their vehicle. He was trying to drag himself to safety after being hit in the leg. *That guy looks like he is hurt pretty bad. I need to grab him and pull him to safety.* James sprang into action, driven by what, he did not know. *Holy shit, this is crazy, we are going to get killed.*

James shouted to the soldier while reaching out his hand, "HEY MARINE! GIVE ME YOUR HAND!"

He managed to grab the soldier's outstretched arm and drug him down the embankment to cover. "I got you, man. Hang in there." James said as another bullet pinged off the Humvee. *Shit, shit, bullets are flying everywhere!*

A Corpsman ran up to them and started tending to the wounded Marine. "You got guts, man, I tell you that!" the Corpsman shouted over the noise.

James just nodded, unable to speak. The adrenaline was overwhelming, and he could hear his heart beating in his ears. He took a few deep breaths to calm himself down. *Holy shit, that was crazy; I can't believe I did that.*

The wounded Marine reached out to James, thanking him for pulling him to safety. James took the Marine's hand in his and placed his other hand on top, saying, "No problem! Happy to help!" James shouted over all the noise. Hopefully, that guy will be ok. *This is fucking crazy!*

All around them, the soldiers were returning fire, with bullets bouncing off of vehicles and hitting the ground in the distance behind them. James could barely hear the shouts from the other Marines, shouting out orders to maintain some semblance of order in the chaos. James watched the heroic efforts of the Marines around him unfold, each one searing itself into his memory.

James continued watching, and noticed a young Marine. *Holy shit, that kid is way too young to be here; he has got some balls; he just ran out there and grabbed that guy by his vest and dragged him to cover with bullets flying all around; he didn't even care about himself. He just saved that guy's life. That was fucking nuts.* The wounded man's leg was severely shredded, leaving a trail of blood to where he now lay.

"Medic! We need a medic over here!" the young Marine cried out while trying to stem the flow of blood that was pouring out the wounded man's leg.

James, thinking quickly, *shit, I can give him my belt.* He removed the belt from his pants, crawled over, and tossed it to the young Marine, "Here, use this as a tourniquet. It should stop the bleeding and buy him some time," James said.

"Thank you, Sir! this will work." The young soldier said.

"No problem, man. I'm glad I could help," James replied. *I hope it helps. That guy was losing a lot of blood.*

To the left of James, two more Marines were carrying another wounded man between them, his arms draped over their shoulders as they moved to safe cover. When they finally set the man down, James could see the man's face was ghostly pale. There is so much blood from that big hole in his chest. *I'm not sure that guy is going to make it. Keep it together; James, don't puke, don't puke.*

"Hang in there, brother! Don't you go dying on us! You are a Marine, and Marines don't die! Do you hear me, Marine!" One of the Sergeants shouted at the mortally wounded soldier. With his last dying bit of energy, the Marine managed to give the Sergeant a thumbs up and a smile before closing his eyes.

Watching this entire scene unfold, James bowed his head and said a silent prayer. *Lord, I pray that you shepherd this soldier to your kingdom and embrace him in your eternal grace ... amen.*

When James looked up again, he spotted Lisa and Tom a few vehicles from where he was. Lisa was still holding on to her microphone while Tom, who had managed to recover his camera, was still filming everything around them. *What the hell? I can't believe they are still broadcasting.*

Tom panned the camera around to take in the scene around them, capturing all the events that were unfolding.

Lisa looked into the camera when it was finally back on her. Her face visibly shaken by what was going on, but still maintaining some resemblance of professionalism, she began narrating the scene to the people watching at home and around the world.

"We are under heavy fire right now! I see ... I'm seeing incredibly selfless acts of bravery happening right in front of my eyes. Marines are risking their lives to pull all the wounded to safety. The acts of bravery are beyond anything I have witnessed before!"

* * *

In the WNN studio, Mitchel Hawkins was struggling with his words. A military analyst they had brought in on the co-panel took over to fill-in coverage, "Mitchel, what this looks like is a well-coordinated attack by one of the current insurgent groups in Iraq," the analyst said as they watched everything unfold live on one of the monitors. "What the insurgents used here is a commonly used tactic called a sandwich attack. It is where they take out the lead and rear vehicles in a convoy and effectively trap the remaining vehicles in the middle."

As they continued to discuss the situation unfolding before them, the live feed continued to display the battle raging on. Viewers across the world watched in horrified and silent shock as the attack played out right before their eyes.

* * *

James lay flat on the ground on his back, the ground hot from the day's sun. His mind was still reeling from what was going on all around him. *Holy shit! This is not supposed to be happening. I'm just a logistics specialist, not a soldier. What am I supposed to do here? Pull yourself together, James!* Then, he rolled to his belly to survey the scene. *Is that my helmet over there? I should definitely grab that and put it on.* He quickly bear crawled over and grabbed it and made sure it was strapped on this time.

A Marine came crawling up next to him, his face streaked with blood and dirt. "Sir! We need to fall back! We are too exposed in this position. We need to find you some better cover!"

James locked eyes with the Marine and nodded, confirming his agreement. As he started to move back, James looked up. *Holy shit, that guy is still alive under the Humvee. Where did he come from? It doesn't matter. I need to help him.* Without hesitating, James changed direction and crawled towards the injured Marine. *This is crazy, this is crazy. Keep going, James. We have to get to him.*

James reached over the embankment, his arm burning as it touched the hot asphalt. *DEAR GOD, THAT IS HOT! Keep going, James!* He stretched until he got ahold of the Marine's vest. A last-second surge of adrenaline helped him pull the Marine out from under the vehicle and down the embankment to safety.

"I've got you, brother. Hang in there," James said as he dragged the Marine back to cover. As he did, bullets whizzed by his head. *Holy fucking shit! I could feel that fucking bullet fly right by me!* James managed to drag the Marine a good 20 feet down the line of vehicles before stopping next to a Humvee whose tires were flat and provided well-needed cover from the onslaught of bullets.

The same Corpsman from earlier appeared next to them. "Good job, Mr. Martinez! I would think you were a Marine if I didn't know any better. Thank you for your help, Sir!"

James sat back and leaned against the embankment, the ground hot against his back. His heart was beating so hard it felt like it was going to burst out of his chest. He closed his eyes for a moment, took deep breaths through his nose, and blew out of his mouth. *Keep it together, keep it together, James. Keep it together, man.* After doing this repeatedly, counting down from 10, his heart rate began to slow. He opened his eyes and saw the Corpsman working on the Marine James had dragged to safety. *Holy shit. I can't believe I did that. That was fucking crazy. What is going on with me?*

Chapter 14

Unraveling

At Balad Air Base, General Sloan was in an office next to the operational command center. He could see screens showing the live feed from WNN through his door. It showed the convoy under attack, his face stone cold as he watched the chaos unfold. *Goodbye, Mr. Martinez and Mr. Simmons. An easy way to kill two birds with one stone.* Then, all of a sudden, sirens went blaring in the background. *What the fuck is going on now?* Sloan looked around, and suddenly, one of the radios on his desk came alive. "We are under attack!" A Marine screamed over the radio. There was a loud explosion that seemed to shake the command center. *Under attack! By who?* Sloan thought.

General Sloan slowly grabbed a radio and said, "This is General Soan; I want a sitrep. What the hell was going on?"

The radio crackled, and one of the guards from the front gate came over it. "General, we are taking heavy fire at the front gate! Insurgents tried to get through and detonated a car bomb, but we were able to stop it before it got through."

More explosions went off in the background, and Sloan could hear heavy gunfire.

"This wasn't the deal, Hassan," the General whispered, looking down at the radio. He walked to the back of the room, took out his encrypted phone, and called Hassan.

The phone rang a few times. "Come on, come on, pick up, damn it," Sloan said quietly as he looked around, making sure no one was looking at him.

Hassan finally picked up. "Ah, General. How are you doing?"

"Cut the shit, Hassan! What the hell are you doing? This wasn't part of the deal. We had a deal!" Sloan catching himself, raising his voice.

"Deal, you say?" Hassan chuckled. "Ahmed, the General said we had a deal." There was some laughter in the background, "You think you can control us, General? Do you think we are merely puppets you can tell to dance anytime you wish? No, General, this is not the case. Today ... Today, we take back our country. Today, we show you what your greed has done. Your corruption has armed your enemies, General. You have given us everything we need, and today, we will show you exactly what we can do with it."

Sloan was holding his phone so tight, threatening to crush it. He clenched his jaw as he spoke. "I hope you understand the repercussions of your actions! This attack, this ... whatever you want to call it, will destabilize the entire region!"

"That is our intended goal, General. We are destabilizing the imperialists' control over our country. The stakes have changed, General, and it is all thanks to you," Hassan said just before terminating the call.

Sloan slammed his fist down on a desk as the line went dead. *I need to get ahead of this. What to do, what to do ... I need to talk to Simmons.* He looked at his phone and dialed Simmons.

After a couple of rings, Simmons answered his satellite phone. "Simmons, listen to me carefully. I need you to make sure Martinez does not make it out of there alive. Do you understand me?" Sloan said in a hushed voice. "Do whatever it takes."

Simmons, who was now by himself. Everyone else was preoccupied with trying to stay alive. "What do you mean? General, I'm not an assassin. How am I going to make sure ..." Simmons looked around again before he spoke. "How am I going to make sure he doesn't make it out alive? Do you have any idea what is happening out here?"

"Yes, I do, Simmons, I'm watching it right now on the TV. This is bigger than just you sitting on the side of the road being attacked. This is a coordinated attack on all of our installations," Sloan said.

Simmons froze at the sound of that. *Attacks at all of the bases? But why? Who? Unless ...* then a thought popped into his head. Then Simmons spoke again. "Was it you that arranged this attack on the convoy? Are you a part of this?" he asked In an accusatory tone.

The line was silent for a moment. Then Sloan spoke, "I don't I like how you asked that question, Simmons. Say what is on your mind."

"Did you orchestrate this attack on the convoy, you son of a bitch?" Simmons asked with anger in his voice. "You did, didn't you? And you didn't warn me at all. So that would mean you were trying to kill me, too. Am I right, Sloan?"

"Well, Simmons, it would appear you have found me out. I wouldn't have had to take these measures had you done your job and kept Marinez in line. But you couldn't even do that. So, yes, your usefulness to me ran out as soon as Martinez found you out and let Colonel Harrington and the DLA Oversight Committee know about your involvement. Hell, now that I'm thinking about it, this might have all been your idea ... Yeah, you were the one selling everything to the insurgents, your fingerprints are all over this. And once this is all over, no one will know the wiser because you will be dead along with Martinez. Thank you, Simmons, for helping me come to this conclusion."

Stunned by what Sloan was saying to him, Simmons sat there for a moment, his mind racing at the implications. Then he spoke, "If I make it out of this alive, I'll expose you for what you did. Don't forget my fingerprints may be all over this, but yours are too, and I have the records to prove it. So you better hide General. You had better find a nice place where no one can find you because once people find out what you did, they will try you for treason, and you know what they do to traitors, right?"

The line went quiet. "I guess we will see what happens, Simmons, but judging by what I see on TV, your odds are pretty slim. I'll take those odds," Sloan replied in a villain-ous tone that he had come to represent.

"Then I guess I'll see you in hell, Sloan, you sadistic son of a bitch!!!" Simmons said as he ended the call.

General Sloan sat there momentarily, thinking about what was unfolding. Slowly, a smile grew on his face. "Yes, I can make this work," he said to himself.

* * *

James leaning against the embankment finally began to come down from the surge of adrenaline he experienced when he was pulling that Marine to safety. All of a sudden his satellite phone started to vibrate in his pocket. He pulled it out and saw there was a priority message flashing across his screen:

MILITARY ALERT
PRIORITY: IMMEDIATE
SITUATION: Simultaneous coordinated attacks reported at the following installations:

- BALAD AIR BASE

- CAMP LIBERTY

- QAYYARAH AIRFIELD

- CONVOY DEST. QAYYARAH

THREAT: ISIS/PMF FORCES EXECUTING LARGE-SCALE ATTACK TARGETING US ASSETS. ENEMY COORDINATION CONFIRMED.

DIRECTIVE: ALL PERSONNEL HIGH ALERT; ALL BASES DEPLOY ASSETS; AIR ASSETS ACTIVATED; ALL UNITS REPORT SITREP; SECURE ALL BASE PERIMETERS.

END TRANSMISSION

A chill ran down James' spine after reading the message. *Holy shit. All the bases are under attack? This isn't just an ambush. It was a part of something bigger than I could have imagined, and somehow, and I'm caught in the middle of it.*

James looked around, finally locating Sergeant Rodriguez, who was busy barking orders at the men who were still capable of fighting. James began to crouch and crawl towards Rodriguez, making sure not to pop his head up too high. When he finally got there, Sergeant Rodriguez turned and saw him.

"Martinez! What the hell are you doing out this far? You should be back over there, out of the way," Rodriguez shouted over the gunfire.

Martinez, holding up his phone, shouted back. "I got an alert on my sat phone! It says that all the bases are under attack as well. ISIS and PMF forces have launched a large-scale attack on all our bases."

Sergeant Rodriguez grabbed Martinez' phone and read the alert himself, his mind reeling at the implications. "We are going to need to dig in. If this is really happening, I'm not sure if help will be coming anytime soon. I'll get on the horn with command and find out what our course of action should be. In the meantime, keep your head down, Martinez! Go back over there and get behind some cover!" Rodriguez ordered.

After James moved, Rodriguez keyed his radio. "Overlord Actual, this is Uniform Six-Two. Do you copy? Over." Static filled the air. He tried again. "Overlord Actual, Uniform Six-Two, priority traffic, how copy?"

There was more static. Rodriguez switched channels. "Any station on this net, this is Uniform Six-Two. Request relay to Overlord Actual, over." He waited, then tried a third time.

Taking Rodriguez's advice, James began heading back to his position, the sound of his repeated radio calls growing fainter behind him.

"Dammit," he heard Rodriguez mutter, still trying different channels. "Overlord Actual, Uniform Six-Two, I say again ..."

As the battle raged on, bullets were flying all around, rockets exploding as they slammed into the already destroyed vehicles. Lucky for them, the armor was holding up. Eventually, James found himself next to Lisa and Tom. They all huddled next to a Humvee. James could see that the light on the camera was still on. *I can't believe they are still broadcasting this all live to everyone around the world. I hope Elena and the kids are not watching this.*

James looked at Lisa and said, "Listen, there is more to this than what is happening here. I just got an alert on my phone. This isn't just an isolated attack. Right now, all the U.S. bases in Iraq are under attack by ISIS and PMF forces."

Stunned by the news, Lisa relayed the information to the camera, "We have just received news that the attack that is currently happening all around us is part of a larger coordinated offensive. We are being told that Balad Air Base, along with other U.S. installations here in Iraq, are currently under attack."

* * *

Back in the WNN studios, the news they just heard from Lisa stunned everyone for a moment. Mitchell Hawkins regained his composure and began to speak to the camera.

"Ladies and Gentlemen, we are receiving an updated report about the situation unfolding in Iraq. Lisa Chen has just informed us that there are reports of a large-scale offensive against all U.S. forces in Iraq. We will bring you more information on this developing situation as we receive it."

* * *

Another rocket slammed into the convoy, causing another explosion that sent debris flying everywhere. James ducked under some cover as pieces of the mangled vehicle flew past him. *Holy shit! This is crazy! What the hell am I doing here?*

"I don't know how many more hits this humvee can take," James shouted.

"These Humvees are built pretty sturdy. They should hold up. Hopefully, the insurgents will run out of rockets soon," a Marine said to James.

James looked around and surveyed the scene. *It is only a matter of time before we run out of either ammo or defenders, with these enemies closing in and chaos all around us. I need to figure out a way to help.* James felt his phone vibrating in his pocket. He pulled it out and looked at it. It was a message from Simmons:

"Stay close, and keep your head down. Keep an eye on the reporter as well. General Sloan is behind this."

James' eyes went wide at what he just read. *General Sloan is behind this attack? What the fuck?* He scanned around until he found Simmons off in the distance, his expression unreadable. *What the hell are these guys into? Was I just a pawn in all of this somehow? Is this part of something bigger that I'm not aware of?*

Over where Lisa and Tom were crouched, Lisa talked to the camera. "We are taking cover behind one of the blown-out humvees." Another explosion rocked a vehicle nearby, causing Lisa to jump and scream. "Looking around,

I can see the civilian, James Martinez, taking shelter nearby. The Marines look like they are trying to hold the defensive perimeter they have set up, but the insurgent attacks are relentless. They seem to be in a good position behind the rocks to our left. The Marines are having a hard time pushing them back."

* * *

Back at the WNN studio, Mitchell Hawkins was sitting at his news anchor desk, his face grim as he watched everything play out live on the monitor in front of him. "What we are witnessing here, ladies and gentlemen, is the face of raw unedited war. The courage being displayed here by everyone there, the sacrifice ..."

* * *

Watching in horror back in Jacksonville, FL, Elena Martinez held a cushion to her chest, tears streaming down her face as she watched everything unfold on the television. Her children had heard the commotion from the TV while upstairs, came down to investigate, and now stood there transfixed on the television, watching their father fight for his life on live TV.

* * *

The onslaught of gunfire from the insurgents was unwavering. The Marines managed to form a better defensive line, which provided a temporary reprieve from the attacks.

James was sitting there trying to work all of this out. The information about Sloan was eating him now. *I won't let Sloan get away with this. I can't. I need to expose him for what he has done and for what he is.* James looked over at Lisa, and a plan started to form. He managed to get closer to her and whispered to her, "We need to stick together. There is more at play here than just this attack."

Lisa looked at James, confused by what he was saying, and asked. "What are you talking about James? I don't understand."

James weighed his options and then decided to tell her what he knew. "I think that General Sloan is behind this attack."

Lisa's eyes went wide, "Brigadier General Sloan? The man that we saw before we left Balad? That General Sloan? What makes you think that? What evidence do you have?"

James began to explain, "During my investigation at Balad, I uncovered a bunch of crates of missing ammunition and some discrepancies with the Humvee inventory. The moment I reported my findings, he was at Balad. I know, that could be just a coincidence. Still, The only person who knew about the missing ammunition was Colonel Harrington. She was not going to report it until we figured out who was behind it all. And then all of a sudden, General Sloan shows up, I mean, that sounds pretty suspect to me. Did you notice the way he was acting just before we left? And then Simmons confirmed my suspicions just a little while ago. Simmons is somehow involved as well."

Lisa sat there for a moment, processing everything. "Now that I think about it, I did mention to Tom earlier that General Sloan was acting odd. He all but threatened Sergeant Rodriguez about questioning him on how late we were leaving," Lisa said.

"Exactly, I think he set all this up. He wanted me here. I think he is trying to kill me, and possibly you, too. You have the ability to expose him on live TV. Hell, he is probably counting on Simmons to be killed as well. Simmons is probably a loose end to him." James paused momentarily so Lisa could process it all before he counted. "We need to get this out," James told her. "Everyone needs to see why this is happening and who is responsible for it."

Lisa understood the gravity of the situation and what James was proposing. "We will do it," she said." I'll need to see the proof. I don't think I can just toss out an accusation like that on live TV without having concrete proof that this was Sloan. Maybe we can get Simmons to confess on live TV or something? But we are going to need to survive this first."

Just then, another attack wave came, everyone ducking as another rocket flew overhead, missing the Humvee and exploding in the distance.

As the sun began to go down, their fight for survival also turned into a fight for the truth. The entire world was watching, and James Martinez, along with Lisa Chen, were determined to ensure that the story that was told was not just about all the attacks going on but also about the corruption that enabled them.

CHAPTER 15

THE SITUATION ROOM

The Situation Room at the White House was humming with tense energy as the multiple TV screens which lined the room's walls, displayed various aspects of the live broadcast of the escalating crisis in Iraq. The main TV at the end of the table was playing the WNN live feed of the ambushed convoy. The sporadic sounds of explosions and gunfire coming from the TV's speakers caused people at the table to jolt every so often.

President Mark Franklin stood at the head of the table, watching the chaotic scenes unfold on the TV. He was surrounded by his top military leaders, most of the three-letter "alphabet" intelligence agencies, and some of his key cabinet members, all of whom sat at the table in shocked silence, watching this large scale attack unfold.

"My God," The President said to himself as he watched a soldier drag another to safety. President Franklin leaned forward onto the table. "How the hell did we miss this? How did we not see this coming?" The President asked, with irritation in his voice.

General Harding, Chairman of the Joint Chiefs, spoke first. He leaned forward to address the President directly. "Sir, this doesn't appear to be random. ISIS and the PMF are hitting us at multiple bases at the same time. Balad and Liberty are confirmed under attack, Sir. And the intel is showing they are just getting started. We could see this intensify even more."

Dr. Emily Anderson, the National Security Advisor, interjected. "Mr. President, we have a developing situation that just came in. CENTCOM just confirmed coordinated attacks against Qayyarah Airfield. The initial reports suggest this is part of a larger offensive that is targeting our key installations in the region. The level of coordination we're seeing is unprecedented since ..."

"What are the casualties so far?" Franklin cut her off.

General Harding's face looked grim, "The numbers are still coming in, Sir," he said. "It is bad, Sir. We are looking at some pretty heavy casualties, military, contractors, and civilians among the wounded and dead. Every base hit ..." He trailed off as he looked at his laptop screen, showing real-time updates.

The room fell silent as they watched the WNN live feed on the main TV. The camera focused on a man dragging a wounded soldier to safety, his movements seeming desperate but determined to get the job done.

"Who the hell is that?" Franklin demanded, pointing his finger at the screen. "The guy pulling that Marine to safety?"

Dr. Anderson was on it instantly, pulling up the information on her tablet. "That is James Martinez, Sir. He is a civilian employee and a logistics specialist out of NAS Jax, down in Jacksonville, Florida. He works for the DLA. He was sent to Iraq to investigate some equipment discrepancies. He wasn't supposed to be anywhere near combat."

"Well, I guess he is now whether he likes it or not," Franklin said. "That man has got more guts than sense, but we will take what we can get right now."

Admiral Jonathan Ross leaned forward and spoke. "Mr President, the USS Eisenhower Carrier Strike Group has confirmed. They are positioning into the Persian Gulf, ETA 2 hours. We should have air support on those bases soon, 5 F35's have deployed off the deck and are enroute as we speak. We will show these bastards what they are really dealing with."

"Thank you for the update Admiral," Franklin said.

Robert Kline, the Secretary of Defense, cleared his throat before speaking. "Mr. President, we need to think about the optics of the current situation. The entire world is watching what is happening on the side of that road live. Are we putting those people at risk ..."

"Speaking of the broadcast," Alicia Navarro, Communications Director, interrupted as she pushed her glasses up, "Should we cut the live feed? Having that news crew broadcast our trapped personnel's position..."

"Hold on," Franklin raised his hand, cutting her off and silencing the room. "Before we make that call, who the hell authorized WNN to broadcast live from this convoy in the first place?"

Harding straightened. "Sir, it was my office that approved WNN's embedment at the request of Senator Katrina Long."

"Why the hell would she request something like this?" Franklin asked.

"Senator Long is currently acting as the chair of the senate committee tasked with overseeing the drawdown. She thought, and we agreed, that it would be good PR to broadcast how our troops were handling the drawdown and how they were doing to the folks back here at home," Harding replied. "We actually are due for an update from her office later this week. Obviously timelines have changed. Let's get her here asap."

"Yes, I would like to speak with her right now," Franklin demanded.

"Me too," Harding concurred.

"Sir, she is in a committee on the Hill," one of the staff members said, already on a secure line with the Capitol.

"I don't care what she's doing," Franklin said. "Inform the Senator this is a matter of national security that requires her immediate presence. Get her here. Now."

At that very moment, Senator Katrina Long was in a deep discussion at her closed-door committee meeting. A young aide quickly and quietly slipped in. She whispered something in the Senator's ear. Long's expression seemed to shift instantly as she processed the message.

Standing slowly, she addressed the room with a practiced grace. "I apologize, Dr. White, but I'm being called away for an urgent matter. I would still like to hear more about this advanced research project you are working on over at MIT."

The 16-year-old MIT student, Dr. White, replied with a nod. "I would be glad to meet with you anytime, Senator Long."

As the Senator left the room, a Secret Service agent approached her. "Senator Long, please follow me if you will, ma'am."

They moved quickly through a series of corridors.

"I have never been down here before. I thought we were going to the White House?" the Senator asked.

"We are ma'am. We are just taking a shortcut," the Secret Service agent replied.

Then they turned down one more corridor into a tunnel behind a door known only to the Secret Service. As they walked, their footsteps echoed in the darkness, which was only broken by the agent's flashlight, until they reached a vehicle that was waiting for them.

Back in the situation room, the debate about the broadcast had begun to get heated. General Harding slammed his hand on the table. "Every second the feed stays live, it shows the convoy's position," he said with frustration. The servicemen and women are sitting ducks. We are broadcasting their exact location and their defensive positions to anyone who wants to watch this."

"And what kind of message does it send the American people if we cut it?" Anderson shot back. "The whole world is watching what is happening right now. If we were to kill the feed ..."

"To hell with the message!" Ross chimed in. "Those are our people on that screen. They are trapped out there!"

"ENOUGH!" Franklin's booming voice cut through the chaos. The room then fell silent as the door at the other end opened. In walked Senator Long, breathing heavy from her hurried arrival.

"Senator, so glad you could join us. Do you care to explain why our servicemen and women are being broadcast live for the entire world to see, like some kind of reality TV show?" Franklin asked with a tinge of anger in his voice.

Long didn't hesitate to answer. She walked right up to the table, her eyes locked on the President. "You want the truth, Mr. President? This goes far beyond just transparency. We have solid evidence that General Sloan, head of operations in Iraq, has been cooking the books over there. He has been selling off our equipment to our enemies to line his own pockets. He has made millions while our troops make do."

The room fell silent for a moment as everyone processed this revelation. Then the room erupted in hurried conversation, discussing the implications of these accusations.

Franklin's face went cold. *Brigadier General Sloan ... Have you seriously betrayed us ...? Are you saying that this attack ...? This doesn't make sense ... What did we miss ... ? How could you ... ?*

"This is an attack of terrorism, plain and simple," said Senator Long, her voice sharp as she spoke. "I had James Martinez sent there to investigate equipment discrepancies. That is why I wanted WNN there, to ensure nothing got buried under a mound of paperwork this time. I never could have imagined Sir ..."

"Thank you Senator, that's enough," Franklin said peacefully.

President Franklin returned to watching the screen as James Martinez helped another wounded soldier. His mind began to race through all the implications and risks. Finally, he stood straight, as he fixed his jacket.

"The feed is going to stay live," Franklin said firmly. "I want word sent that Martinez and the reporter are to be protected. If they are onto Sloan then they need to be protected at all cost." he stated.

"Get a team on this ASAP. If Sloan is as dirty as the Senator says he is, he will definitely have friends in high places that may try to protect him." Franklin concluded.

With that, the room became a whirlwind of action. Phones were being grabbed, orders were being issued, and plans were being made. President Franklin watched the screen, his mind already racing to the next crisis and the next decisions he would have to make.

"Sir," Anderson approached him quietly. "If what Sloan has done goes public, all of the corruption, and all of ..."

"Then we will deal with the fallout," Franklin said, holding his hand up and cutting her off. "For right now, we need to focus on keeping our people alive."

The President sat back and watched James Martinez on the screen. Martinez was still fighting and helping others despite what was happening around him. *Sometimes heroes come from the most unexpected places.*

Chapter 16

The Home Front

In her living room in Jacksonville, Florida, bathed in flickering blue light from the TV, Elena Martinez sat on the edge of her seat. Her eyes locked in on the TV screen, watching the chaos unfold before her in the Iraqi desert.

Miguel and Sophia huddled closely beside her, their young faces expressing signs of worry. Miguel's bottom lip quivering, Sophia, usually the braver of the two, clutched one of Miguel's Blox Fruit plushies she had found on the couch. Her eyes were wide and unblinking as she watched the TV screen.

Elena's phone vibrated repeatedly on the coffee table in front of her, with a mix of calls and messages that went unnoticed. Suddenly, a familiar ringtone broke through her haze. Elena glanced down at her phone to see her mother's contact photo on the screen. With trembling hands, she reached down and picked up the phone to answer it.

"Elena? mija, are you there?" Her mother's voice sounded frantic as she spoke.

"Mom? Yes ... yes, I'm here. What's going on?" Elena replied, her voice sounding distant.

"We have been knocking at the door for five minutes, mija! Unlock the door and let us in, honey." her mother said.

Elena blinked away the confusion. "What do you mean? Where are you? You are here?"

"Yes! Elena, we are here. Please come and let us in," her mother replied.

"Miguel, go let Grandma and Grandpa in, please," Elena said as she set her phone back on the coffee table while staring at the TV.

Miguel nodded and then ran to the front door, his little legs pumping with a purpose. As he left, Sophia moved closer to her mother, her little hands gripping Elena's arm tightly.

Miguel got to the door, unlocked it, and opened it. His grandmother and grandfather came inside, and Miguel embraced his grandfather tightly, looking for some comfort from something that was happening that he didn't fully understand.

"Everything will be OK, Miguel. You will see," his grandfather whispered as he wrapped him in a big, warm hug. Miguel just laid his head on his grandfather's shoulder. His grandfather picked him up as they made their way to the living room.

As Elena's parents walked into the living room, Elena stood and walked over to her mother. Maria, wrapped her arms around Elena to comfort her. "It is going to be alright, mi amor," Maria whispered to Elena while stroking her hair. "God will protect James, you will see." Elena's mother turned to the kids and said, "Come on, you two, let's go to the family room. You two should take a break from watching all of this."

"Thank you, Mom, I really appreciate it," Elena said.

"No problem at all, mija. I love you." Maria said as she walked off with the kids.

Elena's father, Robert, walked over and sat beside her on the couch. Without saying a word, he put his arm around her shoulders and offered silent support as they watched the unfolding battle on the TV.

As the minutes ticked by, they felt like an eternity. Elena thought about happier times, James teaching Miguel to ride a bike, family trips to the park, and lazy Sunday afternoons after church. The stark difference between those memories and what was happening now was almost too much to think about. How many more Sundays would we have together?

All of a sudden, Elena's phone rang. On the screen, she could see it say "DOD" with an unfamiliar number. Her heart skipped a beat as she answered it.

"Hello?" she said.

"ELENA! IT'S ME JAMES!" His voice was loud due to all the chaos in the background.

"James! Oh my god, are you OK? We have been watching what is happening," Elena shouted.

"I AM ALRIGHT FOR NOW. LISTEN, I DON'T HAVE MUCH TIME. I WANTED TO SAY I LOVE YOU AND TELL THE KIDS, TELL THEM ..."

The line all of a sudden went dead.

"JAMES? JAMES!" Elena yelled at the phone, staring at the phone in disbelief. Then she looked at the TV just in time to see another large explosion hit the convoy. The camera shook violently. As the smoke cleared, she saw James taking cover in the background. Still moving, still alive.

Putting her hands over her face, she turned and buried her face in her father's shoulder. "Oh, Dad!" Elena started to cry from the emotional roller coaster she didn't ask to be on.

"He is still alive. He is still alive and moving," Elena's father said to her, trying to comfort her. "James is a survivor. He will make it through this."

Elena sat back, wiping the tears from her eyes. "You are right, Dad. He has to. He promised he would come home to us."

There was a sharp knock at the door, startling them both. Elena got up. *Who could that be?* she thought to herself. Her mind was still reeling from the phone call with James. She walked to the front door to see who it was. As she opened the door, she saw a man and a woman in military uniforms standing on her front porch.

"Mrs. Martinez?" one of them asked, the other officer looking back and scanning the street behind them. "Good evening, ma'am. I'm Lieutenant Commander Hayes, and this is Lieutenant Host. We are from NAS Jax. We have been ordered to escort you and your family to the base ASAP."

Elena, stunned by the request, asked, "Why? Wait ... What do you mean? What is going on?"

Lieutenant Host stepped closer to Elena and lowered her voice before she spoke, "Ma'am, we have orders directly from the President. There are ... concerns about your family's safety and security. The press that is about to show up any minute now. We need to get you to the base."

Hayes glanced at his watch. As if in the queue, a news van pulled up in front of the house. "Mrs. Martinez, I don't want to scare you, but we really need to go. We have a secure home on the base ready for you and your family and a protection detail in place."

Elena was caught entirely off guard by all of this. *Is something terrible about to happen? These two look like some kind of security personnel. This must be serious.*

"How long will we have to stay there?" Elena asked, starting to process everything.

"Just pack light for now. You have five minutes," Lieutenant Host said softly. "And Mrs. Martinez? Leave your phones and electronic devices here. We will provide you with secure communications once we are at the base."

Elena looked back at her father, who nodded at her grimly. His eyes spoke volumes about the gravity of this situation. "Elena, I think this is a good idea. You and the kids should go. You need protection from the outside media, and from what it sounds like, there might be something else you need protection from. We can stay here with Max and take care of him for you."

"All right, Lieutenant. Give me a minute, and I'll pack the kids and get ready to go as fast as I can," Elena said before walking back into the house.

Elena disappeared inside the house. Lieutenant Commander Hayes nodded to Lieutenant Host and said, "I'll go down and watch the perimeter. I saw a black SUV pull up and park down the street. I want to keep an eye on it just in case ..."

"I saw it as well," the Lieutenant replied quietly, moving closer to the door. Her hand rested casually near her sidearm as she scanned the crowd growing just on the other side of the street. "Five minutes here, tops. Then we need to move out."

Hayes walked down to the walkway's edge and stood there casually but alert. Through the earpiece he was wearing, command gave him an update: "Lieutenant Commander, be advised. There is a vehicle matching a watchlist description, three blocks out, heading your way."

"Copy that command," Hayes said without moving his mouth, a practiced talent he had honed as head of the security force at NAS Jax. Haye's eyes never stopped scanning the street and the surrounding area. "Tell backup to stay close and out of sight. Let's not spook anyone just yet."

Inside the house, Elena looked at the TV. There was an image of James, surrounded by chaos but still fighting. *Lord, please protect my husband. I pray that you shield him from any harm and bring him back to us safely.*

"Stay safe, mi amor. I love you," she whispered. "We will be waiting for you."

Elena prepared herself for what lay ahead. As she and the kids prepared to leave their home for the security of the naval base. She could not shake the feeling that their lives had irrevocably changed forever. The sound of more news vans pulling up outside her house and her neighbors' increasingly loud chatter added a surreal nature to this moment.

Looking through her front window, she saw Lieutenant Commander Hayes speaking quietly into his radio. She could see his eyes constantly scanning the street. The Lieutenant remained stationed by the front door.

Elena looked at Miguel and Sophia. *They look so scared.* She pulled them both close, trying to project a calmness that she herself didn't feel.

Sophia looked at her mother and asked, "Mom, where are we going?"

"We are going to take a ride with these nice officers. They work on the base where your father works. They want us to come with them so all those news people outside don't bother us," Elena said to Sophia, "It is going to be OK," she said softly, talking to them both. "We are going to go on a little trip, but we will be back home before you know it. Is that OK?" she asked.

Both of the kids nodded. Still unsure what was happening.

As they started to walk out the door, Elena glanced back and took one last look at their home. She looked at their perfectly manicured lawn, the kids' bikes leaning against the garage, all symbols of what used to be the normal life that they just lived only hours ago. Now, it all seemed almost like a distant memory.

"Ready, Mrs. Martinez?" Lieutenant Commander Hayes asked. As they began to walk, Hayes positioned himself between the family and the street as they moved towards a waiting vehicle. The Lieutenant took a position on their other side, creating a protective barrier for the kids.

Elena helped her kids into a blacked-out SUV. While getting in, Elena noticed the dark-tinted windows and how heavy the door seemed to be when she closed it. *This is an armored vehicle*, she thought to herself.

As they drove away, she looked out the window at her neighbors, drawn out of their homes by the commotion;

their faces painted with confusion and concern at the chaos unfolding. *What about the community we have built here? All our connections to our neighbors—will we survive this ordeal?*

Still clutching Miguel's Blox Fruit plushie, Sophia asked, "Mom, will Dad come home soon?"

Elena hugged her daughter tightly, her voice remaining steady. "Yes, mija, he is very strong, and he is coming home soon." *I know he will.*

Miguel, trying to be strong for his sister by emulating the bravery he saw in his father on TV, added, "And when he does get back, we will have the biggest barbecue ever, right mom?"

Managing a small smile, Elena said, "We sure will, mijo. And we will celebrate like we never have done before."

The ride to the base took about 20 minutes. As the base came into view, Elena thought, *I guess this will be our home for however long it takes for James to come back to us.*

When the SUV pulled up to where they would be staying, they exited the vehicle, and were escorted to a secure house that had been prepared for them. They walked in, and Elena looked around. *This isn't our home, but it is a safe place for us to be for now.*

Later that evening, Elena sat with her kids, reading them a story. Her attempt to calm their nerves and reassure them that everything was going to be OK. Outside, the world around them was in turmoil, but right now, in this moment, they were together, and that was enough for her.

Looking at her children's faces in the soft lamplight, she tried to push away her fears about the uncertain days ahead. She knew James was strong, knew they were strong.

They would get through this because they had to, because they always did.

With that thought in mind, she whispered into the night, "We will be here, mi amor. We are here waiting for you."

Chapter 17

Into The Fray

As the Iraqi sun began sinking towards the horizon, smoke, gunpowder, and the pungent smell of burning rubber were thick in the air. All of the convoy's vehicles were in various states of destruction. Some were still smoldering. Two of the Humvees had their tires blown out. Still, the soldiers managed to winch them together to create a makeshift barricade that they were using for cover.

Leaning against the side of the embankment, James Martinez wiped sweat and grime from his face. His back was pressed against the still-warm ground. The sound of occasional gunfire still filled the air, only interrupted by the occasional groans from a wounded soldier lying in pain nearby. His throat was completely dry, coated by the desert dust that seemed to be on everything around him.

Sergeant Rodriguez, with his face lined with blood and ash, was crouched nearby, returning fire at the insurgents entrenched behind rocks a thousand yards out from their position.

"It looks like they've stopped their rocket attacks on us," Rodriguez said between his bursts of gunfire. "Hopefully, they ran out of them."

Private Riley, also crouched nearby, nodded. "They're waiting for nightfall. They're probably going to sneak up on us under the cover of night like Ninjas."

While looking around, James' eyes stopped on a nearby rifle lying on the ground. *Should I pick that rifle up? I don't think anyone is using it. It must be one of the wounded soldier's weapons.* Without even thinking about what he was doing, he reached out and picked it up. *Holy shit, this thing is heavier than I thought it would be.* He cleaned off the sand as well as he could.

"Pss, hey," he whispered to Jenkins, trying to keep his voice low. "Do you think you could show me how to use this thing?"

Jenkins looked at him with surprise on his face. After a moment of hesitating, he nodded. "What you're holding there is an M4 carbine," he said, moving a little closer. The first thing you want to do is always treat it as if it is already loaded, even when you think it's not."

Jenkins then guided James' hand into position. "What you wanna do here is put your right hand on the pistol grip like this, then put your index finger straight and outside of the trigger guard until you're ready to shoot. Your left hand goes forward on the hand guard. Make sure to keep your grip firm but not tight. The recoil will cause you to shake if you squeeze it too hard."

Jenkins' voice remained steady and professional. "You see this switch right here?" he tapped a lever that was located above the trigger. "That's your selector switch." He rotated it. The click was audible. "Straight up, you're in semi-automatic, one trigger pull, one shot. Fully automatic is all the way forward, but don't use that. You'll waste all of your ammo and hit nothing but the sky. Oh, and make sure you always pull the switch all the way back for safe mode when you're not planning to shoot," Jenkins continued, clicking the switch all the way back.

James nodded, absorbing every word as Jenkins spoke and pointed. *Oh man, I can't believe I'm learning to use this thing.*

Out of nowhere, a burst of enemy fire kicked up some dust near their position. Jenkins didn't even flinch. "You wanna make sure when you shoot that you breathe normally. You wanna take your shot during the natural pause between breaths. And always remember to only fire off two or three rounds max. You have to make each shot count."

James began to trace each control with his fingers as Jenkins named them off. "This is the magazine release right here. Your spare magazines are in these pouches next to you. If you run out, you wanna hit this button. Your empty mag will drop free, and your new mag goes in right here. Hit the bolt catch right here to release the bolt and you are back in business."

"What if it jams?" James asked, trying to make sure he remembered everything. *I hope it doesn't jam, that would suck.*

"Well ... if it jams. You wanna tap the magazine to make sure that it's seated correctly, and then pull back the charging handle and look inside to make sure you cleared the jam. But, don't worry, these babies never jam," Jenkins concluded.

"Okay. So, you've got a red dot sight on the rifle," Jenkins continued explaining, pointing and tapping on the mounted optic. "It's already zeroed, so try not to mess with any of the settings. Just put the dot on whatever you wanna hit." Jenkins helped James shoulder the weapon properly. "Now what you're gonna wanna do is keep both eyes open, and the red dot will look like it's floating out there on the target. That's the way it's designed to work."

Another burst of fire cracked overhead, causing Jenkins to duck, as he continued, "The red dot has got different brightness settings, and you can adjust it with this dial right here on the side. Brighter for when it's daylight and dimmer for when it's dawn and dusk. It's already set, so you're good for right now. But if the sun gets in your eyes, adjust it."

"What if the red dot stops working?" James asked while he practiced acquiring targets without firing. *I have to say this red dot looks really cool.*

"You see these little posts underneath? These are your backup sites. But let's not worry about those right now. Red dots generally have battery life for years, and they can take a real good beating." Jenkins watched James as he practiced with the rifle, noting his form. "Make sure to remember to put the dot on the target, squeeze the trigger smoothly, and follow through. Make sure not to jerk the trigger or flinch. Let the recoil surprise you."

Jenkins looked at James and paused momentarily, then said quietly, "Are you sure about this, Mr. Martinez?"

James crouched there, going over it in his head. *This isn't what I signed up for,* as his hands adjusted the unfamiliar weight and balance of the weapon, *but here we are. I need to step up and help.* He looked at Jenkins directly in his eyes and nodded firmly. "I have no choice now, Jenkins. If I can help defend, then it's my responsibility to do that."

Crouching nearby, a few remaining soldiers exchanged looks. Some nodded with respect for what James was doing, while others had a flicker of doubt in their eyes as they watched James practice with the rifle.

Sergeant Rodriguez, who had been watching Private Jenkins show James how to use the M4, decided that he would give James a test to see how he handled firing the live weapon.

"Martinez!" Rodriguez called out. "You're up. You have your first target. Do you see that boulder about a thousand yards out? The one that is shaped like a shark's fin? Keep an eye out for movement on the left side. They've been using that for cover for a while now."

James gave Sergeant Rodriguez a thumbs-up, then he shouldered the rifle like Jenkins had shown him. He set the stock firmly against his shoulder, and the red dot seemed to come alive and float in space as he scanned the perimeter of the boulder. His heart began to pound in his chest, but his hands were steady as a rock. *H O L Y Shit, am I about to really shoot at someone with this thing? This is fucking crazy, am I crazy? What the hell was I thinking?*

Just then, James caught some movement. *Holy shit, was that someone by that rock? or was it the sun reflecting off of something?* Withoutthinking, he flipped the rifle into semi–automatic mode and squeezed the trigger. The rifle bucked against his shoulder hard. *SHIT, wasn't even close.* He adjusted his aim a little bit and then fired off another shot. This time the impact of the bullet kicked up dust near the target. *Alright, that was closer. You got this, James.* He fired a third shot and, this time, found his target. He heard a distant shout. *Holy shit! I hit someone. Should I be happy about that?*

"Great shot, Martinez!" Rodrigues called out. "Now, I need you to watch the right flank. They like to move around while we are distracted."

Tom's camera was rolling the entire time, capturing every moment of James' transformation from civilian to soldier. Tom had done a great job positioning himself to capture the action and the look on James' face so the entire world could see.

As the afternoon wore on, James settled into a rhythm of scanning, acquiring, squeezing, and adjusting. Each shot felt less foreign. Each time he swapped out the magazine for a new one, the more natural it felt. But he knew that what he was doing, the lives he would potentially take would probably weigh on his conscience for the rest of his life.

Continuing her broadcast, Lisa kept her voice steady. "Our situation here remains critical. We've been under attack on and off for several hours now, with no signs of rescue insight. The toll is ... it's devastating." She paused for a moment, letting Tom pan the camera around for a broader view so that everyone could see the hellscape, along with the faces of the determined Corpsmen working on their wounded buddies.

"What you're witnessing here is something unimaginable," Lisa narrated. "Over to my left, I can see a group of wounded soldiers. The Corpsmen are working on them with whatever medical supplies they brought."

"Unfortunately, not everyone has been so fortunate," Lisa continued, lowering her voice. "I count at least 5 soldiers killed in action," Lisa said softly.

"Despite everything that has happened, the remaining soldiers continue to fight with incredible bravery," Lisa said, her voice slightly rising. "The commanding officer, Sergeant Rodriguez, continues to move from position to position, making sure to check on his men while coordinating our defense."

Tom zoomed in on Rodriguez, capturing the Sergeant's face, as he helped one of his privates adjust his firing position.

"The commitment to fight and defend that we're seeing from these soldiers ... It's unlike anything I've ever witnessed before," Lisa said while choking back tears. "They're not just fighting for one another. They're protecting all of us with such intensity. It's truly awe-inspiring."

While crouched by one of the Humvees, James glanced up to the mounted machine gun on top of it. The soldier that was on it earlier lay dead on the ground nearby. *Maybe I should get Jenkins to show me how to use the big gun up there as well, just in case.*

"Hey. Jenkins," James said, his confidence growing more and more with each shot of the M4. "That gun up there. You think you could show me how to use that one as well?"

Jenkins followed James' gaze, his eyes going wide. "Man, the Ma Deuce, are you serious? And that would be suicide. Anyone who pops their head up there is dead. We're going to stay behind cover and defend until support arrives."

James looked him in the eyes, his voice steady. "Maybe, maybe not. If those insurgents out there decide to rush us after it gets dark, we'll need all the firepower we have to hold them off. And if any more of you guys get hurt, I might have no choice but to use it."

Jenkins sat there for a long moment, staring at James. Then he nodded slowly. "Alright, you crazy son of a bitch," he said, trying to keep his voice low and focused. "That there's a M2 Browning 50 caliber heavy machine gun. It's a whole different beast entirely than that M4."

He pointed as he explained, "It feeds from the left side, right there. The belt goes in there, and the brass and links eject from right there. You'll need to keep your head up. You don't wanna get caught watching the feeding mechanism. Just let it do its job."

Jenkins continued his instructions, James watching intently. "You see that right there? That is the charging handle. You wanna pull that all the way back and then release it. Pull with all your strength, that bitch is tougher than a costco steak. You don't wanna hold onto it and let it jerk you forward. If you get a jam, it's pretty much the same drill as the M4 but in bigger movements. Just remember to keep the barrel facing downrange if you need to clear it."

"The trigger for it is similar to what you have learned, but it has a totally different rhythm. Short bursts, you wanna do three to five rounds. Then let up between the bursts, or the barrel will burn up or you'll jam." Jenkins mimicked the motion. "You wanna squeeze, then release, squeeze, then release. Kind of like a heartbeat.

"Now remember this gun has tracer rounds, and they load every fifth round," he added. "Red lines in the dark, like a laser beam, show you where your rounds are going. You will wanna adjust your fire by walking the tracers onto the target; but remember, those tracers also show where the rounds are coming from and you'll be targeted. Be careful!"

James took in every word Jenkins said, his eyes fixed on the mounted weapon. Jenkins finally finished with a grim warning. "And Martinez? If you do get up there ... you got to remember to keep moving. If you stay still too long, you are just going to be making their job that much easier."

All of a sudden, Sergeant Rodriguez's radio came to life. He moved away from the group quickly and put the radio closer to his ear so he could hear what was being said over the sporadic gunfire.

"Uniform Six-Two, this is Overlord Actual. Do you copy? Over." Command said over the radio.

"This is Uniform Six-Two. Send traffic. Over." Rodriguez replied.

"Six-Two, be advised – Eisenhower Strike Group is moving into position. ETA to station ninety mikes. Additionally, we have a GhostRider scrambling from Al Udeid, call sign Archangel Three-One. Be advised, Archangel will provide air support at Balad. After station time at Balad, they'll need to land and refuel before reaching your position. Estimated time on station for your location is four hours from wheels up. How copy? Over."

"Solid copy, Overlord. Clear on Eisenhower and Archangel's timeline. Any update on ground QRF? We're running low on ammo and medical supplies. Over."

"Affirmative, Six-Two. QRF is Oscar Mike from Balad once they secure the base. ETA is unknown at this time. Be advised, ISR shows multiple enemy groups converging on your position. Estimate battalion-strength opposition. Can you hold it? Over."

Rodriguez looked at his battered group, his eyes lingering on James at the makeshift barricade. His jaw tightened at the news about the delays.

"Roger that, Overlord. We'll hold. Just get support here as fast as you can. Over."

Turning back to the group, he called out, "Listen up, people," just loud enough for everyone to hear. I've got updates from Command."

Everyone gathered a little bit closer, Tom ever present with his camera focused in on Rodriguez.

"I just got word that the Eisenhower Carrier Strike Group is moving its way into the Gulf. They should be in position to provide air support for the region soon." Rodriguez said.

"I got movement!" someone shouted out. It looks like we have a vehicle headed this way from the southeast!"

James turned his M4 towards the new incoming threat, remembering to keep both eyes open as Jenkins told him. Through the red dot, he could see a pickup truck barreling towards their position with what looked like a heavy machine gun mounted in the back. *Alright, James, focus up. You got this.*

"Distance seven hundred yards, and it is closing fast!" Rodriguez shouted out.

"Martinez!" Rodriguez called out, "I need you to focus on that guy in the back with the big machine gun. Jenkins and Harris, I need you two to take out the driver. Everyone else, stay alert and keep an eye on those rocks!"

James took a breath to steady himself. He began to fire one shot at a time, pausing between breaths. The truck bounced across the rough terrain, making it a difficult target. *Come on, man, stay still. Shooting at a moving target is definitely a lot harder ...*

The red dot eventually settled on the guy's position in the back of the truck. James let out a breath, calming himself, and squeezed the trigger twice. The first round missed, but the second round found its mark. It caught the gunner in the shoulder, and James could see a spray of blood fly in the air. The hit spun the man around as he went flying out of the back of the truck. *Fuck me. That was fucking crazy. Did you see that fucking guy go flying out of the truck?*

The truck began to swerve as Jenkins and Harris opened fire, sending a hail of bullets at the windshield. As the bullets hit their mark, the truck began to veer sharply, and off the embankment, it rolled a few times and burst into flames as the fuel tank ruptured.

"Nice shot Martinez!" Jenkens called out. Giving James a thumbs up.

Their victory was short–lived as gunfire erupted from the rocks. James heard Rodriguez cry out in pain. He looked over and saw Rodriguez fall back, clutching his shoulder as a Corpsman began to make his way over to support.

And then things seemed to take a turn for the worse. Recognizing the familiar sound of mortars being launched, while the Corpsman was working on his shoulder, Rodriguez yelled, "Mortar incoming! Everyone down!

The first mortar round landed just short of them, showering them in a hail of rocks, dirt and shrapnel. James pushed up against the Humvee, feeling the impact of each explosion that seemed to rattle his teeth each time they landed. *Dear God! Now they are dropping bombs on us!*

Lisa's voice cut through all of the noise. She was crouching next to Tom and looking directly into the camera. "This is Lisa Chen," she began, trying to shout over all the explosions and noises around her. "We are reporting live from what I can only describe as complete chaos. We just witnessed an amazing moment a few minutes ago. James Martinez, a civilian, has made the decision to take up arms alongside the U.S. Marines to help defend our position against an overwhelming enemy force ...”

After the mortars stopped, gunfire broke out from a different position. Simmons, who had been fairly quiet throughout everything, suddenly jumped into action. He moved to a weakened part of their makeshift cover.

"Simmons, you're too exposed! Watch yourself!" Rodriguez called out, but it was too late. Simmons caught one in the side. He doubled over in pain, stumbling, and fell against the Humvee, where James was crouched.

Reacting immediately, James grabbed Simmons by his flack jacket and pulled him back towards safety, trying to shield him from being hit again. Simmons' face was full of pain, and his breathing started to become a ragged gasp.

Looking at James with guilt in his eyes, "I ... I'm sorry, James." Simmons' voice started to become weaker. "I ... I should have ... told you what was happening ... from the start ... Sloan ... this is his doing."

James stared at Simmons in confusion, “what do you mean this is Sloan's doing?”

Simmons just shook his head, wincing in pain. "I don't know what happened ... I thought I could control the situation. I ... I was wrong." His eyes met James' mixed in pain and regret. "Be Careful, James ... Sloan is a dangerous man

... watch your back ... make sure to look after ... yourself ... And your family."

The light in Simmons's eyes faded away as he clutched James' arm. *This is all Sloan's fault, that piece of shit. How can he treat people like this? Like a piece of garbage so easily discarded. Playing these games just so he could line his own pockets. Simmons didn't deserve to die for Sloan's greed. None of these soldiers did ... I'll make Sloan pay for what he has done.*

"Stay with us, Simmons," James pleaded in vain. The life had already drained from Simmons' body, his limbs falling limp. James gently closed Simmons' eyes with his hand. James bowed his head and said a prayer.

"Lord, please grant him peace," James said softly, with his hand resting gently on Simmons's chest. "Whatever his sins were, Lord, whatever his part in all of this was ... please grant him your forgiveness and take him into your light ... Amen."

Rodriguez, now all patched up, walked over and placed a hand on James' shoulder. "We will make sure his sacrifice wasn't in vain," he said quietly to James.

After a moment, the Sergeant cleared his throat, "Alright, everyone, let's refocus," Rodriguez announced. "Command told me that there is an AC-130J GhostRider inbound to Balad to provide air support for the base. After a refuel, it's headed here."

Private Jenkins let out a whistle. "Did you say a Ghostrider? Those things are badass, man. That would turn things around for us, real fast."

Rodriguez nodded. "Hooyah! Let's push these bastards back and hold this position until the cavalry arrives."

The news of possible support incoming sent a wave of energy throughout the group. James did a spot check of his remaining ammo magazines. *Alright, I got three full mags, and these other three mags seem to be partially full. I think I'm getting used to the weight of this M4 and finally getting this red dot sight figured out. I think I can do this. I just need to push through the fear.*

As if on queue, a burst of enemy gunfire peppered their position, sending everyone ducking for cover. Bullets were pinging off of metal all around them. It was a harsh reminder of the dangerous position they were still in.

Sergeant Rodriguez called out through the chaos, "We need to do all that we can to hold this position until support arrives. Hey Martinez," he continued, looking around for him until he spotted him ... "Are you still down for manning that M2 up there if we need you to?"

James looked up and swallowed hard. *I don't know, am I ready?* The faces of his family flashed in his mind. *If this is what I have to do to get back to them, then so be it.* He looked at Rodriguez and nodded firmly, his voice steady despite the fear he had that threatened to overwhelm him at times. "Yes, Sir. You just say the word, and I'll do it."

As the sun began to dip below the horizon, James adjusted the brightness on his red dot site. He let his finger rest just outside the trigger guard. With the promise of reinforcements on the way, the group had been given a second wind, but as the night came, dangers and uncertainty still loomed before them. The cooling air brought a little bit of relief to their dire situation.

As it grew darker and darker, the red light on Tom's camera continued to glow—a constant reminder that there were people around the world watching this insane situation unfold in the Iraqi desert. Whatever was going to happen in the coming hours, it would be witnessed live by millions of people.

Focus up, James, we can do this. His body ached from hours of stress and fear, but the adrenaline kept him going. He looked up at the M2 mounted on the top of the disabled Humvee again and then back towards the rocky outcroppings where the insurgents were still hiding as the darkness fell.

James Martinez, a civilian who had gone from never firing a weapon his entire life until now, had become a defender of lives in mere hours. He was preparing to stand between his fellow combatants and annihilation.

Chapter 18

The World Watches

The World News Network's studio in New York was in complete chaos. The producers rushed around, relaying all the latest updates to the anchor desk where Mitchell Hawkins was seated. His usually unshakeable composure was starting to show signs of strain.

"We're back in thirty seconds, Mitchell," a floor director said in his earpiece.

After looking up from what he was reading, Hawkins nodded and gave a thumbs-up to confirm. He adjusted his earpiece while glancing at a bank of monitors in front of him. Each one showed a different angle of what was currently happening in Iraq. It was a mix of broadcasts from around the world as people turned in to watch the drama unfold.

"And, in 5, 4, 3, 2, 1." The red light on the camera came on.

"Good evening, and welcome back as we continue our live coverage of this ongoing and unprecedented attack on a U.S. military convoy in Iraq. For those of you that are just now joining us, what started out as a routine mission has somehow turned into a desperate fight for survival that's being broadcast live thanks to our embedded reporter, Lisa Chen."

The screen behind Hawkins came on with the live feed from Iraq. The camera's night vision was now on. It showed James Martinez clutching a rifle and attempting to look over a makeshift barrier.

"Here we see, at the center of this unimaginable event, is James Martinez, who I'm being told is a logistics specialist with no prior combat experience. Who has now become an unlikely hero as he fights alongside the U.S. Marines on the side of that road in Iraq."

The scene cuts to a montage of locations around the world: a crowded bar in New York, a family huddled on the couch, locked in on what was happening on the TV in the suburbs of Georgia, we see office workers crowded around a computer screen in London. In Tokyo, people stood frozen on the street, looking up at the massive public screens watching the battle unfold. In a favela in Rio De Janeiro, local residents gathered around a small TV at a shop. Each scene was interrupted by the occasional gasp or whisper, the stress of which was noticeable even on the TV screen.

"Everything is at a standstill as billions around the world tune in to watch this battle unfold. Early estimates indicate this event's viewership has surpassed any World Cup final in history."

The feed switched to a social media expert in the studio. The tablet that she was holding illuminated her face.

"Mitchell, I'm looking at the online reaction. It's absolutely crazy," she explained, her eyes scanning through the latest updates. "The hashtags #JamesMartinez and #IraqLive are trending worldwide. We're seeing a massive outpouring of support, but we're also seeing some concerning developments. If you look at this post from a user in Tehran:

'James Martinez is nothing more than a puppet for the American war machine. Where is the UN? Why haven't they come out and condemned this man's actions?'

Here is another post, but this time it is from Beijing:

'This does nothing but expose the constant aggression of the U.S. Why are they still in Iraq other than cleaning up the mess that they created?'

The social media expert continued, "It's crystal clear that this event is being interpreted very differently around the world. However, the majority of the posts that I'm seeing are in support of what is going on. Here is one from London:

'James Martinez shows what the best of humanity looks like in the worst situations. #HeroOfIraq'.

And here I have one from Sydney, Australia:

'Let's go, Martinez! Show those bastards what you are made of! We're with you! #JamesMartinez'.

Hawkins nodded. "Thank you. Now, we go to our Pentagon correspondent for the latest update on the U.S.'s military response."

"Thank you, Mitchell. We're being told by military sources that have confirmed the mobilization of significant military assets in the region. The USS Eisenhower Carrier Strike Group is moving its way into the Persian Gulf as we speak. I've also been told that ground reinforcements are being deployed. This includes Abram tanks that are currently being flown to Balad Air Base to be dispatched to the convoy's position. However, the situation remains highly volatile. In addition, we're receiving unconfirmed reports from personnel at the bases that insurgents involved in these attacks may be using U.S. military equipment. While we have not confirmed these rumors as of yet, questions are certainly being asked of both the government and military for clarification."

Back in the studio, Hawkins turned to retired General Liam Fraser, currently serving as an analyst for WNN.

"General, what would be your assessment of this situation?" Mitchell asked.

Leaning forward, his face grave, the General began to speak. "Well, Mitchell, what we see here is unprecedented in modern warfare. We are watching the bravery of these soldiers in real time as if we were watching a reality TV show and watching the actions of Mr. Martinez, who, by all accounts, is not required to help at all. I can say for myself it is pretty remarkable to see." The General paused, letting it all sink in.

The General continued, "But they're also in a very dangerous position right now. The next few hours will be very crucial. Remember that these insurgents are fighting for their warped ideologies, adding another layer to this complex conflict."

Hawkins turned to the camera again and continued, "As the night falls in Iraq with the world watching, we all ask: Will help arrive in time for them? Can James Martinez and the soldiers hold out against the unrelenting insurgent forces? We'll continue to bring you live updates as this situation continues. And we'll be sure to follow up on those disturbing reports of the U.S. Equipment in insurgents' hands in our later segment."

In homes across America, families who had never given much thought to the war in Iraq now found themselves deeply invested. Children asked their parents difficult questions about war and bravery.

And on a Navy base in Jacksonville, Florida, where James' family had been taken for their safety, Elena Martinez held on to her children tightly as they watched their father transform right before their eyes from an ordinary man into a symbol of courage for the entire world.

All of a sudden, Mitchell Hawkins's voice cut through the tension. "Ladies and gentlemen, we're receiving word that the President of the United States is about to address the nation. We're going to bring that to you live."

The main screen split, showing the ongoing battle in Iraq on one side and the Presidential seal on the other. A few Moments later, President Mark Franklin came on the screen, his face serious.

"My fellow Americans," he began, "I'm speaking to you tonight about an unprecedented situation developing in Iraq. In the past several hours, our forces and installations have come under coordinated attack by ISIS and PMF insurgents. Our military personnel are currently engaged in defensive operations against these hostile forces."

The President paused momentarily, allowing the gravity of his words to sink in before continuing.

"We have watched unspeakable acts of violence play out right before our eyes, and we've also seen tremendous acts of courage. We've lost brave servicemen and women. Each one made the ultimate sacrifice for their country and for freedom. We will honor them in our hearts, and their sacrifice will not be forgotten."

His voice began to grow stronger as he spoke.

"What we also have seen is ordinary citizens rising up to become unlikely heroes. James Martinez, a civilian who had never expected to see combat in his life, has shown us what the very best of humanity can be. He, along with the brave service men and women that he's fighting alongside, reminds us that in the darkest of times, the light of human courage shines the brightest."

President Franklin leaned forward, his gaze intense in the camera. "I send a message now to those who are still fighting on that dusty road in Iraq. You are not alone. The thoughts and prayers of every American citizen and the entire world are with you. Help is on its way, stay strong, stay resolute, and we will bring you home."

President Franklin became much more serious, his eyes reflecting his tone.

"Now, I say to the terrorists who perpetrated this attack: Know this. You may have brought death and destruction, but you have ignited our fury. The entire free world stands united against your tyranny. We will not rest until justice is delivered and freedom prevails."

"May God bless our servicemen and women, may God bless James Martinez and those he is fighting beside, and may God bless the United States of America. Thank you, and good night."

* * *

While the President spoke, not everyone watching appreciated what he had to say. General Sloan sat alone in a dimly lit office in the back of the command center at Balad Air Base. The TV screens illuminated his face in a faint glow. The live feed from the convoy battle was on one screen, and on the other, the President was speaking. The irony of the situation was not at all lost on him. Each word the President spoke felt like a personal affront; his pulse was racing as he tried to formulate a plan.

He watched James, the one man he had underestimated in this entire situation. *If Simmons had done his Goddamn job, I wouldn't be in this position.* Sloan thought to himself. "And now, this fucking guy is some kind of damn courageous hero," he muttered while staring at the TV. Sloan's plan to control this situation was unraveling with every minute James was still alive, and now the whole damn world was watching.

"Damn it," he said under his breath, his fingers drumming on the desk. He watched each screen moving back and forth between the two. *James fucking Martinez, with his rifle, mocking me as he stands there like some fucking superhero defending the convoy and the President's stern face with those eyes seeming to look right through the camera at me. This is all Natalie Wright's fault, her incestuous digging, and her constant questions about inventory inconsistencies.*

General Sloan thought he had squashed all of Wright's investigation efforts. If she got wind of this, what he did, if she was still out there ...

Suddenly, his phone rang, breaking him away from his thoughts. He picked up his phone, his voice low and urgent, "What?"

"General, what the hell is going on? This situation is spinning out of control," a voice whispered on the other end of the phone. "The media, the President's speech ... we need to contain this, now. You told us you could handle it. You gave us your word."

Sloan replied, "I know what I said. I don't need you to remind me. I'm working on it. Keep your head down. I'll figure out a way to redirect this somehow. I think we can pin this all on Simmons. I just need to work out the details."

"Figure it out fast, General. I don't want to tell you what happens if you don't," the voice on the other end of the line said.

"Is that a threat?" Sloan asked.

"Take it however you want, Brigadier General Sloan. Just know this: Simmons is not the only one who we can pin things on, and you are not the only one who can orchestrate an accident on the side of the road. Remember who you're talking to." the voice said before hanging up.

Sloan just stood there. *These fucking fools, I made them a lot of money, and now they want to threaten me. They can all go to hell.* As he watched James on the TV screen, Sloan knew his time was running out fast. His control was slipping out of his hands. With every passing minute, the real truth about his involvement was closer to becoming public knowledge.

Sloan started to consider his options. *How can I spin this? I need a way to blame this all on Simmons and have it not blow back on me.* His panic was beginning to boil up to the surface. *This wouldn't just blow back on me alone. My entire network would be exposed. People who definitely would not want to be exposed.*

Rising out of his chair to stand, Sloan began to pace the small room back and forth. *I need to act now, but I need to be careful. There will be a lot of eyes on me. This situation is entirely out of control. What should I do? Is there anyone that I can still trust? Anyone who could help me clean up this mess before it buries me too deep?*

* * *

As the presidential seal faded from the screen, Mitchell Hawkins reappeared.

"Those were extremely powerful words from the president of the United States," Hawkins said. "Now, as we continue our coverage of this unprecedented event, one thing is clear. The world has changed tonight. In what way? Only time will tell. And at the center of it all is an ordinary man named James Martinez, who has shown us all the exceptional potential that lies with each of us."

Now, the main screen was back on once again. The screen was a green hue from the night vision on Tom's camera. In the background, James and the soldiers continued their desperate stand in Iraq. The battle was far from over, but now more than ever, the world was watching, holding its breath, hoping for a miracle in the desert to appear.

Chapter 19

A Family's Vigil

In a secure housing unit at Naval Air Station Jacksonville, Elena Martinez stood in the kitchen, mechanically chopping vegetables for a salad she knew no one would eat. Her eyes kept darting to the television in the living room, where the ongoing drama in Iraq played out in vivid, horrifying detail.

"Elena? Elena, honey, the cucumber's done for," a gentle voice said, bringing her back to reality.

Elena blinked, looking down to see she had reduced the cucumber to a pile of mush. The juice on her hands felt sticky. She managed to give a weak smile to Kim, one of the wives from the Fleet and Family Support Center, who had come to help provide a little bit of support to Elena and her family.

"Sorry, I just ..." Kim reached over and squeezed Elena's arm. "I know, sweetie. It's Okay. We all know."

In the other room, Elena could hear the sounds of children playing. Miguel and Sophia were in there with the other kids, a calculated distraction orchestrated by the kind-hearted Navy wives who had descended on the Martinez family with casseroles, groceries, and much needed comfort.

A knock at the door made Elena's heart leap into her throat. Kim moved to answer it, revealing the base's Commanding Officer, Captain Angelique Phillips, and Chaplain Stephen Clark standing on the threshold.

Elena immediately felt the blood drain from her face, but Captain Phillips, seeing her reaction, quickly held up a reassuring hand. "We're not bringing bad news, I promise," she said quickly.

The relief that flooded through Elena left her feeling weak as if she were going to faint. Elena sank into a nearby chair as Captain Phillips entered. Phillips greeted everyone politely before turning her attention to Elena. "Mrs. Martinez, your husband is showing such bravery out there," The Captain stated. "If you don't mind, I'd like to speak with you privately for a moment."

Elena nodded and stood. She led Captain Phillips and Chaplain Clark into one of the bedrooms. Once the door was closed, the Captain spoke softly. "Mrs. Martinez, I've known your husband, James, for several years now," Captain Phillips began. "I was actually one of the people who recommended him for this assignment. He's always been really great at his job, but what he's doing now ... it's beyond anything I could have ever imagined."

Elena smiled and asked. "You know James?"

Captain Phillips nodded. "I do. He's one of the best logistics specialists I've ever worked with. But this ... what he is doing now, this is something else entirely."

She paused, then continued, "Mrs. Martinez, I've been instructed to make you an offer. We'd like to fly you to Landstuhl Medical Center in Germany. That's where all our personnel from Iraq are sent before they come home. James will be flown there for a medical check-up and debriefing after all of this is over. It's totally up to you, but it might be nice to see James as he gets there. And ... this offer comes directly from the President himself, ma'am."

Elena's mind reeled. The thought of being closer to James made her heart race, but leaving her children behind filled her with dread. "Germany? But ... what about my children?"

"They'll be well taken care of, I assure you. In fact, as we speak, your parents are being brought here to look after them. They have Max too. We'll provide any support they need in your absence," Captain Phillips continued.

Phillips leaned in slightly, her voice low. "Mrs. Martinez, this is the President's idea. We have a plane fueled and ready to go when you are ready."

Elena sat heavily on the bed, her mind running through everything. *I can be there when James arrives to see with my own eyes that he is safe. But it would break my heart to leave Miguel and Sophia behind. They will be OK, though; they will be with their grandparents. I need to be strong for them. I need to be there to support James.*

She looked up at the Captain and nodded. "I'll go. I need to talk to my children first and pack a bag."

Captain Phillips smiled, "Of course. I'll have someone stay and escort you to the plane when you're ready." She paused at the door. "And Mrs. Martinez? Thank you for having such a brave husband. We're all rooting for him."

After the Captain and Chaplain left, Elena moved in what seemed like a daze. She felt the urgency in every action, her hands shaky as she gathered her children. Elena took a deep breath, trying to find the right words. "I need you to listen to me carefully. I need to leave right now, but Grandma and Grandpa are coming here to stay with you. OK?"

"But, where are you going?" Sophia asked, her small hand clutching Elena's.

"I'm going on a trip, mi amor. To Germany," Elena said to them.

"Germany?" Miguel's eyes widened. "But why?"

"I'm going to get your father," Elena explained gently. "Remember how we saw him on TV? How brave he's being?"

Both children nodded.

"Well, when he's done being brave, they'll take him to Germany. And I'm going to be there waiting for him." Elena said.

"But why can't we come?" Sophia asked, her lower lip trembled.

Elena pulled both children into a tight hug, inhaling the sweet scent of their hair and feeling the warmth of their tiny bodies against her. "Oh, my loves. I wish you could. But it's very far away, and you need to stay here where it's safe. Grandma and Grandpa will take good care of you. I'll be back before you know it, I promise."

"Will you bring Dad home?" Miguel asked.

"That's exactly what I'm going to do," Elena assured him, fighting back tears. "I'm going to bring your father home."

She spent the next few minutes answering their questions, reassuring them, and reminding them to be good to their grandparents. Sophia suggested that they draw pictures for their father for Elena to give to him when she finally saw him. While Miguel, with his usual practicality, asked if they could call every day. Elena promised they would.

Sophia looked up, her eyes filled with worry, "Mom, will you be OK without us?"

Elena felt her heart break just a little bit more, "I'll miss you both so much, but I'll be OK because I know you'll be safe here."

By the time she finished packing a small bag, her mom and dad had arrived. Elena's mother wrapped her in a big hug. "My brave girl," she whispered. "You go and bring our James home."

Her father, usually stoic, had tears in his eyes. "We're so proud of both of you," he said. "We'll take good care of the little ones. You just go and focus on James."

Elena hugged her children one last time. "I'm going to go get Dad," she told them. "Be good for Grandma and Grandpa, OK? I love you both so much."

Elena took a final look at the house before getting in the car. Through the window, she could see the light from the TV where her family sat watching the news.

The base was quiet during the drive. There were small groups of people standing around looking at their phones, and all of the flags hung at half-mast. When her driver finally pulled up to the airfield, she got out of the car, grabbed her suitcase, and walked toward the plane, remembering what she'd told Miguel and Sophia: "I'll bring Dad home."

Elena leaned back in her seat and closed her eyes. "I'm coming, James."

Chapter 20

A Night of Fire

As the Iraqi night pressed down on the battered convoy. Tom inched his camera forward, its night vision piercing through the darkness. The world through his lens was a sea of ethereal green, still and silent. Then, a flicker. A shadow where there shouldn't be one.

The muzzle flash came like a bolt of lightning, the crack of the bullet whizzing past Tom's ear before he could blink. He pulled back just in time, jerking the camera back to safety. His heart was almost beating out of his chest from the near miss.

"Holy shit," he breathed. He locked eyes with Sergeant Rodriguez, a silent message passing between them. *The enemy is getting close. Too close.*

As midnight approached, Sergeant Rodriguez gathered what remained of his Marines. His eyes looked hollow from exhaustion as he scanned the faces in front of him. Only three Marines were left besides James, each showing the visible toll of the day's combat. Private Jenkins had a badly sprained ankle he could barely put any weight on. Corporal

Scott had a huge gash on his arm, made evident by the blood soaked gauze that tightly wrapped it, the pain obvious every time he moved. And Private Mallory had suffered a severe concussion from an earlier mortar blast.

"Come in Overlord, this is Uniform Six-Two, status on that GhostRider?" Rodriguez's voice was hoarse as he spoke into his radio, his left arm hanging limp at his side from a bullet that had torn through his shoulder, rendering it useless.

The reply crackled through static: "Uniform Six-Two, Overlord actual, Ghostrider is Fueled and ready. ETA 20 minutes."

Rodriguez keyed his radio again, his good hand shaking slightly. "Overlord, be advised – situation critical." He paused, looking over his battered unit. "I'm down to three mobile combatants, all injured. Five KIA. Three civilians, including two journalists. Need immediate evac." His voice dropped lower. "Running low on ammo. Enemy strength unknown but substantial."

Static crackled before the response came. "Copy that, Uniform Six-Two. Hold position. GhostRider is priority tasking."

"Twenty minutes might as well be twenty years," Rodriguez muttered, clicking off the radio.

James gripped his M4 tighter, the weight now familiar after hours of combat. He'd done what he could, following Rodriguez's lead, learning as he went. He looked at what remained of their unit, they were good men who'd protected them all day. *These guys are hurt and tired. We can barely defend ourselves now and we're going to run out of ammo soon. After that happens, there won't be much else for us to do ...*

James slowly looked up at the mounted M2. *I could try using the M2, but the last guy who got up there didn't fare too well ...* James looked over at the soldier's body, lying motionless. *But the M2 could buy us some time. It could give us the firepower we need to hold the insurgents back. Just long enough until the air support arrives.*

James sat there thinking, *I'm not a soldier ... but that doesn't matter anymore. The question is, do I want to die on this godforsaken dirt road, or do I want to do something to help get us out of here alive.* Watching Rodriguez struggle one-handed with his rifle, seeing the others fighting just to stay conscious. *I need to step up and do what needs to be done.*

Rodriguez produced a flare gun with his good hand, the metal glinting dully in the moonlight. "We light up the sky, give our Ghostrider a target," he said. "We might be signing our own death warrant, but it's our only shot."

James' eyes moved between the mounted machine gun and Sergeant Rodriguez. His mind raced, trying to piece together a plan. *Come on, James, think. We need a plan, that M2 is our only option for holding off those insurgents. But it's practically suicide going up there ...*

James noticed all of the body armor scattered around them, some still on the ones that didn't make it, some discarded. *Wait a minute ... yeah ... yeah ... That might work.* James looked at Lisa and Tom, hunkered behind a Humvee, then back at the soldiers. *I need to get back to my family. I told them I would come home. But I also need to help protect these people at any cost. They have families, too. This is not just about me or my family anymore.*

"Rodriguez, I think it's time," James said, his voice steady, pointing up at the mounted gun. "I'll get up there and man the M2, just like we discussed earlier."

Rodriguez could see the look in James' eyes. This was not the same man who had started the day as a logistics specialist.

Before Rodriguez could say anything, James continued, his words coming out fast as the idea he had earlier finally formed. "Grab all the body armor you can," James said, trying to keep his voice low. *Yes! This might work.*

Everyone around him exchanged confused looks.

"What do you mean, grab all the body armor?" Private Jenkins asked, grimacing as he shifted his weight.

James pointed to the scattered armor. "The body armor, I'll layer it, as much as I can wear. It won't make me invincible, but it might give me enough protection to use the M2 without being immediately taken out." *I'm completely out of my mind right now, but it might be my only chance to stay alive up there.*

A moment of silence followed as the implications of James' plan sank in. "You're crazy, Martinez," Rodriguez said while looking at James. "It might work ... we just need to buy enough time until the Ghostrider gets here." Rodriguez glanced at his useless arm. "I'd do it myself if I could ..."

James nodded, "I know you would, Sergeant. But we need you down here, giving orders and directing that GhostRider when it comes." *Rodriguez is way more important than me right now.*

They began to gather all the armor needed for James to use. As he began to strap layer upon layer of armor onto himself, Corporal Scott chuckled nervously, wincing as the movement pulled at his wounded arm. "Better not catch one in the face, Martinez."

James managed a smile. "Let's hope not." *Am I really about to do this? I'm a logistics specialist, for God's sake, a family man. How the hell did I get here? I would have never in a million years thought I would be climbing up on to a Humvee and firing a 50 cal at people trying to kill me. But here we are ... no time for doubting yourself, James. It's time to hold these guys off until help arrives.*

As the armor layers piled on, one by one, James could feel their weight both physically and metaphorically. He was taking on the protection of the fallen and carrying their sacrifice with him into battle. The logistics specialist was gone and now, in his place stood a man ready to do whatever it took to survive.

Rodriguez, worried for James, asked. "Are you sure about this, Martinez?"

James nodded. "We don't have a choice, Rodriguez. We'll be out of ammo soon and without that M2 to hold the insurgents off ..."

Putting on the last piece of armor he was able to secure, James stood there, a hulking juggernaut figure of kevlar and ceramic plates. *Holy shit, I probably look pretty awesome right now. Focus James!* He slowly moved towards the Humvee, each step heavy with the weight of armor and responsibility. The smell of cordite and sweat filled his nose, mingling with the horrible smell of burning rubber. *Oh my god, this thing smells so terrible.*

Lisa Chen along with Tom and his camera focused on what was happening. They kept watch as the events continued to unfold. When she spoke into her mic, her voice was measured. "This may be our last transmission. We've been completely decimated by the insurgent forces. Air support is on its way, but we might not have enough resources left to hold them off much longer. Please keep us in your prayers."

Lisa paused before speaking again. "Something ... something is ... We are witnessing something happening right now. James Martinez is now planning to enter the turret compartment in one of our Humvees armed with an M2 ... in a last-ditch effort to hold off the enemy."

"Ten minutes," the radio crackled.

James began his ascent to the gun turret, each movement deliberate but silent. Bullets whizzed by, pinging off metal, but none found their mark. Before he hoisted himself up, he paused for a moment, closed his eyes, and bowed his head.

James began to pray, his voice barely audible. "Lord, lend me your strength. I pray for you to protect my family and protect these good people who are here with me now. I ask you to help guide my hands to protect those who can't fight, and forgive me for what I must do. Please, Lord, let us all see the dawn ... Amen."

With those words, a sense of peace washed over him. He then pulled himself up, settling behind the massive gun. His world narrowed to the sight before him and the trigger beneath his finger. The gun's metal was warm beneath his hands, almost as if it were alive.

"Five minutes." Came a call over the radio.

James' eyes caught movement, a sea of shadows surging towards them. "Damn it, I should have been more careful."

He said, chastising himself. His voice cut through the night. "Shoot the flare now!" James said to Rodriguez.

"It's too soon," Rodriguez started to say, but James cut him off.

"NOW! DAMN IT! NOW!"

The red flare launched into the air, arcing high in the sky, and for a moment, the night turned to day. What it revealed was a fresh new nightmare to their reality. There were hundreds of insurgents, a tidal wave of death, advancing on their position.

Time slowed at that moment for James. He felt his finger tighten on the trigger, and the gun came alive in his hands. The world exploded into a cacophony of wrath and destruction.

The 50-caliber rounds burst from the barrel and tore through the night, each one finding its mark with terrifying accuracy. James was no longer a man but an extension of the weapon, a force of nature unleashed upon the enemy. The recoil hammered against his body, his layers of armor absorbing the impact.

"One minute!" the radio cried, faint amid the soundscape of gunfire.

Rodriguez's voice cut through the radio static: "Contact! Heavy Contact! Multiple hostiles. FIRE! FIRE! FIRE!"

"Uniform Six-Two, this is Archangel," a calm voice cut through their comms. "We have you on thermal. Multiple hostiles converging on your position. Standing by."

From high above, the AC-130J GhostRider appeared like salvation itself, its massive form blocking out the stars. "Target acquired. Firing for effect," came the measured voice from above, followed by the flash of its weapons. The gunship's arsenal spoke with the voice of thunder, raining down destruction from the heavens above.

"Good effects on target," the sensor operator reported. "Multiple KIAs. Hostiles breaking formation."

The field before them, moments ago teeming with insurgents, transformed into one of chaos. Explosions were everywhere, painting the night in hues of orange and red. Smoke rose upwards as the AC-130 continued its relentless assault.

"Be advised, large groups moving through the ditch at your two o'clock," warned the fire control officer. "Engaging with the 105."

Amid this apocalyptic scene stood James, a lone figure atop the Humvee, silhouetted against the fiery backdrop. He had become more than a man; he was a symbol, a modern-day Spartan holding the line against impossible odds. The mounted gun in his hands roared in short quick bursts, its muzzle flash a defiant beacon in the night.

"Archangel, Uniform Six-Two, adjust fire grid one-four-eight by three-two-zero," Rodriguez called out. "Danger close!"

"Copy danger close. Spinning hot," came the response. "Twenty seconds."

While this was all happening, Corporal Scott, despite his injury, managed to reload his weapon with one hand, firing off rounds towards any visible threats. Private Mallory, still heavily concussed, relayed coordinates to Rodriguez, ensuring the GhostRider's shots were as accurate as possible.

"Multiple movers, approaching from the north," Archangel warned. "Coming up behind that destroyed technical. Engaging now."

As if sensing the threat he posed, insurgent fire began to focus on James. His position atop the Humvee made him a clear target, a fact that seemed to embolden rather than deter him. Bullets zinged past him, so close he could feel their heat. Others found their mark, sparking off his armor in a shower of light that made him appear to glow in the darkness.

Each impact was a hammer blow, the force reverberating through his body. Yet James didn't flinch, didn't waver. Pain was masked by adrenaline, and fear was a foreign concept to him now. In this moment, suspended between life and death, heaven and earth, James Martinez was immortal.

"Target area sanitized," reported the sensor operator. "No further movement detected."

James' eyes, visible only through the gap in his armor, burned with an inner fire that matched the inferno around him. They were the eyes of a man who had looked death in the face and did not blink. With each squeeze of the trigger and sweep of the mounted gun, James was not just fighting the enemy. He was defying death itself.

The wounded soldiers below watched with a mixture of awe and grim acknowledgment of the situation. They knew the cost of this fight, their injuries preventing them from taking up the gun themselves.

At that moment, as the GhostRider rained fire from above and James held the line below, the tide of battle shifted. The insurgents began to falter when faced with this dual onslaught from the heavens and earth. Their advance slowed, then stopped, then finally broke.

"Be advised, hostiles are retreating," Archangel announced. "Breaking contact to the east. Uniform Six-Two, area is clear. We are going to clear airspace for Warthogs that are inbound," Archangel confirmed.

As the enemy fled, disappearing into the smoke and darkness, a surreal quiet fell over the battlefield. The GhostRider, its mission complete, banked away into the night sky. And James, his armor smoking and dented but unbroken, finally released his death grip from the M2's handles.

He stood there for a moment longer, staring at the fading fires. Then, slowly, he descended from his perch, his body aching from the strain and shock of battle, every step heavy with the burden of his actions. His heart raced, and his breath came in ragged gasps.

James slumped against the Humvee, his limbs feeling like lead, his muscles screaming from the exertion. When he finally looked up, his eyes were changed. They had seen death and dealt it in equal measure. They were the eyes of a man who now knew the true cost of war, grappling with the enormity of what he had just done.

Tom and his camera never veered from the action, capturing every second, broadcasting it back home to the WNN studios. This was not just a story of war anymore, but one of human endurance in the face of annihilation.

Private Jenkins, his face streaked with grime and sweat, slapped James' shoulder. "You did it, man. You crazy bastard, you really did it!"

Lisa and Tom approached cautiously, Tom's camera still rolling. "James," she began, "can you tell us what you are feeling right now?"

James looked at her, then at the camera. His mouth was dry and his voice was hoarse. "I did what I had to do ..." He trailed off, his gaze sweeping over the battlefield, now silent under the breaking dawn. "But the cost ..."

Lisa continued, her voice softer now. "War shows us the blurred lines between the universal struggle for survival. Tonight, we've seen not just the price of that struggle but the courage it requires. This night will reverberate through history, an example of the unbreakable will of the human spirit."

As the first light of dawn came over the horizon, a profound silence settled over the group. It was as if the morning light itself acknowledged the gravity of what had just transpired, and was finally coming to bare witness. In the far distance, the sounds of reinforcements emerged ... the high-pitched whirs of gas turbines of an Abrams tank battalion, accompanied by the deep, rhythmic thump of their clanking tracks. A sound that would have struck fear in the enemy mere moments ago, but now was the sound of hope.

CHAPTER 21

THE HUNT

Back at Balad Air Base, General Sloan had watched the TV screens in his office. His face was pale from the blood that had left it. *This guy Martinez just won't fucking die, will he? He is determined to destroy everything I have built.* His hand trembled by his side. The live feed of James Martinez was playing on one TV. On another TV, a news network was discussing the speculation behind the rumors of the insurgents using US military equipment during the attacks. *It's all going to hell. My whole operation is ruined.*

"Damn it all to hell," he whispered, as the reality of his situation was finally beginning to sink in. *I need to get the hell out of here, but first ... I need to get rid of any evidence.* He went over to his desk. His movements were frantic. He pulled out a shredder from a locked cabinet by the window. He grabbed a bunch of papers, files, and reports, any evidence of his shady dealings, and began to feed them all through the machine, the loud sound of shredding filling the room.

General Sloan stopped in front of a photograph of him and a high-ranking official hanging on the wall, thinking about his past impressions on people high up. *Even you can't help me right now.* With a grunt, he took the photo off the wall, took the picture out of the frame, and shredded that, too. His phone began to vibrate more and more. *There is nothing more that I can do, so stop calling!* Sloan thought as he ignored it. He just focused on erasing his tracks, getting rid of all the evidence.

As he packed his duffle bag with his personal belongings, the cash he had stashed away, along with his passport and a few fake IDs, a pang of regret struck him. He sat down on the desk for a moment, contemplating his actions. *All those soldiers ... they were still my men ... and for what? My legacy? My greed?* He looked at his hands, which were now stained with the blood of all the wounded and dead soldiers around him. *What have I done?*

Obscured just outside the Window of Sloan's office, Major Natalie Wright was peering in at everything he was doing. She had been careful to stay hidden. But now, with Sloan in a panic, Wright knew it was time. She slipped her hand in her pocket, making sure the USB drive was still there. *I have all the evidence I need to bring you down, Sloan. Time to see where you run to.* Her eyes narrowed as she watched him squirm in his office. *The coward is going to run ... but not if I have anything to say about it.*

She pulled out her phone and began to record. *This is the evidence I need.* She made sure to zoom in and try to capture each file as he put it in the shredder. *Perfect Mr. Sloan, show us your deeds.*

* * *

"Senator Long, I'm sending you photos of General Sloan shredding files," Wright pecked out on her phone into her encrypted Signal thread with the Senator.

Wright waited as she stared at her phone. On queue, Senator Long came online and replied, "Just the evidence we need. I'll get a warrant issued for his arrest, don't lose him Sergeant, be careful."

"Wilco, on his trail," she replied.

* * *

After he was finished shredding everything, Sloan left his office and walked out of the building. His foul mood was threatening to get the better of him. He moved through the base with purpose. His eyes kept darting around, trying to make sure he wasn't being followed and ensuring that no one noticed him.

Major Natalie Wright cautiously followed at a distance. Her camera captured every hurried step he made. She had been waiting for this moment for a long time. Her own actions were calculated and patient. She knew the evidence on her USB drive was damning, but the images she was collecting now would be the final nail in Sloan's coffin.

General Sloan's first stop was behind one of the maintenance hangers, where a man named Mohammed, a local contractor known for his shady record, was waiting for him. Their conversation was quiet but heated.

"I need you to get me out, Mohammed. Tonight! I have enough money to make it worth your while," Sloan pleaded, his hand gripping the man's arm tightly.

Mohammed pulled away aggressively while shaking his head. "Do you think you can just buy your way out now? After what you've done? No, General. You have brought too much attention to yourself. I want nothing to do with any of this or with you for that matter."

Sloan watched Mohammed walk away. *I need to find a way out of here and fast. Who else can I go see? Jack? Yeah, he can probably help me.* Sloan continued deeper into the base. He knew exactly where to find Captain Jack Riley. He was a man he had once helped get promoted through less-than-honorable means.

"Jack, I need your help," Sloan said.

Riley looked at him with disdain in his eyes. "I can't do it, Sir. You crossed way too many lines, and a lot of people got hurt. Friends of mine got hurt. One is barely hanging on for his life. So no, I'm not in a position to assist you, Sir. I can't help you," Riley objected.

"You listen here, you smug son of a bitch, after what I did for you. Do you think you can just tell me no? Do you know who you are talking to, Captain?" Sloan said angrily.

"I know what you did for me, Sir, but that doesn't justify your actions. And I know exactly who you are. You're a traitor to your country. When everyone finds out what you've done, they're going to come for you, General. There will be nowhere for you to hide. They'll find you, and you'll be held accountable for what you've done." Riley paused for a second and then said, "Now get the fuck out of here before I call the MPs and have them haul your ass to the brig. I'll give you a head start because I owe you that much. Sir."

Sloan eyed Riley one last time. *I should kick this mother fuckers ass before I go, but fortunately for him, I don't have the time.* Then Sloan turned and left. As Sloan moved on, he began to notice all of the destruction all around him. The remnants of a battle his greed had indirectly fueled.

Soldiers laid out with bandages on their wounds, several ve-hicles destroyed, their twisted metal scorched, and some still burning. Their equipment was now in enemy hands. Each sight was a harsh reminder of the lives he had endangered for his own personal gain.

Wright continued to follow Sloan, her heart racing as she snapped photos, documenting everything. Her camera caught each interaction, each gesture that showed Sloan's growing isolation. Every step she took was a reminder of the soldiers who had died, the trust that had been broken so easily, and the system she was fighting to restore. She knew this wasn't just about Sloan anymore. It was about the whole system he'd poisoned.

Finally, Sloan made his way to a secluded corner of the base near an old, unused supply warehouse. He hoped to meet one of his last contacts but found Major Wright wait-ing for him instead.

"There's nowhere else to run and hide, Sloan," Wright said, her voice steady, while continuing to point her camera at him.

Sloan's face twisted with anger. *How the hell did she find me? Has she been here the entire time?* "You think you have won, huh? You have no idea what you have gotten yourself mixed up in. This won't end with me," he spat.

"Maybe not, but for now, it will. We'll find whoever else you're working for. Right now, I'll be satisfied with you." Wright countered, stepping closer to Sloan. "Your greed has armed our enemies. You have betrayed everything you stood for, and for what? Money? Pathetic!" Wright's mind was racing now. *I need to keep him busy until I can get the MPs here to arrest him.*

Sloan just looked at Wright. His anger building up with every passing second. *I Won't let her stand in my way. She is nothing. Once I'm done with her, I'll find another way out of here.* With a burst of rage, Sloan lunged at Wright, his fist clenched. "I'll make it out of here. You'll see! You are nothing to me!" He swung at her, his punch aimed at her face.

Major Wright tried to dodge out of the way, her training kicking in, but Sloan was on her too fast, his large frame giving him an advantage. He landed a solid punch to her jaw, making her stagger back, blood trickling from her lip.

"You think you can stop me? Then come on, mother fucker," Sloan said, taunting her.

Wright, tasting blood and still feeling the after-effects of the hit, her jaw throbbing, used the pain to fuel her counter-attack. She spit blood on the floor at his feet and wiped her mouth with the back of her hand. Her eyes began to narrow as she looked for an opportunity to strike.

As Sloan came at her again, she ducked under his arm and landed a quick left hook to the liver; this stunned Sloan long enough for her to hit him with a right-hand uppercut to the jaw; Sloan staggered backward, stunned once more, giving the Major just enough time to finish him off with a roundhouse kick to the head, knocking Sloan to the ground.

Wright was on him in a flash; before Sloan could get back up, she punched him with rapid blows to the back of the head and the face, overwhelming him until he fell back down to the ground.

Sloan tried to recover, but Wright was too quick for him; she managed to leverage his back and get him in a choke-hold. Write squeezed with all her might, trying to stem the flow of blood to Sloan's brain to render him unconscious.

Sloan tried to pry her arms from under his chin but the choke hold only got tighter. Wright wrapped her legs around him and pulled back even harder on Sloan's neck. Sloan began to tire his attempts to break free began to slow until he eventually passed out. Holding on to the choke hold for a couple more seconds ensuring that Sloan was indeed passed out, she unlocked her arms and laid there for a second trying to catch her breath before she rolled him off.

Wright rolled over and located her phone. She got to one knee and dialed quickly: "This is Major Wright. I have General Sloan in custody by the old supply warehouse on the north side of the base. Send MPs and medical." She ended the call, still trying to catch her breath. Now, she just had to wait for MPs and Corpsmen to arrive.

Wright looked at Sloan and thought, *I hope you get what you deserve, you piece of shit.*

When the MPs arrived, one looked at the Major and then at Sloan. He nodded to Wright and said, "Good job, Major, we just received his arrest warrant. I imagine this is only the first of many beatings this traitor will get. Corpsmen, see to the Major first; the General seems to be sleeping his ass-kicking off. He can wait."

Major Wright waved off the help, "I'm alright, I'll live." She reached into her pocket, pulled out her phone and the USB thumb drive, and handed them to the MP. "This is the evidence needed to prove this man is a traitor. Make sure it gets into the right hands, and he faces justice for what he has done."

After reviving Sloan from Major Wright's induced slumber, the MPs led Sloan away. His steps were uneasy as he was still trying to shake off the effects of unconsciousness.

Major Wright watched him go; her mission was far from over, but this chapter was now closed.

She took a moment to look over her injuries, the adrenaline now wearing off and the pain starting to set in. She thought of all the servicemen and women who had died because of this one man's greed. *I'll find the rest of them responsible for this. You have my word.*

Sloan, as the MPs were loading him into a Humvee, turned back to Wright one last time, blood trickling down his face, and said, "You have started something you can't stop. The roots go deeper than you know. Watch your back, Major."

Wright just stared back at him, her expression hard. "Save it for your testimony, Sir." She watched as the MPs slammed the door shut.

The base was quiet now, though security remained tight. Wright sat at Sloan's old desk, reviewing the report she had written about Sloan's capture. She knew that tomorrow would bring a new set of challenges. There were still leads to follow and connections to uncover. But for now, this was enough.

Chapter 22

Aftermath

The private military jet touched down at Ramstein Air Base in Germany with a gentle thud waking Elena Martinez from a restless sleep. Her mind was still spinning from the events she had witnessed on the small TV screen during the flight. Her husband, James, had become a hero in the eyes of the world, and she had watched it all happen on live TV.

As she disembarked, a young Air Force Lieutenant approached her. "Mrs. Martinez? I'm Lieutenant Kelly Adams. I'll be escorting you to Landstuhl Medical Center."

Elena nodded. "Thank you. Have you heard anything about James yet?"

"No. Not yet, ma'am," the lieutenant replied. "But we will let you know as soon as we hear anything."

The drive to the hospital went by quickly. Elena's mind kept replaying the images of James, covered in layers of body armor. The scene of him as he was climbing up to use that machine gun. The man she'd seen on that screen seemed so different from the James she knew.

When she arrived at Landstuhl, Elena was taken to a waiting area. She sat there all alone for a while with nothing but her thoughts. After an hour or so she became restless. Unable to sit still, she asked if she could visit some of the wounded servicemen and women. The staff, touched by her request, permitted one of the nurses to escort her through several of the recovery hospital wards.

As Elena moved from room to room, she offered kind words of comfort and gratitude to the injured servicemen and women.

Whispers began to spread throughout the hospital about her presence and what she was doing. "That is James Martinez's wife," Elena overheard someone say as she walked by. Before she knew it, she found herself at the center of everyone's attention.

In one of the recovery areas, a young soldier who had his arm amputated from a mortar round explosion during one of the base attacks sat up in his bed, ignoring the pain. He was eager to meet her as she approached. "Mrs. Martinez, it's an honor to meet you. Your husband ... what he did out there ... we all watched ... he's a legend!"

"Thank you for your kind words," Elena replied, smiling as she reached out and touched him lightly on his shoulder.

"May I have your name?" she asked.

"Oh, it is Lance Corporal Gravatt, Ma'am," he replied.

"Well, it's a pleasure to meet you, Lance Corporal Gravatt. How are you feeling?" Elena asked.

"I'm doing alright, ma'am. I'm better than most. It was just an arm; I have another one," he said with a chuckle while looking at where his arm used to be.

"Well, that is a good attitude to have, but remember to talk to someone as well. What you went through was more than one person should have to deal with alone," Elena said. "Remember, you are not going through all of this alone. There are people around you that are here to help."

"I appreciate it, ma'am, and I will. I promise," he said to her, gratefully.

As she continued her rounds, Elena felt overwhelmed by the outpouring of support for her. Soldiers all over the hospital wanted to shake her hand and tell her how James had inspired them.

The nurse that was with her noticed how tired Elena looked and gently said, "Mrs. Martinez, you should get some rest. I was informed that the base commander had an apartment not too far from here prepared for you. Would you like for me to call you a car to take you there?"

Elena thought about it for a moment. *I'm pretty tired and I should probably call and check on the kids.* "You're right; I'm feeling a little worn out with everything that is happening right now. That would be fine, thank you."

"That's Good. I'll have someone meet you in the lobby to give you a ride," the nurse said.

Elena made her way down to the lobby, where Lieutenant Adams was once again waiting for her. "Mrs. Martinez, I'm here to take you to your quarters. It's just right up the street, not too far." Adams said to her.

"Thank you, Lieutenant," Elena replied.

"My pleasure, ma'am, right this way." Lieutenant Adams said.

When Elena arrived at the apartment, she took a moment to sit on the bed and breathe. As she sat there on the edge,

Elena reached into her purse, pulled out her phone, and dialed her mother.

Her mother picked up on the first ring, "Elena! Oh, thank God. Are you alright? Have you heard anything about James yet?"

"I'm doing OK, Mom," Elena said, her voice sounding a little tired. "I have no news yet, but I should hear something soon, hopefully. Mom, you should see how they're talking about him here. It's ... crazy and overwhelming."

"I'm sure it is, honey. It's a lot to handle. We watched everything on TV, and it was just ... I don't even know what to say," her mother replied.

"How are the kids doing? Are they around so I can talk to them?" Elena asked.

"They're around here somewhere. Hold on, and I'll get them," her mother replied. "Miguel! Sophia! Come here, your mother is on the phone," Elena heard her mother say.

A moment later, there was a rustle on the phone, and Miguel answered. "Hello, Mom? Are you there?"

"I'm here, mijo," Elena replied, glad to hear her son's voice.

"Hang on a second, let me switch it to video," Miguel said. There were some more rustling sounds, and then Elena moved the phone away from her face, and all of a sudden, there was her sweet Miguel's face on the phone.

"OK, way better now," Miguel said, his face lighting up with a smile.

"Oh, it's much better, sweetheart. Now I can see your beautiful face. Where is your sister?" Elena asked.

Just then, Sophia popped into the picture: "Here I am, Mom!" Sophia said, looking around in the background of Elena's video feed. "Where are you at?" She asked.

"I'm in an apartment on base that they're letting me use to get some rest. How are you both doing? Are you behaving for Grandma and Grandpa?" Elena asked them.

"Of course we are!" Miguel said, almost insulted by the question, while looking around to see where his grandmother was and then smiling at her.

"They have been behaving," She heard Elena's mother say in the background.

"Well, I wanted to tell you both I love you and miss you very much," Elena said, feeling guilty for leaving them.

"Do you know when you will be back? Have you talked to Dad yet?" Sophia asked.

"I have not heard anything yet, but I hope to hear something soon, and then, hopefully, we'll both be home," Elena told them.

"Mom, can you give Dad a hug for me when you see him? Tell him I miss him?" Miguel asked.

"I can definitely do that, sweetheart. OK, well, I need to go now. Can I talk to Grandma for a second?" Elena said while trying to hold back tears.

"OK, Mom, I love you," Miguel said.

"I love you too!" Sophia said as well.

The video then changed to Elena's mother's ear on the screen. "Hey, honey."

"Mom, it's on FaceTime now. You don't have to hold it to your ear," Elena said, trying to hold back a laugh.

"Oh, I'm sorry, honey. I didn't realize," Maria said with a little bit of embarrassment. "OK, sweetheart. I can see that you are tired. Get some rest and call us when you can, or get an update on James, OK?"

"OK, mom. I love you, and thank you for everything," Elena said to her.

"No problem. You just be safe and come back home to us with James as fast as possible. Take care. I love you too," Maria said before waving goodbye and ending the call.

After the call, Elena laid back on the bed, exhaustion finally catching up with her, and closed her eyes. "I'm just going to lay here for a few minutes, " she said right before she fell asleep.

* * *

The White House Situation Room was crowded with senior officials as President Franklin received his latest briefing. He stood at the head of the table, studying the tactical displays as reports continued to come in.

"Mr. President," General Harding began, "I'm pleased to say that things are finally turning around in our favor. With the air support from the Eisenhower carrier group now in play, we have successfully pushed back the enemy insurgents. The immediate threat has been stopped."

The President nodded at hearing the good news, his face showing the signs of relief for the first time in hours. "What about our people on the ground, the people in the convoy? Do we have any word on them yet?"

"The latest update is that we have a platoon of Abrams tanks and personnel en route to the convoy's location as we speak, sir," the general continued. "ETA is imminent. Balad Air Base has scrambled two A-10 Warthogs – they've been refueled and are back in the air to provide support while the tanks and troops are en route."

The secretary of State spoke up next, "Mr. President, we're getting word from our allies in the region. The UK and

Israel have expressed their support and are ready to assist if needed. We also just received a message that Russia and China are calling for an emergency UN Security Council meeting. They want an investigation into what started the escalation to this conflict."

President Franklin stood there for a moment, processing what he had just heard. He stood up straight and said, "We'll deal with the diplomatic fallout later. For right now, our top priority is the safety of our people. I think it is time to address the nation again. The American people deserve to know what is happening."

Dr. Anderson, the National Security Advisor, cleared her throat. "Mr. President, if I may. I have a troubling update on the General Sloan situation. Our investigations have been able to trace several vehicles used in the recent attacks back to U.S. military inventory." She glanced at her notes. "The vehicles were officially listed as destroyed in combat or decommissioned, but evidence suggests these records were deliberately manipulated to hide their being sold off to ISIS and PMF insurgent forces."

General Harding added, "Recent Intelligence confirms this report, Sir. We've uncovered financial transactions to off-shore accounts that link back to Sloan and also to a much larger pattern of arms trafficking. This includes not just vehicles but ammunition and other military equipment. It explains the sudden leap in insurgent capabilities we've been seeing."

The room fell quiet as the revelation of this betrayal sank in. The President's expression began to harden before he began to speak. "We need confirmation on all of this. I want the evidence, every piece of it, every transaction, every email, text, every communication tied to this scrutinized."

The President was interrupted when General Harding received a high priority alert on his tablet, drawing everyone's attention to him. "Mr. President, I just received another update on the Sloan situation. It appears that Brigadier General Sloan has already been arrested. Senator Long issued an arrest warrant for General Sloan earlier today. It looks like she coordinated with Major Natalie Wright's to track him down and apprehend him before he could go into hiding. Her surveillance of him while tracking him has provided us with photos and videos of him meeting with some of his accomplices that should provide irrefutable evidence of their involvement with the General. They are all being held securely in the brig at Balad Air Base in Iraq until arrangements can be made to transport them back to the United States. We are coordinating with the CID and the DOJ."

President Franklin nodded in agreement. "Let's make sure they are brought back here ASAP. I pray to god they haven't betrayed our nation, but we will investigate with urgency to find the truth."

CHAPTER 23

THE PRICE OF HEROISM

Sergeant Rodriguez stood on top of a battered Humvee, his battle-hardened face turned towards the brightening sky. Sergeant Rodriguez's radio crackled. "Uniform Six-Two, this is Overlord Actual, over."

"Send it, Overlord," Rodriguez responded.

"Be advised, you have three tanks from Charlie Company, Third Platoon, en route to your position. ETA ten mikes. Medical and QRF following behind. How copy?"

"Solid copy, Overlord. We-" Rodriguez paused. The distinctive hiss and roar of the A-10 Warthog's twin turbofan jet engines made every head turn skyward. Two rugged and brutish looking aircraft maneuvered overhead in perfect formation, their presence a promise of safety and retribution.

The radio crackled again, this time on the air support frequency. "Uniform Six-Two, Hog Flight checking in. We've got eyes on your position. The area looks clear, but we'll maintain overwatch until your reinforcements arrive."

"Roger that, Hog Flight. Much appreciated." Rodriguez turned to the exhausted group behind their barricade. "They'll maintain watch until the tanks arrive," Rodriguez announced. "Tanks are ten minutes out, folks. Corpsmen right behind them. We made it."

A few tired cheers went up. Someone started laughing, the sound carrying an infectious edge of relief.

"Uniform Six-Two, Overlord," his radio sparked again. "The first tank element should be visual in five mikes. Pop smoke when you have eyes on, over."

"Roger that Overlord. Uniform Six-Two, Out." Rodriguez said as he climbed down from the Humvee and looked around, taking in everything that happened.

Lisa Chen, her face covered in dirt and sweat, turned to her cameraman, Tom. "We're live in 3, 2, 1." She took a moment to compose herself before addressing the millions of people watching around the world.

"This is Lisa Chen, reporting live from what I can only describe as a modern day miracle in the desert. We've just received word that help is on the way and should be here very soon." Her voice cracked slightly from the emotions she was trying to fight back. "After the unimaginable nightmare of last night, it appears that this ordeal is finally coming to a victorious conclusion."

As Lisa continued her report, James Martinez just sat slumped against a bullet-riddled Humvee, his thousand-yard stare fixed on some point in the distance. His mind reeled, trying to process the events of the night. *I can't believe we made it. I can't believe what I did ... All those people I killed ... but I helped save these people ... Does that excuse what I did? It was them or me ... Lord, please forgive me for what I've done.*

Rodriguez walked up to James, his boots crunching on debris strewn all over the ground. He extended his good hand, gently shaking James out of his stupor. "Hey, Martinez? Are you with us, man?"

James blinked a few times and looked up, his eyes slowly focusing on the Sergeant's face. He nodded slowly. "Yeah ... I'm here. I'm just ... tired ... but I'm OK." *Am I OK? Will I be OK? What will my family think of me? Of what I've done.*

Rodriguez began to smile, contradicting the exhaustion in his eyes. "You're a goddamn hero, Martinez. What you did last night ... it was ... I have never seen anything like it in all my years of service."

"We're all heroes," James replied softly, looking around at the survivors. "We did this together."

The distant rumble of tanks grew louder ... it was the sweetest music they'd ever heard. Cheers erupted as the convoy of tanks and armored vehicles came into view, a massive dust cloud billowing behind them.

As the tanks rolled in, they took up a defensive position, their massive turrets looking for any lingering threats. Corpsmen poured out of support vehicles, rushing to attend to the wounded.

As a Corpsman approached Rodriguez, he waved them off with a slight grimace. "I'm fine," he said firmly. "See to the others first. There are wounded here who need you more than I do."

Rodriguez helped James to his feet, supporting him as they made their way around the bullet-ridden Humvee. James' eyes swept across the battlefield as they emerged into full view of the rescue convoy, taking in the carnage for the first time in the unforgiving light of day.

Bodies lay strewn across the landscape, some whole, others … not. The sight of what James had done hit James hard, nearly driving him to his knees. A Corpsman approached, a concerned look on his young face, but James dismissed him with a shaky nod. James kept trying to process it all. *Holy shit, there are so many bodies, I can't … I can't … believe this is real.*

"This guy's bulletproof," Rodriguez declared, as he clapped James on the shoulder. "He's more than OK. He's a legend."

Across the road, Lisa and Tom had positioned themselves for what they hoped would be their final report from this hell on earth. Lisa's voice was steady despite her exhaustion.

"What we all witnessed today was a selfless act," she began. "James Martinez, a civilian, found himself forced into a situation not of his choosing. When many of our soldiers were wounded, he stood against insurmountable odds and fought back the insurgents until air support could arrive. His courage and unbreakable spirit, will surely be remembered for gene—"

James stood apart from the group, his gaze fixed on the distant landscape. He caught a faint glint from a rocky outcropping. In that moment of peace, his thoughts turned to Elena, Miguel, and Sophia—to the life he hoped to return to.

Time seemed to slow, the world narrowing to that single point of light.

A flash.

The crack of a rifle, sharp and final. The bullet, an armor-piercing round more than likely purchased from

Sloan's corrupt dealings, pierced through the layers of protection James had put on, finding its mark in the only vulnerable spot.

Pain exploded in James' chest, driving the air from his lungs in a gasping wheeze. The tanks reacted with terrifying speed and precision. Three booming shots in rapid succession reduced the sniper's position to dust and memory, the rocky outcropping disappearing in a cloud of pulverized stone and fire.

James' knees buckled, and they could no longer support his weight as he fell to the ground. His eyes, wide with shock and something deeper-perhaps the recognition of his own mortality-locked onto the camera lens. But his gaze seemed to penetrate beyond, seeing something far distant, perhaps unknowable. *This can't be the end. I have to get home. I promised them I would come home.*

"MEDIC!" Rodriguez's anguished cry was the only thing that could be heard at that moment. He caught James as he fell, lowering him gently to the ground. "No, no, no," he muttered, his hands pressing futilely against the wound. "Not now, Martinez. Not after everything."

Two Corpsmen rushed forward. Their hands moved with urgency, applying pressure, calling for supplies, fighting against the inevitable with every ounce of skill and will they possessed.

Lisa stood frozen, her microphone dangling forgotten at her side. Words, her constant companions throughout her career, failed her utterly in this moment of crisis. But in her mind, she whispered, *This isn't how it was supposed to end.* Tom's camera remained fixed on James, capturing every excruciating second of the unfolding tragedy.

James lay there, his eyes never leaving the camera. In that unflinching gaze, millions around the world saw not just a man but a symbol-of courage, sacrifice, and the best that humanity could offer in the face of its worst.

In homes around the world, the scene played out in terrible, riveting detail:

In a small diner in Kansas, the breakfast crowd watched in horrified silence, coffee cups frozen halfway to their lips. The sizzle of the grill was a discordant backdrop to the drama unfolding on the ancient TV above the counter.

In Times Square, New York, the massive screens that normally blared advertisements now showed a united image-James Martinez, fighting for his life as a nation, a world, watched this all unfold before them.

In a hospital room in Germany, Elena Martinez stared at the screen, her hand pressed to her mouth, a silent scream building in her throat. "No," she whispered, her voice breaking. "Please, God, no." The room seemed to get smaller and smaller around her, the walls pressing in as the reality of what she was witnessing threatened to overwhelm her.

In the White House Situation Room, President Franklin's fist slammed onto the table with a force that made his advisors jump. "Get me an update, now!" he roared. "I want our best people on this! We are not losing him. Do you understand me?" The room burst into action with activity as orders were dispatched to medical teams, intelligence, and anyone who could possibly help.

And on that dusty road in Iraq, as Corpsmen fought with desperate intensity to save his life, Rodriguez leaned over James. "Stay with us, Martinez," he said with an urgent plea. The Corpsmen, their faces grim, as they worked to stem the flow of blood. One whispered, "He's critical, but he's fighting."

James Martinez's thoughts drifted. He saw Elena's face, radiant with love. He heard Miguel's laughter and felt Sophia's tiny hand in his. *I don't want to leave them. They need me. Please, God, don't let me die before I see her one last time. I have to tell her I love her ... Please ...*

With his last conscious thought, James began to pray. *Lord, I know my time has come. Watch over my family and give them strength when I'm gone. Protect my children and guide them through their lives. I'm sorry for my sins. I tried to live a good life, to do what was right. Thank you for the time you gave me with those I love. Into your hands, I commit my spirit. Amen.*

Then darkness claimed him, and James Martinez, the reluctant hero who had captured the hearts of millions, knew no more.

Standing beside Tom, her microphone still in hand, Lisa whispered, "This isn't how it was supposed to end." Her words were lost in the chaos but captured by the camera.

Tom's camera continued to roll for a few more seconds, capturing the Corpsmen's desperate efforts to save James' life.

Back in the WNN studio, a producer saw the tragedy unfold and made the call. "Cut the feed," he said. "Now. We can't ... we can't show this."

The screen went black, the words "TECHNICAL DIF-FICULTIES" appearing in stark white letters against the darkness. But the damage was done. The world had witnessed the fall of a hero, and nothing would ever be the same.

Chapter 24

On the Brink

The desert air thrummed with the rhythmic beat of helicopter blades as the medevac Blackhawk landed near the battered convoy. Dust was kicked up in miniature tornadoes, blocking out the frantic activity around James Martinez's body that lay motionless on the ground. Corpsmen moved with extreme urgency, their hands steady despite what was happening all around them.

"His BP is dropping! We need to move him now!" shouted the lead Corpsman, his voice barely audible above the the sound of the Blackhawk's rotors.

They had packed James' chest wound with a specialized foam designed to halt internal bleeding. His arms were a roadmap of IV lines, each one pumping life-saving blood and fluids into his failing body.

As they loaded James onto the Blackhawk, one of the Corpsmen turned to the onlookers. Lisa Chen, her eyes red from exhaustion and emotional distress; Sergeant Rodriguez, his face grim; and the others who had fought alongside James through the night.

"He is still with us," the Corpsman shouted. "And we are going to keep it that way. We are not going to give up now!"

The door slid shut on the Blackhawk as it lifted off in a swirl of sand and hope. It banked sharply as it set its course for Balad Air Base. On the ground, the survivors watched in silence as their friend was whisked away.

At Balad, a medevac Gulfstream G650 was fueled and ready on the tarmac, its engines idling with its loading bay wide open. A specialized medical team was on board waiting as James was moved from the Blackhawk with choreographed precision.

"Status?" the flight doctor asked.

"Single GSW to the chest, but I'm not sure if there are any more. We were afraid to remove the body armor. It is probably the only thing holding this guy together, judging by all the bullet impacts I see. He has had major blood loss, possible internal injuries," the Corpsman relayed to the flight doctor. "We have stabilized him for now, but he is critical."

"Thank you. Now get off my plane so we can get in the air." the flight doctor said politely but urgently.

Within minutes, they were airborne, the powerful engines of the Gulfstream propelling them toward Germany at maximum speed. The doctors and nurses worked non-stop inside the cabin, which was converted into a flying ICU. Every beep of the heart monitor was a small victory, every stable reading a win in the fight for James' life.

"He is a tough son of a bitch," whispered the nurse as she checked James' vitals for the hundredth time. "Most men I have seen in this kind of shape wouldn't have made it this long."

The flight doctor nodded. "Let's make sure he survives long enough to see his family again. I have seen too many people die today, and this guy isn't going to be one of them."

For three long hours, they pushed the boundaries of modern medicine, their determination matching the Gulfstream's relentless speed.

As soon as they touched down in Germany, James was rushed to a waiting life flight helicopter. The blades were already spinning as he was loaded aboard, and moments later, they were in the air again, racing toward Landstuhl Medical Center.

In the VIP trauma wing, Elena Martinez walked back and forth anxiously, her shoes wearing a path on the polished floors. Every squeak of a wheel or a distant voice made her head turn.

When the doors finally burst open, the trauma team rushed in surrounding James on the gurney. Elena held her breath as she caught her first look at him; there were tubes, monitors, and medical staff working with quick, precise movements. Through the organized chaos, she could barely see her husband's still form beneath all the medical equipment.

The medical team swarmed around James, their voices filled the room with urgent medical terms as they began to remove James' body armor. As the layers came off, bullet fragments began to fall all over the floor; at first, it was a few, then dozens, and then the floor was littered with hundreds of them. The clatter of metal hitting tile filled the room as a rainfall of spent ammunition fell to the floor.

"Dear lord," one of the doctors said aloud, his eyes wide as he took in the sheer amount of bullets. "It's like he went ten rounds with a machine gun and won. I've never seen anything like this before."

A nurse, her hand steady as she hung another bag of blood, shook her head in disbelief while looking down at the floor. "I've never seen anything like this either. How is he still alive?"

As the medical team reached the last layer of armor, they ran into a new, troubling problem. Some of the bullets penetrated far enough through the armor to pierce James' skin that were held back only by the last layer of the kevlar.

As they carefully attempted to peel away sections of the armor, James began to bleed from dozens of small puncture wounds.

"We've got multiple bleeds here!" shouted the lead surgeon. I need pressure here, here, and here. More hemostatic, please!"

The team reacted quickly; they made a quick decision to stop removing the last layer of armor and focus on stemming the new bleeds they had. Bags of blood, nine, ten, Elena lost count, were hung and connected to James' IV, the blood racing through the tubes to replace what he had lost.

Through it all, Elena watched through the glass of the trauma room. She pressed her hands against the window, her face showing a look of desperate hope. Elena could hear the low shouts of the medical team, and she could see them working feverishly. She felt helpless and relegated to the role of spectator in the fight for her husband's life.

Suddenly, James' eyes slowly opened. Confusion clouded his mind, his gaze darting around the room in panic before landing on a nurse leaning over him.

"Mr. Martinez," the nurse said clearly, her voice very calm despite the chaos around her. "Mr. Martinez, you're in a hospital in Germany. You're safe. We are taking really good care of you. Can you squeeze my hand if you understand me? That's good."

James' eyes seem to focus on her words. Then, as if drawn by some unseen force or just aware of her presence, James' gaze found Elena through the window. He weakly raised his hand out towards her, his fingers trembling with the effort, beckoning her to him.

Another nurse by the door, noting the gesture, quickly brought Elena into the room. "Be careful, sweety," she said, "The floor is ... well, just watch your step."

Elena slowly but urgently picked her way across the floor, the bullets rolling under her feet like grotesque blood covered marbles, each one a reminder of what James had gone through. Her hand was shaking as it found his, warm but growing cold. Through her tears, his face blurred and sharpened with each blink, as if her eyes were trying to take a picture of every detail.

James managed a small, pained smile—the same one he gave her on their wedding day, a smile that greeted her every morning with a fresh cup of coffee in his hands. "I love you," he whispered, his voice barely heard over the beeping of the monitors.

And just like that, his hand went limp in hers. The monitor's alarms began to go off startling Elena, each second of that unbroken tone driving deeper into her heart like a dagger. The world didn't just stop for her; it shattered.

She leaned over him, pressing her forehead to his chest, heedless of the blood that smeared her skin. His familiar scent was still there beneath the antiseptic. "Please don't go ... please ... please come back to me," she sobbed, her voice breaking. "We need you. I need you. Please, James, please ... please come back ..."

The medical team sprang into action, gently moving Elena out of the way.

"Starting chest compressions!" one shouted as another prepared the defibrillator. The rhythmic sound of CPR filled the room, along with the whine of the charging of the defibrillator.

Elena watched each compression, counting them silently as she had been taught in that CPR class years ago. One, two, three ... Each push on James' chest was a desperate attempt to force life back into the man she loved. The crack of his ribs under the force made her flinch, but she didn't look away. She couldn't. This was James, her James, and she would witness every second of his fight.

"Clear!" The doctor's voice called out, and James' body arched as the electric current surged through him from the defibrillator pads placed on his chest. Elena felt each shock as if it were hitting her own heart. The monitor remained stubbornly flat, its tone filling the room.

Again and again, they shocked him. Again and again, there was no response. Seconds ticked by, feeling like hours. Elena watched, her world crumbling right before her to the lifeless form of her husband and the increasingly desperate efforts of the medical team.

"How long has it been?" someone asked.

"3 minutes, 27 seconds," came the grim reply, each second adding to the heavy silence.

The lead surgeon, Dr. Marissa Larson, shook her head, her face a mask of defeat. Her hands, usually so steady, trembled slightly as she lowered them. Dr. Larson had seen too many lives slip away in this room, but this one hit differently. She'd followed James' story and felt the pressure of a nation's hopes resting on her shoulders. "We've done everything we can. It's time to call it."

As Dr. Larson opened her mouth to pronounce the time of death, Elena felt something surge within her, not just faith but every moment of love she and James had shared. Her prayer wasn't just words now. It was every moment they'd shared, every dream they'd built, every quiet Sunday morning and chaotic family dinner.

This wasn't the polite prayer of church pews and quiet devotions. This was Jacob wrestling with God, refusing to let go without a blessing. This was a wife refusing to let death take her husband.

"Lord, in your mercy, hear my prayer," she whispered, her voice growing stronger. "Out of the depths, I cry to you, O Lord. Like David before Goliath, like Daniel in the lions' den, I ask for your mercy." The memories flooded through her: James with their newborns, his laughter at family dinners, his quiet strength through every challenge. "Please," her voice cracked, "let him stay with us. Our children need their father. I need my husband."

The room had fallen silent except for Elena's prayers and the monitor's unrelenting tone. The medical staff stood still, caught between protocol and witnessing a wife's raw devotion. Dr. Larson waited, her usual professional detachment wavering as she watched Elena press her forehead to James' hand.

"Through the valley of the shadow of death," Elena whispered, "I will fear no evil, for you are with him. Thy rod and thy staff, they comfort me. Thou preparest a table before me in the presence of mine enemies: Thou anointest my head with oil; my cup runneth over. Surely goodness and mercy shall follow me all the days of my life: And I will dwell in the house of the Lord forever."

Dr. Larson felt tears threatening to break through her professional facade. In twenty years of medicine, she'd maintained her distance, but something about this moment, about the love radiating from this woman for her husband, cracked the walls she'd built.

Nurse Emily, who had been with James since he arrived, gripped another nurse's hand. "I've never felt anything like this," she whispered. "It's like the whole room is holding its breath."

For a long, terrible moment, it seemed as though the hero of Iraq, the man who had defied death all night long, had finally met the one enemy he couldn't overcome. The silence stretched, broken only by Elena's quiet sobs and whispered prayers.

Dr. Larson lifted her head, her own prayer mixing with Elena's. She was about to declare what everyone in the room feared—

The monitor chirped.

The sound was so faint it might have been imagined. Everyone in the room seemed to hold their breath all at the same time.

Another beep. And another.

Suddenly, James' chest heaved as he drew in a ragged breath. His eyes flew open, searching frantically until they found Elena's tear-soaked face. Elena could suddenly feel everything: the cold floor under her feet, the warmth of his skin, and the pulse of his heart fighting its way back to rhythm.

"I ... I heard you," he gasped, his voice barely above a whisper but filled with wonder. "In the darkness ... I heard you calling out to me ... to come back."

The room erupted into shouts, sobs, and the triumphant beeping of the heart monitor. The medical team, moments ago defeated, now moved with renewed energy.

Dr. Larson, her face illuminated with something beyond medical understanding, whispered, "In all my years ... I've never seen anything like this." She felt as if she was witnessing something truly divine.

Nurse Emily, tears flowing freely now, embraced her colleague. "He came back to her," she kept saying, "He really came back."

Elena, overwhelmed with gratitude and joy, pressed her forehead to James'. Through her tears, she saw their future reforming; morning coffee with the man she loved, family dinners, graduations, weddings, and grandchildren. "Thank you," she whispered, her words a quiet offering to both God and James. "Thank you for coming back to me."

Dr. Larson, composing herself, gently touched Elena's shoulder. "Mrs. Martinez," she said softly but firmly, "I promise you, we're not going to lose him again on my watch. But we need to work now. Every second counts."

As Elena stepped back, watching the medical team swarm around James once more, she knew she had witnessed something beyond medicine, beyond science. James Martinez had once again defied death itself, called back by a power beyond understanding, by the love and faith of those who loved him.

The battle for James' life was far from over; the road to recovery would be long and fraught with challenges. But in that moment, as the doctors and nurses worked with renewed determination, hope burned brighter than ever before. The miracle they had all prayed for had come to pass, and now they could only hope it would be enough to see James through the long night ahead.

CHAPTER 25

A NATION'S PRAYER

In the White House Situation Room, President Franklin stood at the head of the table, his tie loosened and sleeves rolled up, evidence of the long night he had endured alongside his team.

"Alright, people," he said, "Let's get a full update. General Harding, you're up first."

General Harding began. "Mr. President, we've secured all affected bases. The insurgent enemy forces have been repelled, but we still see light resistance in some places. Combat ops have transitioned to clearing and securing. Air assets maintain overwatch of all bases."

The President leaned forward. "Casualties?"

"Still compiling exact numbers, Sir," the General replied. "But it's … significant. We've lost good men and women today."

A sad silence fell over the room, broken after a moment by the President. "And the survivors of the roadside attack? Martinez's group?"

"All accounted for, Mr. President," answered Secretary of Defense Kline. "They've been evacuated to a secure location. Many are injured, but thanks to Martinez's actions, casualties were lower than they could've been."

The President's National Security Advisor, Dr. Emily Anderson, spoke up next. "We've got support troops arriving at all affected bases, Sir. They're strengthening security, replenishing supplies, and providing additional medical personnel. We're seeing constant flight activity in and out of the bases, primarily moving the injured to Landstuhl Medical Center."

Dr. Anderson continued, "I've also received word that the German Government has opened up local medical facilities to help us handle the overflow of casualties that are coming in."

President Franklin nodded. "Let's Make sure we let them know we appreciate their help. Now, what about Martinez? What's his current status?"

The room became quiet once again. All eyes turned to Dr. Anderson as she pulled up an updated report on her tablet and began to speak. "Mr. President, the most recent report I have is that James Martinez is currently in critical condition at Landstuhl. He's being prepared for surgery as we speak. The medical team over there ... well, Sir. They say they've never seen anything quite like this before."

Dr. Anderson went into detail about the events of James' arrival at the hospital. She briefed them on the hundreds of bullet fragments that fell from his armor, the critical moment when they removed the armor that then caused additional bleeding, and then the desperate efforts of the medical team to save his life.

Dr. Anderson continued her update. "They're still counting, Sir. Judging by the photos that I was sent of the emergency room floor that was covered with bullet fragments, it looks like he was struck by several hundreds of them. I'm being told that some of them managed to get past the body armor and penetrated his skin, causing a large amount of minor wounds all over his body. They were finally able to stem the bleeding by leaving the armor on before finally stabilizing him."

The President and staff listened as Dr. Anderson went through it all.

"And he was able to survive all of that? How's that even possible?" President Franklin asked.

Dr. Anderson just shook her head and said, "The doctors really don't know how to explain it, Sir. They're calling it a miracle. From what I'm being told, by all accounts, he shouldn't even be alive. But he is. He even was able to regain consciousness for a moment and spoke to his wife just before ... his heart stopped."

Gasps went up around the entire room. The President leaned forward, his eyes wide. "His heart stopped?"

"Yes. Sir," Dr Anderson replied and then continued, "For about four minutes, he was clinically dead. The trauma team had done all they could, and they were about to call it ... when all of a sudden, well as they say, a miracle happened ..."

The room hung on Dr. Anderson's every word as she described exactly what had transpired. She told them about Elena's desperate prayers, the dead silence that fell over the trauma room, and James Martinez's sudden, unexpected revival.

"The monitor started to register a pulse again, Sir. Out of nowhere, it just started beeping, and then James took a breath and opened his eyes. He told his wife he heard her calling him back from the darkness he was in. The medical staff ... they are saying that they witnessed a real life miracle. No one in the room has ever seen anything like it before."

President Franklin sat back in his chair. You could see that he was visibly shaken by what Dr. Anderson had said. "My God," he breathed. "That is ... incredible. I had a feeling it was going to be important to have her there."

Dr. Anderson nodded, agreeing with Franklin's statement. "The trauma team is still in shock, Sir. They have no medical explanation for it. They are telling me he is still in critical condition, but the fact that he is alive is nothing short of astonishing to them."

President Franklin sat there for a moment, taking it all in. When he finally spoke, his voice was full of emotion. "The power of love and faith ... it is a remarkable thing indeed." He looked up. "That man ... he's more than a hero. He's a symbol of everything we are fighting for. Dr. Anderson, I want hourly updates on Mr. Martinez's condition, and I would like to speak to his wife as soon as you think it is appropriate."

Franklin stood up from his chair and addressed the room. "Ladies and gentlemen, we've faced an unprecedented attack today. We've lost a lot of good people, but thanks to the bravery of our servicemen and women in the field and the courageous efforts of one civilian, a man who has seemingly cheated death itself. Our wills have been tested, and we have not been found wanting."

The President looked around the room. "We have a lot of work to get done, people. We need to make sure we take care of our wounded, pray for our fallen heroes, and show the world that we will not be cowed by terror." He paused for a moment before continuing. "I want us all to take a moment. Think about James Martinez and all the other soldiers fighting for their lives in the hospital right now. I want you to think about all the lives Mr. Martinez helped save on that roadside in Iraq. The courage it took for him to stand up and fight. And then let's get back to work, inspired by his example. And believe you me, we're going to get to the bottom of how this happened."

After the meeting ended, President Franklin made his way to the Oval Office. It was time to address the nation once again. He stopped for a moment in the hallway before entering. He reflected on the words he was about to say, how they would resonate with a nation in mourning, and how they would provide a little hope. He thought about James Martinez fighting for his life and for the strength his wife Elena must have to endure all that has happened.

The President straightened his tie as he walked in and prepared to speak. The stress of the past twenty-four hours showed in the lines on his face, but his eyes burned with an inner fire that was clear to see for all.

"We are live in 30 seconds, Mr. President," an aide said.

Franklin nodded. The red light on the camera came on, and he began to speak.

"My fellow Americans. I come before you today with a heavy heart and a great sense of hope. In the past twenty-four hours, we have witnessed the darkest depths of human cruelty and the most inspiring heights of human courage. Our military bases in Iraq were tested today. Our brave servicemen and women held off a coordinated and brutal attack by terrorist forces. This defense did not go without the loss of several servicemen and women, each one a hero who gave their life defending their freedom from those who would take it from them."

The President continued, "But even in our darkest hour, a light shone through the darkness. We saw unrelenting courage from our armed forces, who stood their ground against overwhelming odds. We found it in the international cooperation of our allies who came to our aid without hesitation."

"And we also found it most unexpectedly and brilliantly. We found it in a civilian named James Martinez." The President paused for a moment, reflecting on James' actions.

"Many of you, as I did, watched on your TV screens live as Mr. Martinez transformed into a beacon of hope and courage as he took up arms against those who would do harm against him and his fellow companions on that roadside in Iraq. His brave actions saved the very lives of those who were unable to defend themselves. He helped turn the tide of battle when he bravely climbed atop that humvee and held off the insurgent attack that surely would have led to their collective demise until help arrived from above. But his heroism came at a great cost." President Franklin, seeming emotional, took a moment before continuing.

"I have just been briefed on Mr. Martinez's condition and wanted to share the news with you all. He is currently fighting for his life at Landstuhl Medical Center in Germany. The doctors treating him there have described his survival thus far as nothing short of a miracle. The body armor that

Mr. Martinez was wearing was riddled with the impact of hundreds of rounds as he stood there bravely holding off the enemy with no concern for his own safety but for his companions below. Mr. Martinez was willing to sacrifice himself so that others may live, and we thank him for that."

President Franklin paused for a moment to let people take in his words.

"At this very moment, a dedicated team of surgeons and medical professionals are working tirelessly to keep Mr. Martinez alive. They face unfathomable challenges, but they are dedicated and inspired by the same determination that Mr. Martinez displayed on that roadside in Iraq. They will not give up on him, and neither shall we. To Mr. Martinez's wife, Elena, and their children, please know that you are in the hearts and prayers of a grateful nation. Your husband, your father, has shown us the true meaning of self-sacrifice and heroism."

"To all of those who were wounded mentally and physically in these attacks, to the families of those who we have lost, please know that you have the full support and resources of the United States Government behind you. We will spare no effort to make sure that you and your loved ones receive the care and assistance you deserve."

"And now, I ask all of you watching at home, regardless of your faith or beliefs, to join me in a moment of prayer and reflection."

President Franklin bowed his head.

"Dear heavenly father, we come before You in this hour of need. We pray for Your healing touch upon James Martinez and all of those who were wounded in these attacks. We ask for Your comfort for the families of the fallen so that they may find comfort in Your eternal love in their grief. Lord, we thank you for the miracle we witnessed on that roadside in the desert of Iraq as one man's courage and self-sacrifice inspired a nation and changed the course of that battle. Lord, we pray now that you send down your angels from heaven to descend upon a hospital in Germany and help heal Mr. Martinez and the others who lay there fighting for their lives alongside him."

"We pray that you watch over them, Father. Guide the hands of the doctors and nurses working to save all of their lives. Give strength to Mrs. Martinez and the other families and peace to all the children whose fathers and mothers lay there. Let your holy light shine upon them so that they may feel Your presence even in their darkest hour."

"And Lord, we pray for our nation and the world. In the face of evil, terror, and hatred, help us to respond with love and unity. Let James' example remind us of the hero that lies within each of us, waiting for that moment to shine brightest."

"We ask for all this in your holy name, Amen."

President Franklin raised his head, his eyes shining with tears.

"In the days to come, we will all face many challenges. We will mourn our dead, tend to our wounded, and hold those who sought to do us harm accountable. We will do this united and inspired by the courage that we have witnessed."

"To James Martinez, know this. A grateful nation stands with you. Fight on as you fought for your fellow companions on that side of the road in Iraq. And know that you have ignited a flame of hope and unity that no force of darkness can ever extinguish."

"May God Bless our troops, may God bless James Martinez, and may God bless the United States of America. Thank you, and good night."

As the cameras turned off, the President slumped slightly, the emotion of the moment washing over him. But there was no time to rest. There was work to be done, a nation to lead, and a hero to pray for.

In living rooms and public spaces across America and around the world, people stood in silence, moved by the President's words. In a small church in Georgia, a congregation bowed their heads in prayer, their pastor leading a special service for James and all those affected. In Times Square, a gathering of people formed, with people from all walks of life coming together, some holding candles, others standing in solidarity, and their silent prayers mingling with the city's bustle.

And in a hospital room in Germany, as if sensing the prayers of millions, James Martinez's vital signs strengthened ever so slightly, his body continuing its miraculous fight for survival. Sitting by his side, Elena felt an odd sense of peace wash over her as if the collective strength of a nation was lending her its support.

CHAPTER 26

REFLECTIONS

At Balad Air Base, the med bay was chaotic. Doctors and nurses were moving around fast but carefully to tend to the wounded as they trickled in. The air was filled with the smell of gunpowder and antiseptic, the constant groan of the injured, and the ongoing sound of doctors giving orders. Sunlight coming in through the windows was constantly being disrupted by the movement of people walking by them, casting eerie shadows over the floors as if death's hand was reaching out for its next victim.

Lisa Chen was sitting on the edge of a gurney as a medic cleaned a small gash that was on her forehead; she winced at the pain with each wipe. Tom, her cameraman, was lying on a bed across from her with his leg elevated by a pillow from a sprained ankle that was now in a splint. Despite their injuries, they both kept looking at their equipment as if it were calling to them to get up and capture the unfolding drama that was all around them.

On the other side of the room, Sergeant Rodriguez stood with his arm in a sling, spots of blood barely showing through his bandages. He was talking with a group of officers when his phone began to vibrate in his pocket. He pulled it out, glanced at the message, and then read it aloud to the other officers: "Brigadier General Sloan has been arrested."

A hush fell over the group of officers. "General Sloan has been arrested?" one of the officers asked. "That's what the message says," replied Rodriguez. "I guess we'll find out what that's about in the coming days."

"Excuse me, officers," Colonel Harrington interrupted. "Rodriguez, we're ready to debrief, if you'll please join us in the private briefing room."

"Certainly," Rodriguez confirmed.

Rodriguez stood at the end of the table, pacing back and forth as he began to speak. "It was unlike anything I've ever experienced," he began. "The first IED took out our lead vehicle, and as if timed perfectly, the second IED took out our rear vehicle. The rest of the vehicles were pinned in between, leaving us exposed. We managed to get out and take cover before the rocket attacks started. We were vastly outnumbered and outgunned, and now we know why. The insurgents weren't just using their usual weapons. They were using US military weapons against us ..." Rodriguez trailed off, seeming to look past the commanders he was briefing as if focused on some unknown object in the back of the room. *Why was General Sloan arrested, why did the insurgents have US weapons. Was this related?*

"Sergeant Rodriguez, are you alright?" Colonel Harrington asked him, returning him to reality.

"Yes ... yes, ma'am. I'm good." Sergeant Rodriguez took a breath, refocusing himself before continuing. "As we continued to hold the insurgents off, my men were slowly getting picked off. That's when Martinez stepped up. We didn't even ask him for his help. He just picked up a gun and began to help us defend our position. By the time night fell, we were down to mostly the injured trying to protect us with small arms along with James Martinez. Without him stepping up to help, I have no doubt we would have been overrun, and in fact, moments before the Ghostrider arrived, James got up on the mounted M2 and with the help of our flare, identified hundreds of insurgents that had surrounded us. We were minutes, maybe seconds, away from captivity and or complete annihilation. James unleashed the M2 and pushed them back just in time for the Ghostrider to provide additional aircover. We wouldn't be here without James, Colonel."

Rodriguez's eyes, usually clear and focused, now seemed clouded with the conflict of Sloan's arrest.

"I've served with some of the bravest servicemen and women our country has to offer. But what Martinez did out there … it was beyond heroic. He's the only reason any of us are standing here alive today," Rodriguez said.

Colonel Harrington looked around the table at each of her officers, taking in what she had just heard. "Thank you, Sergeant. I'm sure we will have more questions for you later. In the meantime, try to get some rest."

"One more thing," Rodriguez asked.

"Of course, what is it?" Harrinton asked.

"I got a secure page saying General Sloan was arrested," Rodriguez stated. "Is Sloan implicated in this, is he why the insurgents had US military equipment?"

"Our investigation is underway Sergeant, we hope it isn't true," Harrington responded matter of factly.

I knew it, Rodriguez thought to himself. "Ok, thank you Colonel."

Back in the medical bay, Lisa was finishing up her report. "While the toll of these attacks is a heavy one, the spirit of those who defended us remains unbroken by it. This is Lisa Chen, reporting from Balad Air Base."

As Tom lowered his camera, Lisa's professional demeanor seemed to crack slightly from the pressure of everything that had happened. She leaned against a wall, closing her eyes for a moment, trying to steady herself. "Do you think James will make it?" she asked quietly.

"If anyone can, it's him," Tom replied, reaching out and gently squeezing Lisa's arm. "After what we saw him do last night, I would say that anything is possible."

Lisa looked up and saw Rodriguez walking up to them. "There's something else you need to know," he said to them, keeping his voice low. "I've had a few internal discussions today. This is off the record. But I've come to learn that General Sloan has been arrested, potentially for what happened out there. You guys are going to have the lead on this scoop. But it didn't come from me."

Lisa's eyes widened as the implications of what she had just heard sank in. "Thank you Sergeant ... we'll be paying attention."

Lisa turned to Tom, her eyes shining. "We will tell both stories," she said firmly. The hero and the traitor, the corruption and the courage that exposed it. We make sure everyone understands exactly what happened out here."

"You got it, boss," Tom said to Lisa.

Chapter 27

A Miracle in the Making

The hallway at Landstuhl Medical Center seemed to stretch endlessly as Elena paced back and forth. The constant squeaking of her shoes on the polished floor echoed off the walls.

Hours earlier, a team of doctors had explained to her the challenges that they faced in treating James' wounds. The sheer number of bullet fragments embedded in the armor that was piercing his body made traditional imaging impossible. But they had found a solution. The German government had provided them with a cutting-edge imaging machine that would do the job they needed.

Inside the X-ray room, a team of radiologists and trauma doctors gathered around multiple screens, their faces staring at the screens in disbelief as they studied the results of James' full-body scan.

"In all my years as a doctor, I've never seen anything like this," Dr. Hoffman, the lead radiologist, said. "Look at the amount of fragments spread throughout his body. It's as if he was hit by a wall of bullets."

The 3D rendering on the main display rotated slowly, revealing a ghostly image of James' body. The entire front of his torso and thighs was a constellation of bright spots, each one representing a bullet or a fragment of a bullet trapped either in his armor or flesh.

"It's a miracle he's still alive." Said Dr. Patel, who was one of the trauma surgeons. "Any one of these fragments could've been fatal, but somehow ..."

"Somehow, he survived them all," finished Dr. Hoffman. "Now the question is, how do we proceed with removing his armor without him bleeding out?"

Over the next hour, the team reviewed the scans, working on a strategy to remove the armor and treat James' injuries.

Dr. Patel turned to the group and said, "Alright, our first priority is to remove armor layers piece by piece, enough to first access and repair the chest wound he sustained from the sniper round. Once we've taken care of that, we can then work on carefully removing the rest of his armor in sections, addressing any other injuries as they arise."

The team nodded in agreement, each of them understanding the criticality of the task that lay before them.

As they prepared to go over everything with Elena, Dr. Hoffman made one last observation that seemed to baffle everyone in the room. "Did you all notice the sniper round entrance and exit?" he said as he pointed to the specific area on the scan. "By all accounts, it should've gone straight through his heart. But look right here ... it seems to have passed right between these two ventricles, through his lung, and out his back. The damage to his lung is surprisingly minimal. This bullet should've made a much larger hole and caused a lot more damage."

Dr. Patel shook his head in disbelief as he looked at the scan. "I've seen plenty of sniper wounds in my time here at the hospital, and none of them looked like this one. The medical foam that was used in the field must have done its job containing most of the damage. But this ... this is beyond him being lucky. It's ..."

"A miracle," someone whispered in the background.

Elena's head snapped up as the doors to the X–ray room finally opened, and Dr. Patel walked out, his face unreadable as he walked up to her.

"Mrs. Martinez," he began. "We've completed our scans and have put together a plan of action. Your husband's condition is ... well, very unique to say the least."

Elena's heart seemed to race faster and faster as Dr. Patel explained the extent of James' injuries, the challenges that they would face, and their proposed course of action for treatment. When he described the unexplainable path of the sniper's bullet, Elena felt her knees go weak, and a nurse had to bring her a chair to sit down.

"So, what happens now, Dr. Patel?" Elena asked.

"Right now, we're going to take James immediately into surgery," Dr. Patel explained. "Our first objective is to repair any of the damage that was caused by the sniper round. We plan to remove just enough of the armor to gain access to the wound, clean out the medical foam, and repair all the damage we find. It's going to be a long and complex procedure, Mrs. Martinez, but I want you to know that we have the best team assembled to get this job done right."

Elena nodded, trying to process everything. "And after you're all done with that, what is next?

"After that, we will reassess his condition and plan the next steps for removing the rest of the armor and treating any of the other injuries that we encounter. Mrs. Martinez, your husband has already survived the impossible. We're going to do everything we can to make sure he makes it the rest of the way," Dr. Patel reassured her.

As the medical team prepped James for surgery, Elena found a quiet spot in the waiting room. She pulled out her phone, her hands shook as she dialed her mother's number.

"Mom?" She said as her mother answered, her voice cracking with emotion. "They're taking James back to surgery now. The doctors ... they say it's a miracle that he's still alive."

"Oh, sweetheart," her mother replied, her voice filled with concern. "We've been praying for James, mija. We know he'll make it through this. He's a strong man, and God is on his side."

Elena heard some rustling in the background, and then her father's voice came on the line. "Elena, how are you holding up?"

"I'm okay, Dad," she managed to say, trying to keep her voice steady. "It is just ... all a bit overwhelming ...."

Then, through the phone, she heard Miguel and Sophia's voices. "Mommy, is Dad going to be okay?" Sophia asked.

Elena, forcing a smile into her voice said, "He's going to be fine, mija. The doctors here are the best in the world, and everyone is praying for him."

Miguel chimed in next, "Hey, Mom, we made him a card. I'm going to take a picture of it and send it to you. Can you show it to him when he wakes up?"

"Oh honey, I would love that so much, mijo," Elena responded, her heart swelling with love for her sweet children. "I'll make sure that it's the first thing he sees when he wakes up. He'll love it."

Elena's mother came back on the line, "We've been keeping the kids busy, and they have been so brave, Elena. They're very proud of their dad."

"And we're so proud of you as well," her father added. "You're being strong for all of us."

Elena felt tears of gratitude well up in her eyes. "Thank you, all of you. I needed to hear that and hear your voices right now. Please, keep praying for him."

"We will, honey," Her mother promised.

Elena could hear the children in the background. "We love you, mom! Tell Dad we love him too!"

"I will, my loves," Elena said. "I'll tell him every day until he can hear it from the both of you himself."

After a few more goodbyes, Elena ended the call. She decided to pull up a photo on her phone. It was of James and the kids having a grand time on a sunny day in the park. Looking at their smiling faces, a smile formed on her face, along with the tears she was shedding.

The long vigil of Elena Martinez continued. Somewhere beyond the doors in front of her, a team of the best doctors in the world worked tirelessly to save the life of a man that the world now saw as a hero.

Chapter 28

Reflections and Decisions

Back at Balad, In a quiet corner of the base, Lisa Chen and Tom Ballard sat side by side on a pair of crates, their satellite phones in hand. The adrenaline of the past day had finally worn off, leaving them both exhausted but relieved. The distant sound of jets taking off provided a surreal backdrop to their moment of calm.

Lisa dialed her parents first, her hands shaking slightly as she held the phone to her ear. The moment she heard her mother's tearful greeting, her composure cracked.

"Mom," she said, her voice breaking. "Mom, I'm okay. We're both okay."

"Oh, Lisa!" her mother sobbed. "We've been so worried. We saw the news … the attack …"

Lisa could hear rustling in the background, then her father's voice came on the line. "Lisa? Sweetheart, are you really alright?"

"Yes, Dad," Lisa managed, wiping away her own tears. "I'm fine. It was … it was scary, but we're safe now. Tom and I, we're at Balad Air Base."

"Thank God," her father breathed. "When we saw the footage … Lisa, we're so proud of you, but we were terrified."

Lisa swallowed hard, her mind flashing back to moments where she had to choose between getting the story and ensuring her own safety. "I know, Dad. I'm sorry I scared you. But I'm okay, really. And … and I think we did something important here. We showed people what really happens during combat."

Her mother's voice came back on the line. "Just come home safe, sweetie. That's all that matters now."

"I will, Mom. I promise. I love you both so much." As Lisa ended the call, she looked over at Tom, who was deep in conversation with his wife.

"Babe, I'm alright," Tom was saying, his normally steady voice thick with emotion. "It was … it was intense, but we made it. We're safe now."

He listened for a moment, then chuckled softly, his face easing into a smile as the tension of the battle faded. "Yeah, I know. I'm getting too old for this. But you should have seen Lisa, hon. She was amazing out there."

Tom's expression softened as he continued to listen. "I miss you too. So much. Kiss the kids for me, okay? Tell them … tell them Daddy's coming home soon, and I've got quite a story to tell them."

As Tom ended his call, he and Lisa exchanged a look of understanding. No words were needed; they had shared an experience that would bond them forever.

After a few minutes they decided to set up a conference call with their boss back in New York. The familiar voice of Executive Producer Mark Smith filled the air.

"Lisa, Tom, thank God you're both safe," Mark began, his usual brusque manner softened by genuine concern. "You've done an incredible job under unimaginable circumstances. The footage you've captured … it's historic."

"Thanks, Mark," Lisa replied, exchanging a glance with Tom. "We were just doing our job."

"Well, you did it brilliantly," Mark continued. "The entire world has been watching. Your professionalism in the face of danger … I couldn't be prouder."

They spent the next few minutes updating Mark on the situation at the base and their own conditions. Then Mark asked the question they'd been anticipating.

"Any word on when you'll be cleared to head to Germany? And what about James Martinez? Any updates?"

Lisa filled him in on James' critical condition and their pending transfer to Landstuhl for medical clearance. Then Mark dropped a bombshell.

"I was thinking … if you're up for it, maybe we could arrange a short interview with Martinez's wife? Nothing intrusive, just a human interest angle to complement the story."

Lisa hesitated, her journalistic instincts warring with her empathy. "I don't know, Mark. Mrs. Martinez has been through so much already. I'd hate to bother her."

"Think about it," Mark urged. "If you decide to do it, I trust you to handle it with sensitivity."

After ending the call, Lisa turned to Tom. "What do you think? About interviewing Mrs. Martinez?"

Tom shrugged. "It's your call, Lisa. But if anyone can do it right, it's you."

As they prepared for their transfer to Germany, Lisa's mind raced with potential questions, each carefully weighed for its impact and appropriateness. She wondered how this decision would fit into her evolving identity as a journalist who had seen the true cost of war.

Across the base, in his sparsely furnished quarters, Sergeant Rodriguez sat alone, the dim light of the early evening casting his face in shadow. His satellite phone lay on the desk, and his mind replayed the previous day's chaos. He lightly pressed on his shoulder, sore from the bullet that had passed through, and thought of James Martinez.

He dialed his wife, and she picked up immediately.

"I'm okay, honey," he assured her. "Really, I am."

"Are you sure?" His wife's voice was thick with concern. "What about your shoulder? They told us you were hit."

Rodriguez rotated his shoulder gingerly, wincing slightly. "It wasn't as bad as it could have been, thankfully. The docs said it was a through-and-through. Hurts like hell right now, but they're optimistic I'll regain full movement in my arm."

"Oh, thank God," his wife breathed. "I was so worried when I heard ..."

"I know, I know," Rodriguez said softly. "But I'm okay. Nothing compared to ... well, to what others went through."

There was a pause on the line. "You're thinking about that civilian, aren't you? Martinez?"

"Yeah," Rodriguez sighed. "Amanda, there's a decision I'm having a hard time making; it's a big one." He paused for a moment before continuing "I'm thinking of recommending him for the Congressional Medal of Honor."

He could hear his wife's sharp gasp through the phone. "But isn't that only for military personnel?"

"Exactly," Rodriguez sighed. "There are other medals for civilians, but … Amanda, what you witnessed on TV was only a fraction of what it was really like. What he did … it deserves nothing less than the highest honor."

They discussed it back and forth, considering the impact, and the potential pushback he would get from his superiors and other enlisted servicemen and women. Rodriguez thought of the countless soldiers who had died without such recognition, the tradition, and the honor that came with the Medal. Finally, Amanda said softly, "Pray on it, love. God will guide you to the right decision."

After the call ended, Rodriguez sat at his desk, staring at the Medal of Honor recommendation paperwork. He read through the requirements, his mind replaying the events of that harrowing night.

Gallantry and bravery: Check.

Risk of life above and beyond the call of duty: Absolutely.

Action against an enemy of the United States: Without a doubt.

Confirmed by witnesses …

Rodriguez paused, his thoughts drifting back to the chaos, the sounds of gunfire, and the silhouette of Martinez against the backdrop of that battle on the side of the road. How many had witnessed James' valor? The entire convoy, for sure. But beyond that … millions had watched it live on television. The entire world beared witness.

Now, his mind clear of any doubt, Rodriguez opened his laptop, the screen illuminating his face in the growing darkness. He began to draft an email that could potentially change the very nature of the Medal of Honor.

"To: Joint Chiefs of Staff, Secretary of Defense.

Subject: Unprecedented Recommendation for Congressional Medal of Honor."

Sergeant Rodriguez stared at his screen, knowing the importance of what he was about to write. After twenty years of service, he'd written his share of award recommendations, but nothing like this. He began typing:

"Sirs and Ma'ams,

My name is Matthew Rodriguez. I'm a Sergeant in a rifle company from 1st Battalion, 7th Marines, out of Twenty-nine Palms, California. I'm currently stationed at Al Asad Airbase in Anbar Province, tasked with providing security escorts for supply convoys, and U.S. advisors traveling to meet Iraqi counterparts. This role involves patrolling routes, manning Humvees or MRAPs, and ensuring safe passage through potentially hostile areas where ISIS remnants or local militias might pose a threat.

I write to you regarding an unbelievable act of valor performed by civilian James Martinez during the recent attacks in Iraq, which I'm sure you are all aware of. James was with me and my unit in-route to Qayyarah Airfield when we were ambushed by insurgent terrorist forces. His actions, witnessed not only by myself and the entire convoy but by millions of viewers worldwide, exemplify the highest standards of courage and self-sacrifice.

With the Blessing of the Joint Chiefs I'm formally recommending to Congress that we take the unprecedented step of considering James Martinez for the Medal of Honor. While traditionally reserved for military personnel, his actions during the attack merit this highest recognition.

Multiple after-action reports, combat footage, and sworn statements from military personnel document his gallantry and bravery at the risk of his life, above and beyond the call of duty. The extensive video coverage from embedded journalists provides additional validation of his actions under fire.

I'm requesting Congress draft appropriate legislation to make this award possible to be bestowed upon the civilian James Martinez, provided the appropriate military jurisdiction pre-approves. We have gathered testimony from all military personnel present during the engagement, including the wounded soldiers he helped defend. These accounts, combined with the live news footage, create an unprecedented record of his valor.

Respectfully,
Matthew Rodriguez
Sergeant, USMC
Squad Leader, 2nd Platoon, Company C
1st Battalion, 7th Marines
Task Force Al Asad
Operation Inherent Resolve
DSN: 318-364-4288"

He paused, rereading what he had written. The words seemed insufficient to capture what he'd witnessed that day, but they would have to do. This recommendation would ruffle a lot of feathers in the military community, but Rodriguez knew it was the right thing to do.

His finger hovered over the send button as memories of that night flashed through his mind. The gunfire, the chaos,

James on that turret ... Rodriguez leaned back in his chair, running a hand over his face. The quiet hum of his laptop was a stark contrast to those moments.

"Maybe I should get some input first," he muttered, reaching for his phone. He opened a group chat with his team, the same men and women who'd been there that night:

"Good evening, Team. I'm considering recommending James Martinez for the Congressional Medal of Honor. I know it's unprecedented for a civilian, but after what we all witnessed ... I'd like your thoughts."

For a moment, there was silence. Then Rodriguez's phone lit up with notifications:

"Do it, Sergeant. He deserves it."

"If anyone's earned it, it's Martinez."

"He saved our lives. Nothing less than the highest honor."

Then Private Jenkins's message appeared: "Sergeant, can you share the draft? I want to submit one too."

Before Rodriguez could respond, more messages poured in:

"Send it to me too, Sarge."

"We were all there. We should all speak up."

Rodriguez found himself smiling at his phone. "Alright," he typed back. "I'll send the draft. Use it as a template, but make it your story. Tell them what you saw."

What happened next surprised even him. Within hours, emails started arriving from soldiers he'd never met:

"Sergeant Rodriguez, I'm with the 10th Mountain in Germany. I heard about your recommendation through my old platoon buddy. Request permission to submit one as well."

"Air Force Combat Controller here. We watched it all unfold from our feed. How do we get involved?"

As night turned to dawn, Rodriguez watched his simple recommendation transform into something bigger than himself. Soldiers from every branch, scattered across bases worldwide, were drafting their own letters, each telling their piece of James Martinez's story.

The sun was rising when he finally looked back at his original email. His shoulder ached – a reminder of that night – as he reached for the mouse. With a quiet certainty, he clicked send.

This wasn't just another award recommendation disappearing into the bureaucratic void. This was the first drop of what would become a flood of hundreds of voices, all carrying the same message: James Martinez deserved their highest honor.

Standing at his window, watching the base wake up, Rodriguez felt at peace with his decision. The morning routine played out before him – PT formations, reveille, the everyday rhythm of military life. But something was different now. Every soldier moving across that base was part of something bigger, something prouder, whether they knew it yet or not.

Traditional or not, precedented or not, they all knew the truth. James Martinez was a hero, and it was time the world recognized him for it officially.

Chapter 29

Recovery and Reunions

Back at Landstuhl Medical Center, Dr. Patel approached Elena Martinez, who was waiting patiently in a waiting room just outside the surgical wing. "Mrs. Martinez," he began, "I'm pleased to report that James' surgery went better than expected. We were successful in cleaning out all of the medical foam, and we were also able to repair most of the damage caused by the sniper's bullet. He is still in critical condition, but he is stable for now."

Elena breathed a sigh of relief as she leaned against a wall for support. "Thank God," she whispered. "What happens next, Dr. Patel?"

"The next 24 hours are crucial. We are going to be monitoring him very closely. We'll be watching for any signs of infection or any other type of complications that might arise. As his condition begins to improve, we hope to begin the next stage of removing the armor and bullet fragments from his body," Dr. Patel told her.

Elena, who was hanging on to every word asked, "Isn't removing those so soon after his surgery going to be very dangerous for him?"

"At this point, anything we do is going to be dangerous, but it's necessary that we do it soon," Dr. Patel explained. "The longer the armor and fragments remain, we risk a higher chance of infection and possibly other complications like sepsis. But I assure you, Mrs. Martinez, we'll proceed with the utmost caution and care."

Elena nodded, trying to process everything. "When can I see him?" she asked.

"You can see him right now; they just moved him to a room in the critical care unit. Follow me," Dr. Patel said to her.

As they entered James' room, Elena immediately saw James. The sight of her husband, surrounded by all the machines and covered in bandages, was overwhelming to her. She felt the energy drain out of her, but she kept her composure. She needed to be strong for both her and James now.

She walked over to James' bed, gently stroking his hair, and softly kissed his forehead. "I love you, mi amor," she whispered while taking his hand in hers. "You keep fighting, you hear me?"

A kind-faced nurse, whose name tag read "Anna," wheeled over a reclining chair for Elena to sit in. "You can stay as long as you like, Mrs. Martinez. If you need anything at all, just hit the call button, and one of us will come."

Meanwhile, on another floor of Landstuhl Medical Center, the medical staff was getting ready to examine Lisa

Chen, Tom Ballard, and Sergeant Rodriguez, who had recently arrived. Sergeant Rodriguez was the first to be seen.

"How are those new bandages, Sergeant Rodriguez? Not too tight?" A doctor asked.

"No, Sir. They are just fine, and this new sling is definitely more comfortable than the other one," Rodriguez replied.

"That is good to hear. Well, Sergeant, judging by the x-rays of your shoulder, it looks like you got pretty lucky. The bullet passed right through your shoulder and didn't hit anything vital. You should heal up just fine and regain complete mobility of your shoulder. Just take it easy for the next couple of weeks. When you return to the States, we will set you up for some physical therapy," the Dr. informed Rodriguez.

"Awesome, that is good to hear, Doc. My girls back home will appreciate that news. Now I won't have any excuses when they beat me in basketball," Rodriguez said with a smile.

"You are good to go now, Sergeant Rodriguez. If you have any issues, please let us know," the doctor said.

"Will do, Sir," Rodriguez said as he left the room.

Sergeant Rodriguez made his way to the waiting room, where he found Lisa and Tom waiting. They had already gone through their checkups and were waiting for Rodrguez to finish up his. As Rodriguez approached them, Lisa's eyes moved toward the Sergeant's arm, which she noticed was in a new sling. "Sergeant Rodriguez, how are you doing? How is your shoulder?" Lisa asked.

Rodriguez shrugged slightly, showing a hint of discomfort on his face as he did. "It's not as bad as it looks. The Doc said it should heal up just fine. It was a through-and-through and didn't hit anything vital. He said I should gain full function of it after some physical therapy. How are you two holding up?"

"We are doing okay. We got lucky and only had a few scrapes and bruises." Lisa replied.

Standing next to Lisa, Tom nodded in agreement and then asked, "Have you heard any updates on James Martinez?"

"I overheard one of the nurses saying that he was out of surgery and that he is currently in the ICU in stable condition. But that is all I know so far." Sergeant Rodriguez replied.

Lisa let out a sigh of relief and said, "That is good to hear. At least he is alive and stable. After everything we all went through, it is a miracle we are standing here right now."

"You can say that again," Tom said softly. Silently recounting the past 24 hours in his head.

After a few seconds passed, Lisa cleared her throat nervously. She had been thinking about asking to interview Elena Martinez, but it was causing an inner battle within her about whether or not it was appropriate. Finally, she said, "Sergeant Rodriguez, I ... I have a question to ask you. It is about Elena Martinez."

Sergeant Rodriguez looked at Lisa and said, "What about her?" His tone sounded a little on guard now.

Lisa chose her words carefully before she continued. "My boss back in New York suggested ... Well, he thought it might be a good idea to do a short interview with her. To shed some light on what the family goes through when something like this happens. A lot of times, we just see the effects on the wounded, but we don't see what the family has to go through as well. You know?"

Lisa noticed a frown begin to form on Rodriguez's face, so she quickly continued. "But, I'm not sure if it is appropriate to ask her. That is why I'm asking you first. I figured you might be the right person to ask and decide whether it was appropriate or not."

Sergeant Rodriguez stood there for a moment before saying, "I think Mrs. Martinez has been through enough, don't you? Asking her to do an interview while her husband clings to life. It could add additional unneeded stress on her."

Lisa nodded, "I completely agree with you, Sergeant, And that is precisely why I'm torn about this request. On one hand, I'm worried about causing Mrs. Martinez, as you said, unneeded stress and intruding on her privacy during this difficult time, but on the other hand ..." Lisa paused to gather her thoughts. "On the other hand, I have been thinking about all of the families back home. The families who have servicemen and women serving here, the families who are worrying about them, and whether or not they are going to get that dreaded phone call. And I wonder if hearing from Mrs. Martinez might give them some kind of relief. Show them that they are not the only ones going through all of this."

Sergeant Rodriguez's expression appeared to soften slightly.

Lisa continued, "You see, James Martinez's story has captivated the world. But behind every hero or soldier, there is also a family waiting at home. I thought ... I thought that maybe if Mrs. Martinez was willing to share her experience with everyone, it might help those families feel less alone. It might give them some type of hope, seeing how strong Mrs.

Martinez has been through all of this. If that makes any sense."

Lisa's voice grew more passionate as she spoke, "And it's also not just about the families of the service members. I think it is also about the entire country needing to see and understand the real human cost of what happens during times of combat. Not just see the headlines and statistics but the personal stories and the emotional impact it has on those involved."

Lisa looked Rodriguez in the eyes before continuing, "But I want you to know, Sergeant, that I won't do anything that would cause Mrs. Martinez any more pain or stress than she is already going through. If you think this is a bad idea, or if she's not comfortable with doing it, I'll drop the matter immediately. No questions asked."

Sergeant Rodriguez was quiet for a moment, considering Lisa's words. "I see what you are trying to accomplish here," he said. "Personally, I don't think it is a bad idea. Like you said, it might help people understand the real impact of what has happened," he paused, then nodded. "I tell you what. I'll speak to Mrs. Martinez about your request to do an interview. But whatever she decides, you have to accept that, understood? If she doesn't want to do it, that is the end of it."

Lisa nodded, "Absolutely, Sergeant. I wouldn't have it any other way. And if she does agree to do the interview. I promise that I'll be as respectful and sensitive as possible. She will have full control over what questions she wants to answer and what we will include in the final piece."

Sergeant Rodriguez shook his head in agreement. "You're alright, Chen. You have a good heart in you. I'll talk to Mrs. Martinez and let you know what she says."

As Rodriguez walked away, Lisa knew that if Elena agreed to do the interview, it would probably be one of the most important stories she had ever done. But more than that, she hoped that it might bring some sense of comfort and understanding to those who would watch the interview back home, giving a voice to the silent struggles of other military families around the world.

Sergeant Rodriguez made his way to the ICU, where James was. He had pulled a few strings to get access to see Elena and James. When he got to James' room, he found Elena sitting by James' bedside, holding James' hand. Elena looked up as Sergeant Rodriguez entered the room, surprise registering on her tired face.

"Mrs. Martinez," he said softly, "I'm Sergeant Rodriguez. I was with your husband during the attack in Iraq."

Elena stood, her eyes wide. "Sergeant, please come in. James ... he has spoken of you. He said that you were a really good person, and he thought you had the makings of a great officer." Elena noticed Rodriguez's arm, which was in a sling, and asked, "How are you recovering?"

"I'm fine, ma'am. It is just a scratch compared to what your husband and others have gone through," Rodriguez said, feeling a lump form in his throat, trying to hold back his emotions before he spoke again. "Your husband ma'am ... he is probably one of the bravest men I have ever met. What he did out there for us ... I have never seen anything like it before."

Sergeant Rodriguez recounted James' actions from his perspective to Elena, reemphasizing how, without James' help, they surely would have been done for. As he spoke, Elena's eyes filled with tears of pride at hearing about James' selfless actions, her hand trembling as she still held on to James' hand.

"There is something else," Sergeant Rodriguez added, lowering his voice. "I have recommended James for the Congressional Medal of Honor."

Elena gasped, her eyes wide with shock. "But ... isn't that meant only for military personnel?" She asked.

Rodriguez nodded, "It is, ma'am. But what James did ... it deserves nothing less. And I'm not the only one who thinks this. When I told my team and a few other service members about my recommendation, the call for James to get this award spread like wildfire. Soldiers from all over the world began to submit their own recommendations. Your husband seems to have united the military in a way I have never seen before."

Elena closed her eyes for a moment, taking in how big this news was. She sank back into her chair, seeming overwhelmed by it all. "I ... I don't know what to say, Sergeant."

"You don't have to say anything, Ma'am. You should just know that James isn't just a hero to you and your family. He is a hero to all of us."

As Sergeant Rodriguez turned to leave, he paused. "Oh, and there is one more thing, Mrs. Martinez. There is a reporter, Lisa Chen. She was with us during the attack. She would like to talk to you about doing an interview and tell your story as well. But only if you are comfortable doing it. There is no pressure at all."

Elena looked at James, then back to Rodriguez, her mind racing with all that had happened. "I'll think about it. Thank you, Sergeant Rodriguez. For everything."

Rodriguez nodded and then quietly left James' room, leaving Elena alone with her husband and the steady beep of the heart monitor, which was a constant reminder that against all odds, James Martinez was still fighting.

Chapter 30

A Sacred Honor Bestowed

Back in Washington, D.C., President Franklin once again found himself in the situation room. The atmosphere this time was much calmer, with the relief of the crisis that was now over. General Harding stood from his chair with a tablet in his hand. "Mr. President, I'm pleased to report that the situation at our bases in Iraq has stabilized. The majority of the wounded have been successfully moved to our medical facility in Germany."

President Franklin nodded to Harding at the news. "Do we have a total number of casualties yet, General?"

Harding's expression seemed to tighten as he replied. "Yes, Sir. We do. The final report shows that 47 KIA and 213 service members and civilians were wounded. It's ... a heavier toll than we expected, but it could have been much worse, Sir. Without the quick action of our troops and ... well, the actions of James Martinez, there could have been a lot more casualties."

A murmur of agreement seemed to echo through the room. National Security Advisor Dr. Emily Anderson spoke next. "Speaking of Mr. Martinez. I have an update on his status, Sir."

Franklin gave her a nod to continue.

"Mr. Martinez is out of surgery now and is currently listed in critical but stable condition. The medical team at Landstuhl is monitoring him closely. I'm being told as his condition improves, they plan to begin removing his body armor and the bullet fragments over the next few days."

President Franklin leaned back in his chair, relief crossing his face, "Please keep me updated on his progress."

Secretary of Defense Robert Kline cleared his throat, drawing everyone's attention to him. "Mr. President, there is something else you need to be aware of. It is about Mr. Martinez."

All eyes in the room turned to Kline.

"Over the past 12 hours, we have received an unprecedented number of emails and communications from military personnel around the world. They're all recommending that James Martinez receive the Congressional Medal of Honor. Last I checked, the submission website was still down from all the submissions."

The room fell silent as Kline continued.

"Sir, it all started with Sergeant Rodriguez, who was the convoy CO and who was with Mr. Martinez during the roadside attack. And now, it seems to be gaining traction throughout all military ranks. We are talking about thousands of recommendations, Sir, from every branch of the military and from bases all around the world. Many of these servicemen and women watched the events play out live on TV. They're all telling their own stories of how Mr. Martinez's actions impacted them personally."

President Franklin leaned forward, obviously surprised at this news. "The Medal of Honor? For a civilian?"

"It's unprecedented, Sir, but it has been done before," Kline admitted. "The last civilian to receive the Congressional Medal of Honor was Dr. Mary Edwards Walker in 1865 during the Civil War. It's my personal opinion that Martinez's actions may warrant this type of exception once again. The impact on morale … I have never seen anything like it. The servicemen and women all seem to be united in this."

General Harding nodded in agreement with Kline, "It's true. Mr. President. I've been hearing the same thing from a lot of the commanders at every level. This isn't just about recognizing Mr. Martinez. It has become a symbol of everything our armed forces stand for. Courage, self-sacrifice, duty to your country and fellow man. Even if it's coming from a civilian."

President Franklin stood and began to pace the room as he considered the implications. He stopped by a window and looked out at the Washington Monument, a symbol of the nation's enduring spirit. Finally, the President turned to face the group.

"I think we all know what needs to be done here. But I want to hear it from each of you. We are talking about making an exception for our highest military honor, and I need everyone's honest opinions."

The President looked around the table and eventually landed on the Secretary of Defense. "Mr. Secretary, let's begin with you. What is your honest opinion."

Secretary of Defence Robert Kline sat up straight in his chair. "Mr. President, it's my honest opinion that Mr. Martinez's actions exemplify the very nature of what the Medal of Honor represents. He showed extraordinary heroism in the face of what seemed like insurmountable odds, at significant risk to himself, in a situation where he had no obligation whatsoever to act. His status as a civilian, in my opinion, makes his actions even more commendable. He chose to step into harm's way when he could have found cover and done nothing to help. That level of selflessness and courage should be recognized at the highest level."

President Franklin nodded, "Thank you, Mr. Secretary," and then turned to the Chairman of the Joint Chiefs. General Harding, your thoughts?"

General Harding cleared his throat. "Mr. President, I'll be frank. Initially, I had a lot of reservations about awarding our highest military honor to a civilian. But looking back at Mr. Martinez's action once again Sir, they weren't just brave. They were tactically significant. He turned the tide of the battle on the side of that road in Iraq, which saved numerous lives, and demonstrated courage under fire that would be exemplary even for a trained soldier. Recognizing him would not only honor his bravery but also honor those he saved and the ones we lost."

"Thank you, General," The President said, turning to his National Security Advisor. "Dr. Anderson?"

Dr. Emily Anderson leaned forward. "Mr. President, from a national security standpoint, Mr. Martinez's story presents a unique opportunity in a time when the civilian and military divide is a growing concern. Mr. Martinez's actions remind the American people of the values our armed forces uphold. Awarding Mr. Martinez the Medal of Honor could send a powerful message that shows that all Americans have a shared responsibility to safeguard our nation. It could also inspire the next generation of civil servants and potentially boost our military recruitment numbers, which have declined over the years."

President Franklin thought about what he had just heard and then addressed the Secretary of state. "Madam Secretary, what are your thoughts on the international implications?"

Secretary of State Elizabeth Cameron straightened. "Mr. President, internationally, this could be a huge diplomatic win. Mr. Martinez's actions, having been broadcast live around the world, have already captured global attention. Awarding him with our highest military honor would only strengthen the image of America as a Nation where regular citizens are capable of incredible acts."

Finally, the President turned to his Chief of Staff, "And what about you, John? What's your take on all of this?"

John Davidson, the Chief of Staff, replied. "Politically, Mr. President. Awarding Mr. Martinez with the Medal of Honor is just the right thing to do. His story goes beyond party lines. I don't see anyone being against this. Honoring him could be a rare moment that brings the nation together at a time when it needs it the most. Also, awarding the Medal to Mr. Martinez could set a precedent for honoring civilian contributions to national security in the future. However, we must consider the long-term effects of what the award represents and the potential for future awards to civilians."

President Franklin considered all of their words. "Thank you all. Your insights are appreciated." He paused, looking around the room. "Ladies and gentlemen, we are on the cusp of making history here. Not just in recognizing one man's sacrifice and courage but in expanding our understanding of what it means to serve this nation."

Franklin turned to his Chief of Staff. "John, I need you to draft special legislation for Congress to vote on. We'll need their approval to make this all happen. I want you to get Senator Long involved as well. She chairs the Armed Services Committee. I want her to champion this bill through the House and Senate."

Davidson nodded. "Yes, Sir. I'll get right on it. Senator Long has already expressed her interest in Mr. Martinez's case. She'll be a strong advocate for this honor."

"That's good to hear. Make it clear that this isn't just about Mr. Martinez but about recognizing that heroism doesn't always wear a uniform. I want this bill to set a precedent but with clear parameters attached to it. We are not opening the floodgates for this honor. We are only recognizing a truly unique circumstance," President Franklin stated.

The room hummed with a sense of historic significance. Everyone in that room knew that this decision would be examined, debated, and remembered for years to come. But in that moment, there was a shared sense that they were doing the right thing. They were honoring a hero and, in the process, reaffirming the values that defined their nation.

President Franklin paused for a moment and said "This isn't just about one man's heroic actions. This is about reminding the world what America stands for. Courage knows no uniform. And James Martinez exemplifies the very best of what we, as a nation, aspire to be."

As the meeting adjourned, there was a powerful sense that they had just been part of a historic decision. In a hospital room in Germany, James Martinez fought for his life, unaware that his actions had not only saved lives and inspired a nation but had changed the very definition of military heroism and now, America would honor him in unprecedented fashion.

Chapter 31

A Moment of Reflection

Back in the ICU at Landstuhl. Elena Martinez sat at James' bedside. She hadn't left his side since he was brought to the ICU after his surgery. Her eyes never left his face for fear that she might miss his eyes opening. Elena gently held his hand, stroking the top of it softly. The steady beep of the heart monitor had become a comforting and almost hypnotic rhythm to her. It was a constant reminder that, despite everything, James was still fighting.

She sat there thinking about all the good times they had spent together. She thought about all the trials that she had read about people going through in the Bible. It comforted her, knowing that many of them made it through their difficulties.

A soft touch on her shoulder startled her from her thoughts. A nurse stood beside her, looking down at her with a smile on her face and slight concern in her eyes.

"Mrs. Martinez," the nurse said softly, "why don't you take a break? You haven't slept in a while. You should go for a walk, stretch your legs. We have prepared a room for you to freshen up if you'd like. It's just down the hall, room 205. James will be in good hands while you're gone. I promise you if anything changes, we'll come find you immediately."

Elena hesitated, reluctant to leave James' side. But she knew the nurse was right. She needed to keep up her strength for James.

"Okay, thank you. That sounds like a good idea," Elena said. "I promise I won't be gone long."

The nurse smiled at her, "Take your time. We'll be here watching him for you."

Elena, thankful for the break, made her way to room 205. It was small but comfortable; it had a shower, and there was a change of clothes on the bed that was provided by the hospital staff. Elena walked into the bathroom to take a shower and rinse off. The moment she turned on the hot water, the room began to fill with steam. She climbed into the shower, and the warm water washed over her shoulders; it felt like a physical release of all the tension that she'd been carrying since this entire ordeal started. The warmth seemed to seep directly into her bones, carrying away all of the stress.

After her shower, she headed to the cafeteria, she could smell the scent of coffee and fresh pastries in the air. When she finally walked in, the entire room fell silent. All eyes seemed to turn to her all at once. Every one of the people's faces filled with expressions of both awe and sympathy. Elena felt a wave of emotion wash over her. She was touched by the silent show of support.

With a thankful nod to the room, she made her way to the serving line. The cafeteria staff treated her as if she were one of their own, ensuring she had enough food and everything she needed. When she reached the cashier, the woman who was sitting on the stool simply shook her head and took Elena's hand.

"This meal's on us, Mrs. Martinez," she said. "It's the least we can do."

Overwhelmed by the gesture, Elena managed a heartfelt "Thank you."

Elena looked around the room for a place to sit when she noticed a familiar face. *I think that's Lisa Chen, the journalist I saw on TV with James, sitting over there by herself by that window. Poor thing is just picking at her food. She seems lost in her thoughts. Should I go over there and sit with her?* Elena could see that Lisa had noticed her but seemed hesitant to say anything.

Making a split-second decision. *Yes, I'll go sit with her.* Elena walked over to Lisa's table and asked. "Do you mind if I join you?"

Lisa looked up, surprised to see Elena standing there, and said, "Mrs. Martinez, of course, please sit down."

As Elena settled into her seat, she offered a tired smile, "Ms. Chen, I wanted to thank you. For what you did out there, for showing the world what happened. It was a very brave thing to do."

"I was just doing my job, Mrs. Martinez. It's your husband who's the real hero. I wouldn't be sitting here right now if it hadn't been for what he did. He helped save all of our lives. I'm so grateful for what he did for us," Lisa said, looking down at her plate, trying to hide her face.

"What you did was also brave, Ms. Chen. Don't let anybody take that away from you," Elena said with a smile.

They sat in silence for a moment before Elena spoke again, "So, Sergeant Rodriguez tells me you would like to interview me."

Lisa looked up at Elena, "Yes. I would, but only if you're comfortable with it, Mrs. Martinez. The last thing I want to do is add to your stress. I know you have already been through a lot. I wouldn't be able to live with myself if I made it any worse."

Elena considered for a moment, her thoughts returning to when this all started. When reporters had swarmed their community and forced her to leave her home with her children, she had felt invaded. But right now, she was unsure of the idea of opening up to the world.

"Please, call me Elena," Elena said to Lisa. "What kind of questions would you ask? What do you hope to accomplish with this interview?"

Lisa, choosing her words carefully, said, "I'd like to show the world the side they don't see—the after effects of war and the toll it takes on the families of the servicemen and women who go through it. Beyond the heroics and the politics, there's also a family affected by all this. Your story, Mrs. Martinez, is just as important as James. How you are coping, how this affects your family, and what you want others to know about James as a husband and father."

Lisa paused, letting Elena process what she was saying, and then said, "I think it's important for people to understand the real impact of war and heroism. Not just on the battlefield but on the families left waiting and hoping. If you're willing to share that, I believe it could help a lot of people understand and maybe even bring some comfort to other families going through similar situations."

Elena listened intently, considering everything that Lisa was saying and thinking about all of the implications of what she could offer other families like hers. "I'll think about it," Elena said finally. "I can't promise anything right now, but ... I'll think about it."

Lisa nodded, "That's all I can ask, Mrs. Martinez. Thank you for at least considering it."

After saying their goodbyes, Elena thought about the interview and what it would mean to other people who were in the same situation as her. She thought about James' story and their story and how it was becoming bigger than what was happening to just their family. It affected the entire world. Would sharing her family's experience help others find strength in difficult times?

Elena thought about how her voice could possibly become a beacon for military families, advocating for better support systems and recognizing the silent sacrifices they make behind the scenes that often go unnoticed.

Elena made her way back to James' room, ready to resume waiting by his side, comforting him the best she knew how. But now, she carried with her not just hope for James' recovery but a growing conviction that their journey could inspire and comfort others facing their own battles.

Elena bowed her head and closed her eyes, her hand resting gently on James' as she whispered a quiet prayer, just loud enough for James to hear.

"Lord, I thank you for giving us strength through these trials. Watch over not just James but all those who serve and sacrifice. Be with the families waiting at home, the children missing their parents, and the spouses holding their families together. Give comfort to those keeping vigil in hospital rooms like this one. Lord, Please help guide the doctors and nurses caring for our loved ones.

Bless those who've lost someone, Lord. Wrap your arms around them. And if our story can bring hope to even one family going through what we are, use it for your purpose. Give me wisdom to share it in a way that helps others find strength.

Watch over our children, keep James in your healing hands, and help me be strong for all of them. In your name, I pray, Amen."

Chapter 32

Hope and Healing

Dr. Patel stood at the foot of James Martinez's hospital bed reviewing the latest charts with Elena and a team of specialists. "Mrs. Martiez," Dr. Patel began, "I'm pleased to report that James has shown a significant amount of improvement over the past 24 hours. His vitals seem to be stabilizing, and his body is responding well to our treatment plan."

Elena felt a wave of relief wash over her. "That's wonderful news, Dr. Patel. Thank God."

Dr. Patel nodded, but his expression remained serious. "However, we'd like to keep him in a medically induced coma for a little while longer. It's critical that we do this so that we can minimize the risk of complications. With this number of injuries, we need to ensure his body doesn't go into shock by moving too quickly. It'll be a process of methodically removing the armor and then the bullet fragments. His state will be easier to control while he's still induced."

"If you think it's the best course, doctor, I trust your judgment," Elena said.

"I do. It's my opinion that going this direction will allow us to expedite the process," Dr. Patel told her, "We will begin immediately."

Over the next few days, Elena watched as teams of doctors and nurses worked cautiously to remove James' armor one section at a time. Each piece was removed as doctors tended to the wounds that would begin to bleed. Each piece removed was a small victory and one step closer to James' recovery.

After the last piece of armor was removed, the wounds beneath it were stitched up. James lay in front of them on his bed, his body a testament to the ordeal he had endured. He had hundreds of small wounds covering his legs, torso, chest, and arms that were all carefully stitched closed.

"He looks like a pin cushion," Elena said as her hand gently passed over James' arm, carefully avoiding his injuries.

Dr. Patel smiled and said, "The good news is that there are no signs of infection, and none of the individual wounds are critical; they all seem to be superficial. Now that we have this complete, we can begin to gradually reduce his sedation and wake him up."

"That wonderful, Dr. Patel. Do you think it'll take long for him to wake up?" Elena asked.

"There's no way to tell how long it will take. We can only remove the sedation, and then it's all up to James. We just have to be patient," Dr. Patel told her.

"Thank you doctor, for all you have done for us," Elena said.

"It has been my pleasure, Mrs. Martinez. This has been ... an unusual case, but one that was our duty to help with," Dr. Patel concluded.

As the medical team left the room, Elena felt just a little bit more relieved. James had survived the impossible, and now, finally, it was time to wake him up. She couldn't wait to see his eyes open and look into them.

Standing there a moment longer, looking at James, Elena made a decision. She asked a nurse to request Lisa Chen and Sergeant Rodriguez to come see her.

When Lisa and Sergeant Rodriguez arrived at James' room, Elena greeted them and updated them on James' progress.

"The doctor said he could wake up at any time now. We just have to wait for him to want to," Elena said to Lisa and Rodriguez.

"That is wonderful news, Mrs. Martinez. I'm sure you are ready to speak with your husband and I bet he will be excited to see you when he wakes up!" Lisa said.

"Updating you on James' condition wasn't the only reason I brought you both here. I have decided to do the interview," she said while looking at Lisa and then turning to Sergeant Rodriguez. She added, "If that is okay with the military, of course."

Sergeant Rodriguez told her, "I'll call my superiors right now to ensure there won't be any issues with this." After making a quick call, Rodriguez returned and said, "You are all clear, Mrs. Martinez. Whatever you want to say, you have our support."

They found a quiet conference room to do the interview. As Tom was setting up his camera, Lisa walked up to Elena one last time and asked, "Are you absolutely sure about this, Mrs. Martinez? We can stop at any time if you are uncomfortable with any of this."

Elena nodded to Lisa and smiled, "I'm sure, I think ... I think it is important for people to hear our story of what we have been through."

Lisa smiled back at her and then took a seat. Tom gave the countdown, and the camera began to record.

"I'm here with Elena Martinez," Lisa began, her voice soft and respectful. She is the wife of James Martinez, the civilian whose acts of heroism that we all witnessed on that roadside in Iraq, whose actions captivated the world. Mrs. Martinez, thank you for agreeing to speak with us."

Elena smiled faintly, "Thank you for giving me this opportunity, Lisa."

"Can you tell us a little bit about James? Not the hero the world saw on TV, but the man you know and love?" Lisa asked.

Elena's eyes began to mist over a little bit before she spoke, "James is ... He is one of the kindest, most selfless people I know. He is a great father. James always puts our children first. He has this quiet strength about him, always being protective of those in his life and of those around him. I would have never imagined him being thrust into a situation like this. But looking back, I'm not surprised at all by how he reacted. That is just who James is. He is always thinking of others before himself, always wanting to do the right thing."

"I can definitely attest to that," Lisa said. "When I met your husband, I could tell he was a good person. Can you tell us how these last few days have been for you here at the hospital?"

"It has been a little overwhelming at times, but I have managed to get through it. When I first arrived here at the hospital, I didn't know what to expect," Elena paused, recalling when she watched James being wheeled in when he finally arrived. "When he first arrived, I saw his condition in person ... It was a lot to take in. I didn't know if he was going to make it or not. The doctors were working on him, and it was complete chaos as they worked to save his life." Elena paused again, steadying her emotions, "I felt so helpless watching the man I loved fighting for his life, and there was nothing I could do about it. I just prayed to God to help him and to help me through it, and he did. I believe that," Elena said while nodding her head.

Lisa handed Elena a tissue, and she wiped away her tears before continuing, "The doctors and nurses here have been so great, and all of the support we have received from every-one around us has been very helpful. I'm so thankful to everyone here."

"That sounds so overwhelming; you are such a strong person," Lisa told her. "How has this experience affected you and your family?" Lisa asked gently.

Elena calmed herself before she spoke. "It's been ... a lot. It's been terrifying but also inspiring all at once. The outpouring of support we have received from friends, strangers, and the military community has been incredible. It's shown us the very best of what people are capable of, just as James' actions did."

As they continued the interview Elena talked more about James and their family and what she hoped for the future.

Toward the end of the interview, Lisa asked Elena, "Is there anything you would like to say to the people watching right now? Is there a message you want to say to them?"

Elena nodded, her voice steady despite her emotions at that moment. "I would like to share a Bible verse that has been giving me strength through all of this. It is from the book of Isaiah, chapter 41, verse 10: 'Fear not, for I am with you; do not be dismayed, for I am your God. I will strengthen you and help you; I will uphold you with my righteous right hand.'"

She paused and then continued, "To everyone out there facing their own battles, whether they are on a literal battlefield or fighting personal struggles, have courage. You are much stronger than you know. And to the families of our service members and everyone who puts themselves in harm's way for others, you are not alone. Your sacrifice and strength don't go unnoticed."

As Tom's camera stopped rolling, there wasn't a dry eye in the room. Lisa reached out and squeezed Elena's hand. "Thank you so much," she said softly. "Your words will bring comfort to so many who need it right now."

Elena nodded. After saying all of that, she felt relieved. She had shared her and James' story, her fears, and a little bit of hope for those who maybe needed it.

As they began to wrap everything up, a quietness settled over the room. Almost as if there was a shift in the atmosphere. Elena had a strange feeling that she couldn't quite explain. Just then, there was a knock at the door that startled everyone. A nurse poked her head in the door, smiling from ear to ear.

"Mrs. Martinez!" She said, barely able to contain her excitement, "James is awake! He is asking for you!"

For just a moment, Elena sat frozen, her mind struggling to process the words that she had been waiting for days to hear. Then, as if a switch had been flipped, she leaped to her feet, momentarily forgetting about the microphone wires that were still attached to her.

Tom sprang into action as he rushed over, his hands moving swiftly to remove all of the wires and equipment. "Go, go, go!" he said to her after freeing her from the wires.

Elena didn't need to be told twice. She ran out of the room, her heart pounding in her chest as she ran. The hallway seemed to stretch endlessly before her.

When she approached James' room, she saw a whole bunch of activity just outside the room. There were doctors and nurses moving in and out of James' room, their faces full of excitement. When they saw Elena, they all seemed to part like the sea, creating a clear path to the door. Unable to mask his relief, one doctor whispered to another, "I have been doing this a long time, and this ... this is what it is all about."

Elena made her way into the room, her eyes immediately finding James. His bed had been adjusted to a sitting angle, and there he was. He was awake, alert, and smiling right at her. That smile ... the one she thought she would never see again.

Their eyes met, and at that moment, the rest of the world just faded away. Elena rushed over to his side, carefully enveloping him in an embrace. James' arms, though weak, wrapped around her in return.

It was then that Elena's carefully maintained composure finally crumbled. All the fear, worry, and hope of the last few days came pouring out in a flood of tears. She sobbed into James' shoulder, her body shaking with the release of all the emotion she had been holding in.

James held her tightly, his own eyes tearing up. He stroked her hair gently, whispering soft words of comfort to her. In that moment, it was James' turn to provide the strength she needed, as if all of Elena's willpower had been transferred to him in that single moment.

Just outside the room, Lisa and Tom watched through the doorway, both unable to hold back their own tears at witnessing this powerful reunion happening right before them.

As she looked on, Lisa began to think about everything that had happened over the past few days. The story she had been sent to cover had begun as an investigation to uncover the truth and expose corruption, but now, the story had turned into something much bigger.

Rodriguez, who was standing just outside of James' room, watched from outside the window, his eyes filled with tears, and whispered to himself, "He did it."

One of the nurses, realizing the need for privacy, took charge of the situation. She gently shooed everyone out of the room, pulling the curtains closed to give Elena and James their moment.

Before leaving, she turned to James and Elena. "Take all the time you need, you two," she said softly. "Just let us know when you are ready for the doctors to come back."

As the door closed behind her, James and Elena found themselves alone for the first time since all of this had started. They held each other close. No words needed to be said. James was awake now, and he was going to be okay. In that moment, nothing else mattered.

Outside the room, as the medical staff dispersed and Lisa and Tom quietly made their way back to gather their equipment, there was this sense that a new chapter was about to begin. James Martinez, the hero who had inspired a nation, was now awake. And while there would be several challenges ahead with his recovery, this moment of reunion was a beacon of hope—not just for James and Elena but for everyone who had been moved by their story.

The world had watched James Martinez become a hero; they watched him fall, and now they would watch him rise, strengthened by the love of his family and the support of a grateful nation.

Chapter 33

A Nation's Gratitude

President Mark Franklin sat in the Oval Office, his face grim as he listened to the current update relating to General Sloan's arrest from Jim Kate, his US AG. *My GOD, what have you done Sloan. How did it come to this, was your greed worth more than your men's lives?* The more the President heard, the more disgusted he became.

"Mr. President," Kate concluded, "We have enough evidence here to bring treason charges. We've managed to turn one of his co-conspirators against him. One ... Captain Jack Riley who was also captured and has now agreed to testify against the General. I request permission to have Sloan and Riley both transferred from Balad to Ft. Leavenworth immediately. My office will have formal charges prepared within the next 48 hours."

"Absolutely," Franklin confirmed, "And Kate, I want constant updates on this. I want to know the moment the plane touches down here at home and I want to know as soon as Sloan is secure at Ft. Leavenworth."

"On it Sir," Kate confirmed, "You'll know when we know."

Taking one last look at the compiled case file, President Franklin said, "Sloan, your treasonous actions couldn't overcome the beacon of light that was one, James Martinez." *Your judgment is at hand, sir.*

As AG Kate was walking out the door the President's National Security Advisor, Dr. Emily Anderson, burst in almost running into the AG, her face alight with excitement.

"Mr. President," she said, slightly out of breath, "I've just received word from Landstuhl. James Martinez is awake."

The President's face broke into a broad smile. "That's fantastic news, Emily. How is he?"

"The doctors say that he is alert and responsive. They are very optimistic about him making a full recovery."

President Franklin leaned back in his chair, relieved by the news. "You know what?" he said, "I think that we all needed some good news. This feels like a turning point in this whole ordeal."

Dr. Anderson nodded in agreement. "It does, Sir. The nation could use some good news and hope right now, especially with the recent debates happening right now on military oversight."

The President stood up and straightened his jacket, "You're right. And I think it is time we gave it to them. Emily, please arrange a national address in the press room. I want to speak to the American people this evening."

A few hours later, President Franklin stood behind the White House press room podium. The room's bright lights cast shadows throughout, and the whole room seemed charged with anticipation.

As the President began, the room fell silent. "My fellow Americans, I come to you tonight with good news and a message of hope and gratitude. I'm pleased to report that James Martinez, the civilian whose selfless act of bravery captured our hearts and saved the lives of his fellow companions on that roadside in Iraq, is awake and alert. His doctors informed us a few hours ago that they are very optimistic about his recovery."

Everyone in the press room seemed to show their excitement at the news.

President Franklin continued, "I was also informed that our forces have successfully secured all of the affected bases in Iraq. The threat has been neutralized, and our military stands ready to face any new challenge that may arise."

The President's face shifted to a more serious one, and the room became quiet. "However, our victory came at a significant cost. We lost 47 brave servicemen and women in these attacks, along with 213 wounded. Each of these individuals is a hero, and their sacrifice for their country will not be forgotten."

The President paused, allowing the magnitude of those numbers to sink in among the audience before continuing. "In the face of such a loss, it would be easy for us to give into despair. But the courage shown by our troops, by James Martinez, and by the countless other Americans who were involved reminds us that our unbreakable will is what defines us as a nation. James Martinez showed us that heroism knows no rank or uniform and that it lives in the heart of every American who stands up for what is right.

This message goes out to those who would threaten our way of life, know this: America's will is unshakable. Our spirit is unbreakable. And our commitment to freedom and justice is unwavering.

To the families who lost loved ones, and to those still recovering: your nation honors your sacrifice. We stand with you, today and always. Your loved ones will never be forgotten."

The President paused in a moment of reflection before continuing, "In times like these, I'm reminded of the words from the Book of Joshua Chapter 1, Verse 9: 'Be strong and courageous. Do not be afraid; do not be discouraged, for the Lord your God will be with you wherever you go."

He stood up just a little bit straighter, "We face challenges ahead, but we face them together. And together, we will forge a brighter future."

"In that spirit, tonight I'll be flying to Germany to visit our wounded servicemen and women and to also personally thank James Martinez for what he has done. His courage has inspired a nation and reminded us all of the power of one individual to make a difference."

The President's eyes shone with pride. "America has always been a beacon of hope to the world. Today, we reaffirm that role. We stand united, we stand strong, and we stand ready to meet any challenge that comes our way."

"May God bless our troops, may God bless all those still recovering alongside James Martinez, and may God bless the United States of America. Thank you, and good night."

As the cameras stopped rolling, there was a moment of silence in the room, the President's words hanging in the air, and then a spontaneous applause broke out among everyone in the room. The President's words had struck a chord.

Across the nation, the impact of his speech was felt by everyone. In a small town in Georgia, a veteran watched the speech with his granddaughter, tears in his eyes as he thought of friends lost. "That's what we fight for," he murmured, squeezing her hand.

As Air Force One prepared for its journey to Germany, there was a sense that a new chapter was beginning—not just for James Martinez but for the nation as a whole. The light of the presidential seal seemed to shine brighter, reflecting the hope and call to action that had just been laid before the American people.

CHAPTER 34

COMING HOME

The bustling arrivals terminal at JFK Airport was an assault on their senses after days of being in Iraq. The noise of announcements echoing overhead, luggage banging around on carousels, and mixed scents of coffee and perfume replaced the smell of gunpowder that had remained in Lisa Chen's nostrils for days. She and Tom Ballard appeared from the secure area, both immediately engulfed by their families that were waiting for them to arrive.

Lisa's parents rushed forward, her mother's arms wrapping around her. The familiar scent of jasmine perfume brought unexpected tears to Lisa's eyes as her mother sobbed quietly against her shoulder. Her father held them both, pressing a kiss to Lisa's temple.

To the side, her roommate Jess waited patiently, a bright "Welcome Home" balloon bobbing above her head, adding a splash of color to the depressing gray of the terminal.

Nearby, Tom's reunion played out pretty much the same. His wife clung to him tightly while his young children wrapped themselves around his legs. Lisa had never seen her cameraman's usual composure crack until now, his voice rough as he assured his family he was really home, really safe.

Their eyes met briefly over their loved ones' heads. In that moment of shared understanding, no words were needed. They alone knew what they'd experienced together.

"See you at work, Chen," Tom managed.

Lisa nodded, mustering a small smile. "Yeah, see you there, Ballard."

As Lisa was led away by her family, Jess fell into step beside her, chattering about the welcome home party she'd planned. Lisa listened with half an ear, her mind still partly in Iraq.

The drive home through Manhattan felt surreal. Her father navigated through familiar streets while her mother kept glancing back from the passenger seat as if afraid Lisa might disappear. In her apartment, the normalcy felt almost overwhelming. The refrigerator's quiet hum, the clock's soft ticking, and the faint smell of the lavender air freshener Jess always used.

Her mother immediately took over the kitchen, determined to prepare Lisa's favorite food. The aroma of garlic and ginger filled the apartment as her father settled into an armchair, watching Lisa with understanding in his eyes.

"Sweetie," her mother called from the kitchen, "are you sure you want to go back to work so soon? After everything you've been through ..."

Her father leaned forward, his voice gentle. "Your mother's right, Lisa. Combat ... what you've seen ... it changes you. Trust me, I know. When I came back from Afghanistan, it took years to feel normal again. Even though you were only over there for a little over a week. The trauma you experienced is real."

Lisa sank onto the couch, running a hand through her hair. "I appreciate the concern, really. But I need to get Elena's interview to the studio. This story ... it's very important to me, and people need to see it."

Her father studied her face, recognizing the flicker of ambition in her eyes. "I understand how important this story is to you. Just remember that you have to take care of yourself as well. We're here if you need us, anytime."

The family dinner that followed was filled with careful conversation that skirted what had happened in Iraq. Her mother served all her childhood favorites as if good food could somehow erase the past days.

After they left, Lisa took a quick shower before collapsing into bed. When she finally fell asleep, it brought anything but peace. In her dreams, she was back on that roadside in Iraq. The sound of gunfire filled her ears. She saw James, covered in blood, falling to the ground. Her microphone in her hands felt impossibly heavy as she watched that horrifying moment play out again, but this time in slow motion.

Lisa jerked awake at 3 a.m., her heart pounding and her body drenched in sweat. *Oh my God! Where am I ... what is happening ...* then, slowly, her bedroom came into focus. *Okay ... okay ... breathe ... you are home now.* The familiar posters on the wall, the stack of books by her bedside, the faint glow of the city lights coming through her curtains.

"I'm never going to be able to go back to sleep now." Lisa muttered. With a sigh, she hopped in the shower. *Maybe work will help. After all, WNN never sleeps.* She thought to herself.

The warm water helped wash away the lingering effects of her nightmare but couldn't erase the memories beneath. Dressed and somewhat refreshed, Lisa grabbed her bag and headed out into the pre-dawn New York streets. The city was quieter than usual, though never truly silent. The distant wail of sirens, the smell of fresh bagels from the corner bakery, the rattle of early subway trains. All familiar, yet somehow different now.

The WNN building loomed ahead, its glass front reflecting the first hints of dawn. Lisa put her chin up and squared her shoulders. She had a job to do, a story to tell. Whatever she was feeling could wait.

Inside, the building was mostly empty. The elevator ride to Lisa's floor was silent, but as the doors opened, she noticed a light on in the otherwise dim office. Tom sat hunched over his computer, focused on whatever it was he was working on.

"Looks like I'm not the only one who couldn't sleep," Lisa said softly, approaching his desk.

Tom looked up, startled, then gave her a small smile. "Great minds think alike, I guess. Or maybe just equally messed up minds."

"What are you working on?" Lisa asked.

"Elena's interview footage," he replied, gesturing to his screen. I'm trying to take some notes, marking the best segments. Would you like to join me?"

Lisa pulled up a chair. Together, they watched the interview, occasionally pausing to discuss a particular moment or exchange thoughts on editing choices. When the footage ended, they sat in silence.

"I had a nightmare," Lisa finally admitted, her voice barely above a whisper. "About Iraq. About James getting shot."

Tom nodded, not looking at her, "Yeah, me too. Different details, same horror. One minute, I'm changing my kid's diaper, the next minute I'm back there, smelling the gunpowder, hearing the screams." He paused for a moment, reliving it in his mind, "I've been trying to talk about it with Sarah, but how do you explain ... this?"

They continued talking for a little while longer. Sharing their experiences, their fears about PTSD, and any other lingering side effects of what they had gone through together. It wasn't a solution, but there was comfort in the shared understanding.

As the office slowly came to life around them, early morning workers trickling in, Mark Smith's sudden appearance startled them both.

"Chen, Ballard, you're here early," he said, eyeing them both. "How's the interview coming along?"

Lisa sat up in her chair. "We were just finishing up. Would you like to see it?"

Mark nodded, and they gathered around Tom's computer. As the interview played, Lisa watched her boss's expression change from professional interest to genuine emotion. When it ended, he turned to them, eyes bright with excitement.

"This is perfect. Absolutely perfect. We're airing this tonight on the nightly news." He paused, turning to Lisa, "And I want you on air with Mitchell to discuss it."

Lisa gripped the edge of Tom's desk to keep her balance. "With ... with Mitchell Hawkins? On the nightly news?"

Mark nodded, already pulling out his phone to make arrangements. "You were there. You lived this story. Who better to discuss it with?"

As he walked away, already dialing numbers, Lisa sank back into her chair, her mind reeling. Tom grinned at her.

"Look at you, Chen. Making the big time. Let's go!"

"I can't believe it, this is crazy. Isn't it?" Lisa whispered. "Me, on air with Mitchell Hawkins."

"Believe it," Tom said. "You earned this, Lisa. After everything we've been through ... if anyone deserves it, it's you."

Hours later, Lisa found herself pacing behind the news desk, her nerves threatening to overwhelm her. *Don't freak out, don't freak out, don't freak out.* Lisa kept saying over and over in her head. Mitchell Hawkins, the picture of calm professionalism, watched her with gentle amusement.

"Lisa," he said quietly, "Just breathe. You've got this. You lived this story. Just tell it like you're talking to a friend. I'll guide you along. I promise you can do this."

The crew began their countdown. Lisa forced herself to stop pacing. *Alright, Chen, you got this. This is what you were meant to do.* Channeling the reporter who had stood strong in the face of danger in Iraq.

"In 3... 2... 1... We're live."

Mitchell's familiar voice filled the studio. "Good evening to everyone joining us around the world. Tonight, we bring you an exclusive interview with Elena Martinez, wife of James Martinez, the civilian whose amazing acts of heroism on that roadside in Iraq have captivated the nation. Joining me tonight to discuss this, is Lisa Chen, who was there on the ground during those events. Lisa, welcome."

"Thank you, Mitchell," Lisa replied, "It's an honor to be here with you, Mitchell, telling this story."

"So Lisa, tell us a little about what we are about to watch and what you were able to capture in this interview," Mitchell asked.

"Well. Mitchell, at first, when I was approached by my producer to have this interview with Elena Martinez, I was very hesitant. I thought that she might have already been through enough, and I didn't want to cause her any more stress. But eventually I came to the conclusion that I had to at least ask her. People needed to know what she was going through; everyone was focused on James and what he was doing, and I feel like ... sometimes the families of the people who go through this are overlooked. So I made the decision to request the interview," Lisa said.

"I see. How did Mrs. Martinez react to your request?" Mitchell asked Lisa.

"Initially she seemed very hesitant, but as I explained to her what I wanted to capture in her interview. I wanted to show everyone what the family goes through in these types of situations and how her speaking about it on camera could possibly provide some kind of comfort for those who are going through a similar situation. Mrs. Martinez seemed to understand. She told me she would think about it. A few days later, I received a call that she wanted to see me; when I met with her, she agreed to do the interview." Lisa said to Mitchell.

"Fascinating. Well, like everyone at home, I can't wait to see what she has to say," Mitchell said to the audience. Mitchell and Lisa both turned to a screen next to them and watched.

As Elena's interview began to play, Lisa could feel the emotion building in the studio. Every member of the crew was transfixed by Elena's words. They watched how she spoke with such strength, how she talked about her unwavering love for James. There wasn't a dry eye in the studio when the segment ended.

Mitchell turned to Lisa, "That was absolutely beautiful," he said, apologetically wiping tears from his eyes. "Lisa, I would like to talk about James Martinez, and what you witnessed firsthand. Can you tell us what it was like?"

Lisa nodded and began to speak. She told of how terrifying the ambush was, what it was like witnessing the courage of the wounded soldiers, and the seeing of the remarkable bravery of James play out right in front of her.

"James wasn't a soldier, Mitchell," Lisa concluded. "He was an ordinary man who, when faced with unimaginable odds in the face of death, chose to act. His actions saved several lives, including my own."

"Thank you for sharing that story, Lisa. It really was amazing to hear from your perspective," Mitchell said before wrapping up the interview.

As the broadcast ended, Mitchell reached across and squeezed her hand. "You did great," he said warmly, "Truly great."

Back at her desk, Lisa checked her phone and gasped. Her social media was exploding with notifications. The segment was being shared, discussed, and praised across every platform.

#JamesMartinez and #AmericanHero were trending nationwide. People were sharing their own stories of courage, inspired by James and Elena. The impact of their story was spreading like wildfire.

A military spouse wrote: "Watching Elena Martinez, I see every military family's story. Thank you for showing what waiting, hoping, and staying strong means."

A soldier stationed overseas messaged: "Your coverage reminds us why we serve. James Martinez embodies the best of what we fight to protect."

A civilian posted, "I never understood what families go through until now. This story opened my eyes."

Tears welled in her eyes as Lisa scrolled through the comments when Tom appeared at her desk.

"You okay?" he asked softly.

She nodded, showing him her phone. "Look at this. Look at what James and Elena's story is doing."

Tom read a few comments and smiled. "Sometimes the best stories are the ones that need telling most," he said, squeezing her shoulder. "You did good, Chen. Really good."

That night, as Lisa walked home through the city streets, she felt different. The memories of Iraq were still there, the trauma still fresh in her mind, but something had changed. By telling this story and sharing the courage and love she had witnessed, she found a way to make sense of what she'd been through.

Chapter 35

The Commander-in-Chief

The halls of Landstuhl Regional Medical Center buzzed with energy. President Mark Franklin had arrived, his presence carefully managed to minimize disruption to the patients' recovery. His security detail was discreet, blending into the background. The President had insisted on this, knowing that the soldiers here were more than capable of protecting him, even in their injured states.

As he made his rounds, President Franklin took time with each wounded soldier he visited. He shook hands, listened intently to their stories, and thanked them earnestly for their sacrifices. His body language was open, leaning in to catch every word, his eyes reflecting genuine interest and compassion.

"You've done your country proud, son," he told a young Marine with a bandaged leg, "We're all behind you and you have our support."

The atmosphere in the hospital was electric. Soldiers who had been despondent just days ago now were now full of energy, their eyes shining with pride as President Franklin spoke with them.

Eventually, the President's path led him to James Martinez's room. He paused outside the door to adjust his tie and smooth his jacket before knocking gently.

"Come in," Elena's voice called from inside.

As the door opened and President Franklin stepped in. Elena jumped to her feet, suddenly very aware of her disheveled appearance after days at James' bedside. The President held up a hand, smiling warmly, his eyes kind and understanding.

"Please, Mrs. Martinez, don't worry about it," he said. "There's no need to stand on ceremony here."

He walked up to Elena and said, "Mrs. Martinez, I wanted to personally thank you for all that you have done. The nurses told me what you did for the injured servicemen and women when you first arrived. That was a wonderful thing for you to do for them."

"It was the least I could do Mr. President," Elena said.

He moved to James' bedside, extending his hand. "Mr. Martinez, it's an honor to meet you. Thank you for all that you have done."

James, still somewhat dazed by the presence of the President in his hospital room, shook the offered hand, his grip firm despite his weakened state. "Thank you, Mr. President. I ... I'm honored you came."

A chair was brought in for the President, who sank into it gratefully, his posture relaxing into the comfort of the simple hospital chair. "I hope you don't mind if I sit. It's been quite a tour."

For a while, they talked easily. He asked about James' recovery, about their children back home, his voice soft and engaging. He spoke of the impact James' actions had had on the country.

"You've united us, Mr. Martinez," the President said. "In a time when our nation seemed more divided than ever, your bravery and selflessness have given us something we can all rally behind."

James listened, still somewhat in disbelief that the President of the United States was sitting in his hospital room, praising him. Then, the President's tone became more serious.

"There's something else I wanted to discuss with you," he began. "We've made a decision about the Congressional Medal of Honor."

James' heart skipped a beat. Surely, he had misheard.

The President continued, "We've decided to award it to you, Mr. Martinez."

For a moment, James thought it must be a joke. Then, as the President's words sank in, he shook his head. "Mr. President, I ... I don't deserve that. I'm not even in the military."

President Franklin leaned forward, the light catching the sincerity in his eyes. "James – may I call you James? Let me tell you something. Since the day after the attack, we've been inundated with emails and nominations for you to receive the Medal of Honor. They're still coming in from all over the world. The last count I was given was over 100,000 nominations."

James and Elena exchanged a stunned look.

"These nominations aren't just from the Army or the Marines," the President went on. "They're from every branch of service. The National Guard, the Coast Guard, even our allies overseas. Each one tells a story of how your actions impacted them, why they believe you deserve this honor. It's unprecedented, really. The last civilian to receive the Medal of Honor was during the Civil War. This isn't just about recognizing military service anymore it's about recognizing the spirit of service in every American."

James sat there speechless, trying to process what he was hearing. Elena reached out and took his hand, squeezing it gently, her mind racing with the magnitude of this honor, and how she would explain this to their children.

"I know this is a lot to take in," the President said softly. "But James, what you did over there ... it transcended the usual boundaries of military service. You showed a level of courage that embodies the very spirit of the Medal of Honor."

James looked at Elena, then back at the President. "I ... I don't know what to say, Mr. President."

President Franklin smiled, his eyes crinkling with warmth. "You don't have to say anything right now. Take some time to process this. But know that your country wants to honor you, James. Not just for what you did, but for who you are and what you represent."

There was a pause, a moment where the only sound was the steady beep of the heart monitor. Elena's thoughts drifted to their children, imagining their faces when they heard this news, the pride they would feel.

"There's something else I wanted to discuss with you, James," the President said, breaking the silence. "I've spoken with your doctors here, and they've cleared you for transport back to the United States. We'd like to move you to Walter Reed Medical Center to continue your recovery there."

James' face lit up at the news. "Really? That's ... that's great news, Mr. President. It may not be home, but it's a lot closer."

Elena squeezed James' hand, her eyes shining with happy tears. The thought of being back on American soil, closer to their children and family, was overwhelming. But then James' expression turned serious. He looked at the President, a question forming in his eyes.

"Mr. President, if I may ask ... have the fallen soldiers been transported back to the US yet?"

The President's face softened with understanding, his voice lowering, "Not yet, James. But we're in the process of arranging their return home. Why do you ask?"

James nodded, his decision made, "Sir, I have a request. Would it ... would it be possible for me to accompany them on the flight home?"

Elena turned to James, her eyes wide with surprise. The President sat back, clearly taken aback by the request, his eyebrows rising slightly.

"May I ask why?" the President inquired gently.

James' voice was steady as he replied, "I want to ride home with the real heroes, Sir. To honor them. We're all here because of those who've made the ultimate sacrifice, and if this is as close as I'll come to them, and I suspect it might, then I'll take that."

The room fell silent as the importance of the request James was making sank in. The President's eyes glistened with emotion.

After a long moment of pause, the President finally spoke. His voice thick with feeling, "James, in all my years of service, through all of the ordeals I've faced, and hard decisions I've had to make, I've never had a request quite like this. It's … it's beyond admirable. I don't see any issue with arranging this. Consider it done."

James nodded gratefully, "Thank you Sir, I appreciate that."

"And you know what?" the President added, "James, if you're amenable … I'd like to join you on that flight."

James looked at him squarely in the eyes. The President quickly clarified, "Not as a political gesture, but as the Commander-in-Chief, accompanying our troops home. How would you view that?"

James nodded, too overwhelmed to speak, understanding the profound symbolism of what was about to be on display.

The President stood, and said to James. "Well, it seems we have plans to make. James, Elena, thank you once again for everything you've done and continue to do. I'll see you soon for our journey home."

As the President left the room, James and Elena sat in silence, what had just transpired settling over them. Elena leaned in, pressing her forehead to James'.

"Just when I think I couldn't be more proud of you," she whispered, her voice choked with emotion, envisioning the stories they would tell their children, the legacy they were now part of.

James closed his eyes, holding Elena's hand tightly. The road ahead would be challenging. Physically, emotionally, and in ways he couldn't yet imagine. But in this moment, he knew with absolute certainty that he was doing the right thing. This journey, this honor, was not just for him but for all who had served and sacrificed.

Chapter 36

Bonds of Brotherhood

The clock on the wall of James Martinez's hospital room seemed to tick with an unusual weight. In less than 24 hours, he would be on his way to Dover Air Force Base, accompanying the servicemen and women who sacrificed their lives on their final journey home.

The plan was clear in James' mind. Travel to Dover, escort the fallen personnel to the hangar, and then catch a ride on Air Force One to Walter Reed Medical Center, where he would complete his recovery.

As James pushed through his daily physical therapy exercises, gritting his teeth against the pain and fatigue, a familiar voice cut through his concentration.

"Martinez! Are you trying to make the rest of us look bad?"

James' head snapped up, a grin spreading across his face as he saw Sergeant Rodriguez standing in the doorway. Without a second thought, James wheeled himself over, and the two men embraced like long-lost brothers.

"Sergeant," James said. "It's damn good to see you."

Rodriguez clapped him on the back. "Likewise, you crazy civilian. How about we take a break from you showing off and grab some lunch?"

James chuckled, nodding to his physical therapist who gave a thumbs up. Rodriguez took control of the wheelchair, and they made their way to the cafeteria, talking and joking like old friends.

As they settled at a table with their meals, Rodriguez's tone turned serious. "James, I want to thank you. For everything you did out there. And ... I want to apologize for not coming to see you sooner."

James shook his head. "No need to apologize, Sergeant. We've all been dealing with a lot."

Rodriguez nodded, pushing his food around his plate. "I'm being rotated back to the States, back to California, to finish out my tour of duty. Couldn't leave without seeing you first."

They fell into an easy conversation, recounting shared memories from that fateful night, and discussing the road ahead. Despite the heaviness of recent events, laughter occasionally burst forth, a testament to the bond forged in the crucible of their shared experience.

As they were finishing their meals, Elena joined them, her face lighting up at the sight of the two men together.

"Sergeant Rodriguez," she said warmly, taking a seat. "It's wonderful to see you."

The conversation flowed easily among the three of them. Elena shared updates on the children and the overwhelming support they'd received from across the country.

As their time together drew to a close, Rodriguez glanced at his watch reluctantly. "I hate to say it, but I've got to head out. My flight back to the States leaves soon."

They made their way to the hospital entrance, where Rodriguez would catch his ride to the airfield. As they said their goodbyes, the Sergeant's face grew serious once more.

"James," he said, his voice low and earnest. "What you're doing tomorrow ... escorting our brothers and sisters home ... it means more than you can know. To their families, to all of us. Thank you."

James nodded, unable to speak past the lump in his throat. The two men embraced once more, this time with the knowledge that when they next met, it would be on American soil.

As Rodriguez's vehicle pulled away, James felt Elena's hand slip into his. He looked up at her, seeing in her eyes the same mix of emotions he felt - pride, anticipation, sorrow, and hope.

James' thoughts were on the servicemen and women who didn't make it, remembering Private First Class Miller, a young soldier he'd met briefly before the attack, whose casket would be on that plane.

"Are you ready for tomorrow?" Elena asked James softly.

James squeezed her hand, "As ready as I'll ever be."

They made their way back inside, both lost in thought about the journey that lay ahead. In less than a day, James would be accompanying America's heroes home, a final act of service that would bring his own phenomenal journey full circle.

As night fell over the hospital, James lay awake, his mind racing. Tomorrow, he would bear witness to the ultimate sacrifice soldiers make. And in doing so, he would take the first steps on his own path home, forever changed by the events that had brought him to this moment.

The night passed in a blur of fitful sleep and anxious anticipation. Before James knew it, the soft light of dawn was creeping through his window.

At 0430, a team of nurses and doctors arrived to prepare James for the journey. They checked his vitals, changed his dressings, and ensured he was comfortable in his wheelchair. Elena stood by, her face full of pride and helped James into his suit, carefully accommodating his injuries.

As the clock struck 0600, they made their way out of the hospital. The cool morning air hit James' face as they exited. A motorcade was waiting to escort them to the airfield, the flashing lights of the security vehicles cutting through the predawn darkness.

The ride to the airfield was silent, each person lost in reflection. As they crested a hill, James' breath caught in his throat. The sight before him was unlike anything he had ever seen.

Three massive C-17 Globemaster III aircraft stood in a row, the early morning sun casting their shadows long and dramatic across the tarmac. Their huge cargo bays were open, where solemn teams worked to load flag-draped caskets with utmost care and respect, the morning light glinting off the stars and stripes. Beside them, gleaming in the golden light, stood the unmistakable silhouette of Air Force One. A sleek KC-46 Pegasus refueling aircraft was parked nearby, and on the runway, a squadron of F-22 fighters stood ready, their polished surfaces reflecting the dawn.

"My God," Elena whispered, squeezing James' hand, her eyes filled with sorrow as she watched the caskets being loaded.

As their vehicle came to a stop, James saw familiar faces gathering near the last C-17. The President stood talking quietly with military officials, the morning light highlighting the lines of responsibility etched on his face.

James was wheeled towards the group, a hush falling over the group as he approached. The President stepped forward, extending his hand.

"Mr. Martinez," he said solemnly, "are you ready?"

James nodded, his voice steady despite the emotion threatening to overwhelm him. "Yes, Mr. President. It's an honor to accompany these heroes home."

With that, the final preparations began. James was carefully helped aboard the C-17, positioned where he could see the rows of flag-draped caskets. The President took a seat nearby, his presence a reminder of the national importance of this solemn journey. The engines began to roar, the sound echoing across the airfield, a final salute to those who would never hear it again.

As the massive rear ramp of the C-17 began to close, James took one last look at the impressive array of aircraft prepared for this mission, the sunlight now fully illuminating the scene. It was clear that no expense had been spared, no resource left unutilized, to ensure these heroes received the honor they deserved on their final flight home.

The engines roared to life, the vibrations running through James' body as the aircraft began to move. As they lifted off, climbing into the brightening sky, James closed his eyes for a moment. He thought of the men and women whose bodies lay in the caskets around him, of their families waiting at Dover, of the nation that would be watching their return.

This was more than a flight. It was a sacred duty, a final mission to bring America's fallen home. And as the C-17 leveled off, pointing its nose towards Dover Air Force Base, James Martinez steeled himself for the emotional journey ahead, wondering how this day might shape his future, his purpose, in a world forever altered by what he had witnessed and experienced.

The flight to honor the fallen had begun, and with it, the next chapter in James' own spectacular story.

Chapter 37

A Nation Honors

The tarmac at Dover Air Force Base was filled with energy. Lisa Chen stood in a sea of cameras and microphones, her eyes scanning the massive crowd that had gathered there that day. The turnout was beyond anything she could have ever imagined. Thousands of people lined the airfield, there was a mix of active-duty soldiers, veterans, and civilians from all over the country.

Beside her, Tom adjusted his camera, making sure everything was perfect for this historic moment. Sergeant Rodriguez stood nearby in his crisp uniform talking with other officers and servicemen and women. Thanking them for coming.

Lisa had spent the last 48 hours coordinating with news organizations, veterans' groups, and military contacts. Making sure that everyone came for this honoring event. Now, seeing the fruits of those efforts, she felt extremely proud of herself and to be a part of it all.

"Lisa," a voice called. She turned to see a few of the lead journalists of several major news networks walking up to her.

"Thank you for bringing us all together for this," one of them said, shaking her hand. "It's not often we all work side by side like this. It is an extreme honor to be a part of an event like this."

Lisa smiled, introducing them to Sergeant Rodriguez. As they chatted, Lisa couldn't help but feel a sense of pride in the journalism community. Today, competition had been set aside.

"Thank you all for coming, I'm so glad you all made it." Lisa replied. "Excuse me one moment, I just need to send out a message to someone." Lisa pulled out her phone and sent a quick text to Elena:

"We're all set here. The turnout is incredible. You are going to be blown away!"

Miles away, aboard the lead C-17, Elena's phone buzzed. She read the message, a smile spreading across her face.

"Is everything all set?" the President asked, noticing her expression.

Elena looked up, surprised. "You know about the crowd we organized and the press that are going to be there?"

The President chuckled. "Not much gets by me Mrs. Martinez. And don't worry I'm more than okay with it. This is how it always should be."

Elena laughed softly. "I should have known better than to think we could surprise The President of the United States."

Across the cargo hold, James sat silently, his eyes fixed on the flag-draped caskets surrounding them. He had known about the preparations at Dover, but at this moment, his thoughts were solely with the fallen servicemen and women he was escorting home. *So many of them didn't make it home, and for what? One man's greed.*

One of the President's aides approached him and whispered something in his ear. The President nodded, then turned to Elena and James. "We're about ten minutes out. The pilots will get the aircrafts into formation now."

As if on cue, the massive aircraft began to shift, arranging themselves into a breathtaking aerial formation. Air Force One took the lead, with the three C-17s falling into position behind it, one directly behind and the others flanking it. The F-22s brought up the rear, completing the impressive display.

Back on the ground, a ripple of excitement passed through the crowd as the first speck appeared on the horizon. Lisa's voice, steady and clear, began to narrate the scene for millions of viewers around the world.

"Ladies and gentlemen, the aircraft carrying our fallen servicemen and women are now approaching Dover Air Force Base. As you can see, they're flying in a special formation to honor them ..."

As the formation drew closer, it slowed, allowing those on the ground to fully appreciate the sight. Suddenly, in a coordinated move that left the crowd gasping, all the aircraft released flares simultaneously. The sky lit up with streaks of light, a dazzling tribute to the fallen.

Cheers erupted from the crowd, quickly followed by reverent silence as the magnitude of the moment sank in. Many wiped tears from their eyes, overwhelmed by the display.

Among the crowd, an elderly man in a Vietnam Veterans cap stood with his hand over his heart, his eyes glistening.

"This is how it was meant to be," he whispered to himself, thinking back to the days when such honors were rare for his fellow soldiers.

One by one, the aircraft began their landing approach. The C-17s touched down first, followed by Air Force One, with the F-22s bringing up the rear. As they taxied into position, their cargo ramps facing the assembled crowd, an expectant hush fell over the airfield.

Lisa's voice, now barely above a whisper, continued to narrate for the cameras. "The aircraft have now landed and are taking their positions. In a moment, we expect to see the cargo ramps lowering ..."

As if on cue, the massive ramps of the C-17s began to lower, revealing the solemn cargo within. The ramp of the lead C-17 touched the ground, and for a moment, time seemed to stand still.

President Franklin emerged from the lead aircraft. With measured steps, he made his way to a microphone stand positioned near the aircraft.

The President stood tall. He nodded almost imperceptibly, and the honor guard boarded the first plane, ready to begin their sacred duty.

As the first flag-draped casket appeared at the top of the ramp, President Franklin, having memorized the names of all of the servicemen and women, broke the silence with a voice strong and clear:

"Staff Sergeant Henry Nicolas Lundy."

The casket made its slow journey down the ramp, carried with utmost care and respect by the honor guard. As it passed the President, he stood at attention, offering a crisp salute.

One by one, the caskets were brought forth, and one by one, the President spoke their names:

"Corporal Lisa Elizabeth Marks."

"Private First Class David Lee Wong."

"Sergeant Kevin Michael O'Brien."

Each name hung in the air, a testament to lives given in service to their country. The crowd remained silent, save for the occasional sob that broke through the collective grief. Tears streamed down faces, military and civilian alike, as the magnitude of the sacrifice became painfully clear.

Near the front, a young woman clutched a photograph of her brother, David Wong, her eyes never leaving his casket as it descended. Her tears spoke volumes of the personal loss behind each name.

Lisa Chen, her own cheeks wet with tears, continued to narrate the scene, her voice thick with emotion. Beside her, Tom's camera never wavered, capturing every moment for posterity.

The procession seemed both endless and all too short. Each casket made its way to the hangar where grieving families waited to receive their loved ones. The weight of loss was enormous, a shared burden borne by all present and the millions watching around the world.

As the last casket passed by, President Franklin's voice cracked ever so slightly on the final name. He paused, taking a moment to compose himself. These were more than just names to him. They were his soldiers, his responsibility, and he felt each loss deeply.

With the last of the caskets now in the hangar, the President turned back to the microphone. His voice, when he spoke, carried to every corner of the airfield and into homes across the nation:

"Ladies and gentlemen, I ask you now to bow your heads in prayer."

A hush fell over the crowd as heads bowed in unison. The President closed his eyes and began:

"Almighty God, we come before you today with heavy hearts, yet filled with gratitude for the lives of these brave men and women. They gave their last full measure of devotion in service to our nation, embodying the highest ideals of duty, honor, and sacrifice.

We pray for the families left behind, that you might wrap them in your loving embrace and grant them strength in the difficult days ahead. May they find solace in the memory of their loved ones and in the gratitude of a nation that will never forget.

To our fallen heroes, we say: Your sacrifice will not be in vain. Your courage will not be forgotten. You have shown us the true meaning of heroism, and we are forever in your debt.

Grant us the wisdom to honor their memory not just with words, but with actions. Help us to build a nation and a world worthy of their sacrifice. A world of peace, justice, and freedom - the very ideals for which they gave their lives.

And to you, O Lord, we entrust their eternal souls. May they find rest in your loving presence, and may perpetual light shine upon them for eternity.

Amen."

As the President's "Amen" echoed across the airfield, a collective murmur rose from the crowd as they repeated the word. For a moment, the entire nation seemed united in this single utterance, a shared acknowledgment of loss and gratitude.

President Franklin opened his eyes, surveying the crowd before him. The emotion was evident on his face - the grief of a leader who felt each loss personally, the pride in the courage of these fallen heroes, and the overwhelming responsibility to ensure their sacrifice was not in vain.

As the last echoes of "Amen" faded across the airfield, President Franklin turned towards the C-17 and gave a subtle nod. The crowd, still wiping away tears from the moving prayer, watched in anticipation, unsure of what was to come next.

Slowly, a figure emerged from the shadows of the aircraft's interior. A gasp rose from the crowd as they recognized James Martinez. Defying expectations and his own injuries, James refused to be wheeled out in a wheelchair. Instead, with Elena at his side providing support, he walked slowly but steadily down the ramp.

Elena's heart swelled with pride as she supported James. She remembered the fear when she thought she might lose him, the relief when he woke up, and now this moment of public acknowledgment. She thought of her children watching this on television, how she would explain to them the importance of this day.

As James reached the bottom of the ramp, he and Elena made their way to the President. The two men shook hands firmly, a gesture loaded with mutual respect and shared understanding.

Suddenly, the silence broke. A roar erupted from the crowd, a cathartic release of emotion at the sight of their hero returning home. Cheers, applause, and cries of "Martinez!" filled the air.

James, ever mindful of the delicate occasion, raised his hand to quiet the crowd. His gesture, filled with quiet authority, quickly brought silence back to the airfield. It was clear he had something to say.

With Elena's help, James stepped up to the microphone. His voice, though still bearing the rasp of his recent injuries, carried clearly across the gathering:

"Thank you all for being here today. But please, remember why we've all come. We're here to honor true heroes - those who made the ultimate sacrifice for our nation. I stand before you today only because of their bravery and the bravery of those who fought alongside me."

He paused, his eyes scanning the crowd, taking in the faces of the grieving families, the soldiers, and the civilians who had come to pay their respects.

Through Tom's lens, the camera panned across all of the faces, capturing the raw emotion - the pride in a mother's eyes, the silent tears of a father, the salute of a fellow veteran, and the contemplative gaze of a young child, perhaps too young to fully understand what was happening.

"To the families of these servicemen and women: Your loved ones' sacrifice will never be forgotten. They showed us the true meaning of courage, of selflessness, of love for one's country and fellow soldiers. Their legacy will live on in all of us who were fortunate enough to fight beside them, and in the heart of a grateful nation."

James' voice grew stronger as he continued, "I'm reminded of the words from the Book of John: 'Greater love has no one than this: to lay down one's life for one's friends.' Your husbands, wives, sons, daughters, brothers, and sisters embodied this love in its purest form. And though we mourn their loss today, we also celebrate their incredible spirit and the impact they had on all of us."

He paused for a moment, his final words resonating with hope and conviction: "The Book of Revelation tells us, 'He will wipe every tear from their eyes. There will be no more death or mourning or crying or pain, for the old order of things has passed away.' Take comfort in knowing that one day, we will be reunited with those we've lost. Until then, let us honor their memory by ensuring their sacrifice was not made in vain."

As James finished speaking, a silence fell over the airfield. His words had touched something deep within everyone present.

Elena, tears streaming down her face, helped James step back from the microphone. The crowd, moved beyond words, began to applaud softly, the sound building gradually into a powerful ovation that seemed to shake the very ground.

In living rooms across America and around the world, viewers sat in silence, many wiping away tears. James Martinez, the civilian hero, had once again demonstrated why he had captured the hearts of millions. His words had given voice to the complex emotions of the day, offering both solace to the grieving and inspiration to all.

As the applause died down, the President approached James and Elena, his voice lowered, "Today, we've honored our fallen in a way that echoes our nation's long history of respect for those who serve. From Gettysburg to Normandy,

Dover has always been more than an airfield; it's a sacred ground where we pay tribute to our heroes."

James nodded, his mind drifting to how this moment would shape not only his life but perhaps inspire changes in how veterans and their stories are treated. Elena, meanwhile, squeezed his hand, her thoughts on the advocacy work they might do together, ensuring no family feels alone in their grief.

Together, they made their way towards the hangar where the families waited, escorted by the President. The sun broke fully through the clouds, its warm rays seeming to embrace the airfield, casting a golden glow over the scene - a fitting tribute to the heroes who had come home and to the enduring spirit of those who serve.

In a quiet moment away from the crowd, James and Elena stood together, looking at the horizon. "This isn't the end of our journey," James whispered to her. "It's just the beginning of something new. Maybe we can help others heal, make sure stories like ours are heard, and push for the changes that need to happen."

Elena nodded, her heart full of both sorrow and determination. "We'll do this together, like we've done everything else. For them, for our kids, for everyone who's ever served."

The nation had witnessed more than just a homecoming ceremony. They had seen the very essence of sacrifice, courage, and resilience. And in James Martinez, they had found a symbol of hope - a reminder that even in the darkest times, the human spirit could rise, defiant and unbroken.

Chapter 38

Homecoming

As the last of the crowd slowly dwindled away from Dover Air Force Base, James Martinez sat in his wheelchair, Elena by his side, speaking with the family of the final fallen soldier. The hangar had shifted from a public spectacle to a place of intimate mourning and remembrance. Families stood in small clusters, sharing in their grief creating a bond of silent understanding.

James leaned forward in his wheelchair, meeting the grieving mother's eyes and said softly, "Your son died protecting everything we hold dear. We will make sure he is honored for that."

There was a mother, holding her son who couldn't understand why his father wasn't coming home who spoke to Elena, "Thank you for being here," she whispered, her voice breaking. "It really means a lot to all of us. The words you said on TV, they helped, you should know that."

Elena reached out and took her hand and squeezed it, "I'm glad they helped. Always remember we're here for all of you. You're not alone in this."

James approached a father standing next to his son's casket. The man's eyes were red, but you could see how proud he was through the tears. "My son believed in everything he fought for, he would've been honored to know you, Mr. Martinez," he said. "It really means a lot to us that you're here today to honor them. With everything going on today, it's hard to know how much people really care about those who serve and give their life for this country."

James felt those words deeply, "Thank you for that Sir, I know your son served honorably." *I only hope that my actions can help these families heal. I need to figure out a way to use this new platform to advocate for those no longer able to speak, to push for changes in PTSD support, for transparency in the military, and stronger support systems for veterans and their families. It's the least I can do for them.*

James caught sight of Lisa, Tom, and Sergeant Rodriguez. As they approached, James could see the exhausted looks on their faces from the day's emotional rollercoaster.

"Lisa, Tom, Sarge," James said. "Thank you for being here today. It means a lot to all these families."

Lisa smiled. "It was an honor. We just did what needed to be done. People really needed to see all of this so they could understand the gravity of it."

President Franklin then walked up to the group. Sergeant Rodriguez immediately snapped to attention and saluted.

"At ease Sergeant, there is no need for formality right now," The President said softly. He reached out and shook their hands as he thanked them. "Ms. Chen, Mr. Ballard, Sergeant Rodriguez. Thank you for everything you have done here. Your nation owes you a debt of gratitude. I hate to cut this short but I need to head back to D.C., we have a lot to plan. James, Elena, I'll be on Air Force One waiting, take your time. Good afternoon everyone."

As the president walked away, Sergeant Rodriguez turned to James and said, "Seeing you up there speaking today, James, it's like seeing what service can be. What you did, flying back with all of the fallen soldiers to honor them ... it's inspiring, I'm inspired."

"Thank you Sergeant, that means a lot coming from you," James said.

With promises to stay in touch, Elena and James said their goodbyes and boarded Air Force One.

The flight to Andrews Air Force Base was surreal. James and Elena sat together, thinking about all that has happened and what lay ahead for them.

The President walked up and sat down across from them. Having observed their interactions at Dover, he decided to have a brief but poignant conversation with James. "Mr. Martinez, your bravery is a call to action. We need voices like yours for reform." His eyes twinkled with an idea. "You know, James, from the inside, you could do some real good. You should think about running for office."

James, taken aback, looked at the President. *Did he just say run for office? Me?* "Sir, I ... I would have never considered that in a million years." *Could I really do that?*

The President nodded, a knowing smile on his face. "Just think about it. The United States needs people who've lived through what you did to make real change. I need you on the team, in some capacity ... just think about it." The President looked up at an aide who was standing off to the side, he nodded, "Apologies, if you'll excuse me, I have a call ..." Franklin said as he stood up and walked to his cabin.

James and Elena sat in silent disbelief at what the President suggested. "I don't know James, we've been through so much already," Elena finally broke.

"I know. That's a lot. We'll pray on it," James replied.

As they prepared to land, the President approached James and Elena once more, "I need to head back to D.C.," he said. "We've got plans to make for your Medal of Honor presentation. Exciting times ahead!"

After the plane landed the President walked down the stairs with them and he bid them farewell. James and Elena were escorted to a waiting vehicle that would take them to Walter Reed Medical Center.

As they pulled up to the entrance, James' heart leapt. There waiting were Elena's parents and, to his joyful surprise, his children.

"Dad!" Sophia and Miguel cried out in unison as James was helped from the vehicle. They rushed forward, enveloping him in gentle but enthusiastic hugs.

"Oh, my darlings," James said, his voice cracking as he embraced them.

Elena embraced her parents in a group hug. "This day marks a new chapter for us," she said in a quiet whisper. "Welcome home mija," her dad said softly.

A nurse gently interrupted, guiding them inside to a room bathed in soft light, the window showing the setting sun. The room felt like a sanctuary. She instructed James to sit on the bed as she methodically began to implement her check-up protocols.

"One day at a time," Elena whispered to James.

James nodded, his hand in hers. "Maybe we can start something ... help others like us."

Elena's thoughts wandered further. She envisioned a foundation, scholarships, advocacy – a way to turn their pain into purpose. But she also felt the impending challenge, the public scrutiny, the responsibility to speak for those who couldn't. *How will we navigate this new life?* She continued to ponder, knowing their story was no longer just theirs but a beacon for many. The President's suggestion of office lingered in her mind, adding another layer of complexity.

"You're in great shape Mr. Martinez. The doctor will be here shortly to do a final check, you'll be out of here before you know it," the nurse said as she pecked a few final notes into her computer and prepared to leave.

"One day at a time," Elena whispered again.

Chapter 39

Immortal Warrior

The weeks following James Martinez's return home went by in a blur of rehabilitation, family reunions, and preparation. Now, back in his Florida home, James found himself facing a new challenge. Crafting his acceptance speech for the Medal of Honor ceremony.

In his home office, James stared at the blank page before him. The words wouldn't come easily. *I want to ... no, I need to ... I need to make sure that I honor the men and women who came before me.*

As the days ticked by and the ceremony loomed closer, James slowly shaped his thoughts into words. Between speech writing sessions, he fell back into the routines of home life, cherishing moments with his children that he had once taken for granted. Work remained a distant concern. His boss Frank and Captain Phillips had been clear: "Take all the time you need. Your job will be here when you're ready."

Time flew by quickly, the following week James and his family were in Washington D.C. The night before the ceremony, James stood in the bathroom of their hotel room, his eyes tracing the web of scars that now covered his body, a permanent reminder of what he had endured and survived.

Elena found him there, lost in thought. "Come to bed, love," she said softly, leading him away from the mirror. They talked late into the night, about the ceremony, about the future, about the path that had led them to this moment.

"I still can't believe we're having the ceremony at the National Mall," James mused.

"The White House doesn't do this one justice, but don't let it go to your head, Mr. Martinez," Elena quipped back.

Morning came too quickly. As James and Elena prepared, they could hear the excited chatter of their children in the next room, where Elena's parents were helping them get ready. A knock at the door signaled the arrival of James' military escort.

With a final kiss to Elena and hugs for the kids, James left with the escort. The drive to the White House was surreal, the streets of Washington lined with people hoping to catch a glimpse.

In the Oval Office, President Franklin greeted James warmly. They posed for photos, the flashbulbs capturing this historic moment. "Are you ready for this Mr. Martinez?" the President asked, and with a nod from James, they made their way to the presidential limousine.

As they neared the Lincoln Memorial, James' eyes widened at the sight of the crowd. Hundreds of thousands of people lined the National Mall, stretching from the memorial all the way to the Washington Monument.

"So many people," James breathed.

The President smiled. "They're all here to honor you, James. You've captured the heart of America."

As the limousine pulled up and James stepped out, a deafening roar erupted from the crowd. The cheers washed over him as he climbed the steps of the Lincoln Memorial, the President at his side.

With a gesture, President Franklin quieted the crowd and began the ceremony. His voice, strong and clear, carried across the Mall:

"My fellow Americans, we gather here today in the shadow of Abraham Lincoln, to honor not only the men and women who embody the very best of our nation but also those whose actions reflect our highest ideals of service."

Major Natalie Wright was called forward. "Major Natalie Wright is awarded the Defense Superior Service Medal for her efforts in exposing systemic corruption at great personal risk, demonstrating the profound integrity that is the backbone of our military."

Next, Lisa Chen and Tom Ballard approached. "Ms. Chen and Mr. Ballard are each awarded the Civilian Service Medal. Journalism is a critical service to our democracy," the President declared. "Ms. Chen and Mr. Ballard risked their lives to bring the truth to light, showing that bravery takes many forms."

The President then turned his attention to James. "In the annals of American history, there are moments that define us as a people. Moments that reveal the true character of our nation. The day James Martinez stood against overwhelming odds to protect his fellow Americans was such a moment. His actions remind us that heroism knows no uniform, that courage can be found in the most unexpected places."

President Franklin's voice swelled as he continued.

"James Martinez's story is more than one of individual bravery. It is a testament to the resilience of the human spirit, to the power of faith, and to the enduring strength of the American character. In his actions, we see reflected the very best of ourselves - our compassion, our determination, our unwavering commitment to each other in times of crisis."

The President turned to face James directly.

"James, your country owes you a debt we can never fully repay. But today, we offer you our highest military honor as a symbol of our eternal gratitude. Your actions have not only saved lives, they have inspired a nation. You have shown us that in our darkest hour, hope endures. That in the face of terror, courage prevails. That one person, acting with conviction and love, can change the course of history."

With a huge sense of pride, President Franklin lifted the Medal of Honor and draped it around James' neck.

"By the authority vested in me as President of the United States and Commander-in-Chief of the armed forces, I present you, James Martinez, with the Congressional Medal of Honor. May your example continue to inspire generations of Americans to come."

The crowd erupted in applause as James and the President shook hands. Then, James stepped up to the microphone. The crowd fell silent, waiting to hear from the man who had captured their hearts and imaginations.

"Thank you, Mr. President, distinguished guests, my fellow Americans," James began, his voice steady. "I stand before you today, not as a hero, but as a man who was fortunate enough to be in the right place at the right time to make a difference."

He paused, his eyes scanning all of the faces before him. "This medal doesn't belong to me alone. It belongs to every soldier, sailor, airman, and marine who has ever put on the uniform. It belongs to those who didn't come home, those who made the ultimate sacrifice so that we might live in freedom."

James' voice grew stronger as he continued. "In the face of danger, we all have a choice. We can give in to fear, or we can persevere. We can turn away, or we can stand and fight. On that day, on that roadside in Iraq, I was just a man, thrust into a situation I never expected to face. But in that moment, I remembered something greater than myself."

He began to recount that pivotal moment. "As bullets flew around me and chaos reigned, I prayed. I asked God for the strength to be brave, to do what needed to be done. And in that moment, I felt a calm wash over me. It was as if I heard the Lord speak to me, echoing the words of *Isaiah: 'Then I heard the voice of the Lord saying, Whom shall I send? And who will go for us? And I said, Here am I. Send me!'*"

James' eyes shone with conviction as he spoke, "At that moment, I knew what I had to do. Not for glory, not for recognition, but because it was the right thing to do. Because every life is precious, and if I could save even one, it would be worth any cost."

"To the families of those we lost, know that your loved ones' sacrifices will never be forgotten. And to every American watching today, remember this. Within each of us lies the potential for incredible acts of courage and compassion. We need only the will to act when the moment calls."

James' voice swelled as he concluded. "Let us honor the fallen by embodying the values they died to protect. Let us face our challenges with bravery and perseverance. And let us always be ready to stand up for what is right, to lend a hand to those in need, and to say, 'Here am I. Send me!'"

As James finished speaking, a moment of silence fell over the crowd. The air seemed to vibrate with unspoken energy.

Then, as if moved by some unseen force, the hundreds of thousands gathered began to speak in unison. Their voices, joined as one, rang out across the National Mall:

"MARTINEZ!"

"MARTINEZ!"

"MARTINEZ!"

The effect was otherworldly, as if the crowd had been transformed into a chorus of divine messengers, proclaiming the name of an immortal warrior sent to protect them.

James stood, awestruck, as the sound washed over him. In that moment, he felt connected to something far greater than himself. To the collective spirit of a nation, to the timeless ideals of courage and sacrifice that had shaped America's history.

As the echoes of his name faded, James looked out over the crowd, his eyes meeting Elena's. She stood with their children, tears in her eyes, pride and love radiating from her entire being. In that moment, James knew that his life had been forever changed.

The ceremony concluded, but its impact would ripple out across the nation and the world. James Martinez had entered the annals of American history, not just as a hero, but as a symbol of the amazing potential that lies within every ordinary citizen.

As he descended the steps of the Lincoln Memorial, the Medal of Honor gleaming on his chest, James knew that his journey was far from over. There would be challenges ahead, opportunities to make a difference, and a platform from which to inspire others.

Senator Katrina Long, who had been watching from nearby, approached James afterward. "James, we're so proud of you. You should know that General Sloan is in federal custody," she said quietly. "His court-martial is set for next month. The evidence Major Wright gathered ensures he'll never wear a uniform again and he will spend the rest of his life in prison along with his accomplices. We never would have been able to accomplish this without your assistance."

James nodded, "Thank you Senator Long, Justice matters." James paused for a moment, pondering a question. "Senator Long. Do you think it would be possible to arrange a meeting between myself and General Sloan?"

Senator Long stood there in a moment of contemplation.

"I'll see what I can do, Mr. Martinez," she resolved.

CHAPTER 40

FORGIVENESS

James waited patiently in a secure visiting room at the Fort Leavenworth Military Prison. There was a steel table bolted to the floor, two chairs, and a window with reinforced glass. James sat alone as the sounds of the prison's activities echoed off the hard surfaces surrounding him.

The door buzzed, as General Sloan entered the room wearing an orange jumpsuit, his hands and ankles shackled in front of him. Without his uniform, without his medals, and without the stars on his shoulder, Sloan seemed much smaller now.

"Look who it is ... if it isn't James fucking Martinez, hero of Iraq," Sloan said, smirking at the guard, "We have a celebrity in our midst. A real life superhero." The guard locked Sloan's cuffs to the table before nodding to James and stepping outside. The door closed, the sound of it locking echoed through the room.

Silence hung between them for a moment before Sloan finally spoke.

"I didn't expect to see you here, Mr. Martinez. To what do I owe the pleasure of a visit from the hero of Iraq? Did you run out of babies to kiss already or have you come to gloat?" Sloan asked, his smirk still present, as if permanent.

James stared at Sloan, weighing his words, "I needed to ask you a question."

"A question? I see ... Everyone has questions. I have been asked a lot of questions since my arrest and subsequent arrival here. It has been a three letter agency Q and A session everyday. You would think that I was some kind of celebrity myself. So ... which questions do you have Mr. Martinez? What question would be so important to you, that you had to come all the way out here in person to visit me?" Sloan asked, his smirk failing.

"Was it worth it? Was betraying all you stood for worth it? All the soldiers, people like Simmons ... was it worth it?" James asked, his eyes locked on Sloan's.

Sloan sat back in his chair, his eyes never leaving James', "Ahhh ... the million dollar question. The one that keeps getting asked over and over again by everyone. Was it worth it? You know, I keep asking myself the same thing. Everyone wants to know my answer, hell even I want to know the answer. Was it worth it?" Sloan seemed to look off into the distance past James as if searching for the answer. Sloan locked eyes with James again, "What do you want to hear Mr. Martinez? You want me to say I'm a monster? Would that make you feel better? You want to hear me say that one day I just woke up and decided to betray everything I stood for?"

"I want the truth. The men and women who died because of your greed deserve the truth, their families deserve the truth," James replied

A bitter smile twisted on Sloan's face as he scoffed, "The truth has many layers, Mr. Martinez. More than you can fathom. As for Simmons, his fate was set the moment you found him out, so that is not on me Mr. Martinez, that is on you and Major Wright. Both of you with your holier than thou attitudes, sticking your fucking noses in my business. If both of you had just minded your own business, none of this would have happened and Simmons would still be alive, all those soldiers would still be alive."

A flash of anger crossed James' face. "Don't you dare put their deaths on us. Every decision you made, every piece of equipment you sold to our enemies, every lie you told .... those were your choices, not ours!"

Sloan's tortured smile faded, replaced by an intense look, "You want to know if it was worth it? Here's the truth, Mr. Martinez." Sloan paused, staring at James as he sighed, weighing his words, "At first ... then ... as the years rolled by, the more and more it got complicated ... you think I'm the only one? The military is full of people like me, I'm just the one who got caught." Sloan leaned forward, looking down at his hands. "Was it worth it?" Sloan asked trailing off, "I never wanted American blood on my hands. That wasn't part of it."

Sloan sat back in his chair staring at James, "You know ... It's funny. I had millions stashed away. Properties in three different countries around the world. Respect. Power. And now I'm in this shit hole, eating the same slop as every other prisoner, sleeping on the same thin piss soaked mattresses." Sloan paused, the mask he had put on now ripped off, "No, it wasn't worth it Mr. Martinez."

James studied the man before him, he was not the monster he'd imagined, but something perhaps more disturbing. A human who had lost his way, one small compromise at a time.

"Do you believe in God, General?" James asked quietly.

The question seemed to catch Sloan off guard. "What?" Sloan quipped.

"Do you believe you'll answer for what you've done? Not just to me. Not just to those soldiers in those caskets. Not just for yourself in your court martial case, and not just for yourself as you're tried for treason in front of the people of the United States?" James asked, his eyes locked in a glare on Sloan's.

Sloan's face hardened then gave way, visibly succumbing to the mental anguish from something long buried, reducing him to a scared little boy as eyes filled with tears.

"My father was a chaplain," he said softly, his voice choked in defeat. "He served twenty-five years in the Army. Every Sunday, there he was, preaching about honor and integrity." A forfeited laugh escaped him. "Guess that didn't stick. Eh Martinez?"

"You didn't answer my question," James pressed.

Sloan met his gaze. "Yes. And yes, I believe I'll have to answer for it." He shifted in his seat, the chains clinking softly. "I started answering for it the moment I saw those flag draped caskets unloaded on live TV ... knowing ..." His voice trailed off.

The room fell silent again. The distant sound of a door closing somewhere in the prison reminded them where they were.

"I came here angry," James admitted. "Wanting to see the monster who caused so much pain. But you're just a man who lost his way. I feel sorry for you Roger."

"Don't mistake understanding for absolution, Martinez," Sloan said, a hard edge returning to his voice. "I knew what I was doing every step of the way. I made my choices."

"Yes, you did," James agreed, "And now you'll face the consequences." He sat there looking at Sloan for a moment. "But for myself, I can forgive you for what you did to me, to my family. The rest is between you and God."

"Forgiveness? That's why you came?" Sloan responded, with a glint of surprise.

"I came here for answers. I think I found them. But ... forgiveness was ... unexpected ..." James continued, "I can't carry this hatred for you and what you did anymore. It doesn't serve me any purpose."

"And just like that, huh? And it's over?" Sloan asked, disbelief in his voice.

"No. Nothing's over Roger. Those soldiers that were killed, they are still dead, their families will no longer be able to see their loved ones. You have tormented them for the rest of their time. My forgiveness doesn't change any of that. Your time left here ... everyone's time here ... is temporary. After that, we meet our maker, and we face the consequences of our choices," James said as he stood to move toward the door. "But, for me, I forgive you."

Sloan watched him, something unreadable in his eyes. "Martinez," he called as James signaled for the guard.

James turned back, "What?"

"I'm sorry ... for all of it. Too little, too late, I know, But I'm sorry," Sloan concluded in his somber confession.

James nodded once. "Goodbye Roger. May God have mercy on your soul."

As the fresh air hit his face outside the prison, James felt something release within him—not peace exactly, but maybe the beginning of it. He had come seeking a monster and found a man. A feeble and imperfect man. Perhaps that was understanding enough.

* * *

Two weeks later, James found himself in a different setting. The Senate hearing room of the Armed Services Committee.

The bailiff's voice cut through the hushed room. "Please rise and raise your right hand."

James stood, the Medal of Honor catching the light, his hand raised. The same hand that had manned the trigger of an M2 in the Iraqi desert was now preparing to unveil a deeper truth.

* * *

At Fort Leavenworth Federal Military Prison, a guard walked along the corridor of solitary confinement, a breakfast tray in hand. His footsteps echoed against the concrete halls as he approached Roger Sloan's cell.

"Breakfast," he called, sliding open the viewing slot.

The tray crashed to the floor. "Open cell door S5, now!" he shouted into his radio, staring at Sloan's lifeless body sprawled on the floor, blood pouring from a savage gash across his throat.

* * *

"Do you solemnly swear to tell the truth, the whole truth, and nothing but the truth, so help you God?"

For a moment, James' mind flashed back to that night in Iraq – the moment he had prayed for strength, the moment he had chosen to stand and fight. Now, he was fighting for truth in a different arena, but the principle remained the same.

"I do," James said, his voice resonating through the hearing room.

* * *

Alarms blared throughout Leavenworth's corridors as medical personnel rushed into Sloan's cell. The prison warden arrived, surveying the scene.

"Time of death?" he asked.

"Judging by the current state of rigamortis, I would guess maybe a few hours," the medical examiner replied. "Someone was able to get to him. That could not have been easy."

The Warden turned to one of the guards standing near him, "Lock this place down now, no one in or out." The warden stood there for a moment and then pulled out his phone and typed out a message to Senator Long:

SLOAN FOUND DEAD IN CELL.

* * *

Senator Long's phone vibrated. She glanced down discreetly, reading the message. Her eyes widened briefly before she composed herself and looked back up, watching James take his seat at the witness table.

"Mr. Martinez, please tell the committee what you discovered," Long asked.

As James began to give his testimony, Senator Long's phone vibrated again. She discreetly tapped on the message, from an unknown Signal account, and read it:

"Be careful how deep you dig, Senator."

The message auto deleted after she read it. Long's attention was brought back to the task at hand as she heard James speaking.

"It was never just about missing equipment," James spoke. "It was about a complete breakdown of accountability, a system that allowed those in power to prioritize personal gain over national security ..."

As his words hung in the air there was only the sense of a story still unfolding, a truth yet to be fully revealed. James had found his next battlefield. And this time, it would be fought with words, documents, and an unwavering commitment to the truth.

The End.